THE TREASURES OF EXISTENCE

The year is 1921, but London's glittering 'Roaring Twenties' is just a myth in the provinces. The reality of the aftermath of war is mass unemployment, food shortages and discharged soldiers begging on street corners.

But for David Lawrence, it is passion that is uppermost in his mind, distracting him from socialistic, intellectual pursuits when he falls in love with his beautiful cousin Elizabeth. Physically and mentally opposite, the relationship seems doomed, as not only is Elizabeth an ice-cold madonna to David's hot-blooded philanderer, but her brother Edmund has a deep-rooted hatred of Jews, blaming them for the Depression . . . and David is half-Jewish. And Edmund is dangerous. Born with a cruel streak, he hides his own disgusting vices under a veneer of cool sophistication. A meeting with the handsome Simon Harrow introduces him to new erotic pleasures – and National Socialism. But it is a visit to his sister which explodes unvoiced family prejudices to the surface.

Miserable with her husband's infidelities, Elizabeth confides in Edmund, which proves to be the most dangerous, most destructive thing she could do. As violence erupts in the Lawrence household, it is just a prelude to the violence about to sweep across Europe . . .

The Treasures of Existence

MARGARET JAMES

Macdonald

A Macdonald Book

Copyright © Margaret James 1989

First published in Great Britain in 1989
by Macdonald & Co (Publishers) Ltd
London & Sydney

1ST reprint 1990

British Library Cataloguing in Publication Data
James, Margaret
        The treasures of existence.
        I. Title
        823'.914 [F]

ISBN 0–356–17950–8

Typeset in Baskerville by Fleet Graphics, Enfield, Middlesex

Printed in Great Britain by
Redwood Press Limited, Melksham, Wiltshire

Macdonald & Co (Publishers) Ltd
Orbit House
1 New Fetter Lane
London EC4A 1AR

A member of Maxwell Macmillan Pergamon Publishing Corporation

'If I could explain to you all this, and all that a man can bear and do, and glories to do for the sake of these treasures of his existence! I speak, you know, only of such men as have hearts!' pressing his own with emotion.

'Oh!' cried Anne eagerly, 'I hope I do justice to all that is felt by you, and by those who resemble you. God forbid that I should undervalue the warm and faithful feelings of any of my fellow creatures. I should deserve utter contempt if I dared to suppose that true attachment and constancy were known only by woman . . .

'All the privilege I claim for my own sex (it is not a very enviable one, you need not covet it) is that of loving longest, when existence or when hope is gone.'

Jane Austen *Persuasion* Chapter 23

ACKNOWLEDGEMENTS

While I was writing this book I was fortunate enough to receive the help and encouragement of many relations and friends whose personal reminiscences of the period which the novel covers were of great assistance to me.

I am particularly indebted to my mother, Mrs Mary Laughton, who spent the war years as a member of the Auxiliary Territorial Service. In the course of hours of conversation she brought the 1940s back to life, and she provided me with many insights into conditions in the women's Forces.

I also wish to express my thanks to Mr Robert Boyd, who lent me books, read the first draft of the novel and corrected many of my misapprehensions. Having been on active service in several theatres of operation throughout the duration of the war, Mr Boyd's vivid recollections of the time were of inestimable value to me.

Dr John Stevenson of Sheffield University directed my attention to various publications which were of great interest. Dr Stevenson's own book, *British Society 1914-45* (Penguin, 1984), gives as lucid, readable and perceptive an account of the period as any historical novelist could wish to find.

Chapter One

'HAS THE POST COME YET, MANSON?'

The housemaid nodded. 'Yes, Mrs Barton. There's just the one today.' She set out her employer's breakfast dishes, unfolded a table napkin for her and then busied herself in making coffee. 'It's there, madam – by your plate.'

'Oh, so it is. Thank you, Manson.'

Sitting down to her breakfast on that cold morning of March 1921, Judith Barton took the letter from the small silver tray which lay beside her plate. Recognizing the handwriting, she grimaced; but, nevertheless, she slit open the envelope and drew out the sheet of paper inside.

She skimmed the letter, running her gaze along the lines of neat, schoolmaster's handwriting until she came to the bottom of the page. And there it was – the very thing which she'd been dreading all term.

'It is most unusual for the school to request the removal of a pupil,' she read. 'In Edmund's case, however, it is felt that – ' Turning over, she went on to the end; but she was now only half absorbing the information offered. Pouring herself another cup of black coffee, she laid the letter down beside her saucer, and stared through the breakfast room window.

What had he done now? Surely the imagination of a nine-year-old boy did not encompass the horrors of which her son stood accused? 'Wilful and deliberate brutality towards a fellow pupil,' the headmaster had called it. Edmund had, apparently, made 'an unprovoked attack of

7

extreme barbarity, which has resulted in the permanent maiming of another boy.' Surely, Judith thought, as she gazed at the first daffodils nodding in the wind, surely there must be some mistake?

But then she remembered the many previous occasions upon which she'd been forced, reluctantly, to credit the evidence of her own eyes, when she had been obliged to admit that Edmund was not - well - not quite as other children appeared to be.

There had been the incident of the mice, the two white mice which he'd kept as pets but had then tired of, had shut in a drawer and left to starve, allowing them air and water to prolong their suffering. Then there had been the time he'd chased that other little boy around Kensington Gardens, had caught the child and felled him to the ground, grinding the poor infant's face into the gravel . . .

Judith shuddered at the recollection.

'Is there anything the matter, madam?' Manson appeared in the doorway with a butler's tray in her hand. 'Madam?' she repeated. 'Is there anything - '

'What? Oh, no, Manson - nothing.' Judith managed a feeble smile. 'No, there's nothing wrong. You may clear away, though - I don't want any of this.'

Still in something of a daze, Judith walked upstairs and into her dressing room. She sat down and stared into the looking glass. She'd tried to fob it off for so long. Childish exuberance, that was what she'd called it. Edmund had an over-active mind, a slight excess of those aggressive high spirits which, to some degree, all little boys displayed. But now she was going to have to face the fact that her son was, to say the very least, unusual.

'Mummy? Mum, are you there? May I come in?'

'Er - yes. Yes, darling, do.' Judith made a great effort to compose her features, to look cheerful. 'I'm doing my hair,' she explained. 'Come through.'

There was the sound of footsteps, and a little girl in a white nightgown was reflected in the glass. 'Not dressed yet?' Judith asked, turning round and shaking her head at the child.

8

'I didn't know what to put on.' Elizabeth leaned over and kissed her mother's cheek. 'Will you come and help me choose?'

'Certainly. I'll be with you in a minute. You run along and get into your underclothes, while I finish my hair.'

At least, Judith reflected as she pushed in her last hair-pin, at least Elizabeth seemed to be perfectly normal. Elizabeth, the child as blonde and fair-skinned as her mother was dark – the child who, as far as appearance went, took after her maternal grandmother, for whom she had been named. Taking one last look in her glass, Judith now thanked heaven for this one, perfectly ordinary, uncomplicated daughter.

She took her rings from their box and began to push them on to her fingers. Perhaps it was having no father which was causing Edmund's problems? Colonel Barton had been killed in the last year of the war, during the August of 1918 when an Allied victory seemed at last to be assured. And, looking back, Judith wondered if Edmund's displays of extraordinary viciousness did in fact date from the time of his father's death. .

On the morning the telegram had arrived and the children had been told the news, Edmund had taken himself off to the little wilderness at the bottom of the Bartons' large garden. There, all alone, he had cried and cried, turning his face into a red, sodden sponge. For a week he had been silent, refusing all comfort.

Twice married, perfectly happily each time, and now twice widowed, Judith missed a husband just as much as Edmund must be missing a father. Should she marry again? But whom *could* she marry? Who was there?

She made her way along the corridor to her daughter's pink and white bedroom and sat down at the child's dressing table. Elizabeth, seeing that her mother was pre-occupied, plumped herself down on the wide stool beside her and leaned against her shoulder. 'What's the matter, Mummy?'

'Nothing, darling.' Judith looked down at her hands. 'We're going to see Edmund. He's leaving that school.'

'Oh? Doesn't he like it?'

'Er – ' Judith considered for a moment, and then decided that a six-year-old child did not need to know that her brother was being expelled. 'No,' she replied firmly. 'No – he's not happy there. So we're going to fetch him home.'

'That's good.' Elizabeth smiled. 'When are we going?'

'Tomorrow.' Judith returned her daughter's smile. Well, she reflected, Edmund was invariably pleasant and well-disposed towards his little sister. Perhaps there was nothing to worry about after all . . .

Judith had had her children very late in life. Throughout her first, childless marriage, she had simply assumed that she was barren. And so the birth of Edmund had been an unlooked-for blessing, and the arrival of Elizabeth, born when her mother was forty-six, was something of a miracle. Aware that she was old enough to be a grandmother, Judith now decided that she was too set in her ways and too old-fashioned. Children these days were more outgoing, more adventurous. And perhaps the headmaster had exaggerated, after all.

She hugged Elizabeth. 'We'll have a party, shall we? To welcome your brother home.'

Tired after the long journey from London to Dorset, Judith stepped from her Rolls Royce and rubbed her eyes, wishing away her headache. 'I shan't be long,' she told Elizabeth. She made her way across the gravel drive towards the front entrance of Dean's Mead Preparatory School.

As she walked into the lobby the disgusting odour of education assaulted her. The sour reek of a hundred sports kits, institutional meals and grubby little boys did nothing to raise her spirits. She made her way down the ill-lit corridor, stopped outside the headmaster's study, and tapped sharply on the door.

'Come!'

Judith turned the doorknob and entered.

'My dear Mrs Barton!' Evidently astonished to see her,

10

Mr Kendall removed his spectacles and rose to his feet. Brushing chalk dust from his gown, he came from behind his desk and ushered Judith towards a chair, the seat of which he flicked with a blackboard duster before motioning to her to sit down. As one of the wealthier parents, Mrs Barton merited special attention . . .

Then he remembered why he had written to her; abruptly he stopped fawning on her and went to sit behind his desk. He folded his hands and looked hard at his visitor. He coughed and cleared his throat noisily, but he said nothing.

'What exactly has Edmund done?' asked Judith, breaking the uncomfortable silence by coming straight to the point.

'Well, Mrs Barton - ' The headmaster frowned. 'Well, as I explained in my letter, there was an unfortunate incident - '

'What has he *done*?' repeated Judith, agitated now. 'Headmaster, I wish to know what Edmund himself - '

Mr Kendall leaned forward. 'Mrs Barton,' he murmured soothingly, 'you must understand that the matter has been thoroughly investigated, and - ' He fiddled with the knot in his tie. 'There's no doubt at all - '

'Yes, yes, Mr Kendall - I accept that.' Judith, well aware that prep school headmasters tended not to be squeamish - in fact, rather the reverse - was now almost beside herself. 'Tell me, Mr Kendall,' she pleaded. 'Tell me precisely what happened!'

'Well.' The headmaster coughed again. 'Mrs Barton,' he began at last, 'we have a certain boy here, Hamilton Minor. He's undersized, somewhat sickly; gets asthma, you know. Timid little chap he is. But he's a good worker, tries hard at games - '

'Mr Kendall, *please*!'

'One evening last week, in the dormitory, Edmund attacked him. There was a fight. Your son produced a pair of compasses which he used as a weapon. He stabbed Hamilton repeatedly in the face.' The headmaster looked grave. 'It seems the little fellow may lose the sight of one eye. I'm sorry, Mrs Barton. I'm afraid I can't tolerate that kind of behaviour in my school.'

For a second or two, Judith wondered if she would be sick there and then upon the headmaster's faded Turkey carpet. She put her hand to her mouth and cleared her throat. 'There's no possibility that you may be mistaken?' she managed to articulate, at last.

'None.' The headmaster shook his head. 'As I said, the matter has been thoroughly investigated, and settled beyond any doubt. Edmund himself does not deny that he attacked Hamilton.'

'Has he been punished?'

'Naturally, I have beaten him.' Mr Kendall shrugged. 'I had no choice.'

'I accept that.' Judith stood up and drew her coat around her. Although the room was warm, and the gas fire was popping away merrily enough, she felt cold, chilled to the bone. 'I'll take him now. If someone could fetch him?'

'My dear Mrs Barton, there's no need for immediate removal! The end of term – '

'I'll take him now.'

Judith's chauffeur, who had been hoping he would be allowed to drive into the village for a beer and a sandwich, opened the car door for his employer and her son. After plumping up cushions and tucking travelling rugs around their legs, he started the engine and drove smoothly away from Dean's Mead.

Edmund sat contentedly beside his mother, an expression of absolute complacency lying easily upon his dark, regular features. Glancing at him, Judith saw a perfectly ordinary-looking child. His black hair was neatly combed, his clothes – although worn with the casual negligence affected by most little boys – were clean enough. There was nothing about him to mark him out as a monster. Nothing at all . . .

'Did you really do that dreadful thing to Hamilton?' she dared to ask at last.

'Yes.' Edmund opened his narrow dark eyes as wide as possible. 'He deserved it, Mum,' he added, reasonably. 'He teased me.'

'*Teased* you? But, darling – '

'He said my hair looked like bird's feathers, and that I had a beaky nose. He started calling me old jackdaw – and then all the other chaps did as well.'

'But Edmund, you can't *blind* people just because they annoy you! And you'd promised me, on your honour, that you'd stop fighting – '

'He deserved it!' repeated Edmund. He turned his bland, candid gaze away from his mother and stared out of the window. 'It was all his own fault.'

'But darling, don't you even care – '

'No, I don't.' Edmund shrugged. 'I don't care a bit. Hamilton's a lead-swinger, a pain in the neck – everyone said so. He needed to be taught a lesson.'

Judith realized, with some horror, that Edmund meant what he said. It was as she'd suspected for some time now – her son was indifferent to the sufferings of others. No – it was worse than that: he enjoyed inflicting pain, positively delighted in it. 'What *am* I going to do with you?' she demanded, aloud, but really to herself. 'Did Mr Kendall beat you hard?'

'No!' Edmund giggled. 'He gave me a sermon, then he tickled me, silly old fool. Rogers had a look at me afterwards – there wasn't even a bruise.'

She'd have to find him a tutor, Judith decided. He would have to be educated at home for a few years. He needed the discipline of hard work and the individual attention of a strong-minded teacher; of a man not afraid to lay down the law.

She wondered where she'd find this paragon, and, if she did find him, who would break whose will first. 'We'll have to give you a teacher all to yourself, Edmund,' she observed, watching him.

Edmund glanced at his mother, almost imperceptibly, he shrugged. Then he looked out of the car window again. 'The new Mercedes,' he observed, watching a car over-

13

take their own. 'Wouldn't mind one of those. Oh, come on, Dawson – can't we go a *bit* faster?'

Captain Michael Lewisham MC was a large, fair-haired gentleman of about thirty, a former soldier whose war record was evidently distinguished. He came from a landed country background; but by 1922 a combination of ruinous death duties and agricultural mismanagement had apparently beggared his family beyond redemption. He was consequently reduced to advertising himself as a private tutor.

Mr Lewisham turned out to be a thorough and competent teacher. More than that, Edmund liked him; he even became fond of him. One Sunday morning Judith had the great satisfaction of watching her son and his tutor walking together across the lawn at the back of the house, obviously deep in conversation. And she had been quite touched to see the man lay his hand on the boy's shoulder, while Edmund smiled up at him.

Lessons were not always as harmonious, however, and the first weeks with Edmund had been as difficult for Mr Lewisham as they had for his charge. Trying to define the boundaries, Edmund had deliberately annoyed his new teacher and pushed him as far as he dared. 'I shan't learn Latin,' he had announced, staring his master full in the face. 'It's a waste of time, nobody needs to study that nonsense. So I shan't.'

'You will, Edmund.' Mr Lewisham had nodded. 'You will learn by heart all the declensions on page six and seven of the primer. At the end of the week I shall test you. And if you are not word perfect, I shall beat you.'

Edmund had defied his teacher and learned nothing at all, but he had then borne the marks of correction patiently enough. And Mr Lewisham was no tickler - he crisscrossed Edmund's back and shoulders with a pattern of stripes which took a couple of weeks to heal.

One harsh punishment had been enough, and both teacher and pupil knew it. 'Now that we understand one

14

another,' said Mr Lewisham, breaking his bamboo cane across his knee, 'I shan't need this any more.'

'He's a clever boy,' remarked Mr Lewisham to Judith as the two of them took a walk through the rose garden one June evening three years later. 'He could pass any examination for which he was entered – that is, if he were to put his mind to it! Well, Mrs Barton? For which school did you wish him to try?'

Judith considered. 'You think he'd benefit from going to school?' she asked nervously. 'I'd wondered if – '

'I think he needs to meet young men of his own age, from his own social background.' Mr Lewisham focused his pale blue eyes on his employer and pushed an errant strand of fair hair back from his forehead. 'It might be the making of the boy, you know,' he added, leaving no doubt in Judith's mind that in Mr Lewisham's opinion it was imperative that Edmund go to school.

'Then which school would be best?' asked Judith. 'I hardly think Eton would take him. Perhaps Marlborough?'

'I'd suggest Wellington College. It's convenient for London, and if you wish to visit him there the journey is an easy one.'

Edmund passed the entrance examination of the school chosen for him. 'You will come to see me, sir?' he asked anxiously, as Mr Lewisham helped him select and pack his books. 'Sir, you will – '

'I shall visit you, now and again.' The master turned his fine Nordic features upon his pupil. 'But I shall be going abroad soon, so don't expect to see me for a year or two.'

'Abroad, sir?' Panicking, Edmund stared at the man. 'Where are you going?'

'To Canada.' Mr Lewisham placed a pile of books in a trunk. 'To seek my fortune,' he added wryly.

'Oh.' Edmund shook his head. 'I see.' He looked at the

15

man who had been his teacher and his friend for three years – and he wondered how Mr Lewisham could abandon him so callously. He raked his hair back from his temples and tried to blink away the tears which had gathered in his eyes. 'Why Canada, sir?' he enquired, successfully controlling the wobble in his voice.

'It's as good a place as any.' Mr Lewisham shrugged. 'There's no room in this country for people like me,' he added. 'There's no work, and there's no future. If I were a Jewish financier now, if I were a money-grubber happy to do dubious deals on the stock market – but I'm not, am I?' He laughed bitterly. 'I'm an Englishman, who's no use to England.'

'You're a splendid teacher, sir. Sir, you could – '

'Edmund, my family once owned half of Sussex! I can't become an usher, I can't drag out the rest of my days stuffing Latin grammar into the heads of children! I have my pride, you know – even if that's about all I do possess.' He patted Edmund's shoulder. 'You'll do well,' he said. 'You're ruthless, you're clever, you're nobody's fool. Get your head down, work hard, and you could beat them at their own game. Eh, Edmund? Become a banker yourself, and beat them at their own game.'

Edmund took Mr Lewisham's advice. He worked hard, and he succeeded in recommending himself to his masters as a clever, well-behaved, strong-minded boy, the kind who would become the type of upright English gentleman that the school sought to produce.

For some reason, the darker side of Edmund's nature never came to his masters' attention. His cruelty towards his juniors was never taken to be anything other than the reasonable chastisement which a senior might justly mete out to an annoying little tick. He reached his final year at Wellington without incurring the slightest stain on his character.

His reputation among the boys was another matter. 'Be careful of Barton,' was the advice imparted to newcomers, as the seniors were pointed out to them. 'He's a beast. He thrashes. Black and blue.'

'He's not one of the ones who – you know?' Worried new boys, the vague warning from their prep school headmasters that at big school there would be chaps who might try to take advantage of other chaps still burning their ears, would glance nervously at the tall, dark, thickset senior; and quake. 'He doesn't – '

'Oh, no, he's not a queer. But, in a way, it might be better if he was . . . '

With her son away at Wellington College and her daughter a weekly boarder at a school for girls in Kent, Judith was lonely. And she found herself wondering, not for the first time, if she might get in touch with some of her relations.

For various reasons, she had never actually met her father's other children. Her half brother and two half sisters, the children of her father's mistress, were either in London or Oxford. Could she meet them before she died? Should she try to heal some of the awful wounds of the past and reunite a family broken apart by bitterness and deliberate cruelty? Could she, she wondered rather floridly, be a messenger of reconcilation and love?

And, as she considered further, a sudden longing to see John Harley again filled her heart. The desire to speak to the man whom she'd been brought up to believe was her brother grew, and in the end would give her no peace.

She would make some enquiries. Picking up the telephone one dull, wet afternoon, she rang through to an agency which specialized in tracking down missing or errant relatives and discovering the whereabouts of people who did not, perhaps, want to be found. She spoke to a man who assured her that he could help her.

'Mr and Mrs Timothy Atherton.' Judith turned the sheet of paper over and read the rest of the details it offered. There was a writer called T J Atherton – perhaps he was

17

related to this half sister? She folded the letter and put the paper into a drawer, then she wrote out a cheque to the agency and slipped it into an envelope.

'Elizabeth!' She called to her daughter, who was, since it was Saturday, at home. 'Elizabeth?'

'Yes, Mum?' Elizabeth appeared in the doorway. 'What did you want?'

'Shall we go shopping, darling?' Judith suddenly felt like spending lots and lots of money. 'There are some beautiful new dresses in Whiteley's this week - silk plaids, I'm sure they'd suit you . . .'

Chapter Two

DORA ATHERTON WAS FEELING JUST about settled. The house in which she and her husband Tim had lived ever since their move to Oxford was up for sale. That week the family had moved to a new home, one built to certain specifications and designed to meet the needs of a father who worked at home and who was consequently frequently interrupted and harassed by his two young children.

All the same, it had taken two years to persuade Tim, who hated any kind of physical disruption, that the Athertons both needed and could afford a larger house. He had finally been induced to leave the small Victorian cottage close to the park by the idea of having a study all to himself. 'A place where you can work undisturbed,' Dora had said firmly. 'A room away from Steve and Helen - and me. Wouldn't it be marvellous to have no distractions?'

'Would it?'

'Oh, yes!' Dora had smiled. 'You'd get twice as much done.'

'Mm.' Tim was finding his third book something of a struggle. Since leaving the army, he had written and published two short novels, both flippant social comedies which had appealed to the desperately frivolous mood of the immediate post-war period, and which had done extremely well. But now he was trying something a little more serious, and he was not at all sure that it was going to work. 'I was wondering about getting a proper job, you know,' he'd remarked, eyeing his wife speculatively. 'This scribbling's all very well, but - '

'There aren't any jobs.' Dora had laid down the magazine she was looking at and shaken her head at him. 'And don't call it scribbling. You're a writer now; so get on with that. Write.'

'You really want that new house, don't you?'

'Yes, I do.' Dora had nodded. 'And so do you.'

'There. Isn't that nice?' Dora looked round the room and beamed with satisfaction. 'Don't you feel that you're a real author now, with your own room and your own desk - a private domain all to yourself?'

'It feels odd, having a place that's just mine.' Tim looked round the study. 'I've no excuse not to work now, have I?' he added, somewhat ruefully.

'Oh? Did you have an excuse before?'

'Well, not really.' Tim grinned at his wife. 'But I had you and Steve and Helen wandering in and out of the dining room. I could stop for meals - and any other time I wanted. Now I'll have to get down to it.'

Dora laughed. 'That's the idea! A book a year - that's what Mr Gregson said, wasn't it?'

'What if the Muse won't whisper in my left ear?'

'Muse!' Dora folded her arms. 'Professional writers just get on with it. They work from nine to five like everyone else - they don't have a Muse!'

'Don't they, eh?' Tim glanced through the window. 'Garden's a bit of a mess,' he observed. 'The builders have left enough rubble to build another house. I'd better get out there on fine days.'

'I've arranged for a man to come and see me about it.' Dora looked severely at her husband, daring him to argue with her. 'He can dig the whole thing over, then you - '

'He'll have to sign a written guarantee that he's not a regiments-of-wallflowers and multicoloured-island-beds man,' interrupted Tim. 'I'm not having my garden looking like a corner of a municipal park. And I - '

20

'Yes, dear, I know. I shan't tell him to do anything without consulting you first. We'll have all your favourite roses and clematis, we'll have trees and those lovely pink paeonies – '

'No dahlias. And no revolting egg-yellow daffodils.'

'No.' Dora joined him at the window. 'It's not over-looked at all here. Nice and private. As I said, you'll have no distractions.'

'Don't know about that.' Walking over to the door, Tim nudged it shut and turned the key in the lock. He wrapped his arms around his wife's waist and kissed her forehead. 'A fine and private place,' he murmured into her hair. 'What about it then, Dora? Shall we take advantage of our – ah – seclusion?'

Dora looked up at him. A momentary reflection that this was neither the time nor the place crossed her mind; but was, after a brief consideration, dismissed.

She stepped backwards and sat down on the sofa by the window. 'We shouldn't,' she said, biting her lower lip – but giggling at the same time.

'Why shouldn't we?' Tim was now sitting beside her, undoing the buttons on her cardigan. 'Give me a reason.'

'We just shouldn't.' Dora loosened the knot of his tie. 'Not in the afternoon!'

'The afternoon's the best time.' Tim took his wife's face between his hands and kissed her again, this time on the mouth. Then he tugged his shirt out of the waistband of his trousers, yanked the collar open and pulled the garment over his head.

He lay beside her afterwards, idly tracing the outline of her shoulders through the blouse which she had not had time to remove. 'Dora?' he asked. 'Will you kiss me?'

She did so, very lightly, and giggled when she saw him frown. 'What's the matter?' she asked.

'Again,' he demanded. 'A real kiss, a proper one this time, a nice long one.'

21

'You're insatiable.' Dora laughed at him. 'You get worse as you get older.'

'I get better, you mean.' He pushed her hair away from her face and looked into her eyes. 'I do love you, you know,' he added. 'More and more.'

She ran her hands across his broad back and smiled up at him. 'I love *you*,' she said. 'But, Tim, you must admit that it's a bit excessive – sex on the sofa at half past two in the afternoon. And at our age!'

Tim sniffed. 'I've years of lost time to make up,' he said. 'And I'd always intended to have you on this sofa one day.'

'Is that why you wouldn't let me throw it out?'

'Of course. And now that we know it's ideal – '

'Tim!'

'Absolutely ideal.' Tim grinned at her. 'We artists are entitled to extra treats, you know. Unlike you ordinary mortals, we must have our little whims gratified. If they're not, we sulk and grizzle and our minds go blank. The creative processes fail to function, and – '

'Do they, indeed?' Dora sat up and looked around for her scattered underclothes. 'Well, now that we've had our latest little whim satisfied, could we do a bit of work? Mr Gregson telephoned while you were out; you appear to have promised him a first draft by last Tuesday. So you'd better get cracking, hadn't you?'

'I suppose so.' Tim buttoned his shirt. 'All right, lock me in here and bring me some tea in three hours' time. Will you do that?'

A month into the summer, it seemed as if the family had lived in that new house for years. The children were largely responsible for this. They had made their new bedrooms as idiosyncratically untidy as they had their previous ones, and had filled the rest of the house with the clutter of childhood, with toys and books and the jigsaw puzzles of which Helen was particularly fond. Their nanny's patience was frequently stretched to breaking point. Never before had she worked in a household where the children were positively encouraged to take over the whole of the living space . . .

Stephen loved the new house and had also spent a great deal of time exploring the large, rubbish-bestrewn garden. But playing in mud and dirt, poking sticks into everything and digging holes all over the place did not endear him to Nanny Truman. 'He really is such a *messy* little boy,' she complained to Dora, as she led her younger charge up to the bathroom to be swabbed down yet again. 'I don't know where he gets it from!'

'Oh?' Dora, on her way upstairs to dress for an evening party, did not really want to listen to Miss Truman's grumbling. 'Aren't all little boys naturally dirty?'

'Certainly they're not!' Smoothing her blue dress over her bosom and blinking her bright, bird-like eyes in disgust, the nurse grimaced. 'Your father wouldn't even *think* of blackening his fingernails like this,' she told the miscreant. Observing her charge to be quite unmoved, Miss Truman shrugged apologetically at her employer. 'I do try, Mrs Atherton,' she cried. 'I *do* try!'

'I know you do.' Dora smiled at the woman. 'It comes from my side of the family. His grandfather was an archaeologist, you know – he liked digging holes, too! My mother told me that when Papa was a young man, he liked nothing better than to be up to the elbows in mud – '

'I *beg* your pardon, Mrs Atherton?' Miss Truman stared. 'What did you say?'

'Nothing really, Nanny.' Dora decided against explaining further. 'Nothing at all. Well, little monster,' she added, stooping down to give her dirty infant a kiss, 'go and have your bath. I'll come and read you a story before I go out.'

'Just look at him now! And Helen's such a *good* little girl!' Nanny Truman, sitting with her employer and the two children in the sunny garden which by now had a lawn and some bordering flowerbeds, clucked crossly. She glared at Stephen, who was doing something private and undoubtedly messy in the as yet untended wilderness further away from the house. 'Stephen, I hope you're not getting dirty again!' she cried.

Dora, who was trying to read, glanced over towards her son. 'Stevie!' she called. 'Stevie! Come here!'

Always deaf to Nanny Truman, Stephen responded to the sound of his mother's voice. He grinned at Dora, then he came running. With his smeared face illuminated by a beaming smile, shirt untucked, shoes and socks long since discarded and feet consequently black, he laid his filthy little hands on Dora's white skirt and looked up into her eyes. 'Mummy?' he asked. 'What do you want?'

'We wondered what you were up to, that's all.' Dora shook her head at him. '*What* a little grub!' she added, pushing his black hair out of his eyes. 'What a messy, mucky little urchin!' She grinned at her son. 'You're a naughty boy, Stevie, really you are! A very, very naughty boy! How can you get so dirty?'

'I just do.' His dark eyes wide and guiltless, Stephen continued to look up at his mother. 'I found a penny,' he volunteered. 'An old one, with a picture of the lady's head on it. And I've got lots of other things, too.'

'Have you? Let me see.'

Stephen pushed his hands into his pockets to display a collection of broken china, interesting stones and a rusty shoe buckle. All this detritus poured on to her lap did nothing to improve the beauty of his mother's fine crêpe-de-chine dress, but Dora, almost as interested in her son's finds as he was himself, exclaimed over his treasures.

The bun penny, encrusted with dirt and verdigris, was otherwise in perfect condition. 'It's eighty years old,' remarked Dora, peering at the date. '1845, darling – can you see? That's the year your grandfather was born. Don't lose this, will you?'

'I'll keep it in my special box, with all my other special things.'

Nanny Truman, who had listened resignedly to this stupid conversation, frowned. Stephen's special box, a biscuit tin full of bits of stick, dead insects, foreign coins,

24

used postage stamps and other rubbish, was a particular bone of contention between nurse and employer.

Eventually, she could bear this nonsense no longer. Coughing loudly to express her disapproval, Nanny Truman got up. 'Come along, dear,' she said to Helen, who had been lying on the grass reading a book. 'Come along, darling - it's nearly time for the party. We don't want to be late, do we?' Leaving the little boy and his eccentric mother still enthusing over the heap of stones, the nurse and her more biddable charge went into the house.

Helen Atherton allowed herself to be led upstairs and into the bathroom. She washed her hands and face properly and put her socks into the linen basket. Nanny Truman beamed. 'There's a good girl,' she said. 'Now, shall we go and make you pretty?'

Helen walked into her bedroom. 'My pink, Nanny? Or my blue?' She fingered her two party dresses, hesitating between the shiny satin of the rose-coloured garment and the soft velvet of the blue. 'The pink?'

'Yes, darling.' The nurse smiled benignly at the little girl. 'Yes, wear the short-sleeved one. You'll be much too hot in the velvet. Come here - let me fasten it nicely. Now - a smart bow at the back - that's perfect. Not too tight, is it?'

'No, it's fine.'

'Good. Pop your shoes on. Now, darling - what about your hair? Do you want it in plaits, or shall we leave it loose?'

'May I have it loose?' Helen had suffered a night of torture in curling rags in order to look pretty for the party. She picked up the hairbrush and handed it to the nurse. 'Can you make it go into ringlets?' she asked.

'Well, darling, the curl's almost out now - your hair's so straight and fine - '

'Please, Nanny! Try!'

'I'll see what I can do. Stand still while I get the tangles out.'

Happy to be tending this sweet, obedient child, Nanny Truman's ruffled feathers gradually smoothed themselves down again, and by the time she and Helen were walking along the pavement to the house where the birthday party was to be held, the nurse looked as much like a plump, contented navy blue hen as she usually did.

That year melted into the next. Suddenly the children were not babies any more. Stephen grew rapidly and overtook his sister, growing taller and broader than Helen, whose patience with him was now as sorely tried as ever Nanny Truman's was.

'Clumsy oaf!' she exclaimed one Saturday morning, as her brother trod upon the jigsaw she was doing in the middle of the drawing room floor. 'Oh, Steve! You've broken those pieces in half! Can't you look where you put your big feet?'

'What?' Stephen looked down at the floor and realized what he had done. 'Sorry, Nell,' he said. 'Didn't see them there.'

'You must be going blind.' Crossly, Helen fitted the broken pieces back into the puzzle. 'Perhaps Dad can glue them together again,' she muttered, still scowling. 'But it won't be the same!'

Stephen crouched down beside her. 'Shall I help you with the sky?' he asked, anxious to make amends.

'No, I can do it myself.'

'I'd like to help.' Stephen picked up a piece and slotted it into place. 'Look, I'll do this bit of the sea, shall I?'

'Oh, if you like.' Helen looked severely at him. 'Get your knee off those pieces, or you'll break *them* as well!'

Knowing he was forgiven, Stephen grinned at his sister. Soon both children were totally absorbed.

Since he had started school, Stephen was gradually coming to realize that in *his* sister he had been particularly fortunate. Helen never cried, or whined, she never went moaning and telling tales to Nanny as his friend Robert's sister did.

Helen, in fact, was rather a good sort, and Stephen, always a little in awe of her as his elder, now decided that

26

his sister was very special. Helen, for her part, despised the male sex, but she was pleased enough that her brother was not the sort of boy to pull her hair and tease her, and that he did not think it entertaining to drop live spiders into her lap . . .

An hour later, the jigsaw completed, Stephen retrieved the broken pieces. 'I'll get Dad to mend these,' he said. He stood up and stretched. 'Shall we go and play?'

'Play what?'

'Germans and English?'

'*No* thank you!' Helen got to her feet. 'You always get too rough. I think I'll go and read a book. Why don't you run up the road and call for Robert?'

'All right. But Nell, you could play too – '

'Not likely!' Helen laughed, and opened the drawing room door. 'I'm going upstairs. And don't you dare bring that horrible boy into my room!'

Horrible Robert Lawley, Stephen's best friend, lived twenty yards along the road. Expressly forbidden to step outside the house unaccompanied by a grown-up, Stephen nevertheless did as Helen had suggested. He grabbed his coat and a few minutes later he was running along the pavement, letting himself into Robert's house by the side gate. A quarter of an hour later Robert had given his mother the slip and had absconded from his own home.

Now, at the bottom of Stephen's garden, he was daubing his face with mud in preparation for making a counter attack on Stephen's heavily-fortified trench.

'What was all that commotion just now?' asked Tim, accepting a cup of coffee from his wife and looking enquiringly up at her. 'Sounded like the howling of wolves. Or has war been declared again?'

'I'm afraid so.' Dora giggled. 'Stephen's started an artillery bombardment against Robert, and incurred the wrath of High Command.'

She leaned over her husband and wrapped her arms around his shoulders, letting a stray lock of her hair tickle his face. Tim lay back and relaxed in his chair, stretching his arms out in front of him and flexing fingers which were stiff from a morning's typing.

Dora peered at the paper in the typewriter. 'Is it going well?' she asked.

'I think so.' Tim pulled the sheet out of the machine. 'Don't read, Dora! It's private until it's finished, you know that! So - what was all the row about?'

'Only Stephen upsetting Nanny again, darling. I told you!'

'Oh. Well, in that case I shan't thrash him.' Tim grinned wickedly. 'Annoying Miss Truman's always permissible, even if it does involve making a God-awful racket.'

'Tim!'

'Well - *she* annoys me!'

'She doesn't!'

'Oh, yes she does. Referring to me as the Major, when I've told her a thousand times that I'm *Mr* Atherton. She makes me feel like some gruesome old walrus from a Tunbridge Wells boarding house!'

'Whereas you are in fact a young, handsome, highly successful author who just happens to have been in the army for a few years.'

'Precisely.' Tim drained his coffee cup and replaced it on the saucer. 'Dora, you must go away now. I want to finish this chapter before lunch.'

'Then, sir, I shan't disturb you any longer.' Dora picked up the cup and saucer. 'I'm going over to see Miriam.'

'Right.' Tim picked up a pen. 'Oh, Dora?'

'What?'

'If you happen to see Anthony, could you ask him if I might borrow a French dictionary? He's probably got half a dozen.'

'Very well.' Dora opened the door of the study. 'Tim - doesn't Simnel annoy you, sitting on your desk like that?'

28

'Simnel?' Tim reached across a pile of papers and stroked the yellow cat's neck. 'No. We like each others' company. And it's peaceful in here, isn't it, Sim?'

The cat purred. Although he was Dora's pet, he seemed to prefer Tim's society to anyone else's. Now Simnel got up, arched his back and shook each paw in turn; then he turned round and settled himself comfortably on a heap of foolscap. His motor still running and his amber eyes blinking contentedly, he yawned, folded his paws, ordered his feline thoughts – then relaxed into another sleep.

Dora went back downstairs and into the drawing room. Looking out of the window she could see Stephen and Robert, their mania for homicide temporarily abated, chatting to the gardener and displaying their archaeological treasures to the old man.

Despite never having a moment to spare for conversation with either Tim or Dora, Mr Jarrett didn't seem to mind Stephen disturbing him from his methodical labours amid the vegetable rows and the currant bushes. And although he hated Simnel, and persecuted the poor cat with a violence and fury which the unfortunate animal hardly merited, the gardener never objected or complained when he came across evidence of Stephen's excavations among the runner bean rows or amidst the cabbages.

The man and the children were now squatting companionably on the path, deep in discussion. A neat row of new finds was laid out in regimented columns, and the trio of experts were gazing down at them with all the intensity of museum directors examining Sumerian relics or Egyptian grave goods.

Helen and Miss Truman had gone into town. Dora decided to visit her brother. She put on her hat and coat and left the house. Coming out of the avenue in which she lived, she turned into sunny Banbury Road. Within ten minutes she was at her brother's house.

'How's he getting on these days?' Dora's brother Anthony was seated at his desk jotting down notes from a book, and gave his sister only half his attention. 'Has he finished his latest pot-boiler yet?'

'Nearly.' Dora went over to the bookcase. 'Anthony, may I borrow this?'

'Borrow what?'

'The dictionary.' Sitting down, Dora opened her hand-bag and pushed the book inside. 'He says he'll write a real book one day,' she added.

'There's no money in real books! Tell him to stick to trash.' Anthony closed his notebook. 'Now, Dora,' he said, 'look at me. A classics scholar of – well – some distinction, I can command an advance of fifty pounds for a new book. How much did Tim get for his last?'

'A bit more than that.' Dora smiled at her brother. 'You know, Anthony, seeing you in here beavering away like this, your books all over the place, your cuffs all inky and your glasses buried under a pile of notes – oh, it *does* remind me of Papa! And,' she added with distaste, 'you're just as untidy!' She stood up. 'Where's Miriam?'

'In the house somewhere, I believe.' Anthony waved his hand in the vague direction of the drawing room. 'Go and look for her, will you? Then you can ask her to make me some tea.'

But Miriam, who had heard her sister-in-law come in, found Dora first. 'Rachel and I are going to have some tea,' she said. 'Anthony, I suppose you want yours in here?'

'What? Oh, yes, please.' Anthony was scribbling again. Dora and Miriam left him to his labours and went into the drawing room, chattering to each other enthusiastically as they always did, anxious as ever to discuss their children, their husbands, their servants, their homes – two perfectly unexceptional middle-aged, middle-class women, whose very ordinariness was the most remarkable thing about them.

Chapter Three

IT HAD SEEMED TO DORA, and to the rest of the British nation, that the end of the war must necessarily result in a return to the prosperity and calm which she and everyone else remembered from before 1914. For a short while, it *did* appear that the country would soon be back to normal and that things would go on much as they had before the war had interrupted the established routine.

After 1921 however, everything had seemed, quite inexplicably, to go wrong. Industry stagnated. Businesses failed, bankruptcies mounted. The Twenties, instead of turning out to be the decade of peace and plenty which everyone had expected, were a time of mass unemployment, hunger, strikes and shortages which were unparalleled even by the awkward years at the turn of the century.

Even in Oxford, a prosperous, apparently wealthy place, there was some degree of destitution. Disabled ex-servicemen, unable to find any suitable work and equally unable to support their wives and children on stingy Government pensions, hung about street corners listlessly. Able-bodied unemployed searched the city for jobs which did not exist. Miserable families huddled together in mean little alleys of shabby houses, and in the suburbs beyond Magdalen Bridge there was plenty of charity work for the well-disposed, middle-class ladies of North Oxford to perform.

'Will you help, Dora?' Robert Lawley's mother, a bossy, organizing female, understood the problems of the poor and was prepared to explain to anyone who would listen that if only the *women* would pull their socks up, practise birth control and put a bright face on things, all would be well. She smiled magisterially at Dora. 'May I put your name down?'

'To do what?' asked Dora nervously. She'd been involved in Betty Lawley's missionary work before.

'Well, now. We collect clothes, of course, and on Tuesdays and Thursdays we provide hot meals. Dr Davies holds a free clinic for the mothers and children, for which he needs voluntary helpers.' Seeing Dora grimace at this, Betty Lawley smiled even more firmly. 'Might I put you down for the meals service?' she asked.

'Certainly.' Dora nodded. 'Yes, of course, Betty. I'll be glad to come and give a hand.'

So it was that, twice a week, Dora and two other well-heeled matrons drove down the Cowley Road to a decaying church hall which stank of damp and putrid lavatories. There they set up a soup kitchen which provided a few hundred meals of stew and potatoes for the women and children of the area.

War widows were, for some reason, particularly plentiful in Oxford, and their scruffy, often lice-infested children looked forward to the arrival of the ladies in the blue van. They grinned at their benefactors, touched their forelocks respectfully, and were extraordinarily grateful if any second helpings were on offer.

Dora, however, far from feeling bathed in the warm glow of her own philanthropy, hated her van days. She tried to smile cheerfully as she ladled out the pinkish-grey meat and waterlogged mashed potatoes. But although the children might giggle and grin, their mothers - women of Dora's own age, and often very much younger - were so hopeless, so depressed, so obviously desolate that she found herself almost in tears at the end of those afternoons. The look of baffled misery on each woman's face was a mute accusation, more forceful than any grumbling or complaining could have been. And the silent reproach of all this despair filled Dora with guilt.

'Mrs Gillray, Mrs Hobbs, Mrs Bradley.' The woman in charge of the operation ticked off the names on her list. 'Dora, will you take something in to them? You don't mind, do you?'

Dora did mind, very much, but she agreed to take a plate of food to these women who could not come to the hall. These three were, she knew, recently confined. And their homes, which still had a male provider – except that he couldn't provide, for he was out of work – were even more squalid than the war widows' houses were.

Babies' nappies, never washed unless soiled as well as wet, were left drying over the kitchen fireguards, filling the houses with the reek of ammonia. Dirty toddlers crawled around on cracked linoleum. Babies whined for the nourishment which their mothers, themselves malnourished, could not provide. And Dora, making her twice-weekly visits to these foetid dens, ever afterwards associated poverty with the sour smell of unwashed babies.

Men congregated on the pavements or loafed in little clusters outside the Oddfellows' Hall. Not included in the North Oxford ladies' charity scheme, they were expected to take themselves off to one of the relief centres in the city if they wished to avail themselves of free meals.

As Dora carried a tray which held three steaming plates towards a group of these loungers, one of them, a tall, emaciated creature whose empty sleeve proclaimed him to be a veteran of some now forgotten battle, grinned at her. 'What you got there, missus?' he enquired, barring her way.

Reddening, Dora tried to get past him, but he wouldn't move aside. 'I – ' she began, wishing he wouldn't grin like that. 'I'm just – '

'I know what it is!' Another man stubbed out a minuscule butt of cigarette and carefully stowed it in his jacket pocket. 'I reckon it's M and V.'

'Yeah.' A third man sniggered. 'Yeah, that's what it is! Cor – never thought the day'd come when me mouth would've watered at the smell of M and V!'

'Me neither.' The tall man grimaced. 'Me neither. Here, missus – got any leftovers? Got a bit to spare for an old soldier? For a man what's been wounded in the service of 'is country?'

The other man guffawed, and Dora's face became even more flushed. 'There's a place open in St Aldates today,' she said hesitantly. 'They're serving all the men there. So if you were to go into town – '

'Ain't going *there*!' A man at the back of the group spat on to the pavement. 'Bread, mouldy cheese and a bloody sermon! That's all you gets there!'

Dora was by now thoroughly embarrassed. She looked helplessly at the man still in front of her. 'May I come through?' she asked beseechingly. 'I have to take this to Mrs Bradley, and the food's getting cold – '

'Is it? Oh, well, we can't have *that*!' With exaggerated courtesy the tall man stepped aside. 'On you go, missus. Keep up the good work, eh?'

As Dora walked on she heard the men singing softly. A particularly crude version of 'Mademoiselle from Armentieres' followed her up the road. And, as she knocked on a shabby front door, a refrain about a little tin of M and V rang in her ears like the mockery of demons.

Now and again she was invited into a home, ushered into the back kitchen and asked to sit down to drink a cup of cheap, stewed tea on the surface of which floated scummy blobs of stale tinned milk. Today she sat thankfully in the sanctuary of Mrs Bradley's scullery, glad to have escaped from the men in the street.

Mrs Bradley, a mother of four whose husband had lost his job as a fitter and who showed no interest in trying to get other work, was sobbing. 'They said he's a layabout,' she wept, rocking her grizzling baby backwards and forwards against her shoulder. 'They said he's bone idle! But Mrs Atherton, he's not! He *can't* work!'

The woman's normally thin, haggard face now seemed

to be disintegrating into a swollen, soggy mess. 'He *can't!*' she repeated. 'He's tried - he held down that job at Worrall's for six weeks! But his nerves are that bad he shakes and trembles all the time, and he's no use to anyone really. Oh, I don't blame them for letting him go, but - '

'Was he in the Army?' asked Dora, taking the dirty baby and rocking it. 'Was he shell-shocked?'

'He was at Passchendaele.' Mrs Bradley sniffed. 'He don't say anything about it, but it must have been awful for him. Most of his mates died, you see; he had a bit of shrapnel in his side. That's better now, hardly a scar, but all the same - '

'Does he have bad dreams?'

'He gets nightmares every single night. Screams, he does - he wakes the whole row with his yelling and carrying on.' Mrs Bradley wiped her face with the back of her hand. 'He'll get us all evicted, Mrs Atherton, that's what'll happen next. Then where will we go? And there's the kids as well, *they're* driving me up the wall, always hungry, always wantin' bread and jam, and it's so expensive . . . '

Dora poured the woman some more tea. She had been on the point of saying, 'My husband was at Passchendaele too, and at the Somme. He gets bad dreams as well. He moans in his sleep and talks to himself.' Instead she stirred in an extra spoonful of sugar. 'You could give the children vegetables, maybe,' she hazarded. 'Children like them. And fruit, perhaps - that's cheap enough. Apples, raw carrot - my children are fond of a piece of raw carrot to chew, and it's good for their teeth - '

'Carrot!' Mrs Bradley shook her head. 'No, it's got to be bread, that's what fills their stomachs. Bread and jam, bread and potatoes - that's all they'll eat.'

Dora bit her lower lip. 'You've let your dinner get cold,' she said. 'Shall I heat it through again?'

'No.' Mrs Bradley picked up the plate and slopped the congealed food into a saucepan. 'I'll heat it up for Derek later,' she said. 'He might fancy it when he comes in.'

'But you ought to have it!' Dora looked earnestly at the

woman. 'Mrs Bradley, you're nursing a baby, you need food yourself!'

'I'll have something with the kids later, maybe. When they come in from school.' Mrs Bradley handed Dora the dirty plate and retrieved her baby. 'Thanks anyway, Mrs Atherton,' she said. 'It's been nice to talk to you.'

Dora took the plate. She couldn't blame Mrs Bradley for not wanting the meal. It smelled awful, like dirty under-clothing and old sacks.

Dora began some private charity work of her own, taking parcels of Helen's and Stephen's cast-off clothing, together with spare bedding and old shoes, to a few selected families whom she had come to know well. 'Thank you, Mrs Atherton,' the Bradley children would chorus, as if reciting their twice times table. And their faces would shine as they unpacked a cardboard box full of shrunken woollens, darned shirts and a few discarded toys.

Dora would always hurry away, embarrassed. Mr and Mrs Bradley were pleasant people who must have been a good-looking couple once. Their children, though under-nourished, were well-behaved and pretty. So what had *they* done to deserve this awful hopeless existence, this wretched-ness, this pain?

Of course she could recall instances of pre-war poverty; of course she remembered seeing beggars in the streets, had noticed ragged creatures slinking away down side turnings. But now there were suddenly so many destitute, and even the respectable poor seemed to be poorer still.

Especially in London. Dora and Miriam had decided to have an excursion and had gone up to the capital for the day, intending to have lunch in a nice restaurant and to buy a new dress each. After some discussion and a critical examination of each others' ankles and shins, each had reassured the other that she could wear the new shorter length without looking a total fright . . .

But once she had noticed the beggars Dora couldn't take any further pleasure in their expedition. And then, on the

36

corner of Oxford Street where it turned into Tottenham Court Road, she had seen something which sickened her to the heart. A captain from Tim's regiment - down at heel, his uniform ragged and his cheeks unshaven - was actually begging in the street.

At first, she couldn't believe it. A Guards officer, a member of the elite of the British Army, sitting on the pavement half asleep, an open cigar box in front of him! It was an aberration in nature, a monstrosity . . .

'He probably pinched an old uniform from somewhere.' Tim, unmoved by Dora's pathetic story, helped himself to pudding. 'You gave all *my* stuff to the rag and bone man, didn't you? God, Dora - there must be thousands upon thousands of officers' uniforms in circulation by now! And if you think of it - '

'I kept your badges! I kept your decorations, I took off all your ribbons!' Dora pushed her plate aside. 'Tim, this man had his captain's pips, he had his regimental badges - he had the Mons Star! It made me feel sick to look at him, it really did.'

'How much did you give him?'

'A pound. Well, two, if you must know.'

Tim laughed. 'Well, that was very generous of you, darling. He'll be able to get properly drunk on that. Or he can buy himself a nice girl - perhaps even a couple of nice girls!'

'How can you be so heartless?' Dora reached across and shook him, digging her fingers into his arm. 'How can you *joke*?'

'It's my profession these days.' Tim removed Dora's hand from his sleeve. 'And, talking of my profession, I have half an hour's work to do before I finish for today. We'll have coffee in the drawing room later, shall we?'

'If you like.' Dora looked down at her hands. And Tim left her to brood.

It now seemed to her that her weekly visits to the poorer suburbs of the city and all her industrious collecting and

37

distributing of clothing to the poor and unemployed were an insulting and futile waste of time.

'Dora? What's wrong?' Tim, sitting next to his wife on the sofa, realized that she'd been silent all evening. 'What's the matter, love?'

'Nothing.' Dora twisted a lock of her hair around her fingers and looked away. 'Nothing's the matter.'

'Still fretting about the fellow with the begging bowl?'

'No,' she lied.

'Dora, you do as much as you can to help.' Tim laid his arm across her shoulders. 'There's a world recession at present, though, and – '

'I don't know what that means.' Dora scowled at him. 'I don't understand all this talk of recession and slump, it's all double Dutch to me.'

'There's no market for our coal, cotton or ships any more. That's what it means.' Tim leaned forwards and poured Dora some coffee. 'Things will pick up,' he assured her. 'The car industry, for instance – that's growing, that'll provide more and more work in this town. Your chaps down the Cowley Road – '

'And what are they supposed to do in the meantime? Starve?'

'There'll be hardship for a while yet, I suppose. But that's the way of the world, it always has been.'

'Is it?' Dora sniffed. 'It shouldn't be!'

'Perhaps not. But it *is*. Dora, there were shortages and unemployment, strikes and shut-downs before the war – people went hungry, you know that!' He looked at her earnestly. 'Why do you think so many men joined up in 1914? It wasn't because they were mad keen to be heroes. It was because in the Army they were given enough to *eat*!'

'Mmm.' Dora shrugged. 'I'm going to bed,' she announced. 'I'm tired.'

'All right. I'll be up in ten minutes.' Tim caught at his wife's hand. 'You didn't show me your new dress,' he added. 'Where is it?'

'I didn't buy one.'

'Oh? Why was that?'

Dora pulled her hand away. 'The new fashions don't suit me,' she replied crossly. 'My figure's all wrong.'

'Your figure's perfect!'

'There's too much of it. I'm too fat.' Dora scowled at her husband. 'I'm fat, ugly and old-fashioned. And now, Tim, if you've finished cross-examining me, I'm going to *bed*!'

It wasn't only Dora's figure which was old-fashioned. Her hair was all wrong as well. Thinking how much easier to control it would be if she simply had the great unruly mass of it cut short, Dora pulled the last pin from her chignon and shook out the plait.

If she were to have a new hairstyle, would she perhaps look younger, less matronly? She wondered about a neat, shiny, Marcel-waved bob; some sharply crinkled curls might suit her. Yes, she'd definitely have her hair cut.

As she sat reading in bed one evening, she mentioned her intention to Tim, adding that she was going to lose some weight as well.

His reaction surprised her. He declared that while she was at perfect liberty to diet herself into a wraith and to become a flat-chested, crop-haired harpy, he would then not feel any further obligation to love her as he did.

'You have beautiful hair,' he continued, reaching for a strand of it. 'And a lovely figure. That's what's so appealing about you.'

'Just my looks, you mean.' For some reason, Dora was determined to misunderstand him. 'That's all *you* like about me – '

'It's not all I like about you!'

'Isn't it? Well, Tim, listen to me. *Your* fancy might run to fat, wobbly women, but I don't *want* to be like that any more! If I want to lose some weight, I shall! I could perhaps get into some of those rather nice ladies' trousers then. And I was thinking that it's time I took a little more trouble with my face, used some make-up – '

'Make-up!' Tim glowered at her. 'Very well, then,' he muttered crossly. 'Paint your face, get yourself up as a circus clown with white powder on your cheeks and bright red muck all over your lips, shave your head, bind your breasts! And *I* shall grow my hair long, get myself a velveteen jacket and knickerbockers – I shall wear a horrible flopping cravat, yellow socks and shiny brogues the colour of dried blood! I shall get *my* self up as an Artist, like that fellow we met at Gregson's party! I shall grow one of those damned silly beards!'

'And very odd you'd look.' Amused by the idea of Tim in such fancy dress, Dora's ill-humour left her, and she giggled. 'Tim, you'd never do any of that. But, you know, I'd still love you – whatever you wore!'

'And I'll always love you.' He closed his book. 'But don't mutilate yourself for fashion's sake, eh, Dora? Stay beautiful for mine? No trousers or shingles – please?'

'I can't remember the last time you said "please" to me!' Dora laughed. 'Do you *really* prefer me as I am?'

'Yes. Absolutely.' Tim kissed her. 'Shall I show you just how much?'

'Can't I have just a *little* off?' asked Dora later. She pulled the weight of her hair across her shoulders and let the mass of it fall all over Tim's face. 'Just six inches or so? Darling, it's so *heavy*!'

'An inch or two, perhaps. No more.'

'Tyrant.' Dora kissed him. 'Oppressor.'

'Remember what I said, Dora. I'll embarrass you horribly if you annoy me.'

'Velveteen knickerbockers?'

'Precisely.'

'It's from my sister, Judith Barton.' Dora, holding the letter at arm's length as if she expected it to burst into flames, grimaced at Tim. 'She'd like us to visit her! In London! Well!'

'Oh?' Tim, who seemed unmoved by Dora's agitation, buttered himself another slice of toast. 'We could call in when we're next in town, I suppose.'

Dora looked at him. 'Darling,' she cried, 'I've never even met the woman! I wouldn't know her from Joan of Arc!' She fiddled with her wedding ring. 'I can't just drop by, you know,' she added. 'In fact, I hardly think it's desirable to see her at all . . . '

'I don't see why not.' Tim took the letter and read it through. 'After all, she is your sister. And she only wants to make your acquaintance. There's no harm in that, is there?'

'I'll write to Anna. I'll see what she thinks.' Dora frowned. 'I suppose Judith will have written to Anna and Anthony as well?'

'Only one way to find out.' Tim got up from the breakfast table. 'I'm going up to see Gregson this morning,' he said. 'I could call at – where is it – Albany Row? If I shin up a drainpipe I could take a look at the old bird, give her the once over, then let you know – '

'Don't you dare!' Dora stood up. 'I shall telephone Anna. She'll know what it's best to do.'

'*I'm* not going!' Staring severely at her younger sister, Anna passed Dora a cup of tea. 'Why ever should I wish to meet *her*?'

'Out of curiosity?'

'Mmm.' Anna frowned. 'Well, John doesn't want anything to do with her. When all that business blew up, Judith might have done something to smooth things over between him and her mother. But she didn't, did she? I suppose she wanted Mrs Harley's money. All of it.'

'Well, Tim says he'll go with me.' Now that the idea of meeting her half sister had had a chance to mellow, Dora was quite keen to make Judith's acquaintance. 'Tim will come,' she repeated. 'But Anthony won't. Anna, will *you* reconsider? Don't you think it's time to let bygones – '

'Be bygones? Oh, dear little Dora – you've always been

41

much too willing to forgive and forget! No, I shan't come.' Anna poured her sister another cup of tea. 'I want nothing to do with her.'

'Oh. Well, then – I'll let you know how I get on.'

'Do.' Anna reached behind her for the small package which lay on a side table. 'Would you like to see some pictures?' she asked. 'Caroline and the twins?'

'Please.' Dora held out her hand. Taking the folder, she looked at the photographs. 'Goodness,' she said, genuinely amazed. 'Goodness, Anna, they're the image of their father! Exactly like him!'

'Aren't they?' Anna's face relaxed into a smile. 'You must come down next time they're here and see them yourself. Michael's rather more like Marcus used to be, but Tom has the same colouring – he's blond, with grey eyes. Oh, Dora, they're so beautiful! So perfectly lovely!'

And, her grandmotherly gushing now in full spate, Anna began to entertain Dora to a long recital on the theme of her grandsons' beauty, intelligence and general perfection, which would have wearied anyone less patient than her obliging younger sister.

Having decided against taking their children, and having been unable to persuade Anthony and Miriam to accompany them, Tim and Dora had gone to the house in Albany Row alone. Tim paid the cabman, then he and Dora walked up the impressive steps to ring the doorbell of the London town house.

'Quite a decent pile,' remarked Tim, gazing up at the tall Georgian building. 'Would probably fetch a bob or two.'

'Anna said Mrs Harley was practically a millionairess.' Dora shrugged. 'And if Judith inherited all her money – '

' – she'll be worth sucking up to.' Tim grinned, smoothing his lapels. 'Do I look as fetching as I usually do?'

'Oh, shut up. And when we get inside, do behave yourself.'

'Dora, as if I'd – '

'Don't embarrass me, Tim – that's all!'

'Mr and Mrs Atherton?' The stiff-faced housemaid looked severely at Tim and Dora. 'Mrs Barton is expecting you. Will you follow me, please?'

Turning away, the maid led the visitors into a gloomy hall which smelled of furniture polish, and, unmistakably, of money. 'Come this way, please,' she said, as if talking to a pair of morons. She led Tim and Dora upstairs.

'Dora!' Judith Barton rose from her armchair and walked over towards her sister. 'Dora, how kind of you to come! And Mr Atherton, I'm so pleased to make your acquaintance! Do sit down! Shall we have some tea?'

It was awkward – very awkward. The sitting room was quiet, for the hum of London's traffic was deadened by the thick drapes and blinds which practically obscured the windows. The two women talked of their children, establishing, with little squeaks of exaggerated surprise, that they each had a son and a daughter, and wasn't that a coincidence. There was so much to avoid saying, so many unexploded mines of past family scandals to avoid, that their conversation was necessarily superficial and stilted.

Then, suddenly, Judith turned a brilliant smile on Tim. 'Aren't you a writer, Mr Atherton?' she enquired.

Tim nodded. 'Yes. Yes, I am.'

'I haven't had the pleasure of reading your books. But now that I've met *you*, I shall definitely make an effort to do so! In fact,' Judith added graciously, 'I shall go out and buy some tomorrow. Which do you recommend I try first?'

Tim opened his mouth to reply, caught Dora's warning frown – and shut it again. He pushed his hands into his pockets. 'I don't know your tastes in reading,' he said, at last. 'So I can't really recommend anything.'

Dora breathed a sigh of relief. 'Have you any pictures of the children?' she asked, hoping Tim wouldn't say anything more, wouldn't subject this obviously well-meaning but rather silly woman to any teasing or sarcasm, or goad her into any further fatuity. For she could see that he was making mental notes, jotting down the salient characteristics of an idiotic, overweight, middle-aged half wit who had far too much money for her own good and was too patronizing by half . . .

The visit came to an end. Judith stood up to see her visitors out and led them to the front door herself. Vague invitations to call again were issued. Dora promised to write.

Indeed, she did, enclosing photographs of her own children, remarking that the physical similarity between Edmund and Stephen was extraordinary. But the correspondence soon dwindled into a ritual exchange of Christmas cards. The effort to be friends had been made – but too many years and too many unresolved quarrels and bitternesses prevented any real intimacy between the sisters from developing.

Chapter Four

STEPHEN ENJOYED SCHOOL. HIS OWN particular day school, situated a convenient ten minutes' walk away from his home, had a pleasantly relaxed, unacademic atmosphere which suited a child whose main interests in life were cricket and fighting. While he was aware that some of the chaps in his form were keen to get scholarships to various public schools and were prepared to suck up to the masters in order to achieve this end, he had never felt that he himself was expected to knuckle down and get on with it.

'Atherton's sound enough,' his form master had remarked to the headmaster. 'But he's not scholarship material. Odd, considering the family he comes from. Did you read his governor's latest? Awfully good, I thought.'

Lessons over for the morning, at lunchtime groups of little boys sat on the low stone wall which ran the length of the recreation ground, discussing their sporting heroes, or, less frequently, putting the world to rights. Kicking their heels, these infant politicians parroted the views of their elders, and reflected gloomily on the state of the economy with all the gravity of middle-aged men.

'You two chaps going anywhere this summer?' asked John Charlton one sunny afternoon. 'Anywhere on holiday, I mean.'

'I'm not.' Christopher Ingham, who sat on Stephen's other side, flicked a pellet of pre-masticated paper at a passing junior. 'My father says we can't manage it this year. His business isn't doing so well – Ma says it will have to be belt-tightening all round.'

'Bad luck.' Stephen shook his head in sympathy. 'Perhaps you'll get a week at Broadstairs or something,' he added, trying to cheer Ingham up.

'Doubt it.' Ingham scowled. 'Dad reckons he'll be bankrupt before the end of the year unless things pick up a bit. He blames the working classes, you know – they're always on strike, the idle scum, ruining hard-working chaps like him.'

John Charlton nodded wisely. 'My father blames the socialists,' he said. 'And the Jews. He says the Jews are a dirty, oily, greasy race of money-grubbers who are sucking the country dry.'

Ingham leaned sideways, across Stephen's lap. '*My* father thinks that,' he confided. 'It's the Jews who are destroying his business, he says, undercutting him all the time. And he reckons that if all the Jews were sent back to Palestine, where they belong – without all the money they've stolen from us Christians, of course – everything would be much better.'

'It's not fair to blame the Jews.' Stephen, anxious to enlighten his friends, looked from Ingham to Charlton. 'My cousins' grandparents are Jews,' he continued. 'You couldn't meet a nicer couple. And *they're* not rich. In fact, they're rather poor, as it happens. *They* haven't stolen money off anyone.' He glanced derisively at the boy on his left. 'Your father's stupid, Ingham.'

Christopher Ingham looked narrowly at Stephen, considering this. Then, suddenly, he jumped off the wall. 'Atherton's grandparents are Jews!' he yelled loudly, startling a group of seven-year-olds who happened to be dawdling past him. 'Listen to this, everybody! Atherton says his grandfather's a Yid!'

'I didn't say that!' Stephen glowered at Ingham. 'My *cousins'* grandparents, I said! They're not related to me at all!'

But now John Charlton, whose intellectual capacity was so limited that he would have been hard put to describe the difference between a Zulu and an Eskimo, looked curiously at his friend. 'Not related, eh?' he demanded. 'You know,

Atherton, you've got quite a big nose – haven't you? And that's always one of the signs!'

'Well, I think Atherton's a Jew!' Triumphantly Ingham grinned at Stephen. 'Look at him. Black hair, hooky nose. And his ears stick out! Atherton's a greasy little Jew!'

'And he lisps,' added the omniscient Charlton. 'That's a sure sign!'

'I don't lisp!' Stephen glared. 'I *don't*!'

'You do! Yes, you do! Say seven stupid servants sipped sherry! Bet you can't!'

Stephen, now red in the face from embarrassment and anger, glared from Ingham to Charlton. 'No!' he muttered. 'No, I won't!'

'Go on, Atherton! Say it! You can't, can you?'

'I can! Seven stupid – ' Stephen jumped off the wall and faced Ingham. 'No, I won't say it!' he shouted. 'I'm not a Jew! And even if I was – '

'If you've got Jewish cousins you must have some Jewish blood in you.' Ingham grinned. 'Who are these cousins, anyway? Do they live in Oxford?'

Stephen at last realized the value of discretion. 'Mind your own business,' he muttered.

By now, however, a group of a dozen or more boys had gathered round Stephen and Ingham, all demanding to know what the quarrel was about. John Charlton explained. And then, with much sagacious shaking of their heads, some boys agreed that Atherton certainly had a Hebraic air about him. Ingham, feeling that the mob was on his side, caught at Stephen's hair and yanked his head back. 'Go on, Atherton,' he jeered. 'Own up! You're a Jew, aren't you? A dirty little Jew! Admit it!'

'No!' Jerking free, Stephen hurled himself at Ingham, knocking him to the ground and winding him. He was on top of his tormentor before Ingham had the chance to get his breath back.

The reason for the fight was immediately forgotten in the thrill of the combat itself, and a crowd of children now gathered round the grey flannelled pugilists, cheering them on.

'Come on, Atherton!'

'Kill him, Ingham!'

'Get his head down! Smash his skull!'

'Go on, Ingham, murder him!'

Although Christopher Ingham was taller and heavier than him, Stephen had the advantage in that he had completely lost his temper, and with it any sense of fair play. He thumped Ingham unmercifully, hitting him wherever he could. Bloody about the nose and cut about the eyes, Ingham eventually realized he was no match for an assailant who was half mad with fury. 'Pax, Atherton!' he managed to gurgle, through bleeding lips. 'Pax, damn you! Oh, God, somebody get him off me!'

At last, Ingham's bleats penetrated the red fog of Stephen's anger. Aware that he'd won, he twisted his adversary's forelock around his fingers and banged Ingham's head sharply against the ground. Then he rose to his feet and began, unconcernedly, to dust himself off.

'Jolly well done, Atherton.' John Charlton, the primary cause of all the commotion, clapped Stephen on the back. 'Jolly well fought. Your father's a good fighter, isn't he? Wasn't he a hero in the war?'

Too elated by victory to recognize the oily tones of sycophancy, Stephen nodded. 'He was a major,' he said. 'He won the DSO.'

By now Ingham had got to his feet. He sidled up to Stephen. 'Shake hands, eh, Atherton?' he offered.

'What?'

'Shake hands.' Ingham proffered his own. 'I'm sorry I said you were a Jew,' he added. 'Anyone can see you're not. Jews can't fight – *they're* all cowards.' He put an affectionate arm around Stephen's shoulders. 'Not like you, Atherton. Shake, eh?'

Stephen eyed Ingham's hand and wondered about twisting the fingers right back. But English decency prevailed – he took it and held it firmly for a second or two, before strolling nonchalantly across the playground and into school for afternoon classes.

*　　　*　　　*

48

He walked home from school slowly that day, thinking. It had been a mistake to admit to Jewish connections, he saw that now. *Why* it should matter that his Aunt Miriam – who was far and away his favourite of all his grown up relations – was Jewish, wasn't at all clear to him. But he realized that, in future, her ancestry wasn't something to be discussed with his friends in the playground.

It wasn't as if it was anyone's business, anyway. But, as he walked through the garden gate and up the path to his house, he was still worrying about it.

'You've been fighting again, you little horror!' Dora was in the kitchen talking to her cook. She smiled reproachfully at her son. 'What was it about this time?'

Stephen returned his mother's smile with an engaging grin of his own. 'Nothing much,' he replied. 'A chap was rude to me. So I thrashed him.'

'It rather looks as if he thrashed you!'

'Oh, no. He has *two* black eyes. And a cut lip.'

Helen, who was sitting at the kitchen table drinking a glass of milk, batted her long eyelashes at her brother. Amusement crinkling the corners of her large grey eyes, she flicked her hair back from her forehead, and stared at Stephen with all the assurance of an older sister who is almost thirteen. 'He *is* stupid, isn't he?' she demanded. 'Really stupid. Like all boys.'

Stephen kicked her under the table and glowered at her. But still she grinned at him, as infuriatingly cool and superior as always, as relaxed and languid as her father, who also seemed to find Stephen something of a joke . . .

When Helen went upstairs, Stephen followed her. He looked round the door. 'Can I come in, Nell?' he asked.

'What? Oh, all right.' Helen laid down her book. 'But take your shoes off before you get on my bed.'

Stephen did as he was told, and then joined Helen under her counterpane. They both snuggled right down, making the comfortable dark cave in which they usually hid themselves when they wanted to talk in private. In the stuffy gloom confidences were exchanged, fears admitted and counsel offered.

'So what was it really about?' asked Helen kindly. She looked at her brother. 'Steve, whatever did he say to you?'

'Nothing much.'

'It must have been *something*! Who was it, anyway?'

Stephen sniffed. 'It was Ingham,' he replied. 'He said I looked like a Jew.'

'Oh.' Helen laughed. 'Well, I'm not surprised,' she said. 'You do. Either that, or your ancestors came from India. You don't look English, you must admit.'

'Huh.' Stephen, lying warm and relaxed under Helen's eiderdown, squirmed a little closer to his sister, making himself comfortable. Looking at her he had to agree that, far from appearing to be siblings, they might have been from different races. 'Ingham's a pig,' he said, savagely. 'He thumps the juniors and pinches their sweets. It was time somebody thrashed him.'

'Is he that tall fair-haired boy? The one with the very blue eyes and lots of freckles?'

'That's him.'

'He's a lot bigger than you.' Helen giggled. 'Aren't you brave to tackle him?'

'Oh, shut up.'

Helen pushed his shoulder. 'You are a silly little boy, Stevie,' she murmured, into his ear. 'I don't believe he was rude to you. I think you just enjoy fighting.'

'Mm.' Remembering his victory, Stephen laughed. 'I suppose I do,' he conceded, at last. 'Nell – are we going to Cornwall this summer?'

'I think so. Dad was saying something about taking that house near St Ives for a month. Why?'

'I just wondered. Ingham's not having a holiday this year. I expect that's what made him so scratchy.'

'I expect so.'

'Nell, I – '

'Steve, don't worry!' Helen took her brother's hand and chafed it. 'You're always worrying,' she added. 'You go about looking as if you have the weight of the world on your poor little shoulders. Look, shall we go and have a game of tennis before tea?'

'All right.' Stephen sat up, wincing as he realized that his arm was very sore. 'I'll just go and put some iodine on my elbow.'

'I'll get out the racquets. You will be quick, won't you?'

As he slouched along to the bathroom and dabbed his skinned elbow with the brownish liquid, Stephen reflected that he was quite fortunate in his sister. For a girl, Helen was rather a good chap.

That Sunday the two families sat down to their lunch together, all ranged around the big mahogany table at the Summertown house where the Lawrences lived. And now Stephen noticed for the first time that his cousin David did in fact lisp. Only very slightly, of course; but, once he'd realized this, Stephen could not help noticing it. Rachel's voice was very similar to her brother's. His aunt, whose English was fairly heavily accented anyway, certainly had a full-blooded lisp, always had done . . .

'Stephen?' His mother's voice startled him. 'Your uncle was speaking to you!'

'He's in a world of his own.' His aunt Miriam's soft, pleasant voice brought him back to reality. 'Steve, will you have a wing?' she asked. 'I know how you like them.' She smiled at him. 'Hold out your plate.'

He did so, looking at her pretty face with its sad, dark eyes and sweet mouth. He thought how nice she was. If ever Ingham or any of his horrible friends ever called her a dirty Jew, he'd smash their rotten heads in and tread their eyeballs into the playground dirt . . .

'Stephen!' Now Dora was determined to attract her son's attention. 'Stephen, *will* you pass the vegetables? What's the matter with the child today?'

'He must have had a hard week, poor lamb.'

'Leave him alone.' Miriam patted her nephew's hand. 'Let him eat his dinner.'

Tall, slim, handsome, at eighteen already grown up, self assured and worldly wise, David Lawrence could not have

51

asked for a more devoted esquire than his younger cousin Stephen. No medieval knight could have been worshipped and adored more than Stephen adored David, who, after his own father, was Stephen's idea of what a man ought to be.

After brooding about Ingham's remarks for a week or more, Stephen decided that he would talk to David. He strolled round to the Summertown house one Saturday morning and met David just as he came out of the front door.

'Hullo, Steve.' David grinned at him. 'Looking for your mum? She's in the breakfast room with mine.'

'Actually, I wanted to talk to you.'

'Did you now? Well, you can't just at present. I'm going out.'

'Where are you going?'

David pushed his cousin's shoulder. 'Nosy little devil!' he replied. 'That's none of your business!'

Stephen looked abashed. 'Sorry,' he said. 'Can I - well, could I walk along with you for a bit? I want to ask you something.'

David looked at his cousin's deep frown. He shrugged. 'All right,' he said. 'I'm going down to the Parks. You can come some of the way with me, but when I tell you to clear off, you go - right?'

'Yes, David.' Stephen opened the gate and went out on to the pavement.

'So what is all this then?' asked David, as they walked down the Banbury Road. 'What d'you want to discuss? Some fellow at school upset you? Your mum was complaining to mine that you're always fighting.'

'It's not that.'

'Well, what then?'

'Well - you know your mother's family came from Russia?'

'Yes, I do know that.' David grinned down at Stephen. 'Did you think I wasn't aware of it?'

Stephen ignored the sarcasm. 'Well - Aunt Miriam - she's not English, is she?'

'No, she's not. What's all this leading up to, eh?'

Stephen took a deep breath. 'David, does it matter that you're a Jew?' he asked.

'Does it matter? Well, that all depends.' They had reached the Parks now; and, stooping down, David picked up a stone and skimmed it across the river. 'Depends on where you live, as much as anything. I wouldn't care to be living in Russia or Germany these days.'

'Why?'

'Oh - for various reasons.' David grimaced. 'Hatred of Jews is a hardy perennial which always seems to burst into flower when things go wrong. Whenever anything bad happens, the Jews are traditionally held responsible. At the moment, the country's in a financial mess, so the Jewish bankers are being blamed.'

He pushed his hands into his pockets and laughed, but this was a bitter, harsh sound which came from the back of his throat. 'When Jonathan married Eleanor,' he continued, 'her parents didn't know which to squawk about more - they couldn't decide which was worse, the fact that my brother is an atheist, or that he's a Jew. Oh, yes, Steve - when things get difficult, society always blames the Jews.'

'Why?'

David shrugged. 'They're convenient scapegoats, I suppose.'

'So it's not actually their fault?'

'Oh, God!' David skimmed another pebble across the water. 'What a bloody stupid question!' He glared at his cousin. 'Who's put all this rubbish into your head, anyway?'

Stephen reddened. 'I didn't mean to be stupid,' he muttered. 'Dave, I - '

'Oh, never mind.' David pushed Stephen's shoulder. 'Look, Steve - do you think you could go and ponder the mysteries of the universe somewhere else now? I'm meeting someone.'

Stephen scowled. 'Someone' was probably female. This increasing interest in women was a fairly recent development, and it was one which Stephen definitely hadn't welcomed. 'Is it a girl?' he demanded. 'I bet it's a girl!'

'Yes, it is a girl, you inquisitive little bugger. So buzz off now, there's a good chap.' David grinned. 'She won't want a scruffy little horror like you trailing after her!'

Stephen saw his cousin's eyes brighten. Following their direction, he saw a very ordinary-looking girl, obviously a student, walking across the grass towards them. So he buzzed off.

As he walked home, he wondered why David should prefer to be strolling around the Parks with some boring girl when he could be playing cricket (which he did extremely well), or running races down on the sports field (slim but strong and well-made, David was a natural sprinter). And he wondered why David had never taken up boxing.

For it was a legend at Stephen's school that Lawrence Minor had once taken on Fred Heathcote, a boy almost twice his size, and thrashed him practically unconscious. Lawrence Minor had been something of a celebrity, to whom Stephen Atherton was proud to be related.

But no-one had, of course, been aware that this same Lawrence Minor's mother was a Russian Jew. Even as a child, David had possessed a far better developed sense of natural discretion than that with which his young cousin was blessed.

Chapter Five

BY THE TIME HE WAS FIFTEEN, Stephen Atherton's intro-
spections had still not solved the mysteries of the universe.
But they *had* resulted in the crystallization of a personal
ambition, one which he was determined to realize at any
cost.

He was going to be a professional soldier. Like his father,
whom, from earliest infancy, Stephen had always placed
next to God, he was going to be a Guards officer. And,
once he'd decided this, he knew that there was no other
prospect open to him.

'Yes, I agree that you've got to do *something*,' Helen had
remarked, when he had confided this scheme to her. 'But I
can't think why you want to join the Army! I really can't
imagine anything more ghastly!'

'Can't you?'

'No.' Helen giggled. 'And anyway - what's the use of an
army, in peacetime?'

'There's going to be another war soon. Everyone says
so.'

'Oh, I *see*! You want to be in on it, do you? You want to
be out there with your own little gun, bang bang you're
dead and all the rest of it? Ugh.'

She looked at him. 'Stevie, dear, in the next war - if
there is one - all that'll happen is that our enemies will gas
the lot of us. Aeroplanes will come out of the sky and a
great poisonous cloud will cover the land. We'll be all dead,
finished, kaput. What use will the Brigade of Guards be if

the whole lot of them are lying in neat rows with their toes in the air?'

'Oh, shut up, Nell!' Irritably, Stephen had glared at her. 'I might have known *you* wouldn't understand!'

From very early childhood, Stephen's most precious possession had been a tattered strip of red and blue ribbon, a scrap of material which Tim had left lying in a drawer together with a jumble of other army badges, buttons and insignia - all of which Dora had unpicked from her husband's uniform before she'd got rid of it. And for ten or more years now that bit of cloth, wrapped in silver paper and secreted in a little black japanned box as if in a shrine, had been Stephen's talisman - almost his personal deity.

When he'd asked his father where the medal itself was, Tim had frowned and shrugged his shoulders. 'Don't know, Steve,' he'd replied, offhandedly. 'Ask your mother what she did with it. She's got all that rubbish tucked away somewhere.' And he'd gone on writing, hadn't even looked up.

Such insouciance had impressed Stephen beyond measure. Not only was his father a hero; he evidently regarded heroism as part of a soldier's daily routine.

'I'm going into the Army when I leave school,' Stephen had announced one evening, during a family dinner. 'I'm going into the Guards.'

'Are you, dear?' His mother, who had almost finished her meal and was telling herself that she didn't *really* need another helping of pudding, laid down her cutlery and got up from the table. She murmured something to Helen, who shrugged, then got up and followed Dora out of the dining room. Tim was left alone with his son, who now enlarged on his ambitions, growing more and more florid as he warmed to his theme.

'And so there it is,' Stephen said, bringing his speech to a rounded conclusion. 'I want to be a soldier, like you. And that's what I'm going to be,' he added, leaving 'whether

56

you like it or not' unsaid, but hovering in the air as plainly as if he'd articulated the words.

'Are you, indeed.' Tim leaned back in his chair. '*I* never wanted to be a soldier, you know,' he said carefully. 'I never had any ambitions in that direction. I joined the Army because my father insisted upon it. And – '

'You did very well all the same,' interrupted Stephen. 'And during the war you were in France and Flanders, you were in all the big battles; you must have had quite a time of it – '

'Steve, I was on active service during the war because I had no choice!' Tim lit a cigarette. 'Listen to me,' he continued. 'If it's adventures you want, you won't get them on a battlefield. War isn't glamorous – most of the time it's just intolerably boring. And battle is a bloody awful experience; it's a combination of pain and terror and confusion, there's no glory in it! I can tell you now that during much of my time in the trenches I was just plain scared. And after an action – '

'Why are you trying to put me off?' Stephen scowled at his father. 'Mum said that after the war you wanted to stay in the Army – that you would have done so if your health had been good enough!'

'But that was when the war was *over*, Steve!' Tim laughed at his son's expression of incomprehension. 'Most soldiers don't like war, you know,' he added. 'It gets in the way – it interrupts training and exercises. And it stops one from playing polo and chasing women; which were the two main interests of the chaps in my regiment!

'Look – I wanted to stay in the Army because by then I felt part of it; it was my family, if you understand me. And also, I didn't think I could do anything else.'

'So you don't want me to go into the Guards, is that what you're saying?'

'I'm not sure that you're going to be tall enough. And anyway, if you want an exciting life, I think you'd do better to become an explorer or a field scientist; paddle a canoe up the Amazon, something like that.'

'You think I'm still a little kid, don't you?' Stephen

chewed his lower lip. 'You think I swallow all that *Boys'*
Own Paper rubbish wholesale. You think I – '

'On the contrary, I give you credit for a reasonable
degree of intelligence. But listen – why don't you go up to
Cambridge, eh? Think about the Army again when you're
twenty-one?'

'I want to go to *Sandhurst*, Dad!' Stephen's heavy black
eyebrows knitted angrily. 'I don't want to waste three years
going to drunken parties! I don't want to fool around with a
gang of idiots from public school, half-wits whose idea of
fun is falling out of punts into some muddy old river! And
what's the point of stuffing my head with even more useless
information? Oh, God – I'd be bored stiff at college, it
would be worse than school is now! And anyway, I want to
leave St Anselm's next year, so I shan't qualify for
university entrance.'

Tim, remembering his own three years at Oxford,
laughed at his son's glower. 'You must take HSC,' he said
firmly. 'But after that, if you're certain – '

'Yes, Dad, I am.' Stephen looked anxiously at his father.
'Dad, I'll make you proud of me, believe me I shall! I
shan't let you down, you'll have no cause to be ashamed of
me!'

'Listen, Steve, I'm sure I'd never be ashamed of you,
whatever you – '

'So you'll make some enquiries?'

'Yes, if you're sure it's what you really want.'

'I'm quite sure.' A sudden beaming smile irradiated
Stephen's dark features. 'Thanks, Dad.'

Tim lit another cigarette. 'There's plenty of time to
think about it,' he remarked. 'So if you do decide to stay on
at school, go to university – '

'I know. But I shan't change my mind.' Still grinning,
Stephen looked enquiringly at his father. 'Can I have a
gasper, please?' he asked.

Without really thinking about it, Tim pushed the box
across the table and his son, lighting up, wondered if he
might push his luck so far as to ask for a whisky as well.

*   *   *

58

The Lawrences were happily settled in the large Victorian house which was now so cluttered with the belongings of three generations that Dora called it the old ancestral home. Today they were celebrating a particular success with a special meal.

Jonathan, David's elder brother, had always been determined to do well in the business world and become a bright star in the organization for which he worked. After leaving school, he had elected not to go on to university. Instead, he had gone as a general trainee to a light engineering firm.

This company had survived the recession of the Twenties and in the Thirties it had expanded and amalgamated with other organizations. Now it was part of a great business empire which, although the parent factory itself was in Germany, had subsidiaries and agents all over Europe and America.

'He's one to watch,' Jonathan's superiors had observed. 'Push him a bit – see how he copes.' But Jonathan had not needed to be pushed. With single-minded determination, he had made his way through all the departments of the English branch and had then been sent to the United States for three years.

At first he had been dismissed as a know-all from England who needed to be sat on hard; but, gradually gaining the confidence of his colleagues, he had helped to revolutionize production techniques and had been instrumental in a marketing and promotion drive which had increased turnover threefold. 'We'll be sorry to lose you,' his boss had told him, not altogether sincerely. 'I expect the next time we hear of you, you'll be on the Board.'

'I hope so, sir,' Jonathan had replied, not altogether modestly. He had returned to England, thence to be summoned to head office in Hamburg, where he had received a personal commendation from the managing director of the firm, Helmut Dussell himself.

And now, at the age of thirty, all his hard work had really paid off. His boss in America had been a prophet. Jonathan had been offered a directorship, which made him by far the youngest member of the Board. Now earning more than three times his father's salary, Jonathan had plans to rise even higher.

'I'll be company chairman one day,' he'd told his wife, who'd thought to herself that at the rate he was going he'd have a coronary first. 'There's nothing to stop me now, Ellie. Nothing at all.'

Eleanor had nodded. 'I suppose there isn't,' she had agreed. 'But, darling, you drive yourself much too hard. When was the last time you took the boys out? When was the last time we did anything as a family?'

'I shall let up a little now.' Jonathan was at last willing to believe that he had some security and that the firm needed him more than he needed them. Two or three times in the past month, he had been approached by head-hunters, and he knew well that there was no likelihood of Dussell's allowing their *wunderkind* to be snatched by a rival. He kissed his wife. 'We'll have a fortnight at the seaside this year,' he promised her. 'I shall fish for shrimps with Alec and go boating with Julian.' He laughed. 'You don't believe me, do you?'

Eleanor shrugged. 'And you'll take me out to dinner?' she enquired. 'You'll even make time for *me*?'

'Certainly.' He hugged her. 'You think I'll bring a caseful of files with me, don't you? That I'll sit on the beach costing next year's projects?'

'Mmm.' Eleanor kissed him back. 'I shall see, shan't I? I shall see.'

Coming from such an academic family, in which his father and both his grandfathers had been Classics dons and his brother looked likely to become a university teacher too, Jonathan had had to endure a fair degree of teasing as he'd made his determined way to the top of the management tree.

'You really fancy yourself as a tycoon now, don't you, Jon?' demanded his irritating little brother David, eyeing Jonathan's beautifully cut Savile Row suit and hand-finished Jermyn Street shirt with some degree of amusement. 'You're in all the newspapers these days – "businessman of the year" was what *The Times* called you a day or two ago.'

'Really? I didn't notice that.' Jonathan's dark eyes met David's. Taking in his brother's deliberately slovenly appearance and looking pointedly at the great tear in one of David's jacket sleeves, he grinned in the infuriatingly superior fashion which older siblings tend to assume. 'I wonder why you think it's a crime to try to do well in life?' he demanded. 'I wonder why you're so determined to despise material success?'

'I wonder when you became a mind reader? Was it at about the same time that you decided to register as a fully paid up capitalist?' David lit a cigarette. 'Tell me, what does it feel like to be a member of the Establishment?'

'I couldn't begin to explain. Not to a junior common room pink like you.' With the air of a lion brushing aside a mouse, Jonathan turned away and murmured something to his mother, who shook her head at him and sighed.

'Well, I'd rather be a pink than a bastion of the Tory Party.' David grinned. 'When the revolution comes, though, you needn't worry – I'll put in a good word for you. I'll see to it that Ellie and the children don't go up against the wall, even if you do.'

'I'm sure they'll be much obliged to you.'

'So am I.' David narrowed his eyes. 'And in the meantime, don't turn your back for an instant. All those nasty sharp knives must be honed to perfection by now. Be very careful, won't you?'

'I shall.' Jonathan shook his head. 'Oh, don't fret, little cardboard Lenin; don't worry about me! I do know how to recognize an enemy.' He leaned back in his chair and folded his arms. 'And anyway, Dave, what are you going to do with the rest of *your* life? Don't you fancy the cut and thrust of big business?'

'No, thanks.' David inhaled a mouthful of smoke. 'I don't see myself as a glorified vacuum cleaner salesman. I shall hang about the groves of academe for a few years more.'

'I see.' Jonathan grinned. 'Well, loafing around a college will certainly give you plenty of opportunity to indulge in your favourite hobby!'

'What's that supposed to mean?'

'You'll be free to chase women. I assume that now you've cut your swathe through the female population of Cambridge, you'll be starting on the undergraduates here?'

'*Starting*?' Rachel, the elder of two sisters, giggled. 'Goodness, Jon, he's been in Oxford all summer; he's already broken at least a dozen hearts!' She eyed David sideways. 'How many is it now, Davy? There's poor Alex, she's *really* suffering. There's Jane; and there's Georgina, who's trying to shame him into fidelity. She's wasting her time there! I tell you, Jon – he's insatiable!'

David shrugged. 'They throw themselves at me,' he said, evidently not displeased to be branded a Lothario. He scowled at his sister. 'It's time *you* found yourself a husband,' he told her. 'Look at Kathy' – he glanced at his gentler sister – 'four years younger than you, and already the mother of twins!'

Rachel made a face at him. 'Kathy might not be the only one to have twins,' she retorted. 'They seem to run in this family. I heard a rumour that the Betteridge girl was pregnant – huge they say she is, and only five months gone! Davy, we all know how fond she was of you at one time. So – '

'Bitch!' David glared at Rachel. 'Prurient little busybody, dirty-minded – '

'Children!' Suddenly, their mother's voice cut across what threatened to become an increasingly unpleasant squabble. 'Rachel, don't be so disgusting. And David, I'm surprised at you! Such language! And at the dinner table as well! Now – I think it's time we congratulated Jonathan properly. Anthony?'

'What?' Anthony, who had been in a daydream of his own throughout the meal, started. 'What did you say, dear?'

'We should have a toast to Jon and Ellie.'

'Ah. Yes.' Anthony stood up.

'I'm glad you're doing so well.' Miriam smiled at her beloved elder son. 'But don't work too hard, will you? There are more important things in life than money, and if you wear yourself out – '

'I shan't let him do that.' Eleanor Lawrence touched her mother-in-law's hand. 'Jon's not stupid, you know – he has his priorities right, his children and family come first.' She smiled at her husband. 'Isn't that right?'

'I hope so,' he replied.

Anthony coughed. 'May I have your attention?' he asked. 'Well – what shall I say? To the future chairman of Dussell International? Ladies and gentlemen – '

The Athertons too remained, on the whole, a happy, united family. Although Dora felt that she was steadily losing her son – indeed, had already lost the grubby but endearing little child who was now an uncommunicative, often sullen teenager – she told herself that this growing away from her was natural in a boy.

'He's so like Papa!' she had remarked one day, shrugging helplessly at Tim. For Stephen had been sulking for almost a week now. Obviously, something had annoyed him, but no-one in the family had been privileged to learn exactly what.

'Steve – is anything the matter?' she asked him later that evening, as the family sat together in the drawing room.

'I expect some girl's upset him.' Glancing up at her brother, Helen grinned at Stephen from the safety of the sofa. 'Yesterday,' she told Dora, 'I saw him and Robert with two fourth years from St Clare's. Do you know, Stephen's was quite pretty. Black hair, green eyes.' Helen giggled. 'Who was she, Steve?'

In reply, Stephen's cheeks reddened. He muttered something no-one actually heard, and went on with his book. But, feeling his sister's gaze upon him still, he got up. He went out of the room, slamming the door behind him.

'Surly brute.' Tim laughed. 'Nell, don't tease him. It's

very mean – especially when you know how touchy he is. Dora, where are you going?'

'Just to see – '

'Leave him alone. You'll only make it worse!'

So, increasingly, Dora left her son alone, and for company she became more and more dependent on her daughter. For Miriam, now a grandmother four times over, had very little time to spare and was in any case very preoccupied these days, forever frowning and fretting about some private worry which she refused to discuss, even with her best friend. She was as bad as Stephen sometimes . . .

In her pretty daughter, however, Dora had an agreeable companion. Helen, whose straightforward character and pleasant manners reassured her mother that Stephen's habitual sourness was not the result of parental mismanagement, became her mother's confidante, her friend.

'We'll go up to town today, shall we?' Dora would ask, comfortably aware that Helen enjoyed an aimless wander around the West End as much as her mother did. 'We'll get your father to drive us up and he can go round the bookshops while we have a look in the department stores.'

For it was a form of purgatory to take Tim shopping. 'Yes,' he would say, without even looking at the garment concerned. 'Yes, darling, it's fine. Buy it – then come and have a drink somewhere, eh?'

Helen, on the other hand, would look, consider, exclaim, criticize; and *she* was responsible for the fact that her mother was nicely dressed and properly – if discreetly – made up. It was due to Helen that Dora looked as attractive as she did, attired in the pastel colours and the softly draped garments of the Thirties which flattered her figure so well.

'It needs an inch off the hem. There.' Helen stood back to appraise the results of that particular day's expedition; satisfied, she smiled. 'Yes, I think Dad'll like that. But the black and white dress ought to go back. It's too severe. You'll look like that awful Harper woman in that sort of thing.'

'Who?' Dora, still examining herself in her looking glass, frowned. 'What awful Harper woman?'

'You know – the one in Dad's last.' Helen opened a workbox and took out a pincushion. 'Mrs Harper, the dyed blonde. The one with the Frog fancy man.'

'Oh, her.' Dora sniffed. 'I thought you meant a real person. Well, I don't dye my hair yellow. And your father's too critical anyway. According to him, any woman who even wears lipstick is a trollop. I can't think why.'

'It's his age.' Helen grinned. 'Poor Dad, he can't help being a fossil stuck in the mud of the last century. He associates make-up with a Certain Sort of Woman – and he always will.'

Since he was her father, Helen made a point of reading the fossil's work. But she was, on the whole, unimpressed by it. 'There's no romance in Dad's books,' she complained one day, laying down a first edition of Tim's most recent novel, and stifling a quite genuine yawn. Worldly wise at sixteen, she did wish her father was more in tune with the times. 'There's no feeling,' she continued, shaking her head. 'No emotion!'

'Should there be?' Dora, who was sewing, broke off her thread. 'He isn't out to entertain your age group, you know. He doesn't write for teenage girls . . . '

'Just as well.' Helen held up a copy of the novel she was currently reading, a torrid romance by the most popular author of the day. 'Can't he try something more like this?'

'*The Heart Knows the Answer.* Eleanora Harlowe.' Dora grimaced. 'Well, I daresay he could parody the style, but I'm not sure that he'd deceive many of Miss Harlowe's fans!'

'He wouldn't fool this one.'

'No, I don't imagine he would. Anyway, your father's books are *funny*. He makes his readers laugh. If you want romantic fiction with lots of heaving and groaning, you must stick to what's-her-name you're holding.'

Helen sniffed. 'The trouble is, he's becoming respectable. Soon, he'll be a grand old man of letters and his stuff will be read in schools as set books. And nowhere else!'

'He was talking of trying a political thriller next.' Dora re-threaded her needle. 'Something about those awful people in Germany, what are they called? And I doubt if *that* will be the sort of thing English masters will want to set for examinations.'

'I still think a bit of passion is what's needed. In any sort of book. It's all very well being witty and clever at his victims' expense. It's all very well sending up politicians and sneering at other peoples' stupidity. But tastes change, and I really do think – '

'That your father ought to address himself to the vagaries of the human heart?'

Helen nodded. She chewed her lower lip reflectively. 'I expect he'd be embarrassed to write about things like that, though, wouldn't he? About being in love, and all that.'

Dora considered; and decided that among the many and varied traits of Tim's personality a tendency to be embarrassed wasn't really very marked. 'I don't think so. He simply doesn't choose to write about that side of life, that's all.'

'Well, he should. If he wants to sell.'

The entry into the drawing room of the subject under discussion put an end to Helen's examination of her father's literary shortcomings. Tim sat down on the sofa beside his daughter; then he picked up the novel lying next to her. 'What's this, eh?' he enquired, leafing through it.

'It's mine.' Helen reddened. 'From Elliston's library. Give it back, Dad; it won't interest you.'

'Won't it?' Tim stopped flicking pages and began to read out loud. ' "White with anger, she slapped his face. He caught her wrist and held it. 'Let me go!' she demanded. In response, he pulled her close to him and kissed her hard upon the lips. Her pulse raced." ' Tim raised his eyebrows. 'Good stuff, eh, Nell?' he demanded.

'Dad, please!'

' "Like an imprisoned bird, she was held firmly against his breast. And then, suddenly, she could withstand him no longer. Her heart melting within her, she softened – she gazed into his eyes." Her heart melted within her, eh?' Tim laughed. '*Very* messy!'

Helen had had enough. She snatched the book from him, and stalked out of the room.

'Helen was funny today,' remarked Dora, as she got ready for bed that evening.

'Oh?' Tim took off his watch, emptied his pockets, yawned. 'What did she do?'

'Well, you know how she's always got her nose in a book, usually some highly coloured romantic nonsense like the stuff she was reading today?' Dora grinned at her husband. 'Well, she's decided that *you're* out of step with the times, and unless you pull your socks up, you're going to become a *respectable* writer. A literary genius whose work nobody wants to read.'

'Shall I, indeed?' Tim pulled a face. 'A respectable writer – now there's the proverbial fate worse than death.' He grinned back at Dora. 'Well – did she have any idea how this is to be avoided?'

'Oh, but yes! Darling, she thinks that you ought to inject some passion into your witty little stories. You know – some romance, some emotion.'

'Melting hearts and all that.'.

'Precisely.' Dora giggled. 'Otherwise, she says, you're going to find yourself on the scrap heap . . . '

'I see. And I'd just begun to let myself believe that I was becoming established!' Mournfully Tim eyed his wife. 'Passion, eh?' he demanded.

'Yes. Kisses and stuff. Romance.'

'Ah.' Tim sighed. 'Well, Dora, I'm an old man now. Most of my passion's spent. And as for romance – I'm too ancient to remember what *that* is!'

'That's what I thought.' Dora looked at him speculatively. 'In fact, these days I sometimes wonder if you've *ever* known what it's like to - oh! Tim! What do you think you're doing?'

'Just an experiment.' Grabbing Dora by the shoulders and pushing her backwards on to her bed, Tim kissed her. 'I might be bloody old, Dora,' he muttered. 'I might be decrepit. But I'm not completely past it yet!'

'Aren't you? Oh, Tim, don't tickle, it's mean!' Dora laughed at him. 'Look, I never said you were too old for - '

'You implied it.' Tim began to unfasten his wife's blouse. 'And, for your information, I'm damned well not! Come on, then,' he murmured into her loosened hair. 'Co-operate, can't you? Tremble, or moan - or something!'

Dora giggled. 'Should I slap your face? Or shall I lie here passive and unresisting, letting a great tide of longing surge through my body?'

'Anything you like.' Tim laughed. 'After all, it's in the cause of literary research. And if it saves us from bank-ruptcy - well!'

Helen, in her bedroom along the landing, heard her mother's muffled giggle and her father's answering growl of laughter. 'It's disgusting, at their age,' she thought, as she pulled the hood of bedclothes over her head and got on with Eleanora Harlowe's latest masterwork. 'Quite disgusting.'

68

Chapter Six

DORA HANDED THE LETTER TO TIM, and watched him while he read. As she'd expected, he frowned. And, as she'd also expected, he handed it back to her without comment. 'Well?' she demanded.

'Well what?'

'May she come?'

'I'd rather she didn't.' Tim leaned back in his chair. 'If she's anything like her mother, she'll be an absolute pain. You don't want her here, do you?'

'Not particularly. But I can hardly tell Judith that, can I?' Dora read the letter through again. 'She offers to pay for her keep, she asks very nicely, and - ' Dora looked reproachfully at Tim - 'the girl *is* my niece. Helen and Stephen are her cousins, and she has no other close relations - or at any rate, none that her mother knows. I really do think I ought to say yes . . . '

'Well, I think it's a damned cheek. Oh, for God's sake, Dora - the woman might be your half sister, but she's never taken any real interest in you! So what makes her think she has the right to foist her daughter on us for God knows how long?'

'She doesn't think she has the right to do anything of the sort. Look, Tim - she's going to the USA for six months, then she'd like to visit some of her husband's family in Canada. She's not sure how long she'll be away.' Dora frowned. 'I do see her point,' she said. 'It would be nice for

Elizabeth to get to know her cousins. Darling, shall I write back and agree to this?'

'If you feel you must. But don't be too effusive, eh? Don't overdo the affectionate aunt routine. We don't want to be lumbered with the girl for ever!'

Elizabeth Barton arrived in a chauffeur-driven Bentley, from which a dozen or more pieces of expensive leather luggage were unloaded. She greeted her aunt with regal graciousness.

Over tea in the drawing room, Dora studied her niece. Looking for family resemblances, there was, she decided, a superficial likeness between this girl and her own daughter. But whereas Helen Atherton was fair-haired and fair skinned in a typically English way, Elizabeth was, though also a blonde, physically remarkable.

She was a marble statue come to life. *Her* hair was flaxen; it lay upon her shoulders in a thick, white-gold mane. Her face was classically perfect, serene and expressionless; and her features, individually distinguished, were collectively beautiful. Her skin, very pale and totally flawless, added to the generally marmoreal effect. In fact, Dora had expected the hand which had taken hers to be as cold as stone and the cheek which touched her face to have been as hard as the alabaster it resembled. She had been surprised to find her niece's flesh was warm. Warm, and soft as a little child's.

It soon became apparent that Elizabeth wasn't a pain. She was good-mannered and inclined to be silent unless spoken to. Stephen ignored her completely. Helen, more friendly, chatted to her about clothes and hairstyles. Tim teased her a little, but when he realized that she did not appear to understand his remarks, he took no further notice of her. Only her aunt made a real effort to make their guest feel at home.

'You don't mind her being here, do you?' asked Dora anxiously, about a week after Elizabeth had arrived. 'She's quiet, and she's *very* obliging. She's so eager to please that it's almost embarrassing.'

'Yes, she's pleasant enough.' Tim had observed Elizabeth's beauty, but decided that such loveliness did not compensate for what appeared to be a completely colourless personality. He grinned at his wife. 'She's as emptyheaded and boring as most girls of that age, but she's a decorative enough ornament. She may stay.'

'She *is* very beautiful, isn't she?' Dora sighed. 'Quite lovely; don't you think so?'

'A bit insipid for my taste; I prefer brunettes.' Tim picked up a pencil. 'We'd better keep her away from David,' he added. 'Poor child, she doesn't look as if she'd know how to deal with the Casanova of the Banbury Road!'

'No.' Dora nodded her agreement. 'No, she doesn't.'

The Casanova of the Banbury Road. David Lawrence wouldn't have been displeased to hear himself so named – although he was, of course, perfectly well aware that he was far better looking than that weak chinned Italian adventurer. Twenty-two years old and down from Cambridge, he had taken up a junior lecturer's post at Queen's College and was now – as his elder brother Jonathan had predicted – busily engaged in sorting and classifying the female talent of Lady Margaret Hall, Somerville College, and the rest.

Elizabeth had caught his fancy straight away. Meeting her at his aunt's house a couple of days after her arrival, he had been much taken with Dora's stunning blonde visitor, and was curious to know all about her.

'You've enough on your plate at the moment,' Dora had told him, as he hung around her drawing room one morning, eating his aunt's apples and leafing through all his uncle's magazines. 'You have at least one regular girlfriend, and goodness knows how many other casual ones, so leave your cousin alone.'

'I only wish to be friendly.' David had grinned. 'Dora, what a Jesuitical mind you have. Did you think I'd planned to seduce her or something?'

71

'If you had, it wouldn't surprise me at all.' Dora tried to look severe. 'David, I've heard such stories about you – '

'Lies. All lies.' David stood up and glanced out of the window. 'Well, it doesn't look as if my pretty cousins are coming back for lunch, so I'll take myself off. Oh, Dora, you don't happen to have a spare packet of cigarettes lying about, do you? I seem to have run out – '

'Take a handful from the box.' Dora shook her head at him. 'Would you like to stay for lunch? You're very welcome – '

'I'm meeting Alex.' David stuffed his cigarettes into his jacket pocket. 'I'll see you again soon, though. In fact, I may call round one evening later this week.' He grinned. 'To return the fags, of course.'

'Of course.' Dora laid down her sewing and stood up. 'Well, you're always welcome, you know that. Bring Alex along, why don't you?' she added wickedly. 'She's a nice girl, and I'm sure Elizabeth would like to make her acquaintance.'

As Dora had reminded him, David did have a regular girl-friend. He was at that time very much involved with – in fact, as good as engaged to – Alexandra Lang, a third year modern languages student. But this didn't stop him filing Elizabeth under 'possible', nor from visiting Dora's house rather more often than he'd been accustomed to do . . .

David's tall athletic figure, his finely modelled face and his thick, dark hair (worn, as befitted an intellectual leftie, slightly too long), all made their impression upon Elizabeth. Helen, by now disposed to be fond of her newly-found relation, observed that Elizabeth was inclined to stare wistfully after her handsome cousin's departing back; and she decided that the girl should be put on her guard.

For Elizabeth was, somehow, extremely innocent. Three years older than Helen, she was the kind of girl who didn't understand even the most obvious joke and whose own conversation was absolutely literal. She was so obviously indifferent to any kind of literary pursuit that she made

Helen herself feel something of an intellectual, a woman of the world . . .

'Don't you think he's handsome?' asked Helen one sunny afternoon, well aware that she wouldn't have to explain whom she meant by 'he'.

Elizabeth considered. 'Yes,' she replied slowly. 'Yes, I do. He's very good-looking indeed.'

'And he knows it.' Helen laughed. 'He's very conceited. He projects this image of a man who can't be bothered with his appearance, wearing clothes which are almost coming apart; but it's all an act, you know.'

'An act?' asked Elizabeth, mystified.

'Oh, yes!' Helen giggled. 'He's incredibly vain! And he's perfectly well aware that the ravaged, dragged through a hedge backwards look is particularly fetching on him!'

Elizabeth frowned. 'I don't suppose he earns much money,' she began. 'I don't – '

'He isn't *that* hard up.' Helen folded her arms behind her head. 'Do you know; once, the barber cut his hair too short and he stayed indoors for a fortnight. He wouldn't go out until it had grown again! My uncle teased him about it so much that my aunt became quite upset. No-one's allowed to criticize her baby, you see.'

'Oh.' Elizabeth, still puzzled, shook her head. 'He looks like his mother, doesn't he?' she demanded. 'He's the same build, tall and slim. And he's inherited her lovely eyes.' Elizabeth looked enquiringly at Helen. 'Aunt Miriam looks foreign. French or something. Is she?'

'She's Jewish. Her family came to England from Russia, about forty years ago.' Helen got out of her armchair and stretched. 'Shall we go over to the park? We could get a tennis court, if you like.'

Elizabeth stood up. 'I've never met a Jew before,' she said absently. 'I thought *they* were all short and squat. With black curly hair, big ears and noses; with sloping foreheads and little mean eyes.' She followed Helen out of the room. 'Are you *sure* Aunt Miriam's Jewish?'

'Of course I'm sure!' Helen laughed. 'Oxford's full of Jewish people,' she added. 'Short, tall, blond, dark, fat, thin – the professor of modern history at my uncle's college is a German Jew, and he has ginger hair!'

'Mm.' Elizabeth chewed that over. 'What are David's brothers and sisters like?' she asked.

'All very dark. Jonathan looks exactly like his father; Rachel's quite chubby but very pretty; Katherine's like Aunt Miriam, tall. And you've seen David.'

'Yes.' Elizabeth looked out of the window. 'Yes, I have, haven't I?'

Helen opened the door. 'Well, are you coming?'

'Coming?'

'To play tennis!' Helen shook her head at her cousin. 'Wake up!'

David visited the Athertons again at the weekend, ostensibly to return a book to Tim – but he spent so much of his visit talking to Helen and Elizabeth that Dora became even more convinced that he had designs on the girl. 'Do you want to stay to dinner?' she'd asked pointedly, as he had arrived soon after lunch and it was now six o'clock.

'Dinner?' David had grinned at his aunt. 'Oh, no – no thanks. I'm expected at home. Dad's asked old Rothmann round, and he'll want me to help entertain him.' Turning to look at her again, David favoured Elizabeth with his most charming smile. 'I'll see you again soon, I expect,' he said. And, minutes later, he was gone.

He turned up at his aunt's house one sunny midmorning the following week. He was passing, he said – he'd taken a short cut across the park. 'I've an hour to spare before I have to be in college. Would Elizabeth like me to walk into town with her? She did say she wanted to go to Elliston's some time this week . . . '

'Did she, indeed.' Dora eyed David suspiciously – and David, seeing her frown, widened his own eyes in a parody of innocence, which made Dora frown all the more. 'I'll call her down,' she said. 'But look here, David – don't mesmerize her with your junior don's brilliance! The poor girl doesn't seem to have much knowledge of the real world. She's not used to meeting clever young men, and she won't understand if you tease her. Don't show off and bewitch her – please?'

'Dora! As if I could do any such thing!' David smiled at his aunt; and she, a middle-aged woman very much in love with her own husband, felt a magnetic pull which she could only suppose was that of absolute charm.

In spite of herself, Dora found herself smiling back at him; and thinking that it was just as well for the female sex, and for civilization in general, that most men weren't like David.

Elizabeth came downstairs just then. Looking very neat and pretty in a pastel pink costume, she was obviously surprised and delighted to see her cousin. When she heard the reason for his visit, she positively beamed at him. Dora opened the door for them.

She watched them walk down the road together, her nephew and her niece – one dark and slim, as graceful as a dancer; the other very blonde, and endowed with the kind of figure at which Dora and most other women could only marvel, and remark that it just wasn't *fair* that anyone should look like that . . .

'Do you like Oxford?' asked David, as he and Elizabeth turned out of Aspen Drive and into the Banbury Road.

'Yes, very much.' Elizabeth smiled up at him. 'It's very pleasant around here. These chestnut trees are lovely – and everything's so clean, there's no dirt or soot.' She laughed. 'After London, Oxford almost seems like the countryside.'

'Mm.' David smiled back at her. He wondered idly what to say next. Accustomed to the society of women who considered themselves his intellectual equals and who usually wanted to make sure he knew it, he found Elizabeth extraordinarily relaxing. She was so – so soothing, so comfortable to be with. Her voice was soft, caressing. And she was, of course, absolutely beautiful . . .

Still looking at her, he saw that in sunlight her hair looked even more flaxen, her skin even more smooth and

75

polished. Cosmetics? White lead paint, he wondered, coats and coats laid on an inch thick and then enamelled? No – he could see the fine down on her cheeks, and there was a pinkness here and there which was so delicate that no human artist could have painted it on. And then he noticed a little mole above her left eyebrow. 'What do you teach?' he heard her ask.

'Modern languages,' he replied. 'French and German.'

'Like your father?'

'Oh, no! Dad's a classicist. Like our grandfather,' he added, wondering if she was aware of all that business and deciding that she must be. 'Like our late grandpapa.'

'Oh.' Elizabeth grimaced. 'I never knew *him*,' she said evenly.

'Neither did I. He died when I was about seven. I've only the haziest recollections, but my parents often talk about him.' David grinned. 'He was quite a lad, I believe.'

'Mm.' Elizabeth raised her fine, pale eyebrows. '*My* mother told me he was a flagrant philanderer. He broke my grandmother's heart. He neglected his children, and, after he left his wife, he behaved as if his daughter didn't exist. He can't have been a very nice man.'

'I don't know whether he was or not. But as far as my Aunt Anna's concerned, the saints in Heaven could not compare with her beloved Papa – so he must have had his good points.' David, seeing that his cousin's cheeks were now suffused with an embarrassed flush, decided to change the subject. 'Have you brothers or sisters?'

'One brother. He's older than me.' Now Elizabeth smiled again. 'He's fearfully clever – works for a merchant bank. We were quite close as children,' she added, 'but we don't get on terribly well now.'

'Why's that?'

'He thinks I'm stupid. But *he's* so bossy and self-important you wouldn't credit it!'

David nodded in sympathy. 'Elder brothers can be a bit of a pain,' he agreed. 'I've got one of my own. He works for an engineering company, earns a fantastic salary – and he thinks *I'm* completely hopeless.'

They had now reached St Giles. David's way lay to the left, down Broad Street – Elizabeth's straight on, towards Cornmarket. Glancing at his cousin again, David realized that he would have given a great deal to reach out and lay his hand on her arm, to discover if this human goddess was warm or cold to the fingertips. Aesthetic rather than sexual curiosity held him there, rapt.

But, suddenly, he shook his head. 'I'll see you again soon, I expect,' he murmured, repeating a now familiar formula. 'Dora and Tim come to our house most Sundays, they're invited for lunch this weekend; and they'll bring you with them, of course.'

'That will be very nice. I'll look forward to it.'

Leaving her by the Martyrs' Memorial, he walked briskly away. When he arrived in college, he found he'd come there by some supernatural process, for he'd crossed roads without looking out for traffic and had gone blindly and automatically down familiar streets.

Elizabeth stared after him; and even after he'd disappeared down a side road, she saw him in her mind's eye still.

'Miriam, do tell him to leave her alone!' Dora frowned at her sister-in-law. 'He's running circles round her, he's leading her on quite deliberately. She thinks he's the Lord God Almighty, and she's going to be absolutely heartbroken when he gets tired of her, as he's bound to do sooner or later – '

'I can't help that.' Miram shook her head. These days she had permanent dark circles under her eyes and hardly ever smiled. 'Dora, I haven't the time to worry about David's affairs.'

'Oh.' Dora bit her lower lip. 'What *are* you worrying about?' she asked. 'You're fretting about something, aren't you? You have been for days.'

'Is it that obvious?'

'Yes. So won't you tell me what's bothering you?'

'It's nothing, really.'

'Miriam!'

'It's just that – well, a week or two ago, I was talking to Dr Rothmann's wife. Oh, Dora, she frightened me! The things she told me!'

'Things? What things?'

'Just – things.' Miriam shrugged. 'The Rothmanns and their children left Germany in 1932; but Mrs Rothmann's family is still there. She's anxious that they should leave, but they can't get passports. The authorities won't let them go – and no-one will tell them why.'

'That's silly, Miriam. If they want to leave, they can! Surely?'

'Apparently, they can't.' Miriam shook her head. 'What she said to me made me think of my own childhood. I remembered the fear, the terror, the helplessness – oh, I was always so afraid, Dora! So afraid! And I am now!'

'Nothing can harm you here, in Oxford.' Dora took Miriam's hand in hers. 'Why don't you go and see the doctor? Perhaps you need a tonic or something.'

'A tonic?' Miriam laughed. 'You think it's my age, do you? Menopausal hysteria. That I'm a little out of my mind?'

'I don't mean that at all.'

'Don't you? Well, perhaps I am being silly. Perhaps I am a little mad.' Miriam sighed. 'After all, it's the middle of the twentieth century. Germany's a civilized country; and maybe Mrs Rothmann's got it all wrong . . . '

The first time David kissed her was when the world altered. Now, Elizabeth saw that colours were sharper, heard that music was sweeter or more plangent than she'd ever thought mere arrangements of notes could possibly be. In fact, all her senses were more alert, more acute . . .

As a kiss, it had been no more ardent than a dozen kisses Elizabeth had received before, all from various polite young men at various parties, dances and social gatherings. But, in some indefinable way, David's kiss had been different from theirs. And, thinking about it later, Elizabeth decided that she must have fallen in love.

She found that she was curious about his other women friends. She was well aware that they existed. Her aunt had even mentioned a fiancée; but surely that must be an exaggeration.

'I heard you were engaged to be married,' she said one morning as the two of them sat side by side on a park bench.

'*Engaged*? No, I'm not!' David grinned. 'Well – not officially. Nothing's been arranged, you know.'

'Your mother told me that you and Alexandra Lang – '

'Did she?' David laughed. 'Oh, Mum's been romancing again. The truth is, Alex and I were seeing quite a bit of one another a few months ago – but things seem to have petered out, as they often do.' He glanced at Elizabeth. 'I need to bring Mum up to date.'

'Up to date? How do you mean?'

'Mm?' David leaned across the bench and touched Elizabeth's face. 'Don't you know?' he asked.

'No. David, you'll have to explain.'

'There's nothing to explain. I love you. That's all. I'm in love with you.'

For the first time in his life, David had been caught: he *was* in love. And, to his surprise, he was, at first, perfectly happy about it.

Another man might have savoured the novelty of his condition – but not David. Never one for half measures, he now decided that he needed to be married; even to have children, maybe. Past friendships and attachments were now as unimportant to him as last week's college gossip; and he set about jettisoning them as ruthlessly as the master of a slave-ship might toss a dying slave overboard.

He visited Alexandra Lang in her lodgings and invited her out for a walk. With the callous cruelty of the totally preoccupied, he told her, simply and abruptly, that he was not going to marry her because he was going to marry his cousin instead.

'I'm sorry, Alex,' he said, as if apologizing for treading on her toe. 'I'd have made you a rotten husband. You know that.'

'I do?' Alex, too self-assured and proud to demand what Elizabeth had that *she* did not possess, and certainly too grown up to cry or complain, merely shrugged her shoulders. 'Why do you think you'll make *this* girl a good husband?' she asked.

'I love her.' David, straightforward as ever, smiled beatifically. 'Oh, Alex – I love her! That's why! Still friends?' he enquired, as an afterthought.

'Still friends,' she replied. And she supposed it was true. David wasn't the sort of person one could ever dislike, however badly he behaved . . .

Alex walked along the path, kicking a stone. 'Well,' she thought, 'that's that.' But there were compensations. At least now she could go to Germany for her summer holiday. She could tell Claire and Christine that they could book a berth for her, as well. And she wouldn't have to listen to David droning on about the evils of fascism any more, or be forced to read that Socialist Book Club rubbish.

Not in the least interested in politics, Alex thought of Germany as the land of Schiller, of Heine, of the most marvellous music and of the most delicious food in all the world. Political regimes come and go – and just recently she had been finding David's obsession with the evils of National Socialism rather a bore. If Hitler and his odious band were all as dreadful as David made out, they'd be deposed. One day.

Alex suddenly felt much better. She'd have a splendid holiday. She'd buy herself some tight white shorts and some of those blouses which tied around the midriff. She'd have an affair with a beautiful blond German boy. They'd go for walks through scented pine forests, take off all their clothes and make love on a blanket of pine needles – or perhaps not, they'd be a bit scratchy. Well, she'd see.

80

'And I might get a decent degree now,' she thought. 'If I'm not constantly being distracted, I might manage to get down to some serious work.' David Lawrence needn't think she'd fret for him.

The affair with Alex Lang had been doomed from the start, David decided later. She'd always been too eager, too over-poweringly ready to tear off her clothes and climb into bed – or not into bed, for Alex had never been one to insist on a double sprung divan.

Elizabeth was quite different. The centre of a perfect stillness, she needed to be looked at, appreciated; taken in small sips of exquisite pleasure. He began to understand that the romantic drivellers whose meanderings he had always despised had a point. One kiss from the beloved *was* worth more than a thousand sessions in bed with a succession of casual mistresses; a minute of Elizabeth's marvellously soothing company *was* something he'd travel half way across the world to enjoy.

'Your skin's so pale,' he said one day, touching her arm and watching the blood rush to the spot where his fingers had made a light impression. 'Hold your hand up to the light.'

'Why?'

'I want to see if it's translucent.'

'Of course it's not!'

'It might be. Your ears are.'

Elizabeth laughed. 'You are silly.'

'Perhaps I am. May I kiss you?'

'If you want to.' Obligingly, Elizabeth pushed her hair back from her cheek.

David kissed her. 'As smooth as monumental alabaster,' he murmured, stroking her neck.

'Is that Shakespeare?'

'Don't know. Probably. Shakespeare or Marlowe.' David smiled. 'It's appropriate, anyway. It's a perfect description of you.'

*   *   *

There were, however, lucid intervals. There were times when David panicked, when he decided that he *had* to get Elizabeth out of his mind. Then, he called on other women, took his students out for drinks, or went to parties. He even called on Alex now and then. And, obligingly, Alex let him ramble on about his beloved, drink her coffee and, on one occasion, take her to bed.

If he'd thought that making love to one woman would exorcize the one who had bewitched him, he was to find he was mistaken. He'd told Alex he intended to marry his cousin – and now it looked as if he'd really meant it. 'What shall I *do*?' he asked Alex, rubbing his eyes and looking beseechingly at the naked girl lying beside him. 'Oh, Alex, what shall I do?'

'Oh, for God's sake!' Alex sat up and glared at him. 'If you want to marry her, tell her so!' She pinched his arm. 'Have you even *asked* her if she wants to be your wife?'

'Not yet. I don't seem to be able to – '

'You don't *what*?' Incredulous, Alex clenched her fists and stared wildly around the room. 'Christ Almighty, Dave,' she cried, 'I don't know why I put up with you! Lying here in my bed, moaning and groaning about some whey-faced schoolgirl! I should throw you out. If I had any self-respect at all, I'd spit in your face, I'd, I'd – '

'Oh, Alex, don't!' David laid his face against her shoulder and began to sob. 'It hurts me,' he wept. 'It hurts! You can't imagine how much!'

It did hurt. David wouldn't have believed how much he could suffer; but now all the poets' talk of racks and chains, all their imagery drawn from the torture chamber and the fancied torments of souls in hell seemed horribly apposite. All the elegant grumbling and complaining of mediaeval French troubadours now seemed no more than mild commentary on a dreadful disease. And it wasn't as if he could do anything to help himself. This wasn't an appetite which, once satisfied, would go away.

He was perfectly well aware that what he felt for

Elizabeth would not be appeased or quietened simply by going to bed with her. He knew his own nature sufficiently well to understand that once he'd slept with her he'd probably never be able to have enough of her, and that if she let him make love to her once, then tired of him, he'd go mad . . .

'I want to ask you something,' he said calmly, one Sunday afternoon. The two of them were sitting on the terrace of the Summertown house; the rest of the family had gone for a walk. 'Something important,' he added.

'Oh?' Elizabeth smiled. 'What's that?'

'Will you marry me?'

'What?' She stared. '*Marry* you?'

'Yes!' David took her by the shoulders and shook her. 'You will, Elizabeth, won't you? You will? Oh, God - you must!'

Chapter Seven

HE GAVE ELIZABETH NO PEACE. He cancelled lectures and rushed through tutorials, he rearranged his timetable so that he could squash most of his work into the mornings and leave the afternoons free for her.

'I love you.' He repeated this over and over again, as if it were a magic formula which would ease his suffering. 'I love you, I love you! Elizabeth, do you understand?'

'Yes.' Elizabeth would smile at him. 'Yes, David – I understand.'

'I don't think you do at all.' David, lying full length on his aunt's sofa one dull afternoon, stared at Elizabeth with such blazing ferocity that she wondered if he meant to set her on fire. 'I've always been fond of women,' he murmured reflectively, his almost black eyes still fixed on her face. 'Ever since I was a little child, I've always liked them. I like their company, I like their softness, their warmth, I like – oh, but it's different with you!'

Elizabeth looked at him and shook her head tolerantly. 'How's it different?'

'I want to marry you.'

'Oh – that again.' Elizabeth put down some sewing and drew up her legs, curling in her chair like a beautiful white cat. 'Perhaps we shouldn't get married,' she said. 'After all, we *are* related, and – '

'We're only cousins!' David rolled on to his stomach and hit a cushion, hard. 'For God's sake, we're only cousins!

Less than cousins really - we have one grandparent in common, not two - '

'All the same - '

'Cousins have always married each other. My brother married *his* second cousin! There's *no* reason why we shouldn't marry!'

'I still think - '

'Do you?' David got up and walked over to where Elizabeth sat. He knelt on the floor in front of her. 'I *want* you!' he said, grasping her by the shoulders and shaking her. 'I want you! Oh, God, Elizabeth - I can't work, I can't sleep, my food tastes like ashes in my mouth! If I don't go to bed with you soon I shall die!'

'Ah - so that's it!' Elizabeth shook her head at him again. 'Well, David, at least you're honest about it!'

'Honest? What do you mean?'

'If you don't go to bed with me soon, you'll die.' Elizabeth looked down at her hands. 'You don't want to marry me,' she continued. 'You just want to sleep with me, that's all. That's all it is.'

'THAT'S NOT TRUE!' David shook her violently, forcing his fingers into the flesh of her upper arms. 'It's not true at *all*!'

'Isn't it? You *don't* want to sleep with me, then?'

'*What*?' For a moment, David considered hitting her. He stared at her; but was unable to decide whether or not she was teasing him. Her face, as expressionless and beautiful as a Madonna's, gave nothing away.

'I - ' he began, baffled. He sighed hopelessly. 'Oh, Elizabeth - I think you'll be the death of me!'

Sometimes, instead of having her hair loose around her face, Elizabeth pinned it up in a chignon at the back of her head. She had done so today. Now David reached out and extracted a grip. When Elizabeth did not protest, he pulled out another - and another. And when the whole flaxen roll of hair had come undone and was lying about her shoulders like a veil, he took her in his arms and kissed her very lightly on the mouth.

Then, not daring to allow himself to embrace her any

more, he let her go. 'Tomorrow,' he said softly. 'Elizabeth, it's got to be tomorrow. We must!'

'Must we?' Elizabeth pulled away. 'Aunt Dora's coming,' she whispered, recognizing the footsteps pattering across the hall.

Elizabeth had agreed to go and see where David lived; and now the two of them were in the sitting room of the small house which he shared with another junior lecturer.

It was a charming Victorian cottage in the middle of a terrace of three. Originally a servant's lodging, it still belonged to the college; and it was consequently visited regularly by a charlady, who kept it clean and tidy for the young gentlemen who inhabited it.

After exclaiming at the prettiness of the sitting room, Elizabeth walked into the kitchen. 'Shall I make us some coffee?' she asked.

'Come upstairs,' David replied.

'No - we shouldn't.' Elizabeth reached into a cupboard and took out two cups. 'David, it's not a good idea.'

'Then why did you come here?' His dark eyes sullen with desire, David glowered at her. 'You know what I said yesterday,' he added. 'I *told* you I had to go to bed with you. So now, if you won't come upstairs willingly, I'll drag you. I'll - '

'Don't be so silly, David!' To ease the tension, Elizabeth attempted a light laugh; but to her dismay the sound came out as a sort of croak. To clear her throat, she coughed. Still holding the two coffee cups, she stared back at him; and now, for the first time, she was a little afraid. 'David, you don't really mean it, do you?' she whispered.

He took the coffee cups out of her hands. 'You want me just as much as I want you,' he said. 'Come upstairs.'

He went out of the kitchen and walked up the stairs. And, like one in a trance, Elizabeth followed him.

David drew the curtains, turning the bedroom into a dark

cavern full of shadows. Aware that the slightest friction from his rough cheeks would raise a mass of red weals on her almost transparent skin, he kissed her very carefully. Then he took her hands and placed her arms around his neck. Standing like a statue, she allowed him to take her in his embrace and hold her close. When he undid the first button on her blouse, she remained motionless. 'Sit down,' he murmured, pulling her towards the bed.

He undressed her very slowly, easing off her clothes as carefully as if she were a child who had fallen asleep and he was afraid of waking her. When she was completely naked, he studied her.

Marble. Beneath that white skin there was a pulse and blue veins through which warm blood flowed, but, all the same, it was as if she were made of marble. Even in the half light he could see how very fair she was, white touched with the palest pink. Holding her chin, he tilted her face upwards and opened her mouth with his. 'Ah,' he sighed, 'that's perfect. Perfect!'

No ardent supplicant at a holy shrine could have been more reverent or more fearful of giving offence than David was now. He stroked Elizabeth's face and shoulders, murmuring endearments which might almost have been prayers. He lost all idea of time . . .

Finally, however, he could hold back no longer. He pulled off his own clothes and then lay down beside her, burying his face in her hair.

He realized that he wanted her more than he'd ever wanted a woman before. He looked into her eyes; did she want *him*? 'Elizabeth?' he whispered.

'Mm?' Drowsily, Elizabeth smiled at him.

'Do you want me to stop?'

'Stop?' Still Elizabeth's voice was sleepy. 'No, of course not!' She pulled him closer to her, and twined her arms about his neck. 'Don't hurt me, though,' she murmured.

'I shan't.'

He was very careful, very kind. And when, finally, he ended her girlhood, he did so with such tenderness, such sweetness that Elizabeth herself, inexperienced though she was, understood that this had been something quite new for him, too. 'I love you,' she heard herself say as she plaited her fingers in his black hair. Overcome with happiness, she felt tears come into her eyes. 'David, I love you. Do you understand?'

'Of course.' David kissed her forehead. 'I love *you*!' He lay on his side and gazed at her. Seeing that her eyes were bright with satisfaction, he smiled. She looked as contented as a Persian cat which has just been fed upon chicken. In fact, if she had raised her hand to her lips and licked her fingers, he wouldn't have been at all surprised. Relaxed, she lay against him, stroking his arm.

'Do you still love me?' he asked, a minute or so later.

'Mm, I do.' But then, suddenly, she sat up. 'How many other women have you slept with?' she demanded.

'Why do you ask?' Now David felt inclined to tease her. 'Two,' he said. 'Or maybe it's three – '

'Three! And all the rest!' Elizabeth frowned. 'I suppose, now that you've had your wicked way with me, you'll retract all that stuff about wanting to marry me?'

'No, I shan't do that.' He pulled her down beside him. 'I want to have my wicked way with you again – and again, and again, for ever and ever! I want to be your husband, I want us to belong to each other, to have children perhaps . . . '

In spite of herself, Elizabeth beamed with delight. 'Then you must ask me properly.'

'On my knees? You want me to grovel at your feet?'

'That would be wonderful!'

'Would it, indeed. Well, I'll do no such thing.'

'Why not?' Elizabeth smiled at him.

'Well, I'd feel such a fool. And anyway, I haven't any clothes on.'

'Put some on! There's your shirt.' Elizabeth laughed. 'I'm waiting.'

'Oh, very well. If you insist.' Sighing dramatically, David got out of bed and pulled on his trousers. He knelt before her and folded his hands together in an attitude of prayer. 'Dearest Elizabeth, will you marry me?'

'Yes, David.' Elizabeth flung her arms around him and kissed him. 'Yes, yes, dear David, I will!'

It seemed only polite to invite Edmund Barton down for a few days, so that he might see his sister and meet his cousins; and, in particular, that he might make the acquaintance of his sister's fiancé. Dora sent a postcard to the address Judith had given her, simply asking her nephew to visit for the weekend. It was up to Elizabeth to tell him all the news.

'I've asked Edmund to come down next Friday week,' she told her niece. 'That's the twenty-first. I've invited him to stay the weekend.'

'Have you?' Dreamily, Elizabeth smiled back at her aunt, then, remembering her manners, she sat up straight and acknowledged the compliment properly. 'That's very kind of you, Aunt Dora,' she said, politely. 'It'll be nice to see my brother again.' And then she relapsed into her daydream again, thinking of David.

David's happiness practically shone out of his face; and his dreamy forgetfulness caused his sister and parents much indulgent amusement.

Not that he cared. They could smirk all they pleased, for never, in the history of mankind, had anyone been as absolutely blessed as he was.

When Elizabeth met him the following Tuesday morning, however, she found him totally unlike his normal, lively self. He slouched along the pavement of the Cornmarket glowering down at the stones, viciously kicking a piece of litter along the edge of the kerb. 'What's the matter?' she asked him eventually.

'What? Oh, nothing's the matter,' he replied sourly.

'Yes, there is.' Elizabeth shook his hand. 'Darling, what's wrong?'

David kicked a stone into the gutter. 'Jonathan's lost his job.' He glanced at her. 'That's all.'

89

'Oh.' Relieved that it was nothing more dramatic than that, Elizabeth shrugged. 'Well, I expect he can easily get another one.' She pushed her hair back from her face. 'Why was he dismissed?' she enquired, making conversation. 'I thought he was quite the blue-eyed boy. Your mother was telling me – '

'He wasn't dismissed. He resigned.'

'He resigned? But why? I thought – '

'It was either do as he was told, and resign quietly – or get the sack.'

'All the same, I don't – '

'Oh, for God's sake, Elizabeth! He was kicked out because the bloody firm he worked for is a subsidiary of a German organization. That's why! Jonathan's half Jewish and the Nazis hate the Jews! That's bloody why!'

'But – '

'Someone must have found out that our mother's a Jew, told the company – and that was that.'

'But I still don't understand!' Mystified, Elizabeth chewed her lower lip. 'What's your mother got to do with it? And why – '

'Oh, God in Heaven! Don't you ever read the newspapers? Don't you know what's going on in Germany these days? What's happening to people who don't support the Nazis?' He looked at her, his eyes blazing. 'Do you still want to marry me?' he asked, scowling at her. 'Do you still want to marry an outcast, an undesirable, a piece of subhuman vermin? Do you still want to be the wife of a Jew?'

'David, don't!' Now really distressed, as upset as David himself was, Elizabeth looked back at him. 'You're the person I love,' she said. 'I can't imagine life without you. I wouldn't care if you were black, white or yellow, a Moslem, a Hindu or a Latter Day Saint! I love you!'

'Do you?' David, still surly, favoured her with a supercilious glance.

'Yes!' She pushed her hand into his trouser pocket and twisted her fingers around his. 'Darling, you're getting upset about nothing at all. Look, in business, people are always getting made redundant, moving from one firm to another, it's all part of a game.'

'What do *you* know about it?'

'Oh, my brother tells me things. As a matter of fact, he wrote a few days ago. I'd sent him a letter telling him all about you, your family, the other people here; and he's dying to meet you all.'

'*Is* he?'

'Yes, of course he is! Well, as I was saying, the way I look at it, your brother's young and up to now he's been very successful. So I'm sure he'll soon find another job. In fact, I could ask Edmund – '

'Don't do that.' David pinched Elizabeth's fingers. 'Oh, no doubt you're right about Jon. No doubt he'll soon he on his feet again. But what about the next time, eh? Now that that bastard Hitler's in power, now that our own government seems happy to do whatever the sod tells them, what's going to happen in England?'

'*Nothing*'s going to happen in England.' Elizabeth smiled up at her fiancé. 'David, shall we go to the house for half an hour?'

'What? Oh, no, we can't. I've got a lecture at two-thirty.'

'If we're quick – if we get a taxi in St Giles?' Elizabeth rubbed her shoulder against his chest, letting her hair tickle his face. 'Oh, come on, David. It'll make you feel better, I guarantee.'

David shook his head. 'When I first saw you,' he said, 'I thought you were an ice-maiden. One of those frigid little flirts who sticks her chest out but keeps her legs padlocked together. But – '

'Exactly.' Elizabeth smiled again, more ruefully this time. 'I've never felt like this before,' she said, with a fervour which made the cliché new again. 'I don't know what it is you do to me, but whenever I look at you, I can't help wanting and wanting to be in bed with you, wanting your arms around me, wanting – '

'Taxi!' David grabbed Elizabeth's wrist and dragged her across the road. He jerked open the door of the cab and practically threw her inside. 'Alton Street, number thirty-four,' he told the cabman. 'And we're in a bit of a hurry.'

'Did you write to your brother?' asked Dora a few days later.

'Oh, yes.' Elizabeth nodded. 'I told him all about everyone here. I'm sure he's looking forward to meeting you all.'

'You told him you're engaged?'

'Yes.' Elizabeth smiled her habitual dreamy smile. 'I told him all about David.'

Edmund Barton arrived in Oxford late on Friday afternoon. Elizabeth had promised to join the welcoming party at the railway station, but failed to turn up. Fortunately, Tim and Dora had no difficulty in recognizing the dark young man, for he was a clone of Dora's brother and of her son. This resemblance to Stephen and Anthony did more to recommend him to his aunt than did his manners. For these were, to say the least, cold . . .

Alone with Edmund in the drawing room, Dora poured tea for the visitor and remarked that she was sure Elizabeth would be in very shortly. 'You must be anxious to see her again,' she said, smiling brightly. 'And to meet David.'

'David!' Edmund scowled at his aunt. 'Oh, yes; I'm *very* keen to meet David!'

'Yes, well, you would be.' Accustomed though she was to Stephen's scowls, Dora was somewhat disconcerted by the blackness of Edmund's frown. 'I think - ' she began soothingly, but Edmund forestalled her.

'That bloody philandering Jew,' he muttered, 'what's he up to, eh? What's he think he's playing at?' And now he glared around the Athertons' pretty drawing room almost as if he expected a whole phalanx of philandering Jews to come dancing in through the french windows.

'Don't speak like that!' Dora was so astonished by

Edmund's outburst that she almost dropped the teapot. 'I won't have such language in my house!'

Edmund glowered back at his aunt, but then, recollecting himself, he had the grace to look almost ashamed. He murmured something which Dora took to be an apology.

But she was still annoyed. 'David has asked Elizabeth to marry him,' she said sharply. 'And she has agreed to do so. I won't have you calling my nephew a - what you just did. Do you understand me?'

Edmund shrugged. 'All the same,' he began. He rose to his feet and paced about the room, scuffing the pale drawing room carpet with his shoe.

'Sit down, Edmund.' Dora was now extremely angry. 'Sit down, and stop behaving like an overwrought Victorian papa! Your sister's old enough to decide whom she wishes to marry; and if she's fond of David, why should that upset you?'

'Why?' Edmund slumped down into an easy chair. 'He's only after her money,' he muttered, hitting the arm of the chair with his fist. 'That's all it is. All Jews are the same! Money mad. Grab, grab, grab! If it wasn't for all those damned Jewish financiers, the world wouldn't be in the mess it is today!' Edmund looked narrowly at his aunt. 'This fellow Lawrence - he must know my sister's an heiress, and so - '

'I don't think he *does*, you know.' Dora looked solemnly at Edmund. 'I don't think he has any idea of it. In fact, I doubt if David has given any thought to what they're to live on. Neither of them seems to have any financial sense at all - '

'He's no idea of it, eh?' Edmund broke in. 'Well, he'll know soon enough, because I shall tell him. Twenty thousand a year, that's what my sister has, and when my mother dies, she'll have twenty thousand more. And if that Jew thinks - '

Dora had had enough. Deciding that Edmund was a thoroughly unlikeable young man, she stood up. 'I have some things to attend to,' she said coolly. 'Why don't you go and unpack? Have a bath, if you wish. I expect

Elizabeth will be back by the time you're finished, and then it will be time for dinner.'

She left Edmund standing by the window and went into Tim's study. 'Well?' she asked her husband.

He looked up at her. 'Not my cup of arsenic,' he replied, laying down his pen and taking her hand. 'But no doubt you find him delightful?'

'He's shy.' Dora looked defiantly at Tim. 'A bit shy, that's all. He'll relax when he knows us better.'

Edmund remained sullen all weekend. He was snappish towards his hosts and, when taken to meet David's parents, almost rude to Miriam. He addressed David in mono-syllables and glared at his sister's fiancé so balefully that even Elizabeth, totally preoccupied with David as she was, couldn't help but notice . . .

By Sunday afternoon, Elizabeth had decided that Edmund needed a talking to, and she took her brother for a walk along by the river.

'But I *love* him,' she replied, when Edmund had ex-pounded the folly of his sister's behaviour. 'I love him, don't you see? He's everything I could possibly want in a man; he's kind, he's clever, of course he's irresistibly attractive, he's – '

'He's a Jew.' Edmund scowled at his sister. 'He's on the make, Liz; he's after your money.'

'He *isn't*!' Elizabeth stamped her foot. 'He doesn't even know I've got any!'

'Doesn't he?' Edmund shook his head. 'Look, Liz, he's not stupid; he's probably made enquiries, worked it all out.' Edmund stopped walking and looked severely at his sister. 'Marry that Yid and you'll regret it. I'm warning you.'

'Against *what*?' Elizabeth stared back at him in defiance. 'I'm going to marry David, and that's all there is to it.'

'Suit yourself.'

'I shall!' Elizabeth gave her brother a look of such distaste that he flinched, and drew her cardigan tightly around her. 'You disgust me. I'm going back to the house now. You can find your own way.'

And with that, she turned on her heel and left him.

Returning to London, Edmund lay back in the seat of his first class carriage and turned everything over in his mind. His sister was an idiot. She'd always been a bit dim – like their mother, she was sentimental and silly – but now she'd proved that she was downright stupid. He wondered what to do next . . .

That Sunday evening, he had made a real effort to be affable towards Dora; and this had paid dividends. She had invited him down to Oxford again, in a fortnight's time. For Dora, always anxious to see good in everybody, had now decided that Edmund's boorish behaviour had been the result of shock, or even, perhaps, of jealousy. Clearly, he was overcome by the suddenness of it all . . .

'Come from Friday to Sunday,' she'd said, smiling at him. 'And cheer up, do. Don't worry. Everything will work out, you'll see!'

Edmund didn't doubt *that*.

'Your brother doesn't take to me, does he?' David was lolling on the sofa of the house in Alton Street, his head in Elizabeth's lap. 'In fact, I'd say he hated me on first sight.'

Elizabeth shrugged. 'He's odd,' she replied. 'He always has been a bit strange. But he's fond of me, and so he's probably a bit suspicious of you.'

'Perhaps he's right to be.' David grinned. 'After all, I'm an anti-social element, aren't I? A potential fifth columnist, a crypto-pink. When the Nazis come, I'll definitely be for the camps. And if you're married to me, my darling, you'll be for it, too. You do realize that, don't you?'

'The Nazis won't come.' Elizabeth leaned over and kissed him. 'I want to get married soon. In a month or so – can we arrange it?'

'There's no hurry.' Languidly, David raised his arms

95

above his head and stretched. Then, sitting up, he took Elizabeth in his arms and kissed her greedily. 'There's no hurry to be married, anyway. Not really.'

'There *is*!' Elizabeth, feeling her own desire quickening now, buried her face against his chest. 'You still want to marry me, don't you?' she whispered.

'Yes.' David stroked her hair. 'But – well, whatever your brother thinks, I'm not after your money, and I don't want you tied to me unless you're quite sure – '

'I *am* tied to you.'

'Oh?' David kissed her ear. 'Why's that?'

'Because, David, I'm going to have a baby! That's why!' Elizabeth covered her face with her hands and began to sob.

But David, now having taken that in, smiled. Suddenly filled with a great surge of tenderness for her, David wrapped his arms around her and comforted her. 'Don't cry, darling,' he murmured. 'Don't cry. It's nothing to cry about, after all.'

'Isn't it?'

'No.' David smiled at her, kissed away some tears. 'It's wonderful news!'

It was a mild evening and Edmund had gone out for a walk. He strolled through Hyde Park; then, deciding to call on a friend, he crossed over the Bayswater Road and flagged down a taxi. Suddenly, he changed his mind and told the driver to stop. Getting out of the cab at the top of Charing Cross Road, he walked down a dark, dustbin-lined alley. He let himself in through the back door of a bar.

'Micky?' Finding the person he'd wanted to see, Edmund sat down beside him. 'Micky, what a long time it's been. Well, how are you?'

'So-so.' Micky, a thin boy of about eighteen whose pretty face was elaborately made up and whose eyes were so encrusted with mascara that their lids drooped, stirred a cocktail stick around the dregs of his drink. 'Bearing up, I suppose.'

'Good.' Edmund slid his hand over Micky's and gave his fingers a squeeze. 'Could you come over to my flat for an hour or so?' he asked.

Micky sucked the stick. 'For the usual?'

Edmund shrugged. 'For an hour or so,' he repeated. 'I'll give you – ah – five pounds. And your taxi fare back here.'

'A tenner.' Micky looked at Edmund. 'A tenner, and then you can bash me all you like. Black and blue.'

'Ten pounds, eh?' Edmund considered. 'Micky, you're getting very expensive these days. I'd want my money's worth, you know.'

'Always get it, don't you?'

'Mm.' Edmund thought for a moment. 'Could you stand it, though?' he asked. 'What I mean is – well, the last time we did all that, you looked pretty sick afterwards, do you think you – '

'Anything you like,' replied Micky listlessly. '*Anything.*'

'Right.' Edmund stood up. 'Shall we go?'

'Okay.' Micky slid off the stool. 'But could I have a little drink first? To warm me up?' He hugged his bony body. 'I'm so cold,' he moaned. 'So cold!'

Edmund looked at the boy; he saw how contracted his pupils were, felt how clammy his skin was. 'It's all that stuff you take,' he said severely.

'Yeah, well, got to have it.' The boy giggled. 'Come on, buy me a nice cocktail. You have one too.'

Edmund attracted the barman's attention. 'Give him a brandy,' he said, indicating Micky. 'Nothing for me.'

Edmund let himself into the dark flat, switched on the light and drew the curtains. Micky shrugged off his overcoat. 'Clothes on?' he asked. 'Or off?'

'Off, I think.' Edmund went to his desk and opened a drawer. Taking out a thin leather belt, he twisted it into a loop and swished it through the air. 'Yes, get undressed. Quickly now – I don't want your usual performance.'

Maddeningly slowly, Micky began to unfasten his

buttons. 'Why don't we have a little drink?' he suggested, as he discarded his jacket. 'A little drink, a kiss and a cuddle – that's what you need!' He batted his long eye-lashes. 'And then you might find that you're not cross any more.'

Edmund frowned at him. 'What did you say?'

'I *said*, we could have a cuddle.' Micky's voice, always plaintive, became peevish. 'I haven't quite recovered from last time, you see. You were just a little bit rough, you know, and – '

'Oh, stop fooling about!' Edmund, now thoroughly exasperated, grabbed Micky and pushed him against the wall. 'Get your clothes off! Then lie down! Do you understand?'

'Yes.' Micky's eyes widened. 'But don't hit me too hard,' he begged. 'I haven't been well, I've had such a cough, and – well, a tenner isn't so very much for what you do to me – '

'Shut up!' Now Edmund glared at the boy. 'You'll be paid what you asked for, so you'll do as you're told! But no more talking, do you hear me? I'm warning you now; if you say another word, I'll bloody well *cripple* you!'

Micky saw that his client meant what he said. Obediently, he removed the rest of his clothing and, very meekly, he knelt down on the floor. He bowed his head in submission.

And, as Micky cringed and whined, as he lay on the carpet twisting and groaning in not wholly counterfeited agony, Edmund Barton began to feel a little better.

Chapter Eight

'I THOUGHT HE WAS HORRIBLE. Absolutely horrible.' Buttering a slice of toast, Helen looked at her father. 'And so did you, Dad.'

'I never said so.' Tim shook out the folds of his newspaper and began to read the book reviews.

'You didn't have to.' Crumpling the pages, Helen pushed *The Times* aside; she grinned at her father. 'Your frosty hauteur and your obvious disdain gave the game away completely.'

'Did it really?'

'Oh, yes!' Helen rolled her eyes. 'The way you looked at him! Don't ever look at me like that! I'd die!'

'Idiot.' Tim laughed at his daughter. But then, suddenly grave, he looked hard at his wife. 'Are we going to be saddled with Judith's children for ever?' he demanded. 'After all, it's more than six months since that girl came, and as for the other one – '

'Tim!' Dora looked reproachful. 'Elizabeth will be getting married soon. And Edmund – well, he's only coming for a couple of days. Can't you and Helen put up with him for forty-eight hours?'

'Even forty-eight minutes is much too much for me!' Helen giggled. 'He looks just like a cross ferret,' she observed, grinning at Tim. 'Don't you think so, Dad? His face is exactly like a polecat's. I saw one once in a zoo, you know; and I felt so sorry for it, it was *so* ugly! Now I feel even sorrier. I wonder if it knows it looks like Edmund Barton? I wonder if polecats ever feel despair?'

'I thought he looked very like Stephen,' remarked Dora. 'He and Stephen – '

'Oh, I agree!' Helen glanced at her brother. 'Steve looks like a ferret too. But he's not so sleek as Edmund – Steve's a ruffled, workaday ferret, the sort who lives up a road-mender's trouser leg. Edmund's merely an aristocratic form of the same creature. Brilliantined, but basically just as vicious. And when – '

'Oh, do shut up, Nell!' From across the breakfast table Stephen glared at his sister. 'I wish you could hear yourself sometimes. You *would* die; of embarrassment!'

Dora looked at the clock. 'Elizabeth's overslept again,' she observed.

'It's all these late nights.' Helen looked knowing. 'She and Dave were in the garden at two o'clock this morning; canoodling under the rose arbour, how romantic.' She giggled. 'They seem to spend all their time lying among the bushes. They'll both get greenfly if they don't watch out.'

'Or double pneumonia.' Stephen grimaced. 'They're both quite mad.'

'They're in love!' Helen rolled her eyes again. 'Oh, I wish I were in love! Imagine it – imagine the rapture, the exquisite but welcome torments; the bittersweet pains of unquenchable passion! I wish *I* could experience all that. As Myrtle D'Arcy so truly says – '

'We don't want to hear what some pea-brained romantic novelist has to say.' Stephen got up. 'Is he coming tonight?' he asked his mother.

'You mean Edmund?'

'No, Mum, Mussolini!' Stephen grinned at his mother. 'Of course I mean Edmund!'

'I think so.' Anxiously, Dora looked round the table. '*Please* try to be pleasant,' she said. 'Poor boy, he's so shy – '

'So painfully, abjectly shy! So utterly, heartbreakingly bashful!' Helen sniggered. 'So overwhelmed by all of us!'

'*Stop* it!' Dora folded her arms. 'Stop it, both of you!

100

You'll be nice to him,' she added severely. 'You'll be attentive, and you'll be kind. Do you hear?'

'Yes, Mum.'

'Yes, Mummy dearest.'

Tim shook his head. 'Darling, I shall treat him as he deserves. If he's polite to me, then I – '

'Good.' Dora stood up. 'Well, I'd better go and wake that girl.'

Edmund arrived that evening, greeted his uncle and aunt fairly politely, and sat down to dinner with the family. Stephen, remembering his mother's plea, addressed a remark or two to his cousin – but Edmund ignored him. Not that Stephen minded. He dismissed Edmund as a boring creep, and ignored him in return.

At that time, in any case, Stephen and his friend Robert had schemes of their own which ensured that neither boy spent very much time at home. Weekends were devoted to long journeys across country and that summer the two of them had become addicted to camping, much to Helen's amusement. His sister's ludicrous parodies of hearty German hiking songs, all rendered in a high-pitched falsetto, made Stephen furious. 'I warn you, Nell,' he'd said, glaring at her as she warbled a deliberately fatuous version of something from *The Venturers' Songbook*, 'I warn you – '

'Oh, go and dubbin your boots,' Helen had replied sweetly, and continued to hum . . .

'Family dinner tonight, Steve,' said his mother that Saturday morning, coming into the kitchen just in time to see her son filling a water bottle at the sink. She eyed the rucksack full of clutter at Stephen's feet. 'The meal's at seven.'

'Oh, *Mum*!' Stephen stepped backwards and bumped into the cook, who had just walked in through the kitchen door. 'Mum, honestly – '

'Seven.' Dora looked at him severely. 'And now apologize to Sarah.'

'Sorry, Mrs Gibson.' Stephen steadied Sarah, who shook her head at him and took off her coat. Reaching for a bag of biscuits, he grinned at his mother. 'Robert and I – '

'*Be* here!' Dora glared at him. 'Hello, Sarah. Now, if we make the puddings this morning, we can get on with the rest of the work this afternoon. Mrs Thomas can do all the vegetables when she comes in. How's Mr Gibson today?'

'Better, Mrs Atherton, much better.' Dora's cook, who had worked for her mistress for more than twenty years, hung up her coat and smiled. 'The doctor says he'll soon be up and about again.'

'Is there anything we can do for him?'

'You and Mr Atherton have already been ever so kind.' Sarah took down a bag of flour. 'A week at the seaside – that'll set him up. We'll go to Eastbourne this summer, if we can afford it.'

'I'll speak to my husband.' Dora fetched the big mixing bowl. 'We'll find a nice hotel for you. You can take the children, too, it'll be a break for you all.'

'Mrs Atherton, I wouldn't dream – '

'Sarah, you deserve a holiday.' Dora cracked some eggs into a basin. 'For goodness sake, you've looked after us for years; it's the very least we can do. Think of it as a birthday present.'

Stephen grimaced as he raided the cake tins. Sarah was undoubtedly an excellent cook, but why his mother had to go in for all this soft soap was beyond him. Playing Lady Bountiful was Dora's favourite role, and Sarah understood this – took advantage, too.

Taking advantage himself of the fact that the two of them were now completely engrossed, rabbiting on about Sarah's husband's ghastly diseases again – why were women so fascinated by illness? – he appropriated a bagful of apples. He kissed his mother on the cheek, grinned at her again and slouched out of the kitchen.

*   *   *

102

If he had realized that Stephen and Tim disliked him, Edmund could not have cared in the least. He despised them: the one as an ignorant lout and the other as a tiresome old man. And his aunt was a fool; he lumped Dora with his mother and sister as another example of an empty-headed, vacuous female.

He found Helen the least objectionable member of the household and, to Helen's dismay, he spent the whole of that Saturday morning following her about. Wandering into town with her and then buying her lunch at Oxford's most expensive restaurant, he droned on all the while about the business deals in which he had triumphed . . .

He looked at her as she sat opposite him in the restaurant. Yes, Helen was different. A little sharp, perhaps, but at least she was intelligent. And she was pretty; a wholesome looking girl, not colourless and bland like his sister. Her hair and skin were golden, her grey eyes clear and candid. She was, in fact, what the cheaper newspapers called a smasher . . .

'What are you *gawping* at?' demanded Helen suddenly, as they ate their lunch.

'You.' Edmund laid down his cutlery and grinned at her. 'I was looking at you. Is that not allowed?'

'I can't stop you, can I?' retorted Helen crossly, and went on with her fish. 'God, the *bones*,' she muttered. 'Do you know, King Henri the Second of France once sent his *worst enemy* a fresh salmon – a nice fresh, wholesome salmon – '

'They have bones, too.'

'Not as many as this – this *kipper*!'

'It's not a kipper, is it?'

'I don't know *what* it is.' Helen picked out another bone. 'Anyway, as I was saying, Henri the Second – he sent his enemy this salmon, and inside it was a human heart. D'you want to know whose?'

'Do you want to tell me?'

'It was the enemy's eldest son's. Isn't that awful? And there was a verse enclosed as well, like in a Christmas cracker. I seem to remember that the rhyme was quite witty in French. It doesn't translate well, of course.'

103

'It wouldn't.'

'Have I made you feel sick?'

'No. Did you intend to?'

'I can't eat any more of that.' Helen pushed the fish to one side. 'What are we having next?' she demanded. 'Mum had some beef here once which she said was like old handbag – '

Edmund laughed. 'Then we'll try the lamb.' He looked at Helen again. On the whole, he disliked women. His friendships and his intimacies had always been with men. But old Atherton's daughter was quite interesting; some of the things she said were rather smart; so if he could beguile a tedious weekend with her somewhat abrasive but not unpleasant company, the hours might pass a little more quickly . . .

He poured some wine for her and motioned towards the glass. 'Drink up.'

'No, thanks.' Helen left the glass where it was. 'I don't particularly like white wine.'

'Why didn't you say so?' Edmund, apparently not at all put out by her rudeness, turned round and attracted the wine waiter's attention. 'A light red, please.' He considered the list for a moment. 'Yes, that Beaujolais, I think. The '26, if you have it.'

'I'd just as soon have soda water.' Helen scowled at him. But then, suddenly, she giggled. 'How old are you, Edmund?'

'Twenty-three.' Edmund smiled back at her, pleased to see her more cheerful and noticing that her grin showed up a couple of rather fetching dimples – one on her chin and the other in her left cheek. 'What's funny?'

'You are. You're so pompous.' Helen laughed again. 'That waistcoat,' she went on. 'And your suit. If that's a banker's holiday rig, whatever do you wear for funerals? Haven't you any lighter coloured clothes?'

'I happen to like dark ones. So you prefer your escorts to be got up like peacocks, do you?'

Helen looked at him again and blushed. 'Sorry,' she said candidly. 'I shouldn't be so cheeky.' She took a gulp of

104

wine and found it was excellent. 'This is very nice,' she said politely. 'In fact, everything here is very nice. Thank you for buying me such a delicious lunch.'

Edmund nodded his head. 'My pleasure.'

The day dragged on towards Saturday evening. After dinner, David and Elizabeth disappeared and Tim went into his study. Dora had a headache and went to lie down for an hour. Stephen, of course, had gone out. And so Helen was left to entertain her cousin, who came to sit beside her on the sofa.

Edmund had helped himself to a brandy, and, having drained the glass, he stretched and yawned. 'Shall we go for a walk?'

'I wanted to listen to something on the wireless, actually.' Helen picked up some sewing. 'You go out, if you like.'

'I'm a bit tired, as it happens. Worked late every day last week.' Edmund yawned again, and then he laid his hand on Helen's forearm and stroked her skin. 'Very nice,' he said approvingly. 'Soft, and warm. Very nice indeed.'

'Don't do that.' Helen scowled at him. 'Keep your hands to yourself.'

'I shan't hurt you, you know.'

'That's not the point.' Helen pulled her arm away. 'Oh, honestly, Edmund - *stop* it!'

'Why?'

'I don't like it!'

'Don't you? Well, that's a shame.' Edmund laughed. 'When I think that my sister and your Jewboy cousin are probably going at it hammer and tongs - well, I feel rather left out.'

'I'm sure there are plenty of women who would welcome your attentions. There must be dozens of girls who'd find your combination of wealth and charm irresistible.'

'But you're not one of them, eh?'

'No.'

'Pity.' Edmund continued to run his fingers up and

105

down her arm. 'You'll come to like this, in time,' he said. 'Relax a little – and then we can have some fun.'

'Oh, shut up, Edmund!' Helen glared at him. She was sick and tired of Edmund Barton; he'd annoyed her all day. She decided she would go to bed. Rising to her feet, she walked towards the door.

But Edmund was there before her. As she reached out to grasp the door handle, he took hold of her wrist. Pulling her towards him, he kissed her, his rough cheek grazing her smooth one.

'Let me go!' By now, Helen was really angry. 'Let me GO!' she repeated, trying to wrench her arm free. 'Oh, for God's sake, Edmund, don't be such a bloody pain!'

'What language, from a lady!' Edmund let her go. 'Oh, don't worry,' he muttered. 'I wouldn't force you. Frigid little bitch, I wouldn't waste my time with *you*! You see, I prefer my women to be rather more submissive than you are. I like them to know who's in charge.'

'Do you, indeed.' Helen rubbed her wrist. 'Get out of my way.'

He opened the door for her. With exaggerated gallantry, he motioned to her to go through. As she ran into the hallway she heard him laugh.

She scowled to herself and, quickening her pace, she made for the staircase. Not looking where she was going, she cannoned straight into her father, who had just at that moment come out of his study and into the dimly lit hall.

Tim saw at once that his daughter was angry. Her face flushed, she was breathing heavily and scowling as ferociously as ever her brother did. 'What's up, Nell?' he asked.

'Nothing, Dad.'

'Really?' Tim took her by the shoulders and looked at her face. 'Who scratched your cheek?'

'No-one.'

'Where's Edmund?'

'In the drawing room. Oh, it's nothing, Dad – he was just being a bit of a pest, that's all.'

'Was he, now.' Tim glanced through into the drawing

106

room. He saw Edmund standing there, lolling against the fireplace. 'That's all, is it?'

'Yes.'

'I see.' Tim looked again at his daughter. And now the fact that Judith's lout of a son was not only cluttering up his house, but had also assaulted his favourite child, was just too much to put up with any longer. 'Nell, did he hurt you?' he asked.

'No, Dad, honestly; it's nothing.'

'Nothing, eh?' Tim frowned. 'Go on up to bed,' he told Helen. Then he strode into the drawing room and confronted Edmund. 'What have you been saying to my daughter?' he asked, mildly enough.

Edmund sniffed. He looked Tim up and down. 'That's none of your business,' he retorted coolly.

Tim stared in disbelief. '*What* did you say?'

'I was having a private conversation with your daughter. What I said to her is no concern of yours.' Edmund allowed a faint smile to flicker across his face. 'No concern of yours at all!'

'It bloody well *is*!' Tim walked over to where Edmund lounged and glared at him. 'You've upset Helen,' he snapped. 'I'm asking you what you said to her.'

'You can ask until you're blue in the face.' Edmund picked up a piece of china and began to turn the ornament over in his hands. 'What's it to do with you?'

Wearily, Tim shrugged. What a thoroughly disagreeable fellow young Barton was. Somebody ought to give him a damned good hiding . . . 'Look here, Edmund,' he replied evenly. 'You've annoyed my daughter – and now you're annoying me. I think, in the circumstances, you'd better leave my house first thing tomorrow morning. Don't you?'

'I don't, actually.' Edmund grinned. 'My aunt invited me to stay until Sunday evening; so I shall.' He eyed Tim speculatively. 'Hadn't you better get back to work?' he asked. 'Hadn't you better get on with your latest pot-boiler? You know, Atherton, your industry really impresses me! Scribble, scribble, scribble all day long; don't know how you can stand it.' Edmund replaced the

107

figurine. 'I read one of your books once,' he went on. 'Our greatest British humourist, the dust-jacket called you. God, that's a misnomer if ever there was one! I was bored stiff by page twenty. And as for humour – well! There are more laughs in the last act of King Lear.'

Edmund smiled insolently at Tim. He was enjoying himself now, and hadn't noticed that the older man's eyes had narrowed. A tall, athletic young man who had been a champion fencer at Cambridge, it never crossed Edmund's mind that Helen's ancient father might be capable of physical violence against him.

And now, seeing Tim stand there silent and pale, mortified pride and recent sexual humiliation spurred Edmund on to unwise lengths. Remembering something Stephen had said during his previous visit, something mentioned in the course of Edmund's and Stephen's only conversation, Edmund giggled. 'Great war hero, weren't you?' he sneered. 'Well, then, if you've finished work for the day, why don't you go and polish your medals?'

He turned away from Tim and began to pick at his finger nails. 'Or perhaps you should have your hot milk and biscuits. It must be well past your bedtime.'

'Finished, have you?' Tim caught Edmund by the shoulder and swung him round. 'Don't you dare speak like that to me,' he said, his voice as calm and cold as the frozen Arctic sea. 'Apologize. Now.'

'Stuff you!' Edmund attempted to shake Tim off, but his uncle's fingers were digging into his shoulder, and held him fast. 'Let me go,' he muttered. 'You geriatric sod, let me go!'

'When you've apologized. To me. And to Helen.'

'Go and chase yourself.' Squirming, Edmund tried to get away. 'Oh, for God's sake, Atherton!' he cried. 'Don't be so bloody childish. Let me GO!'

'Do as I ask you, and I'll let you go with pleasure.'

'Oh, go to hell.' Edmund wriggled more desperately. 'Go to *hell*!'

Dora, woken by the commotion, wrapped a dressing gown around her shoulders and came downstairs. As she entered the drawing room, she saw that Tim was holding Edmund fast, and she watched incredulously as Edmund kicked her husband's shin. Even as she stared in astonishment, Edmund tried to punch Tim in the stomach.

Just as Dora was about to cry out, Tim drew back his fist and hit Edmund so hard that the young man went spinning across the room and crashed against the sofa, sitting down heavily. A wail of pain escaped him and he buried his damaged face in his hands, crying with distress.

'Why did you do *that*?' Galvanized into action, Dora ran into the middle of the room and stood between her husband and his victim; catching Tim by the shoulders, she shook him. 'Tim, have you gone mad? You've hurt him!'

Edmund, choking and retching, made some noise of agreement. Blood pouring from his mouth, he moaned that Tim had attacked him, and Dora, watching Edmund's white shirt front turning red, glared at her husband. '*Did* you start this?' she demanded.

Tim shrugged. 'He was rude to me,' he replied.

'*Rude* to you?' Dora gaped at him. 'He's my nephew!' she cried. 'Whatever he said, you shouldn't have hit him! He's my sister's child!'

'And Helen's my daughter.' Tim glanced at Edmund, who was sprawled on the sofa, bleeding on to a cushion. 'Get up, you,' he said. 'Do you hear me?'

Edmund stayed where he was. Dora, flashing Tim another look of baffled anger, sat down beside her nephew. Finding a clean white handkerchief, she held it to Edmund's mouth. 'You stay there,' she said soothingly. 'I'll get some iodine. Don't move.'

Tim opened the door wide. 'Get up, Barton,' he repeated. 'Get out of my house.'

Dora could hardly believe her ears. But then, suddenly, she was afraid. She could feel Edmund's fear; almost tangible, it had communicated itself to her. And now, as she looked at her husband, she understood that he was too angry to listen to reason. Never having seen him so much as cross for ten years or more, she was at a loss. 'Can you get up?' she whispered.

109

When Edmund made no move, when instead he shrank against his aunt, as if to seek protection, Dora looked up at Tim. 'Let him stay until morning,' she pleaded, her voice tremulous. 'Tim, please – '

Tim ignored her. 'Go on, Barton,' he said. 'Unless you want a good hiding, clear off.'

Edmund, still shaking and still bleeding, looked at his aunt. Dora turned away. 'You'd better go,' she murmured.

Edmund got as far as the front door. 'Just one other thing,' said Tim, as he reached for the latch. 'Helen? Helen! Come down here.' He turned to Edmund. 'You'll apologize to my daughter,' he said slowly, as if explaining to an idiot. 'You'll say you're sorry to have upset her.'

Helen, in dressing gown and slippers, appeared at the head of the stairs.

'Go on, Barton.' Tim looked mildly at the young man. 'Repeat after me – '

Sullenly, Edmund did as he was told.

Edmund walked down the road and turned to stare back at the house. He imagined flames at all the windows; in his mind he heard the screams and shouts of people burning to death. Carefully, he rubbed his aching jaw. 'He needn't think he's won,' he muttered. 'I'll settle him – God help me, I'll settle him!'

On the last train to London, he glared back at his curious fellow passengers. Smeared and streaked with blood, his black hair sticking up on end, his dark eyes glittering, he looked positively Satanic – which was not inappropriate, for he was devising the most awful fate for Tim Atherton. The tortures of the damned would be nothing to what Atherton would suffer one day.

And, while he was about it, Edmund decided that he would deal with that uppity Jew as well. David Lawrence and Tim Atherton could start saying their prayers.

Chapter Nine

DAVID AND ELIZABETH WERE MARRIED about half way through Elizabeth's pregnancy. David, who had insisted on a register office wedding, insisted also upon a private affair: his wife's mother and his own parents were the only guests.

Edmund was sent an invitation but did not appear. David's own brother and two sisters were curtly informed that although they could buy him a drink afterwards, he didn't want them hanging around at his wedding. Jonathan, Katherine and Rachel, who were all accustomed to their silly little brother's irritating ways, shrugged and murmured among themselves that they pitied Elizabeth.

'Poor girl,' Rachel sighed, discussing the matter with her sister. 'He'll break her heart - you'll see. I give them six months, no more.'

'He seems very fond of her.' Katherine, whose own husband was, in his wife's estimation, perfection itself, poured out more tea. 'And the wild ones often settle down and become quite domesticated.' She giggled. 'If he's sown his wild oats - '

Rachel sipped her tea. 'Wild oats!' she snorted. 'I tell you, Kathy, he'll never change. Anything in a skirt, anything with a decent pair of legs and nice eyes, and he's undressing it and jumping on it - '

'Rachel, don't be so coarse. Elizabeth's young, she's pretty, she's obviously head over heels in love with him; I'm sure they have a chance of happiness together.'

'We'll see.' Rachel sniffed. 'But I think living here is a mistake. They ought to get their own house – '

'I dare say they will. Elizabeth has plenty of money, hasn't she?'

'Yes, she has. But I doubt if Dave will touch a penny of it . . . '

At first, Elizabeth thought herself in Paradise. Gradually, she grew fatter and fatter; and, to her surprise and great delight, her husband seemed to find her just as desirable pregnant as he ever had while her figure had been slim and elegant.

She was now even more in love with David than she had been before. Lying with him and the unborn child, all three of them comfortable and contented in one warm bed, Elizabeth knew that Heaven existed and that she was in it. 'What shall we call the baby?' she asked him one evening, as she lay curled up next to him, stroking his arm.

'Benjamin.' David grinned at her. 'Benjamin David if it's a boy, Rebecca Miriam if it's a girl.'

'Those are all Jewish names.' Elizabeth frowned. 'I wonder – '

'They're not Jewish names! There must be hundreds and thousands of Bens and Rebeccas who *aren't* Jewish.' Irritably, David plucked at a corner of the sheet. 'You *did* ask me what I thought. If you don't like the names – '

Seeing his face darken, Elizabeth shook her head. 'They're lovely names,' she said, acquiescing, anxious not to upset him. 'Really, they are. Ben or Rebecca it shall be. David, you're not angry with me, are you?'

'No.' Having got his own way, David smiled again. 'No, I'm never angry with you, my darling; I could never be angry with you. Sweetheart, shall we . . . '

But, after the baby was born, Elizabeth didn't want to make love any more. Her body bruised and torn in the course of a difficult confinement, her breasts too engorged

112

and painful to bear being touched; too worn out by Ben's incessant demands to consider David's needs, she lavished all available care and concern upon her infant and seemed hardly to notice her husband at all.

David seemed to accept this state of affairs, and Elizabeth was grateful that he was being so understanding about it. It hardly crossed her mind that he was *too* accommodating. In a state of almost drugged exhaustion, she was far too preoccupied to reflect that a man of David's voracious sexual appetites and extreme selfishness could only be denied for so long . . .

Another woman might have suspected months before it was thrown in her face. Rachel, well aware that her sister-in-law was as innocently trusting as a little child, and not wanting Elizabeth to be hurt, took her brother to task. 'I *do* wish you'd grow up a little,' she muttered, shaking his arm. 'Dave, you're married now. You can't carry on as if you're still a bachelor. You must realize – '

'How I carry on is none of your business.' David took Rachel's hand off his sleeve. 'So, sister dear, you can just shut up.'

'I shan't!' Rachel walked over to the door of the drawing room and stood against it. 'You disgust me!' she cried. 'Really, you do! That poor girl thinks the world of you, and in return you – '

'I *what*?' David scowled at his sister. 'God, Rachel,' he muttered, 'you've got a nerve! You always were an interfering little cow, but just recently you've become insufferable. Talk about frustrated spinsterhood – '

'What?'

'You heard.' He grinned at her. 'What's the matter with you these days? Won't Leon ask you to marry him? Are you afraid you're going to die a virgin?'

Rachel flushed. Her long-standing friendship with Leon Weinstock, a lecturer in her father's department, was a source of much family speculation and interest, but Rachel did not choose to discuss her private affairs with her relations. Leon was a kind, generous man and Rachel was very fond of him, but she didn't want to be his wife, nor his

113

mistress. In fact, the idea of physical intimacy with any man appalled her; so now David had hit a raw nerve. 'I didn't bring you in here to discuss Leon,' she said coldly. 'I just – '

'Wanted to interfere. Wanted to tell me how to run my life. Well, I'll do as I please. And now, if you'll excuse me, I have a lecture at ten. Some of us work for our living, you know.' And with that, David pushed Rachel away from the door and went out of the room. She heard him slam the front door and walk off down the drive.

David continued to do as he pleased. And when Elizabeth finally discovered that her husband had been unfaithful to her, she was devastated. She had smelled the other woman's scent on his clothes; smiling at him, she asked whose it was. And David told her. 'I see Alex now and then,' he admitted carelessly. 'You don't mind, do you?'

She broke down and wept. 'What about fidelity?' she sobbed, dripping tears on the baby's head as she gave him his evening feed. 'David, you're my husband, we have a child. How *can* you want other women?'

'Well, why shouldn't I?' David looked at her, mystified. 'I like you best,' he added, as if this was enough, as if he were genuinely perplexed by her distress. 'I do like you *best*! Won't that do?'

It *had* to do. With a sinking heart, Elizabeth realized that this was to be the pattern of her life with him from now on and, over the next few weeks, she began to wish that she'd never set eyes on David Lawrence.

How did one fall out of love? Surely she should hate him now? After such a blatant betrayal, surely she could at least become indifferent to him? But, try as she might, she could not persuade either hatred or indifference to come. Love of David was, it seemed, an incurable disease – infected, she would now carry the taint of the sickness for the rest of her life . . .

The baby, a black-haired, dark-eyed infant whose sweet

little face enchanted all who saw him, was just as unreasonable as his father. One of those children who needs only a couple of hours sleep out of every twenty-four, he required constant entertainment during the other twenty-two. Left alone for just a few minutes, he would bawl himself into hysteria; only to burble charmingly when his mother, grandmother or aunt came rushing to his side and picked him up.

'He's not hungry.' Elizabeth, at her wits' end, looked despairingly at Miriam. 'He's not wet, he hasn't any wind. I don't know what to do with him!'

'He just wants to play. Let me have him for an hour or two; you go and get some rest.'

'Do you think, if we left him in his pram, at the bottom of the garden – '

'No.' Miriam shook her head. 'No, you can't do that. He'd just cry himself into a fit. Oh, you horror!' she cried, shaking her grandson. 'You little tyrant!'

Ben, pleased to have the undivided attention of *two* adoring women, beamed at his grandmother, and gurgled in delight.

David's socialist principles did not permit the engaging of a nanny and he declared firmly that a small child should be looked after by its mother, who was the person designated by nature for the job. He failed to appreciate just how tired his wife was. 'You should get out more,' he remarked one morning, observing Elizabeth's ashen face and tired eyes. 'Look, leave Ben with Rachel today, and we'll go up to London. I have to see a chap about my book, so you could do some shopping and then we'll go to a concert or something.'

'A concert?' Wearily, Elizabeth shook her head. 'David, I couldn't sit through a concert! Do you know what would be the best present anyone could give me just now?'

'No. What?'

'Sleep.' Elizabeth sighed. 'Sleep, beautiful sleep. Hours of it, days of it!'

'Oh.' David shrugged. 'So you won't come, then?'

'No. Really, I couldn't.'

'Then I'll take Alex.' Getting up from the table, David pushed a pile of books together. 'See you about ten this evening, I expect.'

'You're taking Alex?' Alarmed, Elizabeth grabbed his arm. 'You really mean to take Alex?'

'Certainly I do. Well, if *you* won't come – '

Tears did not move him to sympathy. Only when she was alone did Elizabeth weep. For, by now, she was only too well aware that David hated to see her cry. If she wept too much, he would walk out of the house and stay out, sometimes all night.

But, in spite of this, tears could not be held back. And little Benjamin, now suffering the agonies of teething, added his own plaintive, grizzling cries to his mother's sobbing. Elizabeth, who only six months ago had been delirious with happiness, now wondered how anyone could be so miserable and still live.

David walked into college along the riverside, kicking a pebble. He and Alex had often done this, dribbling a stone between them. He thought of Alex again, remembered how warm and soft she was, how her hair was always so clean and shiny, with a gloss upon it like that of a new horse chestnut. He decided then that he must have fallen out of love.

That morning he'd looked at Elizabeth and noticed that the woman he'd thought was some kind of goddess had a spot at the side of her mouth. Her nose had been shiny and her hair had needed washing, for it was dull and a shade darker than usual. With a tremendous thudding crash the image of Elizabeth, the statue he had placed so carefully upon her pedestal, had come plummeting down and was now lying broken, sprawled in the dirt.

'Why don't you ever wash your hair?' he'd asked.

'What?' Elizabeth frowned, trying to coax Ben to eat his breakfast. 'My hair? Oh, I'll have a bath this evening, I expect. I'll shampoo it then. David, will you be in for supper?'

'Don't know.' David picked up a couple of books. 'I've a faculty meeting at five, and these things always tend to go on a bit. Have yours with Mum and Dad, eh?'

'All right.' Elizabeth nodded. She liked David's parents – these days, she preferred their company to her husband's . . .

It had been suggested that she and David should live with his parents until they found a house they wanted to buy. This arrangement suited David perfectly. With a mother and sister to cosset him, and a wife to see to most of his more intimate needs, he had none of the usual domestic worries of a young married man.

In fact, being married and a father made very little difference to him. Elizabeth had moved into his large first-floor bedroom, that was all . . .

Elizabeth, finding herself lonely, was disposed to make a friend of her sister-in-law. Rachel was sorry for Elizabeth. A plumply pretty, basically good-natured girl who still lived at home and who spent much of her time acting as her father's secretary, she understood why the young mother was unhappy and bewildered and was kind to her.

Elizabeth found Rachel soothing. She knew what David was like, so there was no need to keep up a facade, or to pretend that everything was fine between them. Elizabeth soon realized that Rachel had suspected David's infidelity long before his wife was aware of it.

That bright, sunny morning Rachel came downstairs from her eyrie on the top floor of the house and tapped on Elizabeth's door. She entered and beamed at her nephew, who waved his fat little fist at her and grinned back. His teeth were not plaguing him for the moment, and he was in an excellent humour.

But it was clear to Rachel that her sister-in-law had spent yet another sleepless night, so, picking up her nephew, she touched Elizabeth's shoulder in sympathy. 'Dad hasn't any work for me this morning,' she said. 'Shall I take this little tinker out for a nice long walk?'

'I was just going to bath him.' Elizabeth pushed her hair out of her eyes. 'You could do that for me, if you like.'

'All right. You can have forty winks while I do.' Rachel tickled Ben. 'You're cruel, you are,' she told him, receiving a wide, guileless baby's grin in reply. 'Cruel, like your father. Ben, you're not to turn out like your wicked old Dad!'

'Don't say he's wicked!' Elizabeth, searching for a towel, looked miserably at Rachel. 'Really, you mustn't say he's that!'

'Oh?' Rachel sniffed. 'He's an adulterer, isn't he?'

'He's – ' Elizabeth sighed. 'He's so very attractive, that's the problem. Even as his sister, you must see that!'

'I admit he's pretty.' Rachel frowned at Ben, who was pulling her hair. 'But, honestly, he's so flipping unreasonable it makes me want to spit. So he's attractive to women. But he's married now. He ought to confine himself to one woman. His wife!'

'But – '

'And as for being attractive – well, so are lots of men. He doesn't have to keep on proving the fact, there's no legal requirement to do what *he* does. No-one forces him. He might as well insist that he eats his food because it tempts him beyond endurance, that it's the *food's* fault!' Rachel looked severely at her sister-in-law. 'You should give him a talking-to, Liz. Tell him where he gets off. Why don't you?'

'If I do, he'll just laugh, lose his temper or ignore me.' Elizabeth shook her head sadly. 'He won't take any notice of anything I say.'

'Then he's a beast.' Rachel looked into Elizabeth's eyes, suddenly very serious. 'Liz, you must sort things out between you soon. Otherwise, it'll too late.'

It was a short meeting, over twenty minutes after it had begun, and David, looking at his watch, realized that he

118

had a couple of hours to spare. He decided that he'd go and see Alex again. Busy with her postgraduate studies and anxious to secure a post as a junior lecturer in modern languages, Alex had no time at present to seek out new boyfriends. But she was nevertheless glad to see old ones . . .

As he walked up the road towards the house which Alex shared with three other students, David found he was humming to himself. He rang the bell and when Alex opened the door to him he beamed at her. 'Hello,' he said. 'I was passing, so I thought – '

' – you'd call in.' Alex beamed back at him. Leaning forwards, she kissed him on the cheek, then stepped back to let him enter. 'I didn't expect to see you again,' she added. 'Or at any rate, not so soon!'

'Oh?' David took off his coat and hung it up. 'Well, don't let me overstay my welcome.' He grinned at her. 'May I impose on you for half an hour or so? Could we have a bit of a chat?'

'Certainly.' Taking him into her room, Alex kicked a pile of underclothing beneath her bed. David sat down and Alex plumped herself down beside him.

On his previous visit, they hadn't talked. He had turned up towards midnight, just as Alex had finished having a bath. He had met her in the hallway, pulled her into her room, and more or less dragged her into bed. Sighing and moaning with need, he had pushed off her dressing gown and fallen upon her clean, scented body.

That had, of course, been very flattering and exciting. But today Alex was determined that things should be a little more civilized; they should hold at least a brief conversation before getting down to business. 'So, how's fatherhood these days?' she enquired sweetly.

'Still pretty gruesome.'

'Oh.' Alex grinned. 'How's the child bride?'

David grinned back. 'Elizabeth's fine,' he replied. 'A bit tired, though. Ben keeps her awake at night – he's teething or something. And he keeps being sick. The whole house stinks of vomit and nappies.'

'Ugh.' Alex pulled a face. 'It sounds perfectly ghastly.

I'll never have any children,' she added. 'My mother had six - we were her life, she said. She lived and breathed babies - my poor old Dad never got a look in.'

'Mm.' David sighed. 'I know how he must have felt. If Elizabeth's not fussing over Ben, she's fast asleep.'

'Poor Davy.' Alex leaned across and tickled his cheek. 'Do you want a coffee?'

'Is there anything else?'

'Some white wine?'

'Later, perhaps.' Pulling Alex into his arms, David bit her ear. 'Are you still missing your flaxen-haired Aryan seducer?' he asked. 'Do you still wet yourself when you think of him?' For, although he was now married to Elizabeth, David was well informed about Alex's love life. A stream of postcards had charted the progress of her summer romance, and David was well apprised of everything that had happened in the pine woods that August. 'Well – *do* you?'

'Don't be disgusting.' Alex laughed. 'Davy, you're quite revolting at times.'

'And so are you. Aren't you?' David pinched her hard. 'Was all that stuff you told me true?'

'What stuff is that?'

'About you and Wilhelm.' David gripped Alex's chin, making her look at him. 'About you and that Kraut rolling around in the long grass, pretending to be bloody Adam and Eve. About the pair of you – '

'Yes, it was true.' Looking into David's dark eyes, Alex's own eyes widened. It was no good; she couldn't resist him any longer. With a sudden fluid movement, she pulled off her cardigan and, tossing the garment away, she kissed David full on the lips. 'Poor Erich,' she whispered. 'We *did* talk about marriage, you know. He made me swear to be faithful, he promised he'd be true to me . . . '

'More fool him, Alex.' David pushed down the straps of her underslip. 'More fool him.'

Alex was exactly what David needed: her suntanned body, fit and trim after a summer spent hiking across Bavaria, was desirable enough to have tempted the most abstemious of hermits. She was, moreover, a girl who understood her own desirability – and in addition to that, she was a thoroughly modern young woman, realizing that most men didn't want to make love to passive dummies.

Now she squirmed invitingly against David, rubbing herself against him and undoing his shirt, kissing him greedily, pushing him backwards and lying on top of him until he lifted her away and took over the role of seducer himself.

Kissing Alex, biting her lips until they bled, David grasped her shoulders, forcing his fingers between the bones. He took her violently, pushing his way inside her and not caring that he hurt her, making her catch her breath in pain. All he wished to do was assuage the pent-up frustration of the past few weeks . . .

'Mm,' Alex remarked some twenty minutes later, curling her legs around him so that he couldn't get up. 'Mm, you certainly needed that! When was the last time you – '

'Not since I saw you. More than a fortnight ago.' Theatrically, David groaned. 'Nobody warned me, you see,' he complained. 'Nobody said!'

'I don't suppose they did!' Alex ran her hands across his shoulders and down his back. 'Poor old satyr,' she giggled. 'The honeymoon's over, isn't it? Well, darling – that's all I can do for you today. I have to get up now. Got a paper to prepare.'

Obligingly, David rolled away from her. He lay in bed and watched her dress. 'You're still a lovely colour,' he observed approvingly.

'Thank you.' Alex fastened her suspenders and reached for her skirt. 'You should have seen me in September,' she added, 'I was black!'

'You're golden now. Alex – come here.'

'No.' Alex pulled on her jersey. 'Come on, Dave. Five minutes for a cup of coffee, then I want you out of here.'

'Expecting someone else?'

'No, I told you. I've work to do.'

'It can't be that urgent.' David looked at her. 'You haven't forgiven me, have you?'

'There was nothing to forgive.' Alex sighed and sat down on the bed. 'Was there?'

'Perhaps not.' David reached out and caught her hand in his. 'May I come to see you again?'

'If you like.' Alex shrugged. 'If you want to.'

'I do. Very much.' David ran his fingers up her arm. 'Isn't it obvious?'

'I heard you spent the summer screwing Laura Fenton. *And* that you'd been seen with that red-haired bitch from Somerville; Anthea Cowpat, is it?'

'Cowley. Anthea's very nice, actually. But, my dear Alex, I do prefer you.'

'What about the child bride?'

'She's too wrapped up in Ben to care what I do.' David sniffed. 'It's as you said. Mothers live and breathe babies. Husbands can go to hell.'

'The trouble with *you* is, you can't bear not to be number one.' Alex looked at him sideways. 'The child bride has another interest now – and that's really put your nose out of joint, hasn't it?'

'That's rubbish.' David frowned. 'I don't expect to be anyone's first priority – I never expected to be yours, did I? And if you don't want to see me again, you have only to say, and I'll – '

'You'll find some other poor stupid woman, you'll find another idiot to charm and exasperate.' Alex pushed him away. 'Oh, Davy,' she sighed, smiling in spite of herself, 'Davy, you're too attractive for your own good!'

'Am I?' Warmed by such blatant flattery, David grinned. 'Am I really?'

'You know you are.'

David laughed out loud. 'You don't really need to write that essay or whatever,' he murmured, kneeling up and touching her face.

'I *do*!' Alex turned away.

'No, you don't. Or at least, not until this evening. Oh, Alex, come back to bed! Come and be unfaithful to Hans or whatever he's called!'

'That really gives you a thrill, doesn't it?' Alex

demanded. 'It really makes you happy to think you're screwing a woman who's suppose to be engaged to a German . . . '

'Naturally it does.' David ran his hands down Alex's arms, took her hands in his, pulled her towards him. 'As much as it thrills you to betray your Nazi boyfriend. He'd kill you, wouldn't he, if he knew what you were doing now? He'd slit your throat; he'd burn swastikas all over your lovely body if he knew you'd been to bed with a Jew.'

'David, don't say things like that.'

'Why?' David kissed her, biting her lips again. 'You're a harlot, you are,' he murmured into her hair. 'Anyone's – Jew's or Gentile's, you're a truly indiscriminating whore. Shall I leave *my* mark on you, Alex? Shall I do that? What about a nice little star, a yellow Star of David on your left breast; that would be appropriate, wouldn't it? And then, when Dieter next examines you, when you and he are lying naked in the warm sunshine in some turnip field – '

'Sometimes, I think you're mad.' Nervously, Alex laughed at him. 'Mad. You're talking now as if you hate me, when I know you don't – '

'You don't know anything.' David pushed her on to her back. 'As I said, you're a harlot. I need a harlot. That's all there is to it.'

Miriam, observing that Elizabeth looked close to collapse, offered to look after Ben for a few days. 'Go and see your mother,' she suggested. 'Have a few days away from Oxford, a little time to yourself.'

'But – '

'You need a break!' Miriam jumped Ben up and down on her lap. 'This little one will be fine with me. As long as I attend to him day and night, as long as I entertain him nonstop, he'll be perfectly happy! Go and have a little holiday!'

So, persuaded, Elizabeth went to stay with Judith for a weekend. She met Edmund for lunch, and, over the meal, she found herself telling her brother her troubles . . .

'It's not just the baby, though, is it?' Edmund re-filled his sister's glass. 'It's that Jew.'

'Don't refer to David as "that Jew".' Elizabeth sniffed. 'He's only half Jewish anyway.'

'What's he doing to you?'

'Nothing.'

'Liz!'

'I – '

'Have a brandy. Then tell.'

And so Elizabeth, too tired and too miserable to consider the value of discretion, told Edmund the whole wretched story. As he listened his face grew stony. Looking up, Elizabeth knew – too late – that it had been a mistake to tell him anything at all.

'Oh, I expect it's really my fault,' she said. 'I know how much he needs affection, I know – '

'Nonsense. Well, don't worry about it any more. I'll see to everything now, I'll – '

'You're not to do anything!' Alarmed, Elizabeth shook his arm. 'Edmund, do you hear me? You're not to do anything! Leave David alone! Promise me!'

Edmund shrugged. He promised nothing.

Chapter Ten

EDMUND BARTON LAY ON HIS STOMACH, spreadeagled across the sofa. Chin cupped in one hand, he was listening hard. The drink he'd poured himself sat untouched – a plateful of sandwiches lay uneaten upon the floor.

Looking at his new friend and listening to him talk, Edmund wondered what exactly was so engaging about this particular speaker. He had heard political dogmas trotted out before; yawning, he had ignored most of what had been said. But the present exponent's style of delivery was so arresting, and his personal presence so charismatic that Edmund found himself listening to him with a degree of attention he'd never before given *any* political raconteur . . .

'And so, Edmund, do I convince you?' The blond young man looked hard at his host. 'Do you begin to understand?'

'Mm.' Edmund shifted a little, his eyes fixed on a point where the other man's fair hair was brushed back from his high, white forehead. 'Go on,' he said. 'Go on.'

Simon Harrow, a young man whom Edmund had met at a party a few weeks previously, continued to talk. By now he was well into explaining the ideology of National Socialism, and had given his listener a thorough briefing on the aims and aspirations of a party which Edmund had condescendingly dismissed as just another mob of anti-Semitic thugs.

'And we *don't* hate the Jews,' Simon went on smoothly. 'Good God, Barton, we have room in the Party for anyone, of whatever race or creed. *We* wish to promote the continued stability of the British Empire – *we* want world peace, we want room to breathe, that's all. We distrust the motives of some international financiers, certainly. But, I say again, we don't hate Jews.'

Edmund shifted slightly to make himself more comfortable. 'Most international financiers *are* Jews,' he observed.

'We may be suspicious of the Jewish bankers. They've ruined the world economy, after all.' Simon smiled beatifically. 'But our over-all policy is not anti-Jewish. No, it's nothing so crude as mere anti-Semitism.'

'Isn't it?' Edmund grinned. 'Isn't it really?'

'Of course it isn't. Our over-riding priority isn't the harassment of Jews.'

'That's a pity.' Suddenly in need of some alcohol, Edmund picked up his drink and gulped down a couple of mouthfuls; he refilled his glass. 'What *is* your – ah – your over-riding priority, then?' he asked.

Simon folded his hands together, as if in prayer. 'We wish to avoid a war with Germany,' he said. 'So does every other right-thinking person in this country. The Jews would be delighted if the English and Germans fought each other again, but, good Lord, who else wants to see a repetition of the horrors of 1914?

'*We* want brotherly co-operation between all civilized nations. *We* want full employment here in our own country; an end to strikes, prosperity for all.' Simon looked blandly at his host, realizing that someone like Edmund would not wish to hear that National Socialism also favoured a fairer distribution of national wealth, and state control of the banking system. 'In a nutshell, we want peace and economic stability. How can that be bad?'

'*I* think you just want power.' Edmund shrugged. 'Adolf Hitler must want a war,' he added. 'Or is he re-arming Germany for fun? For display?'

'He doesn't want to fight the British.' Simon now spoke very slowly, as if explaining to a moron. 'The Germans wish to expand eastwards, not westwards. They wish to gather all the Germanic peoples together, into one great Teutonic nation. As an Imperialist power ourselves, surely we should sympathize with that? And so, if the British co-

126

operate with their German cousins, there'll be no need for emnity between us.'

'So we find out what Herr Hitler wants us to do, and do it? Is that it? And we turn a blind eye to whatever he's up to in Europe?'

Simon frowned. 'You may be a financial genius,' he said. 'You may be the bright hope of your banking house, you may be one of the few people in this country who grasps the economic realities of the age in which we live. But politically, Edmund, you're very naive.'

'Am I?' Edmund drained his glass and refilled it yet again. 'How d'you make that out?'

'You believe everything you read in the Jewish-controlled press. You credit all the nonsense you see in newsreels put out by a Jewish-controlled cinema industry. Oh, don't you understand? The Germans are our natural allies, not our enemies! There's plenty of room in the world for both our great nations to flourish! And there's no reason, is there, why the alleged ill-treatment of a tiny minority which is causing the German state some annoyance should embroil *millions* of people in a war?'

'Oh, I don't know.' Edmund swung his legs off the sofa; he twisted round and leaned back against the cushions. 'I don't know. And I don't much care.'

'Don't you?' Simon smiled at his host. 'What's the matter? What *are* you bothered about?'

'What do you mean?'

'You're not a happy man, are you?' Carefully, Simon traced a circle on the arm of his chair. 'You're not a contented person; you have a look about you, a restless, hungry look – '

'Like Cassius?'

'Maybe.'

'That's very perceptive.' Edmund swilled his whisky round his glass. 'Very perceptive indeed. Go on.'

'There's something or someone upsetting you.' His blue eyes clear and hypnotic, Simon leaned forwards and touched Edmund's wrist. 'Tell me what's worrying you,' he invited. 'You can trust me.'

127

Edmund considered. The whisky he'd drunk had made him slightly light-headed, and he found he wanted to unburden himself to this mesmerizing young man. 'Well,' he began, 'I had a bit of a disagreement, you see. Some time ago it was; and this fellow took offence - '

'Is he Jewish?'

'Jewish? No, he isn't. Why d'you ask that?'

'I just wondered. You said it was a pity that our organization doesn't wish to harass Jews, so I thought - '

'Oh.' Edmund sniffed. 'Well, as it happens, there's this other chap, as well. Now, *he's* Jewish. Or half Jewish. And I've a score or two to settle with *him* - '

'Ah.' Simon nodded. 'And there are difficulties, aren't there?'

'Of course there are! A man in my position can't go around socking people on the jaw - '

'Of course not.' Simon smiled. 'But these things can be arranged. What exactly had you in mind?'

'I - ' Edmund thought for a minute. Then, remembering his sister Elizabeth's pale, anxious face, recalling that at their last meeting her whole expression had been a mask of utter, hopeless misery, hatred of David Lawrence welled up and overflowed. He smashed his fist into his other hand.

'Do you know what I'd like to do?' he cried. 'Do you know what I'd suggest? Send the whole lot of them back to Palestine; that's what I think ought to be done. Or to some bit of desert in the middle of Africa, maybe. Or to Madagascar. Yes, that would be best. The place could be patrolled by warships so that the devils could never escape!' He grinned. 'Your pal Mosley would agree with me there. I was reading some article the fellow wrote - '

Simon smiled benignly. 'Don't be so patronizing,' he murmured. 'Don't speak about a gifted and brilliant man in that condescending way. If you'd met him - '

'I haven't.'

'You could.' Simon smiled again. 'I could introduce you. I tell you what - come along to a meeting. We have an informal evening once or twice a week, we sit and talk, have a drink - no-one will put any pressure on you to join

128

the Party, it's not like that.' He slid from his chair and sprawled on the carpet, then turned to look directly at his host. 'Edmund, aren't you cold, so far from the fire?'

'A little.'

'Come over here, then.' Simon patted the floor beside him. 'Come and lie down on the rug, by me.'

'I – '

'Edmund, do as I say.'

So, after a moment's hesitation, Edmund did as he was told. As he lay prone on the hearthrug, Simon laid an arm across his shoulders; his fingers caressed Edmund's upper arm. 'Do you like women?' he enquired suddenly.

'Not much.' Edmund scowled. 'They're necessary on certain occasions. But no, I don't like them. They're so stupid; do you know what I mean? So over-emotional, incapable of rational thought – '

'Quite.' Simon smiled. 'You and I are very similar. We could be great friends – '

Simon's arm was now lying more heavily on Edmund's shoulder; his warm breath was on Edmund's face; and, in the firelight, his fair hair looked almost burnished, a helmet of gold on the head of a young and beautiful knight.

He stroked Edmund's hair, traced his eyebrows. And then, leaning forward, he kissed him lightly on the mouth. 'You don't like women,' he murmured. 'You like me, though, don't you?' And then, abruptly, he took his hand away.

Edmund started; he looked at the dancing orange flames of the fire. He wanted Simon to touch him again. More than anything in the world he wanted those long, white fingers on his shoulder, or entwined in his hair. His spine tingled. 'Yes,' he admitted, his dark eyes bright. 'Yes, I do like you. Very much indeed.'

Simon smiled. 'You'll be an asset to the Party,' he murmured. 'A real asset. I can see that. Now, about those fellows who've upset you – I might be able to help. Why don't you tell me all about them?'

Half an hour later the life histories of both Tim Atherton

and David Lawrence had been poured into Simon Harrow's interested ear; all the details of Tim's and David's careers, their wives and families. This stranger now knew as much about Edmund's uncle and brother-in-law as Edmund did himself.

'An anti-German agitator who writes subversive novels. A left-wing Jewish academic with Communist leanings,' murmured Simon softly. 'Both natural enemies of any civilized society. They'll go on to our files, and when the time comes, Edmund, when the time comes . . . '

Now Simon kissed Edmund again. Slowly, carefully, he began to unfasten the buttons on his shirt. 'Don't move,' he whispered, in the same hypnotic tone. 'Oh, Edmund, I was right about you! We're going to be friends! Very good friends indeed!'

Blinking in the bright sunlight, Edmund Barton walked quickly down Regent Street, crossed it and turned into a narrow alley which led to a dark, dismal court.

He needed a drink badly. He'd never met such a set of rough characters before, and the experience of discussing his precise requirements with such obviously mean-minded individuals had seriously unnerved him.

It had taken months to find them. After several abortive interviews with various shady-looking villains who had nevertheless backed away and made excuses when they had understood what was required of them, Simon Harrow had eventually tracked down a set of thugs who would have been the ideal aiders and abetters of any homicidal lunatic anywhere in the world.

These men had agreed to Edmund's proposals, named their price and, leaving their client somewhat shaken, had departed from the rendezvous. Edmund had walked into the City, flagged down a cab and directed the driver to take him to the West End; back to that area where he felt safe and secure.

He sat in the bar drinking whisky and water. After a while he felt calmer; he found, in fact, that he was very

130

pleased with himself. Yes, it would take Tim Atherton *days* to die. After they had abducted and taken him to the house in Shadwell, Edmund's agents would be able to work on him undisturbed. And then it would be David Lawrence's turn . . .

'Another of these, George.' Edmund grinned at the barman. 'And have one yourself.'

Spring was well advanced. In all the London parks and gardens daffodils waved yellow trumpets in the mild April breezes, and gaudy pink cherry blossom dropped on to the walkways and the scrubby urban grass. One lunchtime Edmund sat in Hyde Park, his eyes half closed, enjoying the feel of the sunshine on his face.

'A lovely day.' A man, sitting himself down beside Edmund, nodded and grinned, expressing the pleasure in the fine weather which all English people seem to feel and which sometimes even causes them to break their habitual reserve and comment upon it to strangers. 'It's almost like summer.'

'Yes, indeed.' Edmund grinned in return. 'Yes, indeed it is. Delightful.'

But it wasn't just the mild weather which was filling Edmund with a warm, glowing sense of contentment – it wasn't just the sunshine which was making him smile. There was something else as well.

He thought of Simon Harrow. He had realized several weeks ago that Simon reminded him of someone. He brought to mind sensations buried deep in childhood and revived past pleasures and happinesses which Edmund had never expected to relive. Simon's blue eyes and fine Nordic features were those of a man whom Edmund had once loved. A man who had come into his life like a miracle – but who had then disappeared completely.

Edmund had never recovered from this betrayal. But now he felt that, slowly, those old wounds were being cleansed. Simon was soothing the hurts Michael Lewisham had caused all that time ago.

'Hello.' The voice of the beloved made Edmund open his eyes wide. There was Simon. Standing with his back to the sun, his hair a halo of fire, he looked like an archangel. 'Asleep, were you?'

'No.' Edmund shifted along the park bench, allowing Simon to sit down. 'I was just thinking.'

'Ah.' Simon grinned. 'Did you meet our friends?'

'Yes.'

'They were accommodating?'

'Very.'

'Good.' Simon pushed his hair out of his eyes. 'Shall we go and have some lunch?'

'That's a splendid idea.' Edmund smiled back. 'What would you like to eat?'

'I rather fancy some oysters.' Simon touched Edmund's arm – only very lightly, there was hardly any pressure in the caress, he could have been emphasizing a point in argument. No passing policeman could possibly have suspected either man of any impropriety. 'Yes. Some of the last oysters, some nice fat Colchesters; that's what we'll have. Then we can spend the afternoon working off their effect.'

'I'll bring the money on Tuesday night,' Edmund promised, eyeing the spokesman of the group with respect. 'I'll come here at about eleven.'

'Used notes, mind.' The man's seamed, pitted face bore all the evidence of a life violent from the cradle. 'Used fivers and ones, nothing else.'

'Of course.' Edmund shuddered; it was the smell of these people which nauseated him more than anything else. The sour reek of poverty made him feel sick. And their unthinking cruelty, their greed and wickedness, were almost visible as an aura around them. 'Then I'll give you names, more details. We must make quite certain – '

'Tell us what you want done, and we'll see to it. You pay – we'll do the rest.'

'Quite.' Edmund tried to smile, to show that he, the paymaster, was in control. 'You'll do as I say. Quite.'

132

'Quaite.' The man grinned, mimicking Edmund's accent, and Edmund found he was more afraid of that black-toothed, evil snarl than he had been of the villain's scowl.

Chapter Eleven

HELEN HAD LEFT SCHOOL AT SIXTEEN. 'Oh, no thank you very much,' she had replied, when her father had suggested she might like to go on to take her university entrance examinations. 'Really, Dad, can you see *me* poring over a lot of fusty old books, writing learned essays and coming to grips with the meaning of life?' She giggled. 'I'm much too stupid to understand the nature of the universe!'

'Don't you like the idea of Cambridge?' In his mind's eye Tim had seen his pretty daughter as a carefree student, her scarf flying out behind her as she pedalled down King's Parade on her way to a lecture. He was annoyed that Helen was prepared to give up three years' pleasure so lightly. 'You could have a good time at college, you know,' he said crossly. 'You could do all sorts of things!'

'*Things*, Dad?' Quizzically, Helen looked back at him. 'Such as?'

'Well, there's the work, of course. But that's not all one goes to university for – there are dozens of societies and clubs one can join. Helen, you could act, perhaps; I've always thought – '

Helen laughed. 'I don't see myself as the definitive Lady Macbeth, thanks all the same. And anyway, Dad,' she added mischievously, 'I've heard what goes on at Cambridge! Parties. Drinking.' She rolled her eyes. '*And* free love! It's a sink of iniquity, and you're proposing to toss your poor little ewe-lamb right into it!'

'Am I right in thinking you don't like the idea?'

'Yes, you are.' Helen grinned. 'I'm going to do a secretarial course and get myself a job.'

'Oh, it's all right,' Helen told her father, when Tim observed that slaving away as Mr Grierson's secretary and personal assistant couldn't be very stimulating. 'It suits me,' she added carelessly. 'Until I get married, it'll do.'

'I don't understand her.' Lying in bed beside his wife that same evening, Tim scowled at Dora and picked at a loose thread in his pillow. '*Why* doesn't she want to go to university? She's bright enough, and she's certainly sharp enough to look out for herself! There's still time for her to change her mind, though. I think I'll have another word with her, persuade her to – '

'You'll be wasting your breath.' Dora smiled at his frown. 'Tim, you'd be talking to the wall! Your children aren't intellectually minded, and that's all there is to it. They take after me, I'm afraid,' she added, somewhat ruefully. 'You'll just have to accept it.'

'Mm.' Tim shrugged. 'I don't think that young people today know *how* to enjoy themselves! For God's sake, Dora – I didn't expect them to go off to college and come home with first class degrees! I just wanted them to have some fun, to see a bit of life!'

Reaching for a packet of cigarettes, he lit one. 'But instead of having three years of freedom, Helen goes and coops herself up in a bloody solicitor's office, like some female Bob Cratchit; and Steve can't wait to get down to endless square bashing. It's beyond me!'

'You'd prefer your children to be a pair of irresponsible parasites?'

'No. But – '

'I think the young of today are more serious than we were.' Dora looked at her husband. 'They worry about things; they don't accept their parents' values just like that. They look at the unemployed and they understand that it's a privilege to be able to earn your own living; that one should take a pride in doing so.'

'You sound like a Labour politician. Listen to me, Dora. There's going to be another war – this year, next year, the year after that. Those Nazi bastards will push their luck too far and even our torpid bloody government won't be able to ignore them any longer. And your son will be in the army. He'll be one of the first to go.'

'As his father was. Tim, Stephen looks up to you; he wants to be a soldier because you were a soldier, your son wants to make you proud of him – don't you understand that?'

'No. Well, in a way, perhaps.' Tim yawned and stubbed out his cigarette. 'Oh, what's the use of talking? Shall we go to sleep?'

A friendship with an earnest young articled clerk further convinced Tim that his daughter was deliberately making her life as dull as she possibly could, mortifying her flesh and her spirit for some masochistic reason understood only by Helen herself.

For Alec Townsend was a plodder. Getting on was what mattered to his family and what mattered to him. He had no interests apart from his work, and Tim decided that the fellow had got his hooks into Helen simply because she was available. There she was in the office, young, pretty and just the kind of girl his mother would like.

But, single-minded though he undoubtedly was, even Alec was slightly more romantic than Tim suspected. 'You're looking very pretty today,' he would tell Helen, meaning it, and blushing scarlet as he spoke.

One day he leaned over her as she sat at her typewriter, his eyes soft with adoration. There was a faintly silly smile playing about his lips. Helen looked up enquiringly at him.

'Er – ' Alec now spent some time arranging various witty remarks in his head; but, finally, he opted for simplicity. 'You look like a film star in that blue dress,' he said at last.

'Do I?' Helen laughed at him. 'Which one? Charles Laughton?'

'Oh, no!' Alec never understood a joke. 'No, not him! I was thinking more of Vivien Leigh . . .'

136

'*She's* a brunette!' Then, with a deliberately hysterical gasp, Helen clapped her hand to her face. 'You've discovered my secret!' she cried. 'My roots are showing! Oh, God, Alec; don't tell Mr Grierson! I'll get the sack! You see, he asked me if I was a natural blonde, and I told him I was – '

'You *are*, aren't you?' Puzzled, and totally unable to cope with this kind of bear-baiting, Alec stared at her. 'I thought – '

'Oh, Alec!' Helen giggled. 'You are silly!'

'I know.' Meekly, Alec accepted the criticism. Then he coughed; and, eventually, he stuttered out what he'd wanted to say. 'Can I – I mean, may I – look, Helen, shall we go to the theatre one day next week?'

Helen scrolled another sheet of paper into her typewriter. 'To see what?' she enquired crisply.

'Ah. I forget what's on. But, if you'll say you'll come, I'll go and get some tickets. Helen, *will* you come?'

'As long as it's not Shakespeare.' Helen looked at him sideways. 'I hate Shakespeare.'

'No Shakespeare,' repeated Alec, frowning.

'Nor Ibsen.'

'Right.' Alec grimaced. 'Shall we say next Tuesday, then?'

'Very well.' Flattered and gratified, Helen laughed. 'You'll have to collect me from home, of course.'

'I'll borrow the new car. And I'll take you home afterwards, naturally.'

'Naturally.' Helen grinned at him. 'Now go away,' she said. 'I've piles of work to do, and you're holding me up.'

Obediently, Alec disappeared.

It was rather nice to be so courted, so deferred to, so adored. And, over the course of the next few weeks, it continued to be nice. It was charming to be brought flowers and to be conveyed about the town in Mr Townsend's smart new Mercedes.

Eventually, Helen began to think that Alec himself was

rather nice. He took her out, but only to places she wished to visit. He bought theatre and cinema tickets, but only for those films or plays which Helen wanted to see. He paid for meals in restaurants.

And he asked nothing in return. In fact, Helen began to think that perhaps he was *too* noble, for he never touched or kissed her, never took any liberties at all. She wondered if she was taking advantage of him . . .

One Saturday afternoon Helen sat in her bedroom, reading. She was stretched luxuriously in a comfortable basketwork chair, the cat on her lap and a library book balanced on Tabriz's head. Lord Dunkerran had just proposed to Flora, had offered her his heart, his estates, his –

'Are you asleep, Nell?' Stephen put his head round the bedroom door, and saw that she wasn't. 'Or just lazing about and reading rubbish, as per usual?'

'Shut up,' replied Helen, without raising her eyes from her book. 'I've just got to a good bit.'

'Pity.' Stephen laughed. 'You have a visitor.'

'Oh?' Helen looked up. 'Who?'

'That little pansy from Grierson's.' Stephen came into the room and grinned down at his sister. 'If you don't want to see him, I'll tell him to clear off.'

'Don't you dare!' Helen gave Tabriz a push, and the cat, startled, dug its claws into her legs. 'Look, tell him I'll be down in five minutes.'

'Going to paint your face?' Stephen giggled. 'Oh, Nell, I shouldn't bother; you look just as hideous tarted up as you do *au naturel* . . .'

The library book missed his head by an inch.

'She's just coming.' Stephen looked Helen's fancy man up and down and decided he could do with some fresh air and exercise. Alec Townsend was a pasty-faced fellow; thin and round-shouldered, he looked as if a puff of wind would blow him over.

138

'All right, Steve; you can take the rest of the afternoon off.' Helen entered the drawing room. 'Go *away*,' she hissed, as she passed her brother.

Obligingly, Stephen sloped off.

'Sit down,' invited Helen.

'Thanks.' Alec plumped himself down on the sofa. 'I say,' he murmured, clearing his throat, 'I hope you don't mind me calling round like this? Uninvited, I mean.'

'It's nice to see you.' Helen sat down beside him. 'Would you like some tea?'

'Er - no, not just at present.' He coughed. 'Are your parents in?'

'My father is, but he's working.' She smiled. 'Don't look so nervous. He doesn't bite!'

'Oh.' Feebly, Alec giggled. 'You told me what he did to your cousin . . . '

'He won't do that to you. Alec, was there something in particular you wanted?'

'I - '

'Oh, come on. Get it out, you'll feel better.'

'Er - I wondered, Helen, if we should get married. Will you marry me? Be my wife, that is?' Alec, now blushing crimson, stared at the floor. 'I mean - '

'I know what you mean.' Helen, looking at him, laughed. 'Oh, Alec! You are funny!'

'Don't say that!' Anxiously, Alec looked back at her. 'Helen, please don't say no straight away! Think about it a little, don't - '

'Really, Alec, you *are* an idiot.' Helen shook her head at him; seeing how red he was, she smiled. She pitied him then. 'But you're a nice idiot,' she added gently. 'A very sweet little clot . . . '

Alec grimaced. 'You think I'm stupid,' he muttered. 'You think - '

'I don't!' Helen covered his hand with hers. 'I think you're very nice. Really I do.'

'Then - will you?'

'Marry you?'

'You'll think about it?'

'I – ' Helen was about to say no, of course I won't. But then, remembering how beautifully Flora had accepted Lord Dunkerran's proposal, she felt an irresistible urge to tease. Looking into Alec's eyes, she was somewhat disheartened to observe that far from being the steely blue-grey of Lord Dunkerran's they were a rather sludgy brown; but, nevertheless, she played her part with spirit. The lines she'd read not ten minutes ago bubbled up inside her and tripped off her tongue. 'My dear,' she declaimed, 'how can I refuse you? You've offered me your heart – how can I not offer mine in return?'

'Oh, Helen!' Alec stared at her. He now looked like a man who had just won a million pounds, become an Olympic gold medallist and inherited a diamond mine, all within the same five minutes. 'Well – that's splendid,' he said, happily. 'Splendid.'

'What is?'

'You are, of course!' Still unable to take in his good fortune, Alec shrugged in a dazed sort of way. 'Helen,' he hazarded, at last. 'Now that we're engaged – can I – may I – kiss you?'

'Engaged?' Helen looked at him sideways. Surely he understood she'd been joking? 'Well – '

Alec took that for consent. He drew her into his arms. Carefully, he planted a chaste, dry kiss on her closed lips.

They were still on the sofa together when Tim came in, looking for a cigarette lighter. He was surprised to find them sitting motionless, side by side in the twilight. He couldn't see his daughter's face – which was just as well.

For Helen's expression was one of utter dismay. She was wondering why on *earth* she'd played along with this charade. Worse still, she didn't seem to be able to explain to Alec that she hadn't *meant* what she'd said . . .

From her extensive reading, she knew what sensations she ought now to be feeling; that she ought to be in some kind of rapture, that her lover's kiss should have kindled some white fire within her. And she was horribly aware that she felt nothing at all . . .

'Hello, Mr Atherton!' Beaming delightedly, Alec

jumped up and held out his hand to Tim. 'Helen's just agreed to become my wife!'

Elizabeth was, by now, accustomed to her husband returning home at any hour of the day or night. So she was not unduly alarmed when, one day in May, David came home at two o'clock in the morning. He stole into the bedroom, tripped over something lying on the floor and swore.

Elizabeth sat up in bed. 'David?' She rubbed her eyes. 'David, is that you?'

'Yes.'

'Just a minute, I'll put the light on.' She reached up, fumbled for a moment or two, then clicked on the lamp above the bed.

David had his back to her. Sitting on the bed, he was undoing his shoelaces. Then he turned round.

'DAVID!' Horrified, Elizabeth stared at him. 'Oh, good heavens! What have you been doing? What on earth – '

'Bad, is it?' Gingerly, David touched his face. Feeling the stickiness of blood, he grimaced. 'Got a mirror?' he enquired.

'Yes – somewhere.' Elizabeth pulled open the drawer of her bedside cabinet. 'Here. Oh God, David, what a mess!' She knelt up in bed, looking at him. 'Where've you *been*?'

David said nothing. He examined his face, squinting into the little mirror.

He saw that one eye was almost completely closed, the bruising around it a promising black and purple. A raw, red gash ran down the length of his cheek, raking it from eye to chin. Elizabeth leaned closer, meaning to examine her husband's wounds. 'Darling,' she said softly, 'who did this to you?'

'Oh, stop fussing.' David handed her the mirror. 'I know what you're thinking,' he said. 'But I haven't been with Alex. Or with any other woman.'

'Then where – '

141

'I went to that meeting. The one at the assembly rooms, I told you about it; it's been advertised all over Oxford.'

'You mean the Union of Fascists thing?'

'That's right.'

'What *happened*?'

'I – look, move up a bit, let me lie down. That's better.' David stretched his arms, flexed his fingers; then pushed a pillow behind his head. 'Pass me that mug of water, will you?'

'Here. David, tell me – '

David gulped down some water. 'Well,' he began, 'we went in. We took up all the back row. There must have been about twenty of us – Jackson, Hyde, Goldstein, some of our students.' David grinned. 'They played the Horst Wessel Lied, and then that oaf got on to the platform.'

'You mean Mr Mosley?'

'Yes. Sir Oswald himself. Well, he started to rant on, so we heckled him. You know; we stamped and gave him the slow hand-clap, that sort of thing. Are there any fags up here?'

'Catch.'

'Thanks.' David lit a cigarette and inhaled. 'Actually,' he went on, 'he's not a bad speaker. He yells a bit, but he *can* talk. So – where was I? – ah, that's it. Things were going on very much as expected. Then Mosley told his stewards to put one of the undergraduates out.'

'Why?'

'Dunno, really. But anyway, we weren't having that. So, we – ah – we remonstrated with the sods.' David rubbed his jaw. 'God, I hope this tooth isn't going to come out.'

'You mean you and your friends attacked the Fascists?' Elizabeth lit a cigarette for herself. 'You and Dr Goldstein and the rest – you started a fight?'

'Sort of.'

Elizabeth frowned. 'Either you did or you didn't. Which?'

'We sort of suggested that they let the student stay. Then there was an argument.'

142

'Weren't the police there?' Elizabeth could still hardly believe her ears, horrified to think that a public brawl should have taken place in Oxford of all places. 'Don't the police do anything?'

David laughed. 'They let us get on with it,' he said. 'Well, for a couple of minutes they did. Then they sort of restored order, as the saying goes.' He lit another cigarette. 'Oh, yes, the police told us off and asked us to calm down a bit. But not before half a dozen of those Fascist bastards had been properly smashed up!'

'I see.' Elizabeth looked at her husband's face, unable to decide which was more appalling; his injuries, or his expression. For David's eyes glittered. He looked almost insane with hatred. The fact that he had apparently been partly responsible for smashing up (as he put it) half a dozen Fascists thrilled him to the marrow. 'How many Black-shirts did *you* hurt?' she asked.

'Lots.' Flexing his right hand, David winced, but then he grinned. 'They got the worst of it, definitely. There were some very nasty head injuries. We hit them with the chairs, you see.'

'Oh, God.'

'See this?' David indicated his discarded jacket. Already shabby, it was now fit only for the dustbin, for it was torn in several places and its lapels were liberally smeared with reddish brown stains. 'That's the blood of a Fascist,' he told her proudly. 'I split his skull open, then I kicked his teeth down his throat.'

'Oh.' Elizabeth now realized that David was more than a little drunk. Presumably he and his friends had been sitting in someone's room, reliving their triumphs over a crate of brown ale. 'Really, David – that's absolutely horrid!'

'Liz, it was *great*!' His eyes sparkling, David sucked his split knuckles. 'Great! We showed them! God, we did!'

Elizabeth pulled on a dressing gown. 'Come to the bathroom,' she said. 'You need iodine on those cuts.'

'Later.' David unfastened the buttons on his shirt. 'Later, darling wife, later.' Pulling the garment over his head, he dropped it on to the floor. Then he leaned over

143

and began to undo the ribbons on Elizabeth's nightdress. 'Elizabeth, I want you to kiss me.'

'David, you're covered in blood, yours and other people's. Don't you think – '

'*Kiss* me! *Now*!' Glaring at her, David took her face between his hands and pulled her closer to him. 'Come on, Elizabeth!' he whispered. 'I want you. Make love to me!'

'But David, don't you think – '

He looked into her eyes. 'You're not an enemy, too, are you?' he asked softly. 'You're not one of those Fascist bastards, who'd kill me and everyone who belongs to me if they got half a chance? My own darling wife, *you* wouldn't betray me?'

Astonished, Elizabeth stared at him. And then, in spite of feeling repelled by what he'd told her, in spite of hating the stink of dirt, sweat, stale alcohol and blood which clung to him, she found she wanted him. She kissed him back. 'You're mad,' she murmured. 'David, you're insane.'

'I am,' he agreed. 'I've been driven mad. And I'll be madder still yet, you'll see.'

Afterwards, still dirty and bloody, David sat beside his wife and stroked her hair, winding a strand of it around his fingers. 'There's going to be a war,' he told her conversationally.

'I don't think so.' Now very much aware of her sore face and lips, dabbing at a place on her neck where David's kisses had drawn blood, Elizabeth winced. 'No-one wants a war.'

'All the same, there'll be one.'

'Will there? Oh, all right, there'll be one.' Tired and bruised, Elizabeth wanted to get David tidied up so they could both lie down together and go to sleep. 'David, I really think you ought to let me clean you up a little – '

'Stop going on about cleaning me up.' David yawned, stretched, and grinned like a demon. 'Elizabeth, don't you

144

understand me? There's going to be a war! The whole of Europe will be in flames; famine and pestilence will stalk the land, millions will perish – '

'So today you were practising? Is that it?'

'In a way.' David giggled insanely, remembering how satisfying it had been to bring a steel chair crashing down upon a Blackshirt's skull. 'They won't have it easy,' he muttered. 'The bastards needn't think it'll be a walkover. We'll fight!'

He turned over, and was soon fast asleep. But Elizabeth, for all her fatigue, lay awake in the darkness, near to tears.

Stephen, on the other hand, was perfectly contented. An anxious few months, during which he had almost fretted himself into a decline over the possibility that he would not grow to the minimum height, had seen him reach it with just a quarter of an inch to spare. And now, six months into training, he knew without doubt that he had made the right decision: he was a natural soldier.

He enjoyed every minute of every day, even the lectures on the history of the British Army delivered so lugubriously by some superannuated major, and the theoretical work in class which some of the other cadets found so insufferably tedious. And as for the practical stuff; the night exercises, the long hours spent on the firing ranges, the endless square bashing which Tim Atherton had always found so deadly – all that was exhilarating . . .

'Who's the blue-eyed boy again, then, Sambo?' demanded another cadet as he and Stephen doubled back to shower and change for dinner one evening. 'Who's always sucking up to Sir, who's the teacher's pet? Who's CSM Firth's little darling?'

'Flattery will get you nowhere,' Stephen, elated by his successes on the weapon training course that day, grinned at his companion. 'And anyway, Fred, you didn't do too badly yourself.'

'Once I'd got my eye in, I was okay.' Fred Ashworth

sniffed. 'But as for *you*! I reckon you've been round the bloody fairgrounds, practising.'

'Since I haven't a grouse moor, old boy, what *else* could I do?' Stephen laughed. 'Going to invite me to the old ancestral home this summer?' he demanded. 'I could give your governor's pheasants a proper pasting!'

'Yes, I'm sure!' Fred grinned back. 'Would you like to do some shooting?' he enquired.

'Wouldn't mind.'

'Right.' They clattered up the stairs, and Fred stopped outside his room. 'I'll tell Mummy to put you on her list.'

'I *say*! *Would* you?' Stephen lowered his eyes in mock diffidence. 'Look here, old chap,' he added, 'I'm not in the book – '

'Your father is.' Fred Ashworth smiled graciously. 'That'll do.'

And, sure enough, *it* did do. A week or so later Stephen received a card from Fred's Mummy, cordially inviting him to stay.

The prospect of spending a few weeks on Lord Ashworth's country estate did not, however, fill Stephen with anticipatory delight. He hated being patronized, and he'd heard stories about Lady Ashworth which made his toes curl.

Although the cadet intake was sharply divided into people who were within the social pale and those who were definitely beyond it, Stephen found again and again that his own position was anomalous.

Through his father he was just about well enough connected to be acceptable to the scions of the aristocracy; and although it was considered very odd that he hadn't gone to a decent school, it was allowed that if one's father was a writer he was bound to be a bit barmy and that wasn't Stephen's fault. On the other hand, Stephen himself felt more at ease with a different sort of cadet, with the sons of merchants and businessmen, who were resolutely

146

shunned by their lordships destined for the Cavalry. He never really joined either faction. Alone among the cadets, Stephen made his friends where he chose.

He became used to being addressed as Sambo, and he put up with it. His black hair and dark complexion had always invited some such nickname. But, apart from that, he would not allow any other teasing. It was soon appreciated that Stephen couldn't take a joke, and would hit anyone who riled him. He continued to do well and to earn the praise of his instructors. The less diligent cadets thought Atherton was quite sickening.

And then it was discovered that CSM Firth's little darling was scared of girls . . .

It was the custom of small groups of the more raffish cadets to sneak off to London, to pick up a few tarts, get properly drunk, and then go on to wherever was convenient. On one of those expeditions Stephen, taken along by an older cadet, had disgraced himself.

Accustomed to the company of nicely brought up young ladies, never having done anything more to a girl than hold her hand or kiss her chastely upon her lips, he had found the liberties taken by the trollops accompanying the young gentlemen that evening profoundly shocking. In the presence of three available sluts, Stephen had been almost tongue-tied. He had reddened, stuttered and mumbled in confusion, quite unable to parry their suggestive remarks. When one had laid her hand upon his lap, he had choked on his drink. Growing more and more embarrassed, he had finally got up, dashed out of the bar and disappeared into the night.

'And,' concluded Michael Carisford, telling the story the following day, 'up he gets and off he trots.' He looked sideways at Stephen. 'Atherton, I've been wondering for some time, and now I'm convinced. You're a pansy.'

'A what?' A year or two before, Stephen would not have given Carisford a second chance, but would have blacked his eye there and then. Now he gave him the opportunity to

147

withdraw his remark. 'What did you call me, you mangy sod?'

Carisford's friends looked up – this might be interesting. 'Fighting talk,' remarked one blandly.

'I should watch what you say, chaps.' Grinning lazily, the rakehell who had taken Stephen on this ill-fated expedition looked from one cadet to the other. 'Otherwise, there might be some unpleasantness.'

'Well – I reckon Carisford has a point.'

'And I reckon Atherton ought to thrash him.'

The end result was, of course, a fight between Stephen and Carisford. 'Go on, Steve! Smash his skull.' A cadet whose parents were in trade and who was consequently cut by Lord Carisford and his friends, was delighted to see Stephen ramming Michael Carisford's head against the skirting board. 'Bash his brains in!'

'Carisford hasn't got any *brains*!'

'Come on, Mike, don't let that little oik beat you!'

'Fiver on Atherton?'

'Christ, Carisford, *hit* him!'

'Carisford'll murder him . . . '

For a minute or two it looked as if Michael Carisford might do just that. But Stephen, heavier and far more aggressive than the other cadet, had eventually socked his opponent into submission. Now, satisfied that Carisford was beaten and that his fine blue eyes would, for the next few days at least, peer at the world from amidst a mess of discoloured flesh, the victor stood up and brushed the dust off his trousers. He grinned at one of his supporters. 'Jack, are you coming over for a drink?' he enquired.

'I think Carisford owes *you* one.' Jack Chesterton, the heir to a chain of grocery shops, nodded towards the vanquished patrician. 'I reckon Carisford ought to cough up tonight.'

'All right.' With some difficulty, Michael Carisford stood up. Generations of aristocratic breeding, and a natural hauteur to which the Jack Chestertons of the world would never aspire, made him as dignified in defeat as he would have been gracious in victory. Descended from

148

gentlemen who, on a battlefield, had invariably invited the French to fire first and who'd sent their enemies bottles of champagne on their birthdays, he smiled as languidly as a badly-damaged face would allow. 'All right, rabble,' he murmured. 'Come on. You as well, Chesterton.'

They walked across the square. 'Here, Atherton,' remarked Carisford, who was wishing his head didn't ache so much, 'your fighting technique reminds me of something I once saw in New York. Nigger chap it was. Great big fellow, proper bruiser.'

'Really?'

'Yes.' Michael Carisford pushed his blond hair out of his eyes. Looking at Stephen's dark features, he grinned. 'Got any black blood, have you?'

'I'm descended from Cetewayo himself.' Stephen grinned back. 'Now, if you wanted to improve the milk and water strain of the Carisfords, if you wanted to thicken their no doubt syphilitic Norman blood – '

'I tell you, Sambo – I'd not let my sisters within a mile of a roughneck like you.' Carisford leaned on the counter. 'Whisky, eh?'

At first, the cadets sat together. But gradually, as the evening wore on, they divided into coteries again, addressing their remarks only to their friends and cronies. Suddenly, Michael Carisford leaned over and grinned at Stephen. 'My father remembers yours,' he remarked. 'Apparently, the two of them were here at the same time.'

'Oh really?' Indifferent, Stephen shrugged.

'Yes.' Carisford nodded. 'Tim Atherton – that's the fellow, isn't it? Younger son of the baronet. Was wounded at Passchendaele. DSO at Mons.'

'That's right.'

'Dad reckons he was a decent fellow.' Michael drained his glass. 'The family's got a place at Evesham, hasn't it? You're related to the Dwyers, and the Cornewalls. Your cousin married Lord Abbeydale's girl.'

Stephen, who hardly ever saw his cousins and seldom thought about them, shrugged an affirmative.

Michael drained his whisky. 'You do a good impression

149

of a lout,' he observed. 'But really, you're one of us. Not like Chesterton, here,' he added coolly. 'He really is *hoi polloi*!'

Stephen grimaced. He wished he had broken Michael Carisford's skull, after all.

'It suits you.' Turning Stephen round, Dora studied him; she brushed his shoulders, straightened his jacket and adjusted his already perfectly knotted tie. 'Yes, Steve, you look nice in uniform. Very nice indeed. You've the figure for it. Now that boy over there,' she went on, 'he's round shouldered and *his* tunic rides up rather – '

Indulgently, Stephen grinned at her, tolerating her fussing. Today, he had even allowed his mother to kiss him without reddening and immediately brushing the mark away. He looked at his father. 'All right, Dad?' he asked.

'Yes.' Tim nodded. 'Fine.' He gazed across the ornamental lake and sighed. 'I was just thinking – it's thirty years since I was last here, and nothing's altered. Nothing at all.'

'Nothing? There must have been some more building, surely?'

'Oh, that. Yes.' Tim folded his arms. 'And of course, all those names weren't on the chapel pillars then.'

'People you knew, I suppose.'

'Some of them.' Tim shrugged. 'And now it looks as if there are going to be plenty more young chaps going the same way.'

'Stop it, Tim.' Dora shook her husband's arm. 'There isn't going to be a war. Mr Chamberlain's arranged it so that – '

'Mr Chamberlain's making it inevitable now, Mum.' Gently, Stephen patted his mother's hand. 'Some time soon, it's bound to come.'

Chapter Twelve

THERE WAS A RINGING SOUND COMING FROM THE HALL. It woke Simon, who was dozing by the fire. Irritably, he got to his feet and shuffled out on to the cold landing. He picked up the service phone. 'Yes?' he muttered.

'Hi. It's Pam.' There was a giggle from the other end of the line. 'Come on, Simon darling, open up!'

'Hello.' The woman walked into Simon's flat and looked around her. She smiled brightly, then kissed Simon on the cheek, smearing his face with her lipstick. She shrugged her coat from her shoulders and let it fall to the floor. 'Well, darling?' she enquired, leaning against him and rubbing her bosom against his chest. 'Anything to report?'

Simon knew what was expected of him. Forcing a smile, he wrapped his arms around her and pulled her close to him. 'I think I've caught a big one,' he murmured into her hair.

'Have you now?' Pam giggled. 'Well, well, well! What a clever boy! Who is it?'

'Fellow by the name of Barton. Works for a bank. Has a large private fortune – at least thirty thousand a year, from what I can gather.'

'I say!' Pam let out a low whistle. 'And he's keen?'

'Not exactly. Not yet.' Simon grinned. 'But he will be. I've promised him a favour or two and I think that we'll be able to ensure that he's – sufficiently grateful. So you can tell Arthur that he's as good as ours.'

'Splendid.' Pam smiled, creasing her make-up. A

woman of at least a certain age, her girlhood long past, she still behaved like a flirtatious adolescent. Now she pushed her violently red hair back from her face, stroking its dyed strands with fingers whose nails were far too vividly carmine. 'Splendid,' she repeated. 'Darling, I hope you didn't have to – ah – compromise yourself too much?'

'I *did* have to make him feel needed.'

'Did you? Well, Simon, I'm sure you managed that very well. Making people feel needed is one of your great talents, after all.' Pam giggled, and then she undid the top button of her blouse. With a gesture which might have been attractive in a woman twenty years younger, she pulled a handful of grips from her hair and shook it loose. 'Clever boy,' she repeated throatily. 'You deserve a reward, don't you? A nice, big, reward.' She undid another button on her blouse and smiled up at him.

Simon sighed inwardly, feeling that he had done quite enough for the Party that particular week. He was tired and the idea of servicing this raddled old tart was not at all enticing. If rumours were to be believed, the horrible old bag had had half the Party traipsing through her bedroom. 'What would Arthur think of all this?' he asked, as Pam fiddled with his tie.

'Arthur!' Pam laughed. 'Arthur's a good man. He's an excellent husband. And he likes his wife to be happy.' She took Simon's hands and laid his arms around her waist. 'He thinks a girl ought to have some fun now and again. Oh, Simon, can't we go to bed?'

Simon eyed her speculatively, his hands upon the clammy silk of her blouse. Of course, he understood his obligations, was aware that just now it would be politically unwise to upset Pam. Gritting his teeth, he leaned forward and kissed her.

She opened her mouth wide and sucked at his lips. 'Ah,' she breathed, clawing at his back. 'Oh, Simon, Simon – you and I . . .'

Simon let her mumble. Closing his eyes, he thought of something else as she wrenched his shirt open, and laid her sweaty palms upon his chest.

Arthur Garbutt was about the only really wealthy backer the Party had left. The heady days of 1934, the hot summer of that year in which everything had gone well for the National Socialist cause, were long since past. The newspaper barons had withdrawn their support and funds were getting horribly low . . .

Simon let Pam lead him into his bedroom. He lay down with her. Once he'd netted Edmund Barton, he decided, Arthur Garbutt and his slut of a wife could go and jump in the Thames.

She was murmuring something now; some stupid endearment which he thought laughable, coming from a hard-faced bitch like her. Her eyes were closed now, and he observed that runnels of mascara and melted eyeshadow had trickled into her crows' feet and smudged and blobbed in her eyesockets. Her powder had caked into orange patches; greasy now, its sticky texture emphasized the creases in her face. And she smelled disgusting: she stank of a mixture of cosmetics, scent, sex and sweat.

Doggedly, Simon went on with his work.

Alec Townsend's possessiveness was beginning to get Helen down. Nowadays, he called at her house at half past eight every morning, walked into town with her, hovered about her all day and in the evening walked her back home.

After dinner he would be at her house again, sitting in her drawing room, talking to her mother or father, stroking her cat and generally making himself a cosy little niche, out of which it was as difficult to prise him as it was to get a Brazil nut out of its shell.

'I think I'll have to suggest he takes up some sort of hobby,' remarked Tim, closing the door on Alec one Wednesday evening and yawning as he locked up for the night. 'Something that'll take him to evening classes once or twice a week. Otherwise, Nell, he's going to drive us all insane.'

'Oh?'

'Well, he'll drive *me* mad.' Tim laughed. 'Really, I

153

didn't particularly *want* that lecture on current divorce law. And what was he rabbiting on about last night? Tithes? Or was it tolls?'

'He *is* a bit boring,' admitted Helen, yawning herself. 'But David, you don't have to stay up until he goes. If you want to go to bed – '

'And leave you and young Lochinvar alone together? Wouldn't be decent.' Tim grinned. 'I shall ask Stephen to chaperone you – when he's next on leave, that is.'

'Don't, Dad. Alec's scared to death of Steve.'

'Is he? Why's that?'

'Oh, Steve's such a thug. He's twice as big as Alec; and he glares at him so!' Helen giggled. 'Poor Alec's quite sure that one day either you or Steve is going to beat him up. He calls our house the Lion's Den.'

'Yet he spends half his life here.' Tim pushed Helen's shoulder. 'Oh, well, perhaps if I do a bit of glaring he might give us some peace. I mean, I can't walk through the drawing room these days without tripping over the fellow!'

The fact that neither her brother nor her father was very impressed by her fiancé mattered to Helen – mattered more, she suspected, than it should have done. And, as time went on, she found that Alec's absolutely slavish devotion, far from making her feel cherished, was beginning to grate . . .

His physical presence began to get on her nerves. First of all it was the little things which annoyed her. The way his hair stuck out at the nape of his neck, the acne scars on his cheeks, his habit of clicking his fingers, the way in which his trousers bagged around his narrow hips – all of these made Helen cross with him. Then there were his affectations. 'Why d'you wear that silly cravat?' she demanded one Saturday morning, reflecting sourly that her father wouldn't be seen dead with a stupid silk scarf around his neck. 'Do you fancy yourself as Noel Coward?'

Alec looked hurt. The gaudy Paisley-printed cravat was

part of the image he wished to cultivate just then; that of the relaxed, knowledgeable man of the world who dresses with a certain elegance and style. 'Why don't you like it?' he asked sulkily. 'It's silk, you know, not rayon. It cost twenty-five shillings!'

Then he went on to give full details of the cost and fabric content of each item of his weekend rig, pointing out that everything he wore was of the latest style and best quality, until Helen felt so sorry for him that she softened. 'It's all very nice really,' she said kindly, brushing some fluff from the crest on his blazer. 'You look very smart, honestly you do. I was only joking before,' she concluded, perjuring herself beyond any hope of heaven.

'Were you, Nell?' Mollified, he grinned at her. 'Oh. Shall we go out, then? Have a bit of a spin, then pick up a spot of lunch?'

Helen grimaced. 'We'll go for a drive, if you like. And we'll take a picnic. I don't like pubs.' For the sight of Alec patronizing a country landlord was one which Helen found particularly hard to stomach . . .

They sat in the car, parked in a narrow Oxfordshire lane beneath a canopy of spring trees. 'Shall we go for a walk?' asked Helen, who had a headache.

'In a bit.' Alec leaned across and touched her shoulder; then, pulling her towards him, he kissed her.

That was another source of friction. Helen was not so naive as to suppose that the moment her beloved's lips touched hers she would hear angels sing, or to imagine that the sensations described in romantic novels were the stuff of everyday existence. But, try as she would to enjoy it, she found that being kissed was absolutely horrible. The sliminess of it revolted her; and the nasty feel of a tongue in her mouth, the idea that the contents of one spit-filled cavity were being mixed up with another, disgusted her.

And, these days, Alec was growing bolder. He fumbled with her clothes, sometimes he almost got as far as unhooking her bra. And when, one day, he had actually

touched her breast, Helen had come out in the most unattractive goosepimples and wanted to scream at him to
leave her alone, she felt sick. Held in Alec's clammy
embrace, she couldn't help reflecting that an animal being
inspected by a butcher must feel much as she did. And she
sighed as Alec continued to evaluate the extent of her
subcutaneous fat.

'I shan't go into the Army until I'm conscripted.' Walking
down the hill towards a pretty Cotswold village, Alec
frowned at his fiancée. 'I don't think there's going to be a
war, anyway.'

'Lots of men are joining the Territorials.' Helen smiled
encouragingly, mindful of her father's hope that Alec
might get himself a hobby of some sort. 'A couple of
Steve's friends have signed up. It sounds as if it might be
rather good fun, you know – weekend camps, night exercises, that sort of thing.'

Alec shuddered. 'No thanks. Look, I was thinking, we
ought to start going round the house agents soon, finding
out what they've got. I'll be fully qualified in eighteen
months' time, I'll be able to afford a wife and family – '

'Will you?' Helen bit her lower lip. 'There's no hurry to
get married.'

'All the same, it's as well to find out what's going. And,
Nell, I was thinking, I really ought to buy you a ring.'

'Don't do that.' Helen shook her head. 'It would be a
waste of money. We ought to save for – er – furniture.
Carpets, and lino. Things like that.'

'Mm.' Alec thought about it. 'Yes, you're right,' he
agreed. 'We should.'

Helen breathed a secret sigh of relief. She didn't want a
ring! To be ticketed and docketed, marked out as Alec's
property! The very idea gave her the shivers . . .

Helen sat on the sofa, leaning on Tim's arm. 'He's a good
man,' she said. 'He's sensible. He's kind. I like him very
much.' She twisted round to look at her father. 'I shall be

happy with him,' she insisted. 'He's not very clever, I agree – but then neither am I.'

'You're not stupid, either.' Tim laid his arm across his daughter's shoulders and pulled her into the warmth of his embrace, letting her rest her head against his collar bone. 'Nell, *do* you love him?' he asked.

'In a way.' Helen shrugged. 'He's grown on me, you know, and nowadays I think I love him as much as I could love anyone.'

'Oh.' Tim looked unconvinced. 'Look, Nell, if you've any doubts, if you're not absolutely sure, you can still call everything off. There's no need to go ahead with it – '

'Alec's mother would have a nervous breakdown if I jilted her son!' Helen laughed. 'Oh, Dad, I don't adore him, I don't worship the ground on which he walks, but I *am* fond of him. And that's all I can expect, isn't it? In real life, that is?'

'Perhaps.' Tim looked at her. His daughter was, next to his wife, the person he loved best in the world. She wasn't in love with that idiot of a lawyer. She even understood that the man was a fool; and yet she wanted to marry him. God alone knew why . . .

He wondered if he should tell her that one day she *would* fall in love, that she was bound to. Then what would she do, immured in a respectable Oxford suburb, the wife of an ambitious young solicitor; the mother, no doubt, of two or three miniature Alec Townsends? A woman with a reputation to lose, a husband to ruin?

They sat together in the darkening room. Helen felt her eyelids drop. Not until a day or two later did she realize that, snuggled up against her father, she had felt warm, safe, contented and that, merely lying in Tim's arms, she had experienced more real pleasure than while in any embrace of Alec's. 'And I can't marry Dad,' she had told herself, looking ruefully at her reflection in her mirror. 'So I might as well marry Alec. He'll do as well as anyone.'

A month or so later, Stephen came home on leave from

college. He was rather more forthright than his father. 'They disgust me,' he said curtly. 'Fellows like Townsend, all those feeble-minded appeasers – they make me sick.' He glanced at Helen, who had reddened. 'Sorry, Nell – but they do.'

'And I suppose *you* think the whole international situation would be improved by a European war?' Helen scowled at her brother. 'You think that killing a few million people who've never done you any harm would ease the tension a little? Well, soldier boy? Isn't that so?'

'Stop it, you two.' Dora poured tea. 'I was talking to Mrs Leitner today. She was in tears, poor woman. She has relatives in Germany who can't get out. They can't get visas from any of the foreign embassies, you see. They've been forbidden to work; they're desperate.

'I really do think it must come to war,' she added sadly. 'It's bound to. I was telling poor Leah that the things which happen in Europe couldn't happen in England, that however much the Fascists here rant and rave there'll never be any persecution of Jews in this country. But she's terrified, poor woman. She thinks the Germans are coming to get her, and she kept asking what harm *she'd* ever done anyone . . . '

'They're obscene.' Stephen glowered at his sister. 'The Nazis are scum. They're a malignant tumour in the body of mankind, which must be excised.'

'Oh, very well put.' Helen sniffed. 'Been reading some of David's Leftie propaganda, have you?'

'Any ordinary person doesn't have to read left-wing propaganda to know that the Germans have overstepped the mark.' Stephen buttered himself some bread. 'It's only morons like your fiancé who bleat on about co-operating with the buggers, living in harmony with our German cousins, all that fascist crap.'

'Stephen!' Dora leaned over and slapped his hand. 'Honestly! You're not among your Army friends now!'

'Sorry, Mum. But really, Nell's so thick she can't even begin to appreciate – '

'I *do* appreciate, as it happens.' Helen looked at her

brother. 'Alec and I were discussing it all yesterday. He sees that things have now gone far enough. He's going to join the TAs.'

'Is he?' Stephen had the grace to look abashed. 'Well, jolly good for him,' he said generously. 'Perhaps he's not such a bad chap after all.'

Chapter Thirteen

EDMUND HAD THE MONEY IN a battered Gladstone bag. Feeling like a character from a short story in the *Strand* magazine, he walked briskly down the Mile End Road, on his way to meet his friends.

It was going to be very expensive. More expensive than Edmund would have liked. He consoled himself with the idea of what all this cash would buy. 'Well known writer disappears,' the headline would run, followed by a small paragraph at the bottom of a page of a national newspaper. Then, a week or so later, 'well known writer brutally murdered' . . .

That would be front page news. The ghastly fashion in which Tim Atherton was going to meet his end would ensure that the gutter press would be *very* interested. Atherton would be more notorious in death than his silly books had ever made him in life . . .

Preoccupied, not really looking where he was going, Edmund did not notice that he was being followed. The woman finally accosted him as he turned down a road near the tube station. 'Hello, love,' she said easily, lazily, touching his arm in an over-familiar way. 'Like to come with me for 'alf an hour?'

Edmund looked at her. Under the soft rays of the street lamp she looked young and fairly pretty; far prettier, in fact, than the usual Cockney tart. And he was attracted by the idea, in spite of himself.

For Simon was out of town, and that week Edmund had

been lonely. He'd wondered about calling on Micky. But these days Micky was always complaining, always demanding more and more money, always grumbling and whining about the state of his health – which was wretched, admittedly. Altogether, Edmund had long since decided, Micky was a greedy little whore who wasn't worth the cash. He glanced again at the prostitute and made up his mind. 'All right,' he agreed. 'Ten shillings.'

'Ten bob?' Sarcastically, the woman laughed. 'Thirty, my hero. Thirty, or nothing doing.'

'A pound, if we can go somewhere private.'

'Twenty-five. That's for a quick one, at my place.' The prostitute grinned at him. 'Girl's got to live, squire.'

Edmund considered; then he agreed. Grasping, avaricious little tart, she'd get more than she bargained for. He'd want more than just a quick one, he decided. And he'd have it.

'Is it far?' he asked.

'Just up the entry, my love.'

It was all over very quickly, the woman made sure of that. She was sitting up again before Edmund had even fastened his buttons. 'All right,' she said. 'That's your lot. Off you go.'

Edmund fished in his jacket pocket. 'I haven't finished yet,' he said. He brought out his leather belt, the one which had been used so often upon Micky's tender flesh. He folded the weapon in half, made a few experimental flicks in the air, then grinned at the girl. 'Ever been thrashed?' he enquired.

'What d'you mean?' The girl eyed the belt with alarm. 'Now look 'ere,' she began bravely, 'just you look 'ere – you've 'ad your money's worth. An' I don't go in for that sort of stuff!'

'Well, one should never forego a new experience.' His eyes glittering and his breathing harsh, Edmund now caught the girl by the shoulder. He grabbed the collar of her dress, tugged at it and tore the thin material from neck

161

to waist. Holding her firm, he raised the belt for the first blow.

But the woman was stronger than she appeared. Used to dealing with lunatics, perverts and villains of all kinds, she could usually look after herself. She twisted out of Edmund's grasp and pushed him hard, so that he slipped on the greasy floor and went skidding towards the sink in the corner of the room. 'Get out!' she shrieked, glaring at him. 'Go on, bugger off! I'll 'ave the cops on you!'

'Damn you!' Having lost his balance, Edmund grabbed at the bedstead, missed and fell heavily against the wall, wrenching his ankle. He got up again; and, wincing, he lunged at the girl. 'Right,' he muttered, seizing her and pinning her face down on the dirty bedspread. 'Right, you little bitch, now you're really going to get it.'

He hit her hard across the back of the head, half stunning her. Then he twisted her arm behind her back and held her down as he lashed her with the belt.

There were footsteps in the street outside. As Edmund hit her for the fourth, fifth, sixth time, the girl had squirmed and struggled, but to no effect. Now, however, the realization that her paymasters were on their way gave her fresh energy. Elbowing Edmund in the stomach, she broke free of him. As he staggered backwards, she twisted round and kicked him in the chest.

He fell against the window. Heavily, awkwardly, his body hit the already broken panes and as the rotten wood gave way he fell backwards through the casement. Unable to right himself, he hurtled through the air and landed on the pavement below with a dull thud.

The man turned him over. He saw the blood trickling from Edmund's mouth and observed that his head was at a grotesque angle to his body. 'Dead, all right,' he muttered to his companion. 'Stark dead.'

Simon Harrow came out of the shadows. 'Sure?' he asked.

'Positive.' The man spat. 'Told you we shouldn've used that stupid little cow. Told you – '

'Shut up.' His face a white mask of fury, Simon pushed

open the door of the lodging house and ran lightly up the stairs. 'Ginny?' he called softly. 'Ginny, where are you?'

'In 'ere.' Ginny was dabbing at her face. 'In 'ere, Mr 'Arrow. Mr 'Arrow, that bloke, 'e's barmy – '

'*Was* barmy.' Simon sat down on the dirty bed. 'He's dead, Ginny,' he told the prostitute. His long, white fingers gripped the woman's bony shoulder. 'Dead, did you hear me? That was very careless of you . . .'

'Mr 'Arrow, 'e was going to kill me! He was beatin' me!' Alarmed, the woman looked at Simon's livid face. 'Mr 'Arrow, 'e was ravin' mad. And anyway,' she added, pointing to the Gladstone bag, 'you've got your money.'

'The first instalment. A mere thousand pounds.' Simon glared at the girl. 'Ginny, my dear, getting the money wasn't part of your job. *You* were supposed to set him up for us, weren't you? To make him feel comfortable; to make him keen to see you again. We wanted to take some nice pictures of you together, didn't we?'

'They never said nothing about settin' him up. Nor about no pictures.'

'Didn't they? They must have forgotten.' Simon grinned, baring sharp white teeth. 'Well, my dear, we shan't have any further use for you now, I'm afraid.'

'S'all right.' Ginny shrugged. 'I can go back on the game. I – '

'Oh, I doubt if you'll be able to do *that*.' Simon snapped his fingers and the man who'd pronounced Edmund dead came in through the door.

'You see, Ginny,' continued Simon smoothly, 'you've let us down. Girls who let us down are punished. You're going to be punished now. And by the time this gentleman here has finished with you, I doubt if you'll be capable of following your vocation for many months. If ever again.'

Half an hour later, Ginny's bubbling cries had died away into the night. The gentleman who had shown her the error of her ways now turned his attention to Edmund.

Expertly, he sharpened his knife. He removed the hands,

mutilated the face and smashed the teeth. He stripped the body and pushed the clothing into a canvas bag. And, when he was as certain as he could be that identification would be almost impossible, he stood up and looked at Simon Harrow.

'I still reckon we should cut 'im up,' he grumbled. 'Either that, or weight 'im down an' chuck 'im in the Thames. S'risky, leaving 'im 'ere. An' we ought to've done the tart in as well.'

'What a bloodthirsty fellow you are.' Simon looked down at his companion's handiwork. 'Just push him behind those dustbins,' he directed. 'And then we'll be off.'

Ten minutes later, the two men strolled into the comparatively well-illuminated Mile End Road. Simon looked in vain for a cruising taxi. Turning up his coat collar, he pulled his trilby down over his eyes. 'Should've brought my umbrella,' he muttered crossly, as the first drops of rain began to fall. 'I do so hate getting wet.'

'He usually comes to lunch every Thursday!' Seriously worried, Judith Barton clutched the telephone receiver hard. 'Darling, are you quite sure he didn't say anything to you?'

'Positive, Mummy.' Elizabeth's contemplation of her own problems left her very little time to think of her brother. She considered replacing the receiver in midsentence. 'Look,' she said wearily, 'if you're that worried, why don't you go to the police?'

'Darling, I rang Scotland Yard. A very nice inspector called round to see me.' Judith sighed heavily. 'He said that in the course of any given year, *hundreds* of adult males go missing; that most of them turn up again in due course, and that practically all of them had intended to disappear. Had I any reason to suspect foul play – that was what he asked.'

'And have you?'

'Darling, don't be silly.' Judith sighed again. 'Well,

Abdale drove me round to the flat. Everything was in order there. Really, Elizabeth, it reminds one of the *Marie Celeste*!'

'Mm.' Elizabeth frowned. 'Well, if you like, I could come up to town for a day or two. We could ring all the hospitals, couldn't we? And ask his friends.'

'I've already done that. I rang the Mounts, the Forrests and the Fishers; and I finally got hold of Jim Firbank. Now, *he* told me something a little odd – it seems that Edmund hasn't been going out much recently, and that he's been seen lunching with some fair-haired fellow – '

'Who?'

'Jim didn't know.' Judith clicked her tongue in annoyance. 'Well, darling, if you could pop up for a day or two, perhaps – '

'I'll come. Ask Abdale to meet the three o'clock at Paddington on Friday.'

'Will you bring Ben?'

'Probably not. David's mother will look after him, I expect.' And, still frowning, Elizabeth rang off.

No-one in Oxford was much disposed to be concerned about Edmund. Elizabeth went up to town, spent an unproductive three days with her mother and returned to the Summertown house as ignorant as when she'd left it.

'You don't seem very bothered,' remarked David, as he and Elizabeth lay in bed together on the evening of her return.

'I'm not, really.' Elizabeth shrugged, pleased that for once her husband was with her and not out on some errand of his own. 'As the police said, most grown-ups who disappear have deliberately made themselves scarce. I expect he'll turn up.'

'What about his job? Weren't the people at the bank concerned?'

'Not terribly. He doesn't seem to have been embezzling money, if that's what you mean.'

'Oh.' David rolled over on to his back, closed his eyes,

and, tired of that particular topic of conversation, he went to sleep.

A month or two later, Elizabeth was summoned to town again. 'There's no will,' said her mother. 'Well – as far as we can tell there isn't.'

'So?'

'So, we're his heirs.' Judith poured tea for her daughter. 'But until however many years have gone by, we can't touch the money. It'll just sit there in his accounts, accumulating.'

Elizabeth sipped her tea. 'You really think he's dead?'

'I don't know what to think.' Judith shrugged. 'I went to see Mr Grainger last week. That's really why I asked you down here.'

'Mr Grainger?' Elizabeth looked alarmed. 'Why?'

'I've been feeling a little unwell. I thought it was just the worry over Edmund.' Judith replaced her cup upon its saucer. 'But it's not that at all.'

'What is it, then?'

'Well, dear, Mr Grainger says it's too late to have an operation. Elizabeth, I *am* an old woman, I've had a reasonably pleasant life, and it appears that it won't be long. I shan't suffer.' Judith shrugged. 'There are painkillers – '

'Oh, *no*!' Elizabeth, now understanding, took her mother's hand. 'How long?' she whispered, still trying to take it all in.

'Oh, a month, two, three – six, perhaps, at the outside.'

'I see.' Elizabeth considered. 'Mummy, listen to me – you must tell me what you'd like me to do. I could come here and look after you, if you wish; I could bring Ben. David wouldn't mind – '

'But *I* would.' Judith smiled wryly. 'Oh, darling, the idea. Just imagine – a young wife separated from her husband so that she can care for her dying mother; a young child living in this great empty mausoleum, with an old woman slowly expiring upstairs! Not at *all* suitable, you must see that!'

166

'Then who *will* look after you? Where will you go?'

'Do you know, darling; I rather fancy Italy.'

'*Italy?*'

'Yes.' Judith patted Elizabeth's hand. 'Years and years ago I had a friend who owned a villa in Capri. As it happens I wrote to her a month or so back and I discovered that she's doddering on, just as I am! Well, dear, I'm going out there. I shall pack a crateful of pills and tablets, then I shall take off into the blue!'

Three weeks later, Elizabeth received a letter with an Italian postmark. Judith's friend Alison informed her that her mother had gone for a swim one morning, and that her body had been found on the beach later the same day.

'And of course,' wrote Alison, 'she meant it to happen like that. She couldn't have put up with the indignities of protracted dying. I intend to do the same myself, when the time comes.'

Elizabeth turned the page. 'Unfortunately for me,' Alison continued wryly, 'it will have to be the cold English Channel. I shall have to launch myself into eternity from Bognor or Ryde. There are ominous rumblings here, talk of internment of aliens; so I'm packing my bags. I'll be in England shortly, and I shall look you up.'

In private, Elizabeth wept; for several weeks she grieved in earnest. But then she rationalized what had happened and decided that her mother had been wise to behave as she had . . .

'She's very calm about it all,' remarked Miriam to her husband. 'Anthony, first her brother disappeared, and now her mother's gone too. Yet she still behaves as if nothing's amiss. She's very – well – odd!'

'Mm.' Anthony shrugged. 'Dave's still giving her some trouble. I think fretting about him tends to push everything else out of her mind. Don't you?'

'Oh, maybe. I tried to talk to him yesterday. He more or

less told me to mind my own business. Anthony, none of our other children are like him! Where does he get it from?'

'I really don't know.' Helplessly, Anthony looked at his wife. 'Perhaps if they had a home of their own?'

'Well, they could certainly afford it!' Ruefully, Miriam smiled. 'Heavens – Elizabeth must be a millionairess now! Or as good as!'

But, when Elizabeth suggested buying a house, David frowned and dismissed the idea. 'Aren't you happy living here?' he demanded.

'Yes, perfectly. But darling, wouldn't you like a place of your own?'

'Not particularly.' David shrugged. 'You may, of course, spend your own money just as you please. If you wish to start buying property – '

'Good grief, David, buying a home for us and for our son isn't exactly *speculating*!'

'I shall stay here.' David took a book from a bookshelf and began to read. 'As I said, it's your money. Do as you wish.'

Chapter Fourteen

ON THE DAY WAR WAS FINALLY DECLARED, Stephen experienced a sense of release; he felt a euphoria that gave him an extra swagger in his walk and caused a satisfied smile to tug at the corners of his mouth. And, looking round him at his fellow officers, he realized that most of them felt just as he did.

The autumn was spent in England. Stephen's battalion trained and drilled; and waited. Rumours that the whole strength was to be sent overseas ebbed and flowed; preparations to move were made, orders given, but then, inexplicably, countermanded. And when, finally, the expedition to Norway was mounted, the battalion was left behind. In fact, most of the officers – Second Lieutenant Atherton among them – were given leave.

'Perhaps it'll all fizzle out before the summer,' said Dora. 'What with the blockades, and the French holding the Maginot Line, I don't see how the Germans can hope to last out much longer . . . '

Stephen did not deign to comment on this. He looked at his father and, almost imperceptibly, he shrugged his shoulders. 'Is there any more tea?' he asked tonelessly; reflecting that his mother might as well retain her comforting illusions for as long as possible.

Stuck in England waiting for the raids which didn't come, Stephen and his friends cooled their heels, and hung about the bars and cafés of a sandbagged, blacked-out, but still undamaged London. Copying the behaviour of the aristocratic young blades of the most fashionable cavalry regiments, all the subalterns in the capital now seemed to be engaged in staging ridiculous stunts and in showing off to girls, ordering clothes they could not afford and drinking more than they could carry.

Stephen and Michael Carisford, now in the same regiment, in the same battalion and, by chance, posted to the same company, got on each others' nerves. Both frustrated and under-employed, they took turns in daring each other to perform increasingly ludicrous exploits. 'When I was at school,' remarked Carisford one evening, 'I regularly climbed the main tower; and I – '

'Ran the housemaster's gown up the flagpole. Oh, *what* a jolly jape.' Stephen leaned back in his chair and laughed. 'God, Carisford, you're pathetic! Any idiot can climb a bloody clock tower!'

'Actually, Sambo, this was rather more than just a bloody clock tower.' Carisford tipped back his drink. 'Two other chaps in my year tried it – one fell off and broke his neck, the other lost his nerve and had to be rescued the following morning.' Lazily, Michael Carisford grinned. 'So you see, Atherton – '

'Any steeple in London.' Stephen grinned back at his brother officer. 'Name any steeple in London, and I'll have a cheesecutter on the top of it by midnight tomorrow.'

'Tenner on Atherton?' One of Stephen's friends looked around him. 'Well?'

'Tenner on Steve.' Another officer laughed. 'Come on, chaps, cough up.'

'Fiver.'

'Tenner.'

'Twenty quid. Look here, Sambo, you'd better not bugger it up – '

Bets were taken rapidly now, and amid much noisy speculation and argument a book was made up. It was established that, if he lost his nerve and failed them, Stephen's supporters stood to lose several hundred pounds to Carisford's . . .

Michael Carisford placed his bet. 'Right,' he muttered. He looked at Stephen. '*Any* steeple, you said?'

Stephen shrugged agreement. 'Okay.'

'D'you know St Catherine's Eastgate, in the City?'

'I could find it.'

'In the dark?'

'I eat as many carrots as you do.'

'Right, then. My cap on the weathervane by Tuesday morning.' Michael Carisford giggled. 'Atherton, I hope you've made your will?'

'It's inside my pay book.' Stephen grinned. 'I've left you my copy of King's Regulations, properly amended. It's the only up-to-date copy in barracks; well worth having.'

'Can't wait.'

'Thought you'd be thrilled.' Stephen yawned. 'Now – if *I* manage this stunt, what about you having a go at St Simeon-by-Chancery?'

'I – '

Seen to hesitate, Michael Carisford was assailed by a barrage of abuse. 'Go on, Mike, you windy bugger!'

'Anything Sambo here can do – '

'Carisford always was all talk.'

'Christ, he's *scared* – '

'Oh, all right, all right! I'll do it!' Michael Carisford glowered at Stephen. 'We'll see who's all talk,' he muttered, as he left the bar.

On the nights that followed, with various examples of regimental headgear stuffed in their pockets and accompanied by various seconds and abetters, both Stephen and Michael Carisford proved their manhood by scrambling up half a dozen church spires. Subsequently, tiring of this dangerous pastime and spurred on by Michael Carisford's taunts, Stephen drank revolting combinations of various sorts of alcohol, and he picked fights with men half as heavy again as he was himself. But scrapping with other Guards officers didn't calm him down. Itching and aching to go overseas, he wanted to fight Germans.

The regiment stayed in barracks. Spring came on rapidly, and still they were there.

Then, all of a sudden, Stephen's battalion received its orders. A weekend's embarkation leave was granted and then, loaded down with huge supplies of extra kit, the men found themselves en route for France.

At the beginning of May, it looked as if there might be some action at last. The battalion took up its position on the Belgian border, joining the rest of the main British Expeditionary Force, ready to march into the Low Countries if and when the order came.

It looked as if the days of playing at war would shortly be over. The officers and men of the BEF were in no doubt that soon they were going to receive what would, for most of them, be their first experiences of real combat. Over the following week or so soldiers in a state of nervous expectancy moved to and fro along the border, bringing up supplies, siting their batteries and assuring each other that Jerry wouldn't get past this lot. In the evenings, they visited estaminets and tried to get drunk . . .

'God, this stuff's worse than the rubbish we get at home.' Scowling, a couple of officers downed their weak beers and ordered more. 'Come on, Mademoiselle,' shouted one after the barmaid. 'Chop chop! Get your skates on!'

'What's the wine like?' his friend asked another drinker.

'Bloody terrible. Tastes like dishwater.'

'Why're *you* drinking it then?'

'Well, old chap, it does make one drunk.'

'*Does* it?' The officer laughed. 'In that case – Mademoiselle! Deux verres de vin bloody blanc, s'il vous plaît. Et get a bloody move on!'

'Look, let's go and find a couple of tarts.' In the bar, the young captain sitting next to Stephen grinned. 'There's a place down the Rue Lacoste apparently – chap in the Warwickshires was telling me about it, and he reckons it's okay.'

'Oh, really?' Stephen held out his wineglass to be refilled.

'Yes. It's clean – and the girls are as pretty as it's reasonable to expect. Coming?'

172

Stephen stretched his legs out in front of him. Affecting a nonchalance he did not feel – for panic was already reddening his cheeks and making the hairs on the back of his neck rise – he shook his head. 'No,' he said, manufacturing a yawn. 'No, I don't think I shall.'

'Windy, Steve?' The captain grinned again. 'You know, Mike Carisford was telling me – '

'Carisford's a cretin. I don't fancy a dose, that's all.' Stephen drained his glass. 'By this time I expect half the BEF's been through your reasonably pretty mademmoiselles on the Rue Lacoste. And God only knows what they'll have picked up from those louts in the Warwickshires!'

'Mm.' The captain nodded. But then he stood up. 'Last chance, old man,' he said sombrely. 'This time next week we'll probably be dead. Make hay and all that!'

'All the same, no.'

'Suit yourself.'

'I shall.'

Left alone in that corner of the bar, Stephen stared gloomily into his drink. He half wished he'd gone with the other officer.

But girls were so unapproachable! A terrifying blend of wide-eyed innocence coupled with deliberate sexual allure, most of them even sharper-tongued and more disdainful than his own sister, they both fascinated and appalled him. As they had done since he was fourteen.

'He's shy! Bless his little heart, he's scared of me!' Stephen still remembered the look of scorn on that girl's face; could still see Carisford's tart grinning at him in that awful mocking fashion.

The lights in the London bar had been dim, the girl had been tipsy; but she had obviously noticed that Stephen was blushing. Disengaging herself from Carisford's groping embrace, she had leaned forward and stroked Stephen's face. 'You're only a little boy, aren't you?' she'd enquired, giggling. 'Look, I've got a friend, she likes baby soldiers. Would you like to meet her?' Her other hand had brushed his thighs . . .

Stephen had got up, pushed the table back and more or

173

less fled from the bar. No, there was no more or less about it. He had, as Carisford had implied, run away.

The orders to march into Belgium came on 10 May. The BEF, however, had hardly had time to fire the first salvo before the invading Germans were upon them. On the days that followed the Allied armies were beaten back; bombed and strafed, mortared and machine-gunned, the British Army was defeated before it had even begun to fight.

For Stephen's battalion the order to retreat came on the morning of the twenty-sixth. The Germans had by now broken through north of Menin and were pouring across Belgium unchecked. The men's instructions were to retire to the coast to help to form a bridgehead around Dunkirk.

'They reckon we've 'ad it,' muttered a disgruntled corporal as he and his platoon crammed a lorry with as much ammunition as it would hold. 'They reckon we're runnin' away.'

'Good thing too.' One of the man's fellow NCOs wiped his face on the back of his hand. He glared at the sweating men who were piling supplies into another vehicle. 'Come on, you idle sods, you lazy little fairies!' he yelled. 'Bloody well *MOVE*!'

Now the awareness that they could easily become completely surrounded and taken prisoner – or worse – made tired soldiers shift themselves at a speed which they wouldn't have thought possible. Soon, the orderly retreat had become a panic-stricken rout. The tattered remnants of the only force which lay between Britain and invasion were running, stumbling, struggling towards the coast; abandoning vast stockpiles of stores, weapons and ammunition, the men were fleeing for their lives.

Smashing through the Ardennes, the enemies' tanks had, by the last week in May, penetrated deep into Northern France. The British Army, the greater part of which had taken up its defensive position between the Belgian and French forces, was now trapped in a wedge of

174

countryside along the Belgian border – and the enemy was fast closing in.

Already some German tanks had reached the coast. Boulogne had fallen. Calais, despite the heroic efforts of the Rifle Brigade, went the same way. And now the Germans made plans to advance towards Dunkirk, intending to cut off the BEF's last retreat.

Then – for some reason never properly understood – the enemy advance was delayed. Even as the Citadel in Calais was being bombed into surrender, even as Stephen's company was making its tortuous way from Armentieres towards the blazing funeral pyre of Dunkirk, the full might of the German forces was held back.

The British troops were completely unaware that Fate – or Hitler – was giving them a last chance. Covering the withdrawal, the Guards were doing their best to hold up the enemy, and although they knew only too well that against dive-bombing Stukas and German tanks their Lee Enfield rifles were of little use, they made valiant efforts to cause as much damage to the enemy as possible.

The company in which Stephen was a platoon commander had stopped for ten minutes' rest. Fairly well concealed in leafy hedges, the men squatted on their haunches or lay down on their sides, glad to close their eyes for even a few moments.

Then, all of a sudden, there was the familiar hum of a dive-bomber. 'That one! There!' Pointing into the sky, Stephen jerked the arm of the guardsman who was carrying their only remaining Bren gun. 'Get him! Oh, God damn you, FIRE!'

'But, sir – ' Weary from lack of food and sleep, the corporal with the machine gun hesitated. It wasn't possible, surely, to shoot down a Stuka just like that? 'Sir – '

'For God's sake, give it to me!' Stephen grabbed the weapon, aimed it; and, as the plane swooped over them again, he fired. So did the German gunner. A hail of bullets raked the company, claiming another two victims.

175

Stephen was unhurt. As the wounded men's mates began to examine their friends' injuries and do what they could for them, he stared morosely into the clouds, watching the plane grow smaller. And then, suddenly, he grinned. 'I got him!' he shouted. 'Oh, great Jesus, I got him! Look!'

It seemed that he had. The retreating plane dipped. And, as the men watched, a bright orange ball of fire ballooned out of its fuselage. Now, Stephen was crowing with triumphant laughter and gradually the other men joined in.

'D'you see that?' Excitedly, a lance-corporal elbowed his mate in the side. 'Bloody hell, d'you see that? He got the sodding thing! He got a fucking Stuka with a Bren gun! You all right, sir?' he added solicitously, seeing that Stephen was rubbing his shoulder and grimacing with pain.

'Fine.' And Stephen, like his men tired, hungry and weak from the effects of dehydration, grinned back, elated.

Later that day all his euphoria had evaporated. He was now the only officer capable of issuing orders, for the other platoon commanders were dead, picked off by field guns or dive-bombers as they made their way along the route. The company commander, Captain Anson, had been wounded in the chest the day before, and could hardly speak. Clearly he was going to die.

The company had been strafed and machine gunned from the air all the way from Armentieres. They had started out with ten vehicles, but by now all of them had been shot up and the men who could still walk were going forward on foot. By evening, it was obvious that Captain Anson could not last much longer.

Supported by two guardsmen, he had stumbled on through the heat of the day; but when evening came, he was done in. 'You'll have to take over, Steve,' he muttered, lying on his back in the ditch where the remains of the company were sheltering, taking half an hour's break.

'We'll carry you, sir.' Stephen offered the man the last

176

dregs from a water bottle. 'Sir, we'll make a stretcher of some sort, we'll – '

'You can't. Go on – you *must* go on. Get the men to the coast.'

'But, sir, we can't just leave you here – '

'You've no choice.' Weakly, Captain Anson sighed. 'Look, you're not on your own, Rosie will help you. Rosie'll see you through.'

'I know, sir. But – '

'So chin up!'

Stephen forced a half-hearted grin; but he did now feel slightly better, for the mere mention of Company Sergeant Major Rosewood cheered him. He knew that, with the assistance of the great, hulking CSM, he would have a chance. 'But all the same – '

Captain Anson managed a faint grin in return. 'I'll be okay,' he murmured. 'Jerry'll find me, get me patched up. They'll look after me. Geneva Convention and all that,' he concluded wryly.

So they left him, and footslogged on into the unquiet night.

The following morning, a couple of Stukas spotted them and dive-bombed the company, causing two more deaths and several injuries. Then land forces arrived on the scene and a burst of fire from Spandaus was followed by an artillery barrage. A rain of mortar bombs and shrapnel shells made a bloody shambles of the once peaceful country road.

Inching forwards in an attempt to discover if they were completely surrounded, Stephen was foolish enough to raise himself upon one elbow, and almost immediately he was hit. He jerked upright, spun round; then fell over and rolled back into the ditch in which the other men had taken cover.

'You shouldn've done that, sir.' CSM Rosewood shook his head gloomily. 'Where'd they get you?'

'In the side. It was a shell splinter, I think. Sorry, Rosie.' Still more surprised than anything, Stephen stared

177

at the bright red stain which was now spreading across his already filthy battledress. Realizing with dismay that he must be badly hurt, and would now be unable to lead a counter attack, he looked helplessly at the sergeant major. 'Should we stay where we are for the present?' he asked weakly.

'Might be best.' The CSM grimaced. 'Bastards might think they did for the lot of us, and move on. Well, you can live in 'ope.'

Later that day, the survivors of the now decimated company did what they could in the way of treating each others' injuries. CSM Rosewood fashioned a splint for a corporal, then improvised a bandage for the one remaining officer. Leaving the shards of metal embedded in Stephen's side, he bandaged the lieutenant's chest. 'Can you walk, sir?' he enquired.

'I think I can.' Stephen got to his feet and took a few unsteady steps. 'Yes, no problem there.' And then, to take his mind off his injuries, he discussed their situation with the CSM.

'Should we spend the night here, d'you think?' he asked. 'Rosie, if we get a few hours' sleep – '

'I reckon we ought to carry on.' CSM Rosewood nodded sagely. 'Otherwise, we might be left behind all together. Look, sir, we got no ammunition, we got no water, we got no food – '

'But the men are dead beat! And if we're captured, it might be for the best – '

'Nuts to *that*, sir!' Wolfishly, CSM Rosewood bared his teeth. 'Guardsmen don't never give up.'

'I didn't mean we should surrender – '

'No, sir, I didn't think you did. You ain't been trained to take that line.'

'So – '

'We don't want to risk getting cut off, so we should get on, as fast as we can.' CSM Rosewood shook his head. 'You think Jerry's a gentleman, sir,' he muttered. 'You think 'e's as upstandin' and honourable as you are your-self – that's *your* trouble! But I tell you, sir, he's an animal!'

'Yes, but – '

'An *animal*!' CSM Rosewood snorted. 'And, sir, don't you start to spout all that Geneva Convention crap to *me*! If Jerry catches us, he'll shoot us, then finish us off with bayonets.'

The sergeant major made a stabbing motion, followed by a twist and a jerking withdrawal. 'Nasty way to go, sir. A very nasty way to go.'

'Then we'd better get moving.' Stephen felt an arrow of pain pierce his side, and winced. 'We'd better shift now.'

'That's the ticket, sir.' The sergeant major grinned. 'Shall I get the lazy buggers back on their feet?'

'Very well, Sergeant Major.' Stephen tried to grin back. 'Very well, Sergeant Major Rosewood. Carry on.'

A stroke of luck – a miracle, even – occurred the next day. Stumbling more dead than alive into a bombed and deserted village, the company discovered a French Army lorry. Parked in a farmyard, complete with a reasonable set of tyres and half a tankful of petrol, it was a gift from Heaven. In this vehicle, the seventeen remaining members of the company travelled a further twenty miles, picking up a dozen or more stragglers from other regiments as they went on, passing pathetic columns of civilian refugees for whom they could do nothing. When the fuel ran out, they smashed the lorry's engine, ripped its tyres and abandoned it.

They were now within five miles of Dunkirk. Although Stephen was tempted to press on towards the town, he realized that his men were exhausted and would not make it unless they first had some rest. 'We'll get going again at nightfall,' he told Sergeant Major Rosewood.

'Sir.' The sergeant major lay down, closed his eyes and fell into a deep sleep.

The men were woken by the drone of overhead aircraft.

Bracing themselves for bombs and bullets, they were astonished when sheets and sheets of white paper came fluttering down, coming to rest upon them as gently as snow.

'Leaflets, sir! They're dropping fucking leaflets!' A young private, whose arm was practically severed from his shoulder, actually laughed. 'Stupid sods,' he added derisively. 'Let them wait, that's all! Let the buggers wait!'

'Stupid sods,' agreed Sergeant Major Rosewood. He wiped his face with the back of his hand. 'Stupid bastards. We ain't finished with them yet! Well, sir, since they've woke us up – '

For Stephen's men the actual retreat to Dunkirk was over within a week; but by the time they reached the coast, it seemed that they had been struggling through the French countryside for an eternity.

Their progress was now horribly slow. Tired and famished, the men dragged their weary bodies on so tardily that at times it seemed that they were almost standing still. As they entered the outskirts of the town, a volley of shots from a rise of land to their right flank left Sergeant Major Rosewood clutching his shoulder and swearing ferociously. 'Come on, you idle bleeders!' he growled, exhorting the rest of the group. 'If we stand here like ruddy targets, they'll do for us all! Shift yourselves!'

Dunkirk was, by now, nothing more than a hell on earth. On the road, the men had got used to diving into ditches and praying hard, as Messerschmidts dive-bombed them and Stukas and Heinkels appeared out of nowhere and machine-gunned them to glory.

But now, inside the defensive perimeter, there was no cover. On the beaches men dug foxholes and during air raids they crouched in these shallow pits, unable to do anything but curse the enemy and hope for the best. The sand did, at least, absorb the shocks of the explosions . . .

Rations were very scarce and drinking water was almost

unobtainable. For although water had been stockpiled in containers for just such an emergency, it was nothing like enough to go round the thousands and thousands of men who needed it now. Attempting to slake their thirst with either white wine or champagne, there wasn't a soldier on the beaches who wouldn't have sold his mother for a pint of fresh water.

'All right, Mr Atherton?' Sheltering against a broken wall, those men of Stephen's company who were wounded or otherwise incapacitated huddled together, listening to the planes which were now coming over again. The corporal who had spoken touched Stephen's arm. 'Sir, you awake?'

Stephen nodded. 'Yes. Just about.'

'Shall I have a look at you, sir?' The corporal indicated Stephen's side. 'If you'll pardon me, sir, it don't smell too good; and I think that dressin' ought to come off – '

'No.' Stephen shook his head. 'No, don't remove the bandage. I'll start to bleed again if you do.'

'I expect it's septic in there, sir.' The NCO was persistent and now he fished in his trouser pocket. 'Look, sir, a fellow from the Shropshires back along there give me these field dressings specially. Wouldn't it be better to have that thing off?'

'Well, perhaps.' Foul with clotted blood and black with dirt, the bandage which Sergeant Major Rosewood had fashioned nearly a week ago was now as stiff as plaster of Paris. Very tempted to have it removed, and aware that the NCO was probably right when he asserted that the wound must be septic, Stephen now seriously considered the man's offer . . .

'No,' he said, at last. 'No, don't do anything. I'll keep this dressing on. You hang on to those bandages.'

Just then a terrific thud shook the beach, and a high-pitched scream issued from somewhere on their right. 'You may need them yourself before this lot have finished with us,' he added, closing his eyes.

Despite the racket overhead, Stephen spent the rest of that day in a light doze. Growing weaker by the hour, he now alternated between fitful sleep and bleary-eyed consciousness, which two states eventually blurred into one pain-filled haze.

It was the middle of a hot afternoon when he felt the CSM shaking his elbow, jerking him awake. 'Come on, sir,' he said gently. 'Our turn. We're goin' on a little boat trip round the bay.'

'What?' Stephen opened his eyes. 'I can't,' he mumbled. He focused his eyes on the sergeant major's face. 'Rosie, I'm sorry, but I can't get up. My legs won't work, you see.'

'Yes, they will.' The sergeant major slipped one arm around Stephen's waist and levered him into a sitting position, making him wince. 'Come on, lad,' he repeated, his voice low and soothing. 'I heard all about you back in Blighty – you're the fellow who scrambles up church steeples an' what have you; you're the chap who socked Fred Wainwright in the jaw Now, all you got to do today is come down for a little paddle in the sea – '

'I *can't*!' The sergeant major had touched his injured side, and if his mouth had not been too dry to allow it, Stephen would have cried out in agony. 'You go,' he muttered. 'Take the men. Make sure they carry as many weapons as possible, see that the Bren isn't left behind, get the rifles – '

Babbling to himself now, Stephen was already losing consciousness again, had already closed his eyes. 'My legs won't work,' he repeated helplessly.

The sergeant major pulled the lieutenant to his feet. Half dragging, half carrying him, he lugged his officer to the shoreline, where a row of lorries formed a temporary jetty for small boats.

The walk to the water's edge, short though it was, proved just too much for the injured man. Opening his mouth, intending to order the sergeant major to see that the men got on first, the words simply wouldn't form. Another spasm of pain convulsed him. And, slumping forwards, Stephen fainted.

'Take this officer.' Sergeant Major Rosewood manhandled the lieutenant into the little pleasure boat. 'Careful now – he's hurt very bad.'

When Stephen came to, the little cruiser was bobbing on the open sea. All around him men were lying packed closely together; everywhere there were soldiers cursing, bleeding, and despite the absolute calm, vomiting over the pale wood of the cabin where he lay.

'Will you have a drink?' A man of about fifty, a tall, good-looking gentleman clad in white trousers and a navy pullover, leaned over him. 'A whisky, eh?'

'Whisky would be very nice.' Stephen tried to sit up. 'But could I have some water in it, please? My mouth's so dry – '

'Certainly.' The man disappeared and returned again with a mug.

'Thanks.' Stephen swallowed a mouthful of the drink. 'Is this your boat?' he asked.

'Yes.' The man laughed. 'My pride and joy.'

'It's a bit of a mess now.'

'It'll clean up.'

Stephen nodded. 'I suppose so.'

'Don't worry about it.' The man regarded Stephen curiously. 'Bad out there, was it?' he asked conversationally.

'On the beach?'

'Yes.'

'Well – bad enough.'

The man grimaced. 'I was in the last show,' he said. 'Thought I'd seen everything. But those beaches – God, I don't know how we're *ever* going to get them all away! This is my third trip, you know.'

'Is it?' Stephen was impressed. 'It's very – ah – patriotic of you. I mean – well – ' He tailed off, feeling abashed. 'What I mean is – '

'Least I can do. Oh, *God*!' The man stood up. 'Oh Jesus Christ, not *more* of the buggers!'

But, even as he spoke, aircraft could be heard coming

183

overhead. A huge explosion to starboard rocked the little boat; and through the porthole at his side Stephen looked on helplessly as the cabin cruiser a few hundred yards away went down. Already overloaded, the boat he was in could give no assistance to the men floundering in the water.

The owner of the little pleasure craft cursed. 'Better get a move on,' he muttered grimly. And, agonizingly slowly, pursued by German bombers all the way back to England, the boat ploughed on.

Tired, filthy and unshaven, the troops who arrived back in England were a raggle-taggle of an army who frightened the ladies gathered on station platforms to provide tea and sandwiches.

'What a bloody shambles,' muttered a sergeant, as he drank his first cup of tea for a fortnight. 'What a bleeding monumental balls-up.' He grinned at his mate. 'But what a sock in the eye for Jerry, eh? What a shiner!'

Stephen stared at the nurse who leaned over him, at the vision who, in that low, caressing voice reserved for the seriously ill, was telling him that she was going to change his dressings. He watched while she got on with her work.

She swabbed the torn flesh and then bandaged the wounds, apologizing when he winced. 'Comfortable?' she asked kindly, as she finished.

Stephen closed his eyes. He didn't want to talk to her.

'He's passed out again.' The nurse looked enquiringly at the ward sister. 'Shall I ask doctor to have a look at him?'

'Is his pulse normal?'

'Almost.' The nurse released Stephen's wrist. 'Yes, it's what it should be.'

'Let him sleep, then. Now, Rawlings, *have* you finished those charts?'

Stephen lay on his side and listened to the nurses talking. He wished that he *could* sleep; that the demons which were tormenting him would go away. But they wouldn't. They never would now . . .

For he'd failed. Failed himself, and failed his men. And his battalion had failed as well, failed to repulse or even to delay the enemy.

Stephen himself had been a liability. Wounded as a result of his own stupidity, he'd been brought back to England like a parcel. As a soldier, he was useless. He could have cried; had he let tears come, he would never have been able to stop them.

The final twist of the knife came in the form of a letter from his mother. He heard from Dora that Lieutenant David Lawrence, who had joined up just two days after war had been declared, had arrived back in England on one of the last boats out of Dunkirk; was safe and perfectly well.

But it was not David's preservation which was galling Stephen to the heart. It was the fact that during the flight across France David and his battalion had ambushed and destroyed a whole convoy of advancing Germans, and, as if this was not enough, had then laid a booby trap and subsequently blown up the staff car of one of the German top brass.

David and two other officers had been recommended for the Military Cross.

Chapter Fifteen

'HE'LL PULL THROUGH.' COMFORTING HIS wife, who had been horrified to see her only son in such a dreadful condition, Tim kissed Dora's face. 'He'll survive; don't worry! In a few weeks' time he'll be up and about – '

'Will he?' Dora sniffed. 'Oh, Tim!' she cried miserably, 'he looked so ill! Ill, and wretched!' She dabbed her eyes with her handkerchief. 'And there's something bothering him – '

'I expect his stitches hurt. Now look, Dora; you're not to fret. Steve'll be okay.'

But Tim was more concerned than he cared to let Dora know, having observed that at present his son was anything but okay. He realized that Stephen's mental state must be even more traumatized than his physical one.

'I'll make you proud of me.' Tim could remember Stephen saying that as clearly as if it had been yesterday. And the crestfallen look in his son's eyes, the expression of total despair on Stephen's face, had pierced Tim's heart. He'd wanted to take his son in his arms and hug him, to tell him that it just didn't matter. But that, as he was well aware, would only have made everything worse . . .

The fear of invasion from France – which, despite the Battle of Britain having been fought and won, was to persist for six months or more – had culminated in a terrified panic when on 12 September the government had put out a near-hysterical invasion alert. Among other things this broadcast resulted in the more resolute fathers and husbands confidently assuring their wives and daughters that they would slit their throats before they let them fall into the hands of the Jerries . . .

Tim, however, had behaved throughout as if there was nothing to worry about. But, although he was apparently so unconcerned, he and Anthony *had* spent some time closeted together in Anthony's study, discussing matters which they refused to divulge to the rest of the family.

'We were just chatting,' Anthony said innocently, pushing his spectacles on to the top of his head and peering myopically at his sister. 'We were nattering, that's all.'

'Rubbish. You're cooking something.' Dora scowled at him. 'Come on, Anthony, you've both been looking secretive lately. What were you gassing about?'

'We were just gassing! And looking at dirty postcards.' Anthony shook his head. 'Honestly, Dora,' he went on, more gravely, 'it's better if you don't know.'

'Men! Oh, all right. Have your little secrets; I don't care. I shall get it out of Tim eventually!'

But getting information out of Tim proved to be impossible; and although Dora wasn't in the least bit fooled by her husband's bland assurance that he and Anthony had been discussing the implications of Soviet neutrality, she was eventually obliged to save her own face by accepting this absurd explanation. And, in spite of Tim's continued nonchalance and his advice that she should not worry about invasion, horrible nightmares of goose-stepping German soldiers now haunted her dreams, causing her to wake up sweating with fear.

'If they do come, what will you do?' she asked Tim one night, as she lay curled up next to him. Holding on to his reassuringly solid arm, she had been glad to find that what had disturbed her sleep had only been another dream.

'Shoot as many of them as I can, before they shoot me.' Tim grinned. 'Better get my old service revolver out and practise.'

'You'd shoot Germans? You'd stand at your own front door and fire at them as they came up the path?'

'Of course.'

'But if you do that, they'll definitely kill you!' Dora's eyes were wide. 'Tim, don't you think – '

'No, I don't.' Tim pulled the bedclothes around his wife and made her comfortable again. 'I expect I'm on their list anyway. My last novel but one wasn't very complimentary about old Adolf and his merry men; so I shall be for the high jump. They'll torture me, so, since I'm probably due for the piano wire treatment, I might as well go down fighting – '

'Oh, God!' Dora blenched. 'Honestly, Tim, it was foolish to write that story! I said so at the time!' She shook his shoulder. 'Why did you have to be *funny* about the Nazis?' she demanded. 'Why couldn't you have written a different book altogether, come to that?'

'I thought I made a good point or two. In fact, I'm rather fond of that particular effort.' Tim shrugged. 'Oh, darling, I wrote what I did, and that's that. Dora, can't you see? Back in 1935 Adolf and his bunch of maniacs were irresistible!'

'You really think they'd kill you? Just because of a few jokes?'

'Don't know, do I? We'll have to wait and see. But I don't think the Gestapo has much sense of humour.' Tim kissed Dora and smoothed her hair back from her forehead. 'Look, love, you must go back to sleep. Believe me, it won't seem so frightening in the morning.'

Tim went out the next day, returning home with a parcel tied up in brown paper and a lot of hairy string.

'What's that?' asked Dora.

'Paper,' he replied. 'Blank paper, offcuts from the *Oxford Times*. Chap who works in the editorial office offered it to me, so, since paper and everything else will be in short supply soon, I thought I'd have it.'

Dora didn't believe this story, but she let it go. 'I've been thinking about Miriam,' she said.

'What about her?'

'Oh, for goodness sake, Tim!' Dora glared at her husband. 'She's Jewish! With her face and features, it's obvious that she is, and they hate the Jews!' Dora began to sob. 'I *love* her!' she cried. 'She's my best friend; she's the nicest, kindest person I've ever known! Oh, Tim, they'll torture *her* as well! They'll take her away! It'll be just like Mrs Leitner said, they'll come for the Jews and they'll take Miriam –'

'They won't do anything of the sort.' Tim sat down beside his wife. 'Look, Dora, if the Nazis come, we'll protect Miriam. We'll find a way to hide her, they won't catch her. In fact –'

'That's what you and Anthony have been discussing, isn't it?'

'Sort of.'

'Where will you take her?'

'It's better if you don't know exactly, not just at the moment. But we've made plans for Miriam, and for Katherine and Rachel, and the grandchildren.' Tim saw that Dora was eyeing his parcel. 'Have a look if you want to.'

Dora unfastened the string and took out a package containing a wad of papers. 'Birth certificates,' she muttered, puzzled. 'And whose is this marriage certificate? Who's Eileen McCarthy? Tim, I don't understand!'

'Well, darling.' Tim smiled at his wife. 'If it becomes necessary, you and your friend Eileen will be taken to a nice seaside town somewhere in Wales, to a house which Anthony and I happen to have bought, and where Eileen can recover from the effects of a serious illness. You'll be going to look after her. And Eileen's children –' Tim looked at some other papers – 'Mary and Christina, not to mention *their* children too, will be coming with you. Later on, perhaps –'

'Tim, it's impossible!' Dora threw the birth certificates back on to the pile. 'All this cloak and dagger stuff – it's ridiculous! If you seriously imagine that people will be fooled; that no-one will betray us –'

'Then what do *you* suggest?'

'I don't know. But – '

'Dora, it probably won't come to this. But if it does, you and I will get Miriam and all her family away. We'll – '

'You'd risk your life for your sister-in-law?' Dora looked incredulously at Tim. 'You'd risk being shot, or worse, just to protect Miriam?'

'As I told you, I'm probably for it anyway; and I can only be killed once. Now, Dora, have a look at these – they're pretty good, aren't they? All signed and stamped, properly creased and aged – works of art, you must admit. And the identity cards and ration books – see this? It's the work of a master, isn't it?'

'It all looks convincing enough.' Dora thumbed through Eileen McCarthy's ration book. 'Yes, it would fool me. Not that *that* means a great deal.' She sniffed. 'What about Miriam's voice?' she demanded. 'She does have a very strong accent. And these days she's always muttering to herself in Yiddish!'

'She'll have to be careful, that's all.' Tim shook his head. 'Dora, it'll be very difficult, I know that. But the alternative's unthinkable . . . '

When it became clear that the Germans were not coming – or at least, not immediately – everyone shrugged and told their friends and relations that of course they weren't afraid of Hitler and his mob.

By the time the autumn had arrived in good earnest, and a spell of miserable, wet, dirty weather had brought with it the promise of a foul winter, the threat of invasion had receded. Painted over hoardings in railway stations and misleading signposts at crossroads had all become something of a joke.

Chapter Sixteen

'YOU'RE LOOKING MUCH BETTER TODAY.' Helen sat down on the edge of her brother's bed and grinned at him. 'In fact, I'd say you were malingering now.'

'Dead right, I am.' Pleased to see her, Stephen returned his sister's smile. 'What have you brought me?' he demanded.

'A horrible sponge cake which I made myself; a nasty cheap magazine which was all I could get, I'm afraid; and a few books.' She ferreted in her bag. 'Dad's made us clear the shelves of rubbish. These are some I saved from the pulpers.'

'What's happened to *my* books?' Stephen asked. 'Nell, you didn't let him – '

'They're quite safe; all tucked away under my bed, along with some of my stuff.' Helen giggled. 'He'll never think of looking there.' She looked around the ward. 'Now, if I ask that old dragon over there nicely, is there any possibility of you being allowed on to the verandah for an hour?'

'I should think so.' Stephen pushed back his blankets and got out of bed. 'Oh, God, Nell, I shall be glad to get out of this place!'

'Can't wait to get back to the jolly old barracks, eh?' Helen laughed. 'Goodness, Steve, you're a glutton for punishment! I suppose you're dying to get back overseas?'

'Of course I am!' Stephen fished under the bed and found his slippers. 'Christ, I haven't finished with Jerry yet!'

'There speaks a proper little hero!' Helen pulled a face. 'Alec's off to a transit camp on Monday,' she said. 'He spent his embarkation leave weeping on my shoulder. Poor thing, he's scared stiff, but he's trying to be brave!'

'He's all right, Alec is,' said Stephen gravely. 'It's chaps like him, men who don't want to be soldiers but who join up anyway, who really *are* heroes. Nell, it's all right for me; *I* want to go.'

'God knows why.' Helen grinned. 'I think you're just too stupid to be afraid.'

'Oh, shut up.' Stephen pushed her shoulder. 'Go and fetch me a dressing gown. There are some in the dayroom, down the corridor.'

Stephen's wounds healed cleanly and he left hospital in August. Only a series of long, white scars running down the length of his left side showed where the shell splinters had sliced into his flesh. Soon, he told himself, he'd be back in action, and he'd be able to redeem himself and prove he *was* a soldier.

But, when he was discharged from a convalescent home at the beginning of October, there was a nasty shock awaiting him. He was informed that from then on he would be temporarily attached to the Hampshire Regiment; and, to his absolute disgust, he was detailed to report to an army camp near Portsmouth, where he would receive further orders.

'I say, Steve, that's pretty rough,' remarked a fellow ex-convalescent whom Stephen had met for a drink. 'The Hampshires, eh? Why the Hampshires, I wonder?'

'I don't ruddy well know.' Stephen downed his weak whisky and water. 'I'll speak to the CO,' he muttered. 'They can't *do* this! Not to *me*!'

'Perhaps it's all a mistake,' soothed his friend. 'Administrative balls-up, most likely.'

Demanding an interview with his commanding officer, Stephen was informed that as active service overseas was out of the question, he ought to be happy to go where he was needed. 'A spot of home service, Mr Atherton,' said the colonel. 'That's what you need. Get you fit again, eh?'

'But why am I being sent to *Portsmouth*, sir?' Stephen frowned. 'Sir, couldn't I go to the Depot or something?'

'You're only fit for light duties. Right now, the Portsmouth job is just the ticket. Tailor-made for you.'

'But – '

'But *what?*' Annoyed that this presumptuous young subaltern should dare to argue with him, the Colonel glared at the young man. 'Stop bloody scowling!' he barked. 'For God's sake, man! Anyone would think you're being cashiered!'

'Being attached to the Hampshires is damned near the same thing!' In his chagrin, Stephen did not even realize that he had sworn at the colonel, contradicted his commanding officer and laid himself open to a variety of charges. 'Sir, I'd hoped – '

'Look, what the blazes d'you expect us to do with you?' Angrily, the colonel banged his fist down on the desk. 'I suppose you were expecting a transfer to the Suicide Squad? Fancy yourself as a Commando, do you?'

'No, sir, not at all. Just the same – '

'Well, then!' The colonel glowered at the lieutenant. 'Do as you're bloody well told! Come on, now, Steve,' he added, rather less roughly. 'You're not going to be any use in combat for some time – the MO reckons you'll be out of all that for at least a year or two. You might as well accept it.'

Stephen arrived in Portsmouth in the middle of a drizzly, cold October. He reported to the barracks, a dismal collection of Nissen huts and rotting wooden cabins a couple of miles from the centre of the town. Here he was informed that he would be working with a section responsible for the paperwork involved in sending soldiers overseas.

'You'll liaise with Captain Armstrong,' said the major who was to be Stephen's new commanding officer. 'Her mob does most of the clerical work.' He grinned. 'They're a good crowd, those ATS girls. Better than the men – more accurate, and they work harder. And Lois Armstrong's a decent sort. I'm sure you'll get on.'

Sourly, Stephen nodded. Ten minutes later he was walking across the barrack square towards his new quarters.

The winter set in with a vengeance, and from then onwards air raids added to the general atmosphere of gloom and misery. At night, Portsmouth was lit up as if for a jubilee, for the Germans were doing their best to destroy the docks. Everywhere else there was blackout.

The camp was a dismal place in which to be. Surrounded by dripping trees, it could have been in the heart of some ancient forest. During those evenings on which he was not on duty, Stephen lay on his bed reading, or trying to read. Still too disgruntled to be sociable, he resolutely shunned the company of his fellow officers. He listened to the wind, heard the whines and crashes in the distance and cursed his fate.

Wrapped up in his private misery, he hardly understood that almost everyone else in England was experiencing the same baffled fury as he was; a fury which could only be expressed by swearing about the Germans and wishing that Hitler would choke on his own poisonous spit. And as he crouched in a dug-out along with dozens of other army personnel, listening to a raid which that night was uncomfortably near, Stephen seriously considered going back to London, there to confront his CO and *demand* that he be taken back into some kind of active service . . .

Surely there was *something* else he could do?

'Lieutenant Atherton, welcome aboard!' The woman beamed at him and shook his hand as firmly as any man could have done. 'Glad to have you with us!'

As his commanding officer had predicted, Stephen found Lois Armstrong a good sort. The woman was straight-forward and sensible; she ran her section with a more than

194

military precision and she was always fiercely protective towards her girls, as she called them. Provided Stephen did not undermine her authority, she was perfectly charming towards him. But when he asked a clerk to do some typing for him one day, Lois heard about it, and she gave him a dressing down the like of which he'd never received before.

'So, Lieutenant Atherton,' she concluded, displaying a set of perfectly white teeth, 'you will refer any future requests for clerical assistance through the proper channels. Through my office, in other words. Do I make myself perfectly clear?'

Stephen replied that indeed she did. He wondered if she were married, for she wore no rings, and if she were widowed, what her husband had died of . . .

Good crowd or not, the ATS clerks were not particularly impressed by the new officer who had just been posted to Dorrington Barracks.

'He's a bastard,' muttered Rose Davies one morning. 'Nothin' but a bleedin' bastard.' Rose, a habitually cheerful East Londoner, picked up a folder of work which she had been instructed by Lieutenant Atherton – whose orders were, she observed, properly endorsed by Captain Armstrong – to do again. And to do properly this time. 'Bastard! Don't he know there's a bloody war on?'

'I dare say he's noticed.' Rose's friend Agnes Lyall, a handsome redhead whose air of world-weariness belied her eighteen years, grinned. 'Look,' she added, 'just do it right, then there'll be no aggravation. You're a lazy cow, Rose – you know you are.'

'*I'm* lazy?' Rose glowered. 'God, Ag! *You* can talk!'

Agnes laughed. 'Go on,' she said, opening another file, 'just get on with it. Do it all nice and neat an' his lordship might take you out for a drink – you never know.'

'That'll be the day.' Crossly, Rose began to batter her typewriter, cursing the shift keys, which *would* stick. '*He* don't never ask girls out,' she continued tetchily. 'D'you know what, Ag?'

'What?'

'I reckon he's a five.'

'A what?'

'A five to two. A Jew. Oh, for God's sake, Ag, a bleedin' Yid!' Rose nodded wisely. 'Have you looked at him sideways?' she demanded. 'Them eyebrows an' that nose – they're a dead giveaway. He reminds me of Mr Abramowicz who used to keep the corner shop down our road.'

Agnes considered. 'Mm,' she conceded. 'P'raps. Well, then, if he's a Yid, he's bound to be a bit tight. Tell you what; you ask *him* out! Stand him a drink, eh? Might bring a smile to 'is miserable face!'

'You *what*? Stuff that!' Rose made a mistake. 'Now look what you made me do!'

Walking back towards Dorrington Hall, the Victorian country house which gave the camp its name and which stood like an affronted dowager among the forlorn trees and decaying Nissen huts, Agnes and Rose resumed their discussion of Lieutenant Atherton.

'*I* reckon he's one of Them,' said Agnes, as the two girls went up the stairs to their dormitory.

'One of what?'

'Them. Queer – you know!' Agnes winked. 'A pansy!'

'Oh!' Rose giggled. 'No,' she said. 'No, I don't think he's queer. He's just a bit shy.' She unfastened her cuffs. 'He was talking to Ellen Dyer yesterday – she reckons he was quite chatty. Talked about the war, the weather, passed the time of day and that.'

'Well, we'll see.' Agnes grinned. 'I'll sort him out. I'll get him to take me to the flicks.'

'You reckon?'

'Yeah.' Agnes giggled. 'I quite fancy him, in a way; I always like a dark man.' She sat down on her bed. 'Here, have you noticed how hairy his hands are? I wonder if he's like that all over?'

'Sounds as if you're goin' to find out,' replied Rose. She

196

sniggered. 'Tell you what – take 'im round the back of the cookhouse an' give 'im the once-over. An' then you can tell me if 'e's a five, an' all.'

'I might just do that, Rose.' Agnes giggled. 'That'd shake you, if I did!'

Agnes laid her plans. When Stephen next came into the office she beamed at him. 'Good morning sir!' she cried chirpily. 'And what can we do for you today?'

Stephen raised his eyebrows. 'Can you do this right away?' he asked, giving her a folder. 'Captain Armstrong has okayed it.'

'*Yes*, sir!' Cheekily, Agnes giggled. 'Shall I bring it over to you personally, sir?'

'Well, yes, that would be splendid.' Stephen coughed. 'In an hour or two, if you could.'

'Oh, I shan't take *that* long!' Agnes got up and walked over towards a filing cabinet, brushing past Stephen. As she bent over to open a drawer, she bumped her bottom against his thigh. 'Sorry, sir!' she exclaimed, widening her green eyes. 'Did I hurt you?'

Stephen reddened, and scowled at her. Stupid little tart. He noticed that Rose Davies was trying not to giggle, and he was not at all surprised when a positive explosion of sniggers followed him into the corridor.

He walked back across the square, thinking. He had decided to ask Ellen Dyer if she'd like to go to the cinema with him. A small, serious blonde girl who seemed rather overwhelmed by the experience of being in the army, she frequently looked so lost and miserable that Stephen thought that perhaps they might cheer each other up. Small, lost and miserable. No, there was nothing threatening about Ellen . . .

But no power on earth would have induced him to respond to Agnes Lyall's inviting grins. Agnes was exactly the sort of woman he despised.

*　　　*　　　*

197

In the middle of December David Lawrence turned up in Portsmouth, telephoned his cousin, and arranged to meet him for a lunch-time drink.

Sitting beside the newly-decorated hero, Stephen looked enviously at the white and purple ribbon on David's tunic. 'Tell me again what happened, Dave,' he said. 'You got as far as Aubaille, then – '

'Oh, shut up, Stevie!' David giggled. 'Good God, you're embarrassing, you really are! Like a little kid! Please, sir, did you have a Tommy gun? Did you shoot lots an' lots of Germans? Sir, sir – '

'I only asked you – '

'You'll have a chance to get yourself a bit of tin.' David gulped down a few mouthfuls of weak beer. 'We haven't really started yet, you know!'

'I suppose not.' Mortified, Stephen changed the subject. 'How's Elizabeth?' he asked.

'Don't know.' David shrugged. 'Haven't seen her this leave.'

'Haven't *seen* her?' Astonished, Stephen blinked. 'What *have* you been doing?'

'Ah, well, it's none of your business, but there's this lady down in Fareham. I just had to call in before I go back overseas.'

'And you've been staying with her?'

'In a manner of speaking.'

'My God!' Stephen gaped. 'Who is she?'

'Her name's Annette. Her husband's in the Navy. She has brown hair, blue eyes and the most fantastic pair of legs you ever saw. I met her at a reception centre just after Dunkirk, and she gave me her address. Said if I was ever passing, to call in.'

'Oh.' Too amazed to comment further, Stephen simply stared.

David shrugged again. 'Well, you nosy bugger, is there anything I've left out? Oh, yes. Knew there was something. She's bloody marvellous in bed. God, she's even taught *me* a thing or two these past few days!'

Stephen could think of nothing to say to that. And now,

looking at his cousin's appalled expression, David laughed. 'Don't look so horrified,' he said. 'Christ Almighty, Stephen, *you* don't live like a flaming monk, do you? Not among all those ATS girls?'

'*I'm* not married!' Stephen scowled into his watery beer. 'Dave, I'm not a father, I'm not – '

'Oh, give it a rest! You're as bad as my mother!' David giggled. 'Vy haven't you been home to see your Mamma?' he demanded, rolling his eyes. 'Vy haven't you written to your vife? Oy vey, such a son I have already, that he should break his mother's heart!'

'Aunt Miriam doesn't talk like that!' Stephen pushed his cousin's shoulder. 'Dave, you're a shit. An absolute shit!'

'I'll be going to Oxford in a day or two. So I'll see Ben and Elizabeth then.' David drained his glass. 'Ah, women, Stevie!' he said, grinning. 'Pebbles on the beach! Tell you this; they might moan, they might grizzle fit to drive you insane, but they don't suffer! Not like we do! Read any of the poets – Shakespeare, Donne, Byron especially – they'll tell you!'

'Elizabeth's not some poet's tart. She loves you!'

'Does she now?' David pushed his hands into his pockets. 'Oh, you're not a married man, what do you know about it?'

'Well – '

'Bugger all, that's what. So I'll tell you this, for nothing. I'm married to a saint. A saint, Stevie. And saints love everybody! God, you've no idea how hard it is to live with perfection!' Yawning, David leaned back in his chair. 'Now, are you going to buy me the other half before the fellow calls time?'

Despite his devil-may-care demeanour, David was not looking forward to going to Oxford. Elizabeth would be reproachful and her light eyes would be red-rimmed and tearful. She'd hang about his neck and ask him why he hadn't come sooner.

And she did. David arrived back in Oxford at midnight

199

and as soon as he had thrown his kitbag on to the floor she was there in the hall, a warm, soft vision in a white night-dress and pale blue dressing gown, a beautiful woman smelling of soap and shampoo, who was hugging him and covering his face with kisses. 'Why didn't you come earlier?' she demanded. 'I've been expecting you all day! Ben and I – '

'Oh, God, Elizabeth!' He sighed wearily. 'I couldn't get away any sooner! And besides, there were some friends I wanted to see before I go overseas – '

'Friends? What friends?' Elizabeth stopped kissing him and stared. 'Women?'

'Some of them were women.' David sniffed. 'They were just friends, Elizabeth! People who like me!'

'But I *love* you! Don't you understand that? Oh, I know you have lots of friends, I know there were other women before me, but I'm your wife!' She sniffed pathetically. 'Don't you love me?' she asked.

'Of course I love you!' David kicked the coat rack. 'Christ Almighty! Why do women always want to be told they're loved?'

Elizabeth looked down at the floor. 'I sometimes think we should never have married,' she said miserably. 'I don't think you're the marrying kind, David, you're one of Nature's bachelors – '

'Do you want a divorce, then? I'll give you one if you do.'

'A divorce? No! No, why d'you say that? David, I want you!'

'All to yourself?'

'Yes! Of course!'

'Well, I'm afraid that's something you may not be able to have.' David lit a cigarette.

Elizabeth understood that she was wasting her breath. She had not intended to quarrel, and now she tried to smile. Wanting to wipe the last five minutes from the record, she leaned forward and kissed her husband's face.

'Well, it's lovely to see you,' she said bravely. 'We'll have a pleasant couple of days together, shall we? Ben and I have lots to show you, he's been doing so well in nursery school, he's made you - well, I won't spoil it by telling you.' Elizabeth shrugged. 'If you've been with anyone else,' she added, 'I don't think I want to know about it.'

David scowled. 'Were you in bed?'

'Yes.' Elizabeth nodded. 'Actually, I was rather tired.'

'Are you going back to sleep?'

'Well, that was the general idea.' Wearily, she smiled. 'Come with me, if you like.'

'Wouldn't you rather I slept on the sofa?'

'No, of course not, but - '

'Well, stop bloody nagging, then!'

David followed his wife upstairs. Undressing quickly, he left his clothes in a heap on the floor. 'Liz,' he murmured, 'come here.'

'What is it?'

He took her face between his hands and looked into her eyes. 'You said you loved me,' he said softly. 'Elizabeth, was that just talk?'

'No. No, it wasn't.' Elizabeth laid her arms around his neck. Almost against her will she found herself responding to him. And afterwards she fell asleep perfectly contented, curled up close to him, relaxed and happy.

He left Oxford the following day. Offering no excuses or explanations, he packed his kit and after an early breakfast he walked out of the Summertown house. Leaving no details of how his wife might get in touch with him, he was gone.

'He'll write soon,' she told herself. 'As soon as he has a Forces address, he'll let me know roughly where he is.' Yet she knew she was deceiving herself . . .

By February 1941 Elizabeth realized that she must be pregnant again. But by then David was in Africa - somewhere in the desert, fighting the Italians, or so she assumed. And he had not written to her.

Chapter Seventeen

'YOU WERE DAMNED UNLUCKY TO be caught just there,' remarked the medical officer. 'Or lucky, depending on which way you look at it.' He took his stethoscope from around his neck and picked up his fountain pen. 'All right, get dressed again.'

Stephen pulled on his shirt and began to fasten the buttons. 'Well?' he demanded. 'Well, sir, what's the verdict?'

The MO frowned at his patient. 'You're much as I'd have expected you to be,' he replied evenly.

'Oh.' Stephen looked hopeful. 'I was assuming I'd be passed fit – '

'Were you, indeed?' The doctor raised his eyebrows. 'Whatever gave you that idea?'

'Well, I don't feel so tired these days. I don't have any pain.' Stephen picked up his tie. 'I *am* fit!' he added desperately. 'Sir, I'm perfectly well now! Whatever the report you have there says, I *am better*!' Stephen looked beseechingly at the doctor. 'Look, sir – I want to go back to my regiment! Please, couldn't you recommend – '

'You'll stay at Dorrington for the present. The duties you have here are eminently suitable for a man in your state of health. You – '

'But I'll go *mad* if I have to spend another month in this camp!' Stephen's eyes glistened. 'Surely I could go to the training battalion or something? Couldn't I help with – with weapon training, with – '

'Oh, God give me strength!' The MO sighed and eyed Stephen over his spectacles. 'Look here,' he said carefully. 'You must understand, once and for all, that I can't recommend a man with only one effective kidney and a badly damaged lung for any kind of active duty.

'Training battalion, indeed! Good grief, man, your breathing's so bloody laboured it's agony to listen to it! Your left lung's practically useless, and your right one was just caught, too. You're lucky to be alive!'

He drew breath. 'I doubt if you could run across the sports field and not go blue in the face. And that's without your kit!'

'I'll never be fit to be killed, then.' Sulkily, Stephen fastened his cuffs.

'No, that's right, you won't.'

'And I'll be spending the rest of the war in some office, I suppose.'

'I expect so.' The doctor finished writing and glanced up at Stephen. 'Damn it all, man!' he barked. 'You've done your bit! You were at Dunkirk, weren't you?'

'Yes.'

'So you've had a crack at Jerry. Broken a couple of mothers' hearts, no doubt. Now it's someone else's turn to kill a few of the Hun.'

The doctor replaced Stephen's medical notes in the folder. 'Now, I've got a dozen other men out there, so if you've nothing else to say to me – '

Stephen grimaced. He walked out of the doctor's room and along the corridor. He thought of David – of glamorous, dashing Acting Captain David Lawrence, MC – who was now probably scooting across the desert sands, giving the Eyties what-for and no doubt performing yet more heroic exploits.

He felt sick with envy. Scowling, he walked back across the parade ground and entered his office.

There, he found Lois Armstrong waiting for him. 'Yes, what is it?' he enquired, almost rudely.

Lois let that go. 'We've a new draft starting on Monday,' she replied sharply. 'All girls fresh to the

Service. I thought you and I ought to get our heads together and decide how they're to be deployed.'

'I see.' And, although Stephen understood that she was paying him a compliment by consulting him, he would have liked to have told her that he didn't give a damn what happened to the new draft.

'Excuse me, sir.' Blushing furiously, Ellen Dyer put her head round the door and looked at Stephen. 'Sorry to interrupt, but there's a phone call for you. It came through to the main office, and the switchboard's gone wrong - so they can't transfer it. Could you come, sir?'

Stephen looked at Captain Armstrong, who nodded. With Ellen Dyer at his side, he walked briskly over to the main office. 'Anything wrong, sir?' asked Ellen boldly. Now that she had been to the pictures with Stephen, she felt that such an enquiry after his mental state wasn't impertinent. 'Sir, you look a bit down in the mouth. Is there – '

Stephen silenced her with a look. Striding into the office, the scowl on his face the blackest anyone had ever seen, he picked up the receiver. 'Atherton speaking. What is it?' he growled, so angrily that he seriously alarmed the innocent clerk at the other end of the line who merely wanted to know if he'd finished with a confidential file.

'Right, Leon. Lunch on Monday. I'll meet you in Cornmarket at about twelve.' Then, amused by something her friend Leon had told her, Rachel Lawrence laughed. 'I *must* go now,' she said. 'Take care.'

And, replacing the receiver, she was about to go back upstairs when the front door bell rang.

'Someone to see you, Liz!' Having admitted the visitor into the house on the Banbury Road, Rachel went in search of her cousin. She poked her head around the drawing room door and spotted her quarry. 'Liz? Did you hear me?'

'What?' Elizabeth, who had been talking to her mother-in-law and playing with Ben, glanced up. 'Sorry, Rachel. What did you say?'

'You've got a visitor.' Rachel grinned. 'A rather fetching young officer. I've put him in Dad's study.'

'An officer, you say?' Elizabeth frowned. 'Who *is* he?'

'No idea. Probably a German spy, so be careful what you say.' Still grinning, Rachel pulled on a woolly hat. 'See you all later,' she said, and was gone.

The fair-haired young man, a second lieutenant in some regiment the badges of which were unfamiliar to Elizabeth, smiled at her. 'Hello,' he said easily, holding out his hand. 'Simon Harrow's the name.'

'Elizabeth Lawrence.' Politely, Elizabeth shook hands. 'Ah - I'm sorry, Mr Harrow, but I'm afraid - '

'Friend of Edmund. We were at Wellington together.' The young man continued to smile. 'Rack your brains! He must have mentioned *me*!'

'Well, I'm sure he must have done, but all the same I don't think . . . ' Obediently giving her brains the suggested racking, Elizabeth shrugged in apology. 'Mr Harrow, I'm sorry - '

'Not to worry.' Now, without invitation, the young man sat down. 'Hope you don't mind me dropping by like this,' he continued affably, 'but since I was passing through, I thought - well, Edmund always said if I was ever in Oxford I might look his sister up.'

'Did he?' Now Elizabeth stared. 'Really?'

'Really.' Simon Harrow folded his arms. 'So, tell me, how is the old chap? Haven't seen him for - oh, it must be three years now!'

'I - ' Elizabeth looked at the visitor. She didn't think she liked him. Why, she could not have said, but there was something about his manner which disconcerted her. 'My brother's away,' she replied shortly.

'Out of England?'

'Well, I'm not sure.' Reddening now, Elizabeth twisted her hands together. 'The fact is, Mr Harrow - '

'I get the picture. Hush, hush, all that sort of thing. Oh, well!' Simon Harrow rose to his feet. 'Mrs Lawrence, it's been nice to meet you. I was rather hoping you could give me some news of old Edmund; but, there you go!'

205

Elizabeth observed that the young officer's face had clouded over. 'Was there any – any particular reason why you wanted to see my brother?' Looking hard at the young man, she wondered if it would hurt to confide in him. 'What I mean is – '

'Well, as a matter of fact there *was* a reason.' The young soldier pursed his lips. 'But it's a bit embarrassing . . . '

'Please, Mr Harrow!' Now Elizabeth was almost sure he could help her. 'If you know anything about Edmund – '

'I . . . ' The young man shuffled a little, then coughed. 'The matter is, Mrs Lawrence; well, the thing is, he owes me money.'

'Oh, I see.' Disappointed, Elizabeth shook her head. 'A lot of money?'

'No! Not very much at all!' Blushing, Mr Harrow blinked hard at Elizabeth. 'Only five thousand odd. But the thing is, I'm a bit strapped for cash at present and I thought that if you could let me know the old fellow's whereabouts, I could – oh, this is *most* disagreeable!'

'I don't know where my brother is.' Stonily, Elizabeth stared down at the floor. Then, feeling some obligation towards Edmund's creditor, she glanced up again. 'Um – Mr Harrow?'

'Yes?'

'Have you any – er – documents relating to the debt? If you have, and if I could help in any way – '

'*Could* you?' Brightening visibly, the young man smiled. 'Well, that would be most awfully decent of you! Look, here's the guff.' Fishing in his breast pocket, the young officer produced a pile of papers. 'Have a dekko at these,' he invited. 'See what you think.'

The documents were mostly IOUs. Written on gaming club notepaper, they looked genuine enough. Elizabeth recognized the bold black up and down strokes of her brother's signature. She hadn't known he was a gambler, but there was no doubt that he could have afforded to blow a few thousand now and then. She looked helplessly at Simon Harrow. 'Well,' she began, 'if my brother owes you all this money, he'd certainly want the debt discharged.

Perhaps, if you could leave these papers with me for a day or two?'

'Could I?' The man beamed. 'I say, that's very decent of you! Could I call back on – say – Tuesday week?'

'Tuesday?' Elizabeth considered. Was Tim Atherton in Oxford at present? She needed someone to advise her . . .

'Yes,' she said, at last. 'Yes, come back then, come on Tuesday afternoon. I'm sure I'll be able to sort something out by then.'

Elizabeth saw her visitor out. Glancing at the hall table, she turned over a couple of letters which had come by the late post. Nothing for her. Nothing from David . . .

She sighed. Why didn't he write to her? Oh, for God's sake, *why*?

David checked on the sentries and, after making sure that the duties rota was properly made up, he took himself off to the makeshift officers' mess for a drink.

Marriage had been a terrible mistake – he saw that now. Infatuated, he'd married the kind of woman whose very virtues had made him chafe to be free of her. He knew she loved him. And, worse than that, she understood him, she forgave him. What could have been more intolerable?

A clean break, he decided. A clean, uncomplicated break. That would be best. If she assumed he was dead, she would begin to forget him – she would meet other men, perhaps even fall in love again.

It didn't occur to him that a saint would never even so much as dream of betraying her husband . . .

Later that evening, David sat in a dug-out in Bardia, celebrating the Allies' recent victory over the Italian army. 'Whisky, Dave?' demanded the battalion CO.

'Thank you, sir.' David took the drink and swallowed it, then downed another.

Now, the whole thing was completely clear in his mind. She'd forget him, of course she would. After all, she'd hardly noticed when her mother had died, and he could still remember the stoicism with which she'd accepted her brother's disappearance. And his parents wouldn't worry. They had his brother and sisters to think about, not to mention their numerous grandchildren. If he didn't write to them, he doubted if they'd even notice.

'Yes, fill it up.' He nodded at the man by his side. More than a little drunk by now, David felt blissfully happy. Some other officers had begun to sing a scurrilous version of a popular song, and he joined in.

With a perversity which was, even for him, extreme, by the end of the evening David had convinced himself that he'd never be missed by anyone in Oxford.

Standing in the chilly African darkness looking up at the stars, he grinned.

'Mr Lawrence?' A sergeant came up to him and saluted. 'Sir, there's a message for you. We're to leave at 0500 hours tomorrow, and – '

The sergeant continued to explain, and David listened, commented, approved; gave his orders. Then he pushed his hands into his pockets and began to whistle.

He was free. For the first time in years – in his life, perhaps – he was free. He kicked a stone and watched it bounce, then giggled to himself. He was as free as a bird, and by this time next week, he might even be dead. He laughed out loud.

Elizabeth's anxiety about her husband was superceded by worries about her brother for the next few days. She hadn't thought of Edmund for months and months; but now she found she was thinking of him all the time. Where was he? What was he doing?

She looked at the papers again. Edmund Barton apparently owed Simon Harrow five thousand, two hundred and twenty six pounds, nine shillings. 'Forget the odd couple of hundred,' Mr Harrow had said generously. Elizabeth pushed the papers into her handbag and walked to the Athertons' house.

'Hello, Elizabeth. What can we do for you today?' Tim Atherton took his niece into the drawing room and helped her off with her coat. 'Dora's in the garden. Make yourself comfortable here while I go and fetch her.'

'Actually, Tim, it was you I wanted to see.'

Elizabeth gave him a brief account of Simon Harrow's recent visit, then extracted the documents from her handbag. 'Have a look at all these,' she said. 'Tell me what you think of them.'

Tim took the papers and scanned them quickly, then looked back at his niece. 'You think it's really his signature?' he asked, his eyes narrowed. 'Liz, you reckon – '

'I think so.' Elizabeth frowned. 'Look, Tim – if Edmund really owes this poor man all that money, the debt ought to be discharged without any more delay. Don't you think so?'

'Not necessarily.' Tim handed the papers back to Elizabeth. He lit a cigarette. 'I think we ought to go to the police.'

'The police?' Elizabeth's eyes were wide. 'You think Mr Harrow's a swindler?'

'My dear girl, it's something we ought to consider!' Curbing a desire to take his companion by the shoulders and shake some common sense into her, Tim allowed himself a faint smile. Remembering now that he had a friend in the Metropolitan Police who owed him a favour or two, he nodded at his niece. 'Leave it with me for a day or two,' he said. 'I'll see if I can find out anything about this – what's his name?'

'Simon Harrow.'

'Thank God it's not Jack Smith. Right.' Standing up, Tim patted Elizabeth's shoulder. 'Let's go and find Dora, shall we? I expect she's down on the vegetable patch digging for victory, plucky little thing that she is!'

Tim's enquiries turned up some interesting information about one Simon Harrow. A couple of days after Elizabeth had called to ask her uncle for advice, Tim was able to tell her a few things about Mr Harrow's past.

'Of course, we don't know if it's the same chap,' concluded Tim, lighting a cigarette. 'Fellows like that – well, for one thing they usually have half a dozen aliases. But if it *is* the same bloke, you must see that he's likely to be on the make.

'He *might* have known Edmund. But as for being at school with him, well, in this fellow's case that's a load of rot. Some suburban elementary had the honour of providing our Mr Harrow with his education. And as for the gambling club – '

'Yes?'

'The place was bombed out last month. All the membership records have been destroyed. I reckon Mr Harrow knows that. And so – '

'You think he's a con man?'

'I think it's highly likely.' Having successfully resisted a temptation to shout, of course he's a bloody con man, you moon-faced half-wit, Tim shook his head. 'Look, Elizabeth,' he continued heavily, 'when this fellow comes back, would you like me to be part of the reception committee?'

'Would you? I'd appreciate that. Actually, I was going to ask you . . . ' Blushing, Elizabeth rummaged in her handbag and found her handkerchief. 'I don't really want to see him by myself,' she said, dabbing at her nose. 'There's something about him which isn't very nice. And although Anthony's so kind, he's – '

He's as useless as you are at dealing with the real world. 'I'll be there.' Reassuringly, Tim smiled. 'Don't worry, Elizabeth. We'll sort Mr Harrow out.'

Tim walked back home feeling annoyed, both with himself and with his niece. He found conversing with her such a strain. Sometimes he wondered if she was all there. No, that wasn't fair at all. But even so . . .

'Mr Atherton, how do you do?' Exuding charm, Simon Harrow smiled and offered Tim Atherton his hand. 'And Mrs Lawrence,' he added, turning to Elizabeth. 'I hope you're well?' He looked enquiringly at Edmund's sister.

'Have you had a chance to look at all that stuff?'

'Yes.' Looking nervously at Tim, Elizabeth tried to remember her lines. 'Yes,' she said, 'I have. It seems everything is in order.'

'Good.' Simon Harrow's grin had not faltered. 'Then?'

'I'll act on Edmund's behalf.' Sitting down at Anthony's desk and opening the top drawer, Elizabeth looked at the young officer. 'Would a cheque be all right?'

'That would be splendid.' Sitting down now and glancing round Anthony's study, Simon Harrow fetched a great sigh. 'You know, Mrs Lawrence, this is awfully decent of you. I must say – '

'Must you?' Tim took a seat opposite the visitor and eyed Simon Harrow narrowly. 'Your badges, Mr Harrow,' he began equably. 'I don't recognize them. To which regiment would you happen to belong?'

'Ah.' Obviously ready for that particular question, Simon Harrow leaned back in his chair. 'I'm in military intelligence,' he replied. 'On special reserve. Hush hush.'

'I see.' Tim smiled. 'Something to do with the fellows in Aberporth Place, perhaps?'

'Perhaps.' Enigmatically, Simon Harrow smiled back. 'Sorry, old chap – can't explain. Careless talk and all that stuff.'

'Quite.' Tim shook his head. 'You weren't in the army before the war, Mr Harrow?'

'No.' Still Simon Harrow's grin did not waver. 'I was in – commerce. Before that; well, I've done all sorts of things. I've been in banking, in retail – '

'You were a member of the BUF. You were a close associate of its founders. You were acting as a steward during a meeting in Dagenham in the course of which a policeman was badly injured; so badly, in fact, that he later died.' Tim leaned forward in his seat. 'Mr Harrow, does your present commanding officer know about these particular episodes from your varied career?'

'I dare say he does.' Simon Harrow sniffed, grimacing now. 'The BUF wasn't a criminal organization, you know,' he said carefully. 'It was a properly constituted

211

political party. Admittedly during some of its public meetings things got a little out of hand. But I myself was never involved in violence. And the party membership as a whole was never predominantly composed of the sort of thug which the popular press described.'

'No.' Tim lit a cigarette. 'No, I don't suppose it was. All good chaps and true, weren't you? Patriots who loved your country.'

'Exactly.' Simon Harrow nodded. 'As you see, *I* am now in uniform. In England's hour of need, I – '

'Have come to her aid. Very decent of you.' Tim's grey eyes met Simon Harrow's blue ones. 'Mr Harrow, would you tell my niece and me what's happened to her brother?'

'How can I do that?' Simon Harrow spread his hands. 'How can I tell you something I don't know myself?'

'It would be difficult, I admit.' Now Tim rose to his feet and walked over to the window. 'Mr Harrow, how's Ginny Reilly these days?'

'Ginny who?' Simon Harrow frowned.

'Reilly.' Tim turned to face the other man. 'Ginny Reilly. Two or three years ago she was involved in an – an accident. Wasn't she?'

'Was she?'

'Yes.' Tim stubbed out his cigarette. 'You see, Mr Harrow, although you've obviously forgotten all about the poor woman, she hasn't forgotten you. One night in parti-cular is very vivid in her memory. And what she told the police about it led them to suspect that you – or a friend of yours – were responsible for her injuries.'

'Her name means nothing at all to me.' Now Simon Harrow stood up. 'Mrs Lawrence, if you've finished?' He walked towards Anthony's desk.

'Just a moment.' Tim picked up the cheque and looked hard at the young lieutenant. 'The Metropolitan Police,' he continued, 'have some notes on a certain Mr Simon Harrow. And it appears that Miss Reilly's case is tenta-tively linked with that particular file.'

'Is it?'

'Mm.' Tim shrugged. 'Miss Reilly was a prostitute, it

212

seems. Her accident, however, left her quite badly scarred, and her injuries currently prevent her from pursuing her calling. In a statement made to the police, she provided them with a good description of her assailant, and of his friend. But, unfortunately, the police failed to trace either of them.' Tim frowned. 'Simon Harrow. Not a common name, is it?'

'No, it isn't.' But now Simon Harrow glared. 'Mr Atherton,' he began stiffly, 'I don't know quite what you're accusing me of, but I don't think I like your tone. Okay, so I was once a member of the BUF. But this Jenny Reilly business is – '

'Nothing to do with you? Oh, I never insisted that it was.' Tim picked up the bundle of IOUs. 'All the same, I think I'd better tear these up, hadn't I?' Tim tore the first document across. 'Perhaps I should put a match to the lot of them?'

Simon Harrow shrugged. 'I don't admit anything,' he said carefully. Then, rallying, he squared his shoulders. 'Mr Atherton,' he continued, 'has it occurred to you that I might sue you for slander?'

'Might you?' Tim laughed. 'Go ahead, then. Try.'

'Mm.' Simon Harrow picked up his hat. 'You can prove nothing against me,' he said stiffly. 'But you obviously doubt my probity. And so, in the circumstances, I feel I should not accept the kind offer which Mrs Lawrence has made to discharge her brother's debts. As an officer in the British Army I wouldn't wish to appear to be claiming money under false pretences.'

'A wise decision, Mr Harrow; very wise.' Tim walked towards the door. 'I'll show you out, shall I?'

Simon Harrow walked down the Banbury Road. Philosophical enough to understand that he couldn't always win, it was relief, rather than any other emotion, which was uppermost in his mind.

He looked at his watch and scowled. Talking to that old fool Atherton, listening to the stupid sod playing

Sherlock Holmes, had taken up rather more time than he'd expected. Now he'd missed the fast train back to London. Damn . . .

He had an urgent appointment that evening, and he had to get back to the capital somehow. Walking into the bus station, he made some enquiries. To his delight, he learned that if he caught a bus to the next town, he might be able to get on an express train from Swindon, which would get him back to London in plenty of time for his rendezvous.

The bus left Oxford on time. Grinning, Simon Harrow flopped back into his seat. He was always lucky! People had remarked on that, and Pam's words came back to him: 'You were born to have your own way, Simon . . . '

'If you was to jump off 'ere, sir, you'd get to the station in five minutes. If you runs along the line, that is.' The bus driver had stopped the vehicle and was calling to Simon, anxious to assist an army officer. 'Sir? Did you 'ear me?'

'What?' Simon came out of his daydream and gave the man his attention. 'What did you say?'

'Get off 'ere.' Indicating the moonlit level crossing, the man grinned. 'Look – that's the main line to London. If you scoots along the track, you'll be at the station in two ticks. You'll catch the train wiv ten minutes to spare.'

'Thanks.' Getting off the bus, Simon grinned back at the driver. 'Thanks a lot.'

'You're welcome, mate. Watch how you go.'

The moon was well up and Simon could see the railway line clearly. In the distance were very faint lights, mere pin-pricks in the blackout – presumably that was the station. He set off along the track, trotting easily, confident that he would make it. Jogging comfortably, he was quite enjoying the exercise.

Suddenly, however, the bank of cloud behind him obscured the moon and everything was plunged into darkness. He stumbled; picking himself up, he decided that if he ran along the sleepers themselves, skipping from one to the other, he had less chance of falling over.

He heard the train coming. But, in the near total darkness, he misjudged the speed at which it was travelling. He was just about to jump out of the way when it caught him . . .

The locomotive hit him squarely in the back, throwing him forwards. His clothing caught on the buffers, and he was dragged along the line. And, as the train arrived at the station a mere hundred yards further on, the passengers were appalled to see what was stuck to the engine and splattered against the wheels. It was with great difficulty, and with much retching, that a couple of railwaymen detached the body from the train.

Edmund's perfidious lover was still alive; but, his face torn away, his legs broken and his chest a mass of gashes which cut through to the bone, he would not remain so for much longer. A doctor was summoned, but he arrived far too late to do anything for the mortally injured man. In front of a crowd of horrified travellers Simon Harrow lay on the station platform and bled to death.

Chapter Eighteen

HELEN MET TOM RICHARDSON IN a café in the town. A tall, thin, fair-haired man, he came up to her table and, after asking if the seat opposite her was taken, he sat down and watched her consume her cheese and potato pie.

Between mouthfuls, she found herself glancing at him. His face, she noticed, was gaunt, and the skin stretched across his cheekbones pallid; but his blue-grey eyes were wide and candid, and these gave his otherwise unremarkable face some distinction.

She guessed he must be about twenty-five. Although he was not in uniform, she decided that he was obviously in the Forces, for he had that sort of bearing. There was the kind of relaxed strength about him which she found so attractive in her father; and which was so painfully lacking in Alec, who was nervous and permanently fidgeting.

The man sat there for a few minutes, stirring his tea and staring at her. Helen felt as if she were being watched by a large, friendly dog – a collie, perhaps, or a setter. When he opened his mouth to speak again, she almost expected him to say 'wuff', instead of, 'I hope you don't mind my saying so, love, but that's a very pretty frock you're wearing. And with your fair colouring, that blue really suits you.'

Helen smiled. 'Thank you.'

Encouraged, relieved that she wasn't either offended or alarmed, the man smiled back. 'It's natural, your hair, isn't it?' he asked.

216

'Oh, yes.' Knowing perfectly well that he was referring to the colour, she giggled. 'It's not a wig!'

'It's beautiful. Like a wheatfield; hundreds of different colours, all blended together.' His pale face reddened then. 'I'm sorry, miss,' he added. 'I shouldn't be so familiar.'

'That's all right.' Helen looked at him. 'Are you stationed near Oxford?' she enquired.

They chatted for a quarter of an hour or more. She discovered that he was on sick leave from the Army. A sergeant in the Royal Artillery, he'd joined up as long ago as 1931, and had been wounded in France. 'It's all up to the MO now,' he said. 'In three months' time I'll either be passed fit and sent back overseas; medically downgraded and found a job in England - or kicked out.' He looked curiously at Helen. 'And what about you, love?' he asked. 'D'you work?'

'Yes. In an office.' Helen stirred her second cup of tea, which had long grown cold. 'I used to be a solicitor's secretary, but now I'm in a reserved occupation. I'm a clerk at one of the ministries. And I work in a market garden at weekends.' She looked at him, a smile twitching her lips. 'I hope you don't think I'm not doing my bit?'

'Far from it.' The man returned her smile. 'I know it's a bit of a cheek,' he went on. 'But would you like to go to the pictures with me one night?'

'The pictures?' Helen laid down her spoon; she considered.

'Yes. I'd like to take you to the cinema. If you've an evening to spare, that is?'

'Oh.' Recovering from her surprise, Helen nodded. 'That would be very nice,' she replied. 'Thank you very much.'

They went to the cinema together and spent a couple of hours watching Clark Gable throw women about as if they were sacks of potatoes; then, afterwards, they walked back up the Banbury Road. When they reached the turn-off for

217

the avenue in which she lived, Helen told Tom that she would go the rest of the way by herself.

'I'll see you safe home,' he said. 'Can't have you wandering about in the dark, all alone.'

'Oh, I know the way! And look, the moon's out tonight, it's hardly what you'd call *dark* - is it?'

'I suppose not.' He laughed. 'All the same - '

'I'll be fine, don't worry.' She wanted to get away now; she could see his face in the moonlight and had realized that if she stayed with him any longer he would try to kiss her. And that would spoil what had been a very pleasant evening . . .

He hadn't touched her in the cinema. That had been a relief. Used to Alec's damp hands on her wrist, on her neck - and sometimes, daringly, under her stocking-top - it had been nice to watch the film in peace. 'Look, it's late,' she said. 'I really must go; my mother will be worrying - '

'Yes. Well, Helen, shall I see you again?'

'What? Oh, yes. If you like.' She looked up at him. 'When?'

'Meet you for lunch tomorrow?'

'Yes. Twelve o'clock. Outside Parker's?'

'Fine.' Tom grinned. 'There's a much better caff than that one you were in when I first met you. Down by the bus station - the Holly Bush it's called. Know it?'

'I've passed it. I've never been inside.'

'They do a very good cottage pie. So, twelve o'clock tomorrow, then.' And, without asking permission, without any preamble, Tom leaned over Helen, and kissed her. His hand on her shoulder, he touched her lips with his. 'Good night then, love,' he said a minute later. 'Thanks for a nice evening. Watch how you go.'

Helen didn't know why she was waiting until his shadow had completely disappeared. But, all the same, instead of walking briskly home, she stood motionless in the cover of some overhanging trees, watching him. Unable to move, she was equally unable to tear her eyes away from Tom's receding figure . . .

218

Her lips felt as if they'd been scorched. Her shoulder, where he'd touched her, was burning, was threatening to sear through her clothes. She felt a strange sensation in her stomach; it was as if she had just been on a terrifyingly fast fairground ride. And she wanted Tom to come back, to kiss her again. 'Just so that I can find out,' she thought. 'Just so that I can decide if it *really* felt like that . . . '

She looked up at the moon. 'After all, you *do* send people mad,' she muttered, as she finally hastened home.

'Hello, love. How are you today?' Tom's manner of speaking was charming. His soft, Northern accent was, Helen had decided, quite delightful. His liberal use of 'love' – and pet, and sweetheart – could have been irritatingly over-familiar, but in Tom's case it was gratifying. He spoke and behaved as if she really *were* his love, his pet, his sweetheart . . .

And when he kissed her – as he often did now – Helen almost purred. He was so nice to lean against, and in his warm embrace she felt safe and protected; for, in spite of being so thin, he was large-boned and reassuringly solid. 'You're a lovely kid,' he told her one evening, smiling at her as they stood on the corner, in the gloom of the black-out. 'So, where's your regular boyfriend these days?'

'Overseas.' Helen told herself that there was no point in lying. 'He's with the Berkshires,' she added. 'In the desert.'

'Poor devil.' Tom looked at her, his face very pale in the moon's feeble light. 'Engaged, are you?'

'No. Well, not really.' *That* was a thumping great fib. And now Helen added another. 'He said I wasn't to sit at home and miss him,' she told Tom. 'He said I was to go out and meet other people . . . '

'Did he, now?' Tom smiled ruefully. 'Well, all the same, I'd better not get too fond of you, had I?'

He originally came from Merseyside. The family, he

explained, was dispersed. His father had died when Tom was a little boy; and his mother had distributed her six children around her friends and relations, then disappeared. Having lost touch with his brothers and sisters and having no real home, it had seemed logical to join the Army, where at least he would belong, if only to his regiment . . .

He'd kept an address which a friend had given him, and when he came out of hospital he'd taken the train to Oxford. He'd looked up the friend, who had helped him find a room in a lodging house off the Iffley Road.

'It's not a bad place at all,' he said complacently, as he walked back to Helen's office with her one lunchtime. 'Landlord lives off the premises, which is always a good thing. An' I see Arthur from time to time – I tell you, his wife does a smashing steak an' kidney pudding!'

'Arthur?' asked Helen, having lost the thread of his narrative.

'The mate who helped me find my digs.'

'Whose wife is a good cook.' Helen laughed. 'She must be well in with her butcher if she can still make a decent steak and kidney pudding.'

'Mm.' Tom grinned. 'Oh, she's a pretty lass. An' a nice smile works wonders with most men, as I don't doubt you know.'

They walked along in silence for a few minutes. Helen was mulling over what he'd said. 'D'you get lonely?' she asked suddenly. Now, when she was with Tom, she tended to soften her precise North Oxford accent and slur her words together as he did. 'Tom, d'you miss being in the Army?'

'No. Well, yes. A bit.' He took her hand. 'There's good pubs in Oxford, though, and there's the cinemas. I've got a few mates now; I see them of an evening. I play darts, billiards. I get by.'

'Yes. I see.' Helen thought about an unknown world of cheap lodging houses and city pubs, of bolt-holes where otherwise homeless, rootless people congregated because they had no families or firesides of their own. She had never really understood that Oxford was a working man's town; that this other Oxford had a life all of its own, outside and totally independent of the university. There were factories in Oxford; she knew that, but she had hardly appreciated that the factory workers themselves lived so close to the dreaming spires. So very near, but in a different world altogether . . .

'Have you been round the colleges?' she asked.

'The colleges?'

'Yes.' Helen laughed. 'There are dozens of them. You must have noticed!'

Tom looked puzzled. 'Why should I want to go round the colleges?' he demanded.

'Well, it would give you something to do. Architecturally, some of them are quite interesting. Magdalen's perfectly beautiful; there's a deer park, you know, and there's the river – '

'Oh.' Tom sniffed. 'I don't go much for all that sort of thing,' he said shortly. 'It's not really for the likes of me.'

Helen looked at him. 'What do you mean?' she asked.

'Well, I don't want to go gawping round a lot of old buildings. What's the point?'

'The point? Well – ' Thinking about it, Helen decided that really there *wasn't* any point in Tom wandering around the university, guidebook in hand, a staring tourist. After all, he was so far outside the intellectual, middle-class society to which Helen herself was accustomed that he was hardly aware of what the university was *for*.

So, naturally, he'd never wanted to venture inside a college. He'd never thought to stroll into a courtyard and gaze around him at the grey towers rising from the manicured lawns; he'd never considered entering a college chapel and listening to the choir as they practised, to the organist as he rehearsed for Evensong. The university did not exist for him . . .

Helen wondered what it was exactly that she liked about him. Obviously, he *was* very likeable; it was plain that he easily made friends. When he first took her into a pub, he

221

was greeted by a shout of welcome, then by a couple of quieter voices asking what he would have, and did the young lady fancy a port and lemon?

And, without a veneer of education or acquired good manners, Tom was a naturally gentle man. Or at least, he was where women were concerned.

'Why do you take me out?' she asked him one evening, as they walked home from a couple of hours spent in the bar of an Oxford pub playing darts, for which Helen had discovered she had a talent. 'Why do you spend all your money on me?'

'What a daft question!' Tom laughed. 'Why d'you think?'

'Because you fancy me?'

'I should say so!'

'What else?'

'Oh, I don't know.' Tom laid his arm across her shoulders and hugged her. 'I think you're a nice girl,' he said. 'You're not spiteful, you're not grabby, you're not a moaner. You don't criticize me, you don't carry on if I'm a few minutes late; you're a pleasure to be with. That enough?'

Helen smiled. 'I suppose so,' she replied.

Tom had met Helen at a time when her life was particularly empty. Her schoolfriends had either married young, joined the Forces, or were in the Land Army. They were, at any rate, out of Oxford.

Temperamentally the absolute opposite of her brother, Helen had a horror of communal life, of any kind of regimentation. Having left the Brownies after her probationary six weeks, she'd never belonged to any organization since. The idea of being in the Army, of wearing regulation underclothes and getting up at crack of dawn to do PT, of sharing a hut or dormitory with a dozen other women, appalled her.

'Oh, *no*, Mum!' she'd cried, when Dora had suggested that Helen might like to follow her friend Jane Fellowes

222

into the Wrens. 'Can you imagine *me* marching in step and saluting the jolly old flag? Splicing the mainbrace and swabbing the decks?'

'Well, dear . . . ' Dora had laughed. 'Not really, I suppose.'

Her contribution to the War Effort was, Helen was well aware, minimal. Her job at the ministry was undemanding. At weekends and on some evenings she went over to an Anglican convent in the Woodstock Road, where she and a dozen other gently-bred North Oxford girls dug for victory in the huge garden, growing vegetables to feed the occupants of a sister house in the East End of London and to distribute to the Londoners as the need arose. Helen's sprouts and carrots were made into vegetarian pies and her potatoes provided a basis for the nourishing soup which was doled out to the destitute of Whitechapel.

She was often bored, and frequently lonely. Dutifully, she wrote to Alec, answering his turgid letters with equally stilted missives of her own. Until she'd met Tom, her life had been very, very dull.

Tom and Helen now embarked on a long term pub crawl, marking the bars and saloons of Oxford out of ten. Dressed in slacks and a jacket, her hair piled up under a headscarf, Helen enjoyed these excursions into a different world. Confident as she was that if things got at all rowdy Tom was more than capable of protecting her, she observed Oxford's rough characters with interest and downed half pints of milk stout as nonchalantly as if she'd drunk beer from childhood.

As Tom observed, it was almost impossible to get tight on the beer they served nowadays, and it was only on very rare occasions that Helen was alarmed by the sight of a drunken thug making a nuisance of himself. She improved her game of darts so much that she could beat Tom. She learned to play billiards, and she was soon chalking her cue and sizing up the game with the eye of a master. Made welcome by Tom's mates and tolerated by everyone else, because she was with a large young man who looked as if he'd take exception to any rudeness shown towards his girl-friend, she had a thoroughly good time . . .

'I wonder about where you live, you know,' she remarked, coming out of the smoky warmth of the Carpenter's Arms one evening into chilly, starlit darkness. 'Are you comfortable there?'

'Comfortable?' Tom considered. 'I hadn't really thought about it. Tell you what – why don't you come and see?'

'Could I?'

'Course you can.' Tom grinned. 'It's a nice night for a walk. Come an' have some coffee, then we'll see if we can get a bus back up your way.'

They strolled down the High Street and over Magdalen Bridge. Passing the place where the road forked into three, they went on into the unknown hinterland of the Cowley and Iffley Roads.

They might have been in a different city. Helen had never been any further east than the river bridge and had never wondered what lay beyond Magdalen's tall tower. Now she looked at the shabby buildings, cheap shops and tall, gaunt lodging houses. In the cold starlight they looked, perhaps, shabbier and uglier than they really were . . .

'Here we are.' Stopping outside a large Victorian villa, possibly built for a family but long since turned into a lodging house, Tom produced a key. He unlocked the main door and led Helen into a narrow hallway. 'Careful as you go up the stairs,' he said. 'Carpet's very worn – lots of holes and that.'

'What's that horrible smell?' Helen wrinkled her nose. 'Tom, I think there's a gas leak somewhere.'

'Oh, these old houses always smell of gas.' Tom led her past a noxious bathroom. 'It's really a mixture of rubbish, drains and old cooking. Don't worry, pet; the place isn't going to blow up.'

On and on they climbed, until at last they reached the

224

top landing. 'Duck,' advised Tom. 'The roof's very low just here.'

They stood outside a door, the corner of which was cut away to fit into the slope of the ceiling. 'Here we are,' said Tom, unlocking it. 'Bit puffed, are you? It's a hundred and three stairs. I counted once.'

Tom's room was tidy and clean – but it was very bare. Bare, comfortless, and very, very cold. He lit the gas fire, which popped sulkily then began to glow, giving out a disgusting smell.

He made some coffee, boiling the water on a gas ring, infusing the cheap, bitter grounds in a cracked jug. They drank it sitting side by side on the narrow single bed. 'Why did you want to come here, love?' asked Tom gently.

'I was curious about you.' Helen sipped her coffee, glad of the warmth of the cup in her cold hands. 'I wanted to be able to picture you here.' She looked around the room, and sighed. 'I'll get you some decent curtains,' she declared. 'Some nice curtains, and a bedspread. It'll make it seem more like home.'

'Home!' he laughed. 'Some home!' He put his arms around her and kissed her. 'Oh, you're a nice lass, aren't you?' he asked, still smiling at her.

A nice lass? Helen hoped so. She relaxed in his arms; she kissed him back, encouraging him, enjoying being caressed.

She snuggled closer and closer to him. The gas fire had begun to make its presence felt, and she was warmer now. Tom, in fact, was sweating slightly; she could smell fresh perspiration, a sharp, animal scent. It excited her. She rubbed her face against his chest – and the nebulous plans she'd been making all evening suddenly resolved themselves. She made up her mind.

'Tom,' she began diffidently. How did one ask a man to take one to bed? 'Tom – shall we – '

But, even as she spoke, he took her arms from around his neck. He stood up. 'I'd better take you home now,' he said. 'Do your coat up, like a good girl.'

'No!' Alarmed, Helen stared at him. 'No, I can't!'

'Can't do your coat up?' He grinned at her. 'Come on, pet, don't be silly.'

'I mean, you can't take me home.'

'Well, I'll not let you walk all that way by yourself!' He picked up her handbag and held it out to her.

'Er – look, Tom.' Helen laid the bag on the bed. 'I don't want to go just yet.'

'What d'you mean, love?' Leaning over her, he touched her cheek. 'Don't tease me, there's a good girl. If you stay here any longer, I'll want to go to bed with you, and that won't do – will it?'

'Why not?'

'Oh, Helen! You're not a tart, are you?'

'No, I'm not. But, all the same, I'd like you to take me to bed.' As she spoke, Helen could hardly believe she was saying such things. 'Tom, will you?' she asked. 'Please?'

'I think you'd better go home.'

'No!' Her eyes blazing, Helen shook his arm. 'You can't reject me!' she cried, her voice fast becoming a wail of panic. 'Tom, you *can't* turn me down; I'll die if you send me away now! Oh, Tom, *please*!'

'Look, Helen – '

'Don't you want me?'

'It's not that at all.'

'Then, what's to stop us?' Helen shrugged off her coat and held out her arms to him. 'Tom, come here. Please?'

He could not resist that. Sitting down again, he took her in his arms. A minute or two later, he unfastened the buttons on her blouse and slid his hands inside, beneath her underclothes. 'Are you sure?' he asked softly. 'Stop me now, if you're not sure.'

The feeling of his warm hands on her bare flesh was electrifying. Helen was certain that she was burning. It was as if something inside her had ignited, starting a conflagration which was now blazing out of control. She clung to Tom, kissing him feverishly and biting his ear.

He'd pulled off his own shirt and now he started to undo her slacks. To his surprise, Helen's excitement now

226

affected him – he became clumsy and, as he tugged, a button came off. He swore.

'Don't pull, you'll tear them. Let me.' And then, after wriggling out of her trousers, Helen more or less dragged Tom on top of her.

He took her almost without thinking, without any further touching or stroking of her body. Simply holding her in his arms, his face lying comfortably against her own, he came inside her as easily and naturally as if he belonged there, as if he and she were two halves of a perfect whole.

Helen, expecting pain and difficulty, caught her breath in surprise at just how easy it was. Afterwards, she tangled her fingers in his hair. 'Tom?' she murmured drowsily, pulling his head back. 'Tom?'

'Yes?'

'You're heavy.'

'Sorry.' He made as if to move.

'No, don't move.' Now Helen hugged him. 'So heavy, but that's nice. Stay here, keep me warm . . . '

'You're unbelievable.' Looking into Helen's eyes, Tom shook his head. 'Incredible! I've never had a lass like you . . . '

'Why do you say that?' Helen, now assuming that she'd got something horribly wrong, looked back at him in alarm. 'Tom, what do you mean?'

'I've never met anyone like you before. That's all. Oh, Helen, love – talk about dynamite!' He raised himself on one elbow and gazed at her. 'And you never said it was your first time,' he added solemnly. 'Why didn't you?'

'Why should I have done?' she asked. 'And how could you tell?'

'In your case, it was obvious.' He looked concerned. 'I must have hurt you!'

'You didn't. Really, you didn't hurt me at all!' Helen, afraid that he did not believe her, shook his arm. 'Oh, Tom, don't look so cross! What difference does it make if you *were* the first?'

'A lot,' he replied. 'Helen, how old are you?'

'Twenty-two. Nearly twenty-three, actually.'

227

'Just a kid.' He rubbed his face and looked at her. 'I'd thought you were older,' he said tonelessly. 'I thought you were nearer my age.'

'How old are you?'

'Twenty-nine. Oh, God, I'd never have done that if I'd thought – Helen, why did you want it to be me?'

'I'm not sure. But I did want, very much.'

'You still shouldn't have. You ought to have kept yourself for your husband – you know that, don't you?' He sighed. 'I've spoilt you now.'

'It doesn't matter, Tom, honestly.' She smiled at him. 'And someone has to be the first, after all.'

'Did you like it? Tell me the truth.'

'I loved it. Truly.' Helen took Tom's hand and kissed it, then rubbed it against her face. 'It was bliss! Utter, utter bliss!' As she spoke she realized that such a remark sounded precious; it wasn't at all the sort of thing Tom would say. She kissed him. 'Tom, you taste so nice,' she added simply.

'Do I?'

'Yes.' Helen smiled at him again, willing him to smile back. 'You don't smoke, do you?'

'No.'

'Why don't you?'

'The MO told me to give it up. On account of my lungs. When I was hit, you see – '

'Yes, I see.' Gingerly, she touched the scars on his shoulder blades. 'Your poor back; it's a mess, isn't it?'

'Don't know, haven't looked. Oh, don't touch me! Helen, I wish we hadn't *done* that!'

'You mustn't say that. Please, Tom!' She frowned at him. 'Do you really think I look thirty?'

'You look – self assured. That's what deceived me. But you've the face and body of a twenty-year-old.' He smiled at her. 'Just now, you look about seventeen.'

'I ought to go home.'

'Yes, you must.'

'I'll come again. I'll find you some better curtains, a nicer rug, a cushion or two.'

228

He fastened her coat for her. 'I'm not stopping here for ever, you know,' he said. 'Don't go to any trouble, love.'

'Have you a wife?' she asked him, one day.

'No.' He shrugged. 'I had a girl just before the war; her family wasn't really in favour, though. Her Dad liked me, but her Mum thought I was too rough for her Annie.'

'How d'you mean, rough?'

'Oh, you know. No family, no background – no school certificates. No birth certificate, even, come to that!'

'And Annie was persuaded?'

'I think her Mum must've had a word. She stopped writing. I didn't follow it up.'

'She was no loss,' Helen said firmly.

'P'raps not.' Ruefully, he grinned. 'Helen, what's your family like?' he demanded. 'What's your old man do?'

'He's a writer. He writes novels. T. J Atherton – have you heard of him?'

'Oh, yes. I've heard of him. Never read any of his stuff, though – far too highbrow for me!' Still grinning, Tom laughed. 'Now tell me what your Dad really does.'

'He's a writer. Honestly!'

'You're not having me on?'

'No, of course not!'

'I see.' Tom whistled. 'Well, what a turn up! I expect you get dozens of people asking you if you're any relation, eh? D'you let on?'

'Sometimes. It depends.'

'*I'd* thought you were an ordinary working girl.'

'I *am*!'

'You sure of that?' Tom laughed again; but this time he didn't smile. He sounded bitter. 'I reckon you're really one of those peculiar debby types you read about in the papers. The sort who fancies a bit of rough trade.'

'Rubbish.' Unable to decide whether or not he was joking, Helen glared at him. 'God, I wouldn't have told you if I'd thought you were going to make such a fuss!'

'Sorry.' Tom patted her shoulder. 'Sorry, love. Well,

princess - where would you like to go for your tea? Can't afford the Savoy this evening, I'm afraid; my governor hasn't sent my allowance. But there's this little place by the railway station where they do a frightfully decent grill, and the wine list's not too bad either - '

'Oh, shut up. Would you rather I went home?'

'Course not. Come on, your ladyship! If we get a move on we'll be able to nab a table near the orchestra.'

Helen let him pull her along Queen Street. She wondered what his reaction would have been if she'd told him that one of her uncles was a baronet and the other a university professor. She decided that he probably hadn't believed what she'd told him about her father. After all, Oxford was full of Blackwells, few of whom were related to Basil Blackwell himself . . .

Helen arrived home later that evening to find a letter from Alec waiting for her. She slit it open and skimmed through it. As usual, it was a series of grumbles: the heat was intolerable, trivial little cuts always seemed to go septic and become festering sores and the flies settled on food and devoured it even as a man tried to eat it. Alec loathed the fearless African flies, who had no fear of being swatted and who buzzed about getting in everything. He concluded the long succession of gripes by revealing that he was still very bored and by asking Helen to write back very soon. He sent his best wishes to her parents.

She folded the lettercard and sighed. Alec was stuck in the desert with nothing but her letters to cheer his dismal existence, and the idea of writing to tell him she no longer wished to marry him appalled her. The cruelty of it would be too much for him to bear.

She imagined him opening such a letter - reading it twice, disbelieving. His thin face would pucker. Then his friends would cluster round him, and cries of 'what's up, mate?' would result in Alec telling them all about her. And then the other soldiers would console him, telling him that all women were cows, bitches, tarts . . .

230

No, she couldn't do it. Infidelity behind his back was one thing, but throwing it in his face was something else altogether.

Tom was now as necessary to Helen as the air she breathed. She went to bed with him as often as he would let her. Airily, she dismissed his reservations, telling him that she was well aware that she was being unfaithful to her fiancé, and that he did not need to keep pointing it out.

'What if you start a baby?' he asked her one evening as he lay beside her, in love with her against his will, wanting her in spite of the fact that she belonged to someone else. 'Helen, if you fall for a kid – '

'I shan't.' She tickled his shoulder. 'You use those things.'

'They're not foolproof. Look, sweetheart, it's still possible to be caught.'

'Don't you want to sleep with me any more, is that what you're saying?'

'No!' He pulled her into his arms and looked searchingly at her. 'Oh, love, you know I don't mean that! But – '

'Don't start talking about me being spoken for.'

'I wasn't going to. Listen to me; you ought to go to see the doctor. There are things a woman can use – '

'You seriously expect me to go and see my dear old family doctor and say, ''oh, Doctor Golding, I'm having a torrid affair with a wonderful man and would you be so good as to fix me up so that I don't get pregnant?'' Eh?' Helen giggled. 'Good heavens, Tom, he'd have a heart attack!'

'All the same, you must do something. I'll find out where you can go. And I'll pay whatever they charge.'

Helen kissed him. 'You're a good man, you know. A lovely man. I don't deserve you.'

'Mm.' He kissed her face and stroked her hair back from her forehead. 'You're a smasher,' he said. 'The nicest woman I've ever known. There's no-one like you.' He frowned at her. 'God knows what you see in me.'

231

'I need you. My love, you're necessary – that's all.'

Helen went to a clinic in a seedy part of town, queued up with a dozen sallow factory girls, and got herself fitted with a contraceptive device.

'My husband's very ill,' she told the doctor, as she fiddled with the brass ring on her finger. 'He got shot up at Dunkirk, you see – he needs constant nursing.'

The doctor finished measuring her patient and went over to a drawer. 'In that case, Mrs Taylor, why – '

'He's still – well – he's still a man, if you see what I mean.' Helen blushed. 'It's his legs, you understand,' she went on wildly. 'I can't afford to have any children, not just now.'

'No. I quite see that.' The pleasant lady doctor bent over Helen and fitted the device. Satisfied, she removed it again and went to wash her hands. 'Well, Mrs Taylor, I hope your husband's health will eventually improve. I assume the Army is looking after you financially?'

'Oh, yes.' Scarlet in the face now, Helen nodded. 'When do I need to come back here?'

'I'll see you in three months' time; you can let me know how you're getting on then.' The doctor smiled. 'You shouldn't have any problems. Now, you're quite sure you understand what to do?'

'Oh, yes!'

'Good. If you *do* feel any discomfort, or if anything doesn't seem quite right, come back and see me, won't you?'

'Thank you, doctor. I shall.'

Helen almost ran into the street. She stood on the pavement breathing hard. She felt violated, and now she had dreadful stomach cramp; brought on, she supposed, by nervousness. As she clutched the bag containing the device and its accompanying tubes of jelly, she wondered if she'd completely taken leave of her senses.

*　　　*　　　*

Dora remarked on Helen's frequent absences and asked her where she went, evening after evening. 'Of course, you're old enough to spend your free time as you please,' she went on carefully. 'But it was three o'clock this morning before you were in, and your father and I – '

'I see a friend, that's all,' said Helen curtly.

'Oh.' Dora poured her daughter some tea. 'Who is he?' she asked. 'What does he do?'

'Why do you assume it's a he?'

'Isn't it?'

'Yes, it is, actually.' Helen sniffed. 'He was in the Army,' she muttered, 'but he's on sick leave at the moment. He's waiting to hear if they'll take him back. In the meantime, he's living in Oxford, where he has some friends.'

'I see. Why don't you bring him round for dinner?'

Helen frowned. 'I can't do that.'

'Why ever not?'

'He's – he thinks he's not very well educated.' Helen looked down at her plate. 'He wouldn't be comfortable here.'

'Nonsense!' Dora giggled. 'Oh, darling, *I* never went to college!'

'All the same, I shan't bring him here.'

'Please yourself.' Dora sipped her tea. 'I suppose you think I'd embarrass you,' she added crossly.

So Helen's parents did not meet Tom. It wasn't that she was ashamed of him – not at all. In him she had recognized the truly essential qualities of kindness, gentleness, and almost limitless generosity – for he appeared to consider it natural that he should pay for meals and cinema tickets, although he was obviously hard up.

She didn't want him scared away. Not until she was absolutely sure of him.

Chapter Nineteen

SOON AFTER SHE ARRIVED AT Dorrington Camp at the
beginning of November 1940, nineteen-year-old Lucy
Hollander realized that she was somewhat different from
the other girls in her company.

For one thing, she had been to a private school, and
there she had acquired a precise, rather *too* elegant accent
and style of diction. Amid the regional burrs and metropolitan argots, Lucy's King's English stood out and
appeared pretentious and over-refined. She was marked
down as a snob before she had even unpacked her kit . . .

Then, on her third day in barracks, she had been rash
enough to confide that her Daddy – she ought to have called
him her Dad, or her old man – was a stockbroker. To her
amazement, this information provoked positive howls of
laughter from the others in her dormitory. 'Reallay?'
demanded a private. 'Then you must be *frightflay* well orf!'

'May Dadday's a stawkbrokair,' giggled another girl.
'Oh, gollay!'

'What's she say?'

'Her Daddy's in the Citay.'

'So's mine.' A sharp-faced Cockney girl, who had
recently received her first stripe, sniggered. 'He takes 'is
barrer up Chancery Lane.'

The first speaker turned back to Lucy. 'Will you be able
to give me buckshee advice on my investments, then?' she
asked, grinning.

'I beg your pardon?'

'Ay beg yawr pahdun. I mean, d'you know a lot about the stock market? Well up on Rio Tinto zinc, are you?'

'I don't know what you're talking about.'

'*Don't* you? Funny – you don't look that stupid!' The girl laughed. 'Your locker's in a right mess,' she added. 'So – '

'You'd better tidy it.' The NCO looked severely at Lucy. 'An' there'll be kit inspection tomorrow morning, so get all your stuff smartened up. You ain't got your lady's maid to clear up after you now, you know.'

'You'll 'ave to polish your buttons, too. Shine 'em up so's you can see your face in 'em.' A girl with a strong Liverpool accent leaned over and picked up Lucy's cap. 'Your badge is filthy,' she went on scathingly. 'You'll be on a charge if you don't get it buffed up decent.'

'You'll be on jankers.'

'In the glasshouse.'

'On fatigues.'

'Whitewashin' great big 'eaps of coal.'

Astonished and unused to being teased, Lucy simply stared at her tormentors. Wondering what on earth she'd done to deserve such treatment, she blushed – and resolved to keep her mouth shut from then on.

Her silence, however, merely convinced the rest of the women that she was stuck up. And worse was to follow. She acquired a reputation as one of the snobby ones who would only go out with officers. This was entirely undeserved, but, once she had rebuffed the advances of a loutish corporal, it was assured.

The other women wondered aloud why such a toffee-nosed cow hadn't joined the WAAFs; that was, after all, the service in which all the okay people were to be found . . .

Lucy and the other ATS girls were never short of company. A steady stream of people passed in and out of the main office of Dorrington Camp; messengers brought work or took it away; the sergeant in charge of their little section arrived to harass them; Captain Armstrong made her rounds – and now and again a male officer wandered in.

'Two,' remarked Agnes Lyall one morning, as the door closed behind an elderly captain who had seen service in the

First War. 'Two out of ten, an' that's only cos' I'm feelin' generous.'

'Oh, Ag.' Ellen Dyer shook her head. 'I like Captain Grange. He's always so polite. An' he give me a bar of chocolate last week.'

'That's nothin' to what Captain Andrews give *me*.' Agnes grinned. 'Chocolate! Huh!'

'Captain Andrews never gave you nothing.' Ellen opened a folder. 'He don't even speak to you!'

'Yes, he does.'

'Rubbish. And anyway – '

'Talking of blokes,' interrupted Rose Davies suddenly, 'I reckon madam over there's got her eye on Lieutenant Atherton. Fancies him, don't you, Luce?' she demanded. 'When he was in here a minute ago you was blushin' something shocking!'

Lucy bent over her work.

'She types 'is reports out ever so carefully,' continued Rose, grinning. 'Checks everythin' twice, I seen 'er. Touchin', ain't it?'

'You want to watch him, Luce.' Agnes Lyall wound another sheet of paper into her machine, then looked hard at Lucy. 'Yes – you want to be careful there. He's a *proper* terror!'

'What do you mean?' asked Lucy.

'Tell 'er, Ellen.' Agnes Lyall sniggered. 'Tell 'er what you told me!'

Ellen Dyer giggled. '*You* tell her,' she muttered, grinning.

'*I* ain't tellin' her!' cackled Agnes. She began to type. 'Oh, I dare say she'll find out for 'erself!'

'I think you're all very silly,' said Lucy, blushing furiously.

'Ay think you're all vay sillay!' mimicked Agnes. 'Oh, pipe down, Lady Muck.'

Lucy's face and neck were now crimson. Ellen grinned even more broadly. Agnes caught Ellen's eye and winked. So Rose Davies had been right . . .

*　　　　*　　　　*

Agnes Lyall knew nothing whatsoever about Stephen's sexual habits or preferences, but she was delighted to see that Rose's hunch had been correct. By now, teasing Lucy Hollander had become the company's favourite pastime, and dark hints were continually dropped about Stephen's sexual rapacity. Ellen Dyer, taken to the pictures on two occasions, had felt bound to declare that he had tried it on; and she had been universally believed. 'He's *awful*, Luce,' she murmured, one wet Tuesday morning. 'I won't tell you where he put his 'and – '

Soon, Agnes and Ellen were thrilled to notice that the mere mention of Lieutenant Atherton was sufficient to make Lucy flush scarlet. 'He's after you, Luce,' muttered Agnes, as Stephen walked out of the office one morning. 'Your days are numbered, kid!'

'Oh, really, Agnes, you *are* stupid!' Poor Lucy was, by now, almost beside herself. 'Listen, I don't like him, I don't fancy him, he's – '

'Don't you, eh?' Agnes grinned. 'But 'e fancies *you*!'

'He doesn't! He hardly knows who I am!'

'That a fact?' Agnes nodded at Ellen. 'Just you wait and see, your ladyship. Just you wait and see.'

It transpired that, after a fashion, Agnes Lyall was right. Stephen finally asked Lucy out about a week or so after that exchange.

For Lucy, that evening in the local cinema was traumatic. Expecting to be jumped upon and mauled as violently as the young RAF sergeant on her left was attacking *his* evidently complaisant companion, she spent three hours in a state of absolute terror. Sitting bolt upright in her seat, staring fixedly at the cinema screen, she replied to Stephen's few remarks in curt monosyllables. She kept her gloves and coat on, crossed her legs and folded her arms. She hardly looked at him, but whenever she did glance in his direction, she felt a horrible blush staining her face and neck. She wished she'd never agreed to go out with him at all.

A polite kiss on the cheek as he left her outside Dorrington Hall was something of an anti-climax. As well as being relieved, she felt somewhat cheated – and so, when he asked if she'd like to go out with him again, she accepted rather too eagerly . . .

As for Stephen, he walked back towards the officers' quarters feeling rather pleased with the way the evening had gone. He'd particularly wanted to see that film, and Private Hollander had let him watch it in peace. She'd sat beside him as quietly as a mouse and had spoken only when he'd addressed her. All in all, she had behaved in so lady-like a fashion that Stephen had been charmed . . .

'Hello, Steve.' As Stephen walked into the officers' mess, he was waylaid by Captain Andrews. 'Had a good time?'

'Fine, thanks.' Stephen grinned. 'I always think Leslie Howard – '

'Get your leg over, did you?'

'What?'

'You heard, Mr Atherton, you heard!' Fred Andrews winked. 'Nice little piece, that Hollander girl. Quite fancy a bash at her myself. When you've finished with her, of course,' he added hastily.

Stephen reddened. 'I don't think she's that sort of girl,' he said stiffly. 'I don't think she'd know – '

'Ah, don't come all that holy innocent stuff with me!' Fred Andrews tapped Stephen's lapel. 'I tell you, Steve – whatever they *say*, all those ATS girls are the same, all tarts underneath; why else would they have joined the Army? And pretty Private Hollander – '

'She's a decent girl!' Stephen glared at the captain. 'She gave me no reason to think – '

'Tease, is she? Oh, well, in that case . . . ' Fred Andrews shrugged sympathetically. 'Never mind, put it down to experience. Now, I'll tell you something – Agnes Lyall, she's the little ginger one over in the general office, and *she's* – '

Captain Andrews rattled on for several minutes, explaining why he thought Agnes Lyall would be a good bet; and then, growing philosophical, he went on to categorize and define the characteristics of womankind in general. He looked complacently at his junior officer. 'So, Steve,' he concluded, 'I – '

'I think it's time I turned in.' Stephen manufactured a yawn. 'Ah – goodnight, sir.'

'What?' Fred Andrews blinked. 'Oh – right. Goodnight to you.'

As he walked across the parade ground, Stephen scowled to himself. Fred Andrews was an oaf. The Hampshire hogs which adorned his uniform were an appropriate emblem for him and his kind . . .

Lucy kept a diary. Now, little red hearts marked the days she went out with Stephen, and soon the pages of her private journal could show a respectable number of these pretty scarlet symbols . . .

She wasn't scared of him now. Indeed, if the other girls hadn't insisted that he was a wicked seducer, she'd have said he was diffident and shy, even a little afraid of *her*. On the other hand, there *was* something dangerous about him. Although she still didn't know what he'd done to Ellen Dyer, his narrow dark eyes and sulky face, his wide mouth which could suddenly smile and transform his expression completely, were not the features of a milk and water type. She believed him capable of passion.

'You don't mind this?' he asked her, taking her hand as he and she walked through the town one Saturday afternoon.

'No! Oh, no – it's nice.' Lucy looked up at him and smiled. Indeed, it was delightful to have her hand in his; and to show she meant what she'd said, she gave his fingers a gentle squeeze. 'I like to hold your hand,' she added, blushing, feeling silly for telling him so. 'It feels right.'

'Good.' Stephen said nothing more for a few minutes. Then, turning to his companion, he smiled back at her. 'Would you like some tea?'

'Er – yes. Yes, I think I would.' Lucy giggled. Tea! She

had wondered if perhaps it would be today that she'd be dragged into a bar and plied with strong drink, then taken to a house of ill fame, and . . .

Her education had not been broad enough to suggest to her what might come next. She giggled again.

'What are you laughing at?' demanded Stephen.

'Nothing.' Lucy pointed across the road. 'That place is open,' she added. 'Shall we go there?'

The air raid siren had gone. The familiar series of short wails had pierced the evening air, and soon all the personnel of Dorrington Camp were in shelters or dug-outs, grumpily preparing for a few hours' discomfort and annoyance.

Stephen had not heard the siren. Engaged in some clerical task of such extreme tediousness that he had been yawning over it all day, he had actually fallen asleep at his desk.

The crumping of bombs woke him. Opening his eyes, he blinked and gazed around him; but, in the absolute darkness of a moonless, starless night, he was able to see nothing. The camp was silent; and he reflected that, by now, everyone must be in the shelters. Listening hard, he realized that the docks were probably getting it, and he told himself that it was unlikely that the bombers would come this far out tonight.

He considered running across the parade ground to a dug-out; but then he decided that he couldn't be bothered. 'Oh, damn it,' he thought, yawning. 'Might as well get into the cupboard, and read.'

This cupboard – a large, square, windowless cubicle at the back of the wooden hut – had a door which was a good enough fit to prevent much light escaping. The place had originally been used to store large scale maps, but now it was empty. Six or seven feet square, it was big enough to stretch out in. Stephen groped in his desk, found a novel, some bars of chocolate which he'd forgotten he had, and a torch. He felt his way across the room.

If the hut received a direct hit he would be neatly incinerated, but, nevertheless, he crawled into the cupboard and made himself as comfortable as he could. Lying on his greatcoat and eating chocolate, he now enjoyed the deceptive security of a hedgehog which has made a cosy nest in a bonfire on November the fourth . . .

The raid went on, and on, and on. Stephen lay on the floor, reading and yawning. Having eaten almost four weeks' supply of hoarded chocolate, he wanted a drink; but of course he couldn't have one. He felt dozy; but he knew that if he extinguished the torch he wouldn't be able to sleep. There was too much noise for that.

He tried to concentrate on his book. But the novel, one by Thomas Hardy, was boring. He found, as he turned the pages, that he didn't really *care* what became of Tess – and as for Angel Clare, what decent man would treat a girl like that? The whole thing was so far-fetched as to be ridiculous, and Stephen couldn't see why his father thought Hardy was so marvellous . . .

The bangs and crashes of the raid made Stephen slightly uneasy. Some of the bombers seemed to be directly overhead now. But he had been in far too many raids to feel afraid. Fatalism had long since replaced panic. Now, as he lay in his den, he thought of the townspeople who were no doubt sheltering in far less comfortable surroundings. Poor things, they trekked out of the built up areas every night, walked into the blackness and the freezing cold, huddled together in sheds and church halls – and then wandered miserably back again, not knowing if their homes would still be intact when they got back to the town. Yawning violently now, Stephen rubbed his eyes. Perhaps he would go to sleep, after all . . .

Suddenly, there was a scratching sound. A rustling, clawing noise disturbed him, and, blinking, Stephen looked up. It took him a second or two to realize that someone was trying to open the door of the cupboard. 'Wait a sec!' he shouted. 'I've a light on in here!' He switched off his torch and pushed open the door. 'Come in,' he said, to whoever it was. 'There's just room for two.'

241

A figure stumbled into the darkness and collapsed in a heap.

'I saw the light. I – oh! Not another one!' The pretty ATS girl, the one who typed his reports so neatly and whom he had taken to the pictures a few times, was sitting in the corner shaking with terror. In the torchlight she looked like a frightened schoolgirl, for her long, dark hair had come down and was lying loose about her shoulders, she was hatless and there were traces of tears on her cheeks. The bomb exploded, and she shut her eyes.

Stephen stared at her. 'What on earth are you doing, wandering around by yourself?' he demanded sharply. 'Why aren't you in the shelter?'

'Why aren't *you*?' Opening her eyes wide now, Lucy stared back at him, then she blushed. 'I'm sorry, sir,' she mumbled. 'I didn't mean to be cheeky.'

'Well, you were.' But then, suddenly seeing the absurdity of it all, Stephen laughed. 'I fell asleep at my desk,' he explained. 'I must have missed the siren. My mother always said I'd sleep through the last angel's trumpet call and it looks as if she was right. So, what happened to you?'

'I was in town. I couldn't get a bus back to camp, so I began to walk. I'd got about half way when the raid started. I ran and I ran. I kept falling over things, I cut my knees; I didn't know where I was.' Lucy pushed her hair back from her face. 'When I reached the perimeter fence I climbed in – there's a gap, you know – and I saw a very faint light in this hut. I thought I was imagining things.' Lucy shuddered. 'Oh God! I was so scared!'

'Are you cold?'

'Yes, I am.' Lucy shivered.

'Well, then, don't loll about on that concrete floor. Come and sit on my coat.' Stephen made room for her. 'Would you like some chocolate?'

'No thanks, it gives me spots.' Lucy leaned against Stephen and hugged herself. 'And I couldn't eat anything just now, anyway.'

Her breathing was still very harsh and she was still trembling and so, to comfort her, Stephen slid one arm around her shoulders. As he pulled her closer, Lucy did not resist him. And it seemed only natural that his other arm should find its way around her waist . . .

It occurred to him that perhaps he was being over-familiar. 'Do you mind if I hug you like this?' he asked politely.

'No, not at all. It's lovely.' She snuggled closer to him and sighed. 'I don't feel so scared now.'

'Good.' He kissed her cheek and stroked her hair. 'You do smell nice. Very nice, in fact.'

'I'm sure I don't. I'm all sweaty.'

'Can't smell the sweat. But there's a definite scent of clean hair, and of something else which is very appealing.' Stephen kissed her again.

He'd never kissed her in the cinema. While practically every other couple of seats had held a squirming pair of lovers, Stephen and Lucy had always sat side by side in the darkness, chastely watching the film. He had occasionally taken her hand and held it between his, resting it lightly on his lap. But he'd never done anything more exciting. And his goodnight kiss, the fleeting brush across her cheek before he'd returned her to her quarters, had been nothing to get worked up about.

In fact, she'd wondered if he was really a pansy, who took girls out to make other people think he was normal. Or if she was plain unattractive. She couldn't decide which was worse.

But now he was kissing her more passionately than he'd ever done before. His mouth on hers, he was parting her lips and licking her teeth. He even had one hand pressed against the pocket of her tunic and was caressing her breast. She began to kiss him back with enthusiasm.

There was a whine, a thud and a terrific explosion which shook the hut to its unstable foundations. Lucy started and pulled away from her companion; but then, her eyes wide, she grabbed Stephen's arm and pinched it hard. 'Stephen, what – '

'It's all right. It missed. In fact, it must have landed miles away.'

'Really?'

'Really. So don't worry.'

Stephen's voice had been low and soothing; and Lucy felt a little calmer almost straight away. She leaned against him and pushed her face against his breast pocket. 'Do you think they'll bomb the camp?' she asked, in a whisper.

'No, not a chance. That one was a stray; I expect the plane's on its way home to the Fatherland by now.'

'Oh.' Lucy shivered. 'It's just that when I hear them crump it makes me feel so sick.'

'I know. They frighten me as well.' Stephen wrapped his arms around Lucy and held her tightly. 'Is that any better?'

'Yes, it is. Much.'

'Good.' Stephen kissed her cheek again. 'Isn't your hair long?' he murmured. Feeling it brushing the back of his hand, he let it tickle his fingers. 'Long, and heavy!'

'I know.' Lucy grimaced. 'It's murder to keep pinned up, but I *won't* have it cut. Oh, I know what you'll say,' she added. 'If the redcaps catch me looking like this – '

'You'll be on a charge. You will anyway; they'll have noticed you're missing.' Stephen realized that the girl was shivering violently now. 'Are you still cold?' he asked.

'Not really.' She giggled faintly as he touched her behind one knee. 'I'm ticklish there,' she explained.

'Are you?' Stephen smiled at her. 'Where else?'

She took his hand and, blushing at her own temerity, she showed him. Soon, he was kissing her again, even more urgently now; and, holding him close to her, she could feel his heart thudding against her chest. He was breathing very hard, and making curious moaning noises. He was sweating, his forehead was beaded with perspiration, his face and his lips were salty . . .

Then, to her great delight, she realized that he desired her, wanted her; and she wasn't at all surprised when, a few minutes later, she heard him say, 'Lucy, may I make love to you?'

In spite of his evident agitation, his voice was as calm and neutral as if he'd asked her to make a top copy and three carbons. Lucy looked at him . . .

She was certain that the last hour of her life had come. The planes seemed to be within a mile or so of the camp. Muffled thuds and crashes echoed all around the perimeter; and Lucy now decided that if her death was imminent, she would like to die doing something enjoyable. She wound her arms around Stephen's neck and pulled him as close to her as she could. 'Please,' she murmured. 'Please, I'd like you to. I want it to be you.'

She didn't really know what would happen now. Afraid to let him see how ignorant she was, she continued to hug him. She wondered what he expected – what, if anything, a woman was *supposed* to do . . .

Stephen unfastened some of the buttons on his jacket. He fiddled with Lucy's own tunic – but then, instead of kissing her some more, instead of cajoling and whispering nice things in her ear, he pushed her over backwards; and before Lucy could protest at such rough treatment, he fell on top of her.

He tugged at her starched collar and, after some ineffectual fumbling, he managed to get her tie undone and to unfasten a few of the buttons on her shirt. His face against her neck, his teeth bruising her flesh, he kissed her throat. Then, pushing her hair back from her face, he stared down at her. His eyes glittering, he now looked quite mad; and he held her shoulders so tightly that he hurt her. 'Oh, Jesus!' she heard him mutter. 'Oh, God! Lucy, I can't – '

And then, to her own amazement, Lucy took the initiative. She unfastened her skirt and eased her hips out of the awful regulation bloomers. 'Take your time,' she whispered. 'Don't be in such a hurry. Stephen, there's no need to rush – '

But it appeared that there was. Stephen was shaking her as if she were a doll, his grip on her so fierce that he was almost crushing the bones in her upper arms. In considerable pain now, Lucy shut her eyes. A minute or two went by. And then, with a great, sobbing groan, Stephen finally relaxed. He lay on top of her, holding her in his arms, and trembling.

Lucy opened her eyes. Calmly, and – considering her

245

state of disarray – with some dignity, she looked at him. She saw how distraught he was. 'Don't be upset,' she said kindly. 'Stephen, don't – '

'I'm not upset,' he muttered. 'Not at all.' Raising his weight from her, Stephen sat up and stared back at the girl beside him. 'I made a right mess of that,' he added sourly. 'A right sodding mess.'

'Not really.' Instinctively aware that it must have cost him a great deal to make even that back-handed apology, Lucy touched Stephen's hand in sympathy. 'It can't be easy,' she added. 'Not the first time.'

'It wasn't.' Stephen grimaced. 'It bloody well wasn't.'

'Never mind.' Lucy smiled at him. 'Well, I wasn't much good, either.'

'Lucy, you've – er – ' Stephen looked at his hands. 'I mean – you haven't done this before?'

'Of course I haven't! Wasn't it obvious?'

'No.' Vehemently, Stephen shook his head. 'Lucy, did I hurt you very much?'

'A bit.' Lucy bit her lip. 'Well, no; not really. I mean, I've always been quite energetic, I go riding and all that; it's supposed to help when – well, you know.'

'Does it hurt now?'

'No, not at all.'

'Good.' Relieved, Stephen managed a faint smile. 'Thank you, Lucy,' he said. 'Thank you, for being so kind.'

Lucy leaned forwards and kissed his face. 'It'll be better next time,' she said. 'It must be, it's bound to be.' Then she undid the rest of the buttons on her shirt and unhooked her bra. 'Touch me,' she invited. 'And let me touch you. Don't be afraid.'

He did as she suggested. Unfastening his own tunic and shirt, he pulled her into his arms. He stroked her long, dark hair and kissed her, then he took her face between his hands and looked into her eyes. 'Oh, Lucy, Lucy!' he murmured a few minutes afterwards, 'I think you're a witch!'

'Thank you very much, Lieutenant Atherton. A witch indeed! Let me tell you, sir, I haven't a single wart on the

246

whole of my body!' She held out her arms and turned to and fro for him to see. 'Look, if you like!'

'You're still a witch. A beautiful, beautiful witch. Lucy, put your arms around me again . . . '

Lucy did.

Ten minutes later the sirens began, a long, mournful wail which indicated the all clear. Lucy began to gather her scattered clothing. 'Time to go,' she said, as she fastened her skirt.

'Mm.' Stephen, still half naked, watched her disappear inside her hideous army clothes. 'I hate uniform on women,' he remarked. 'In fact, I don't think women should be in the army at all.'

'If this particular woman doesn't get back to her dormitory, perhaps she won't be for much longer.' Lucy grinned. 'Good night, sir,' she said. And, picking up her coat, she left Stephen sitting in the map cupboard, thinking.

Chapter Twenty

BEFORE HE HAD ANY FURTHER CHANCE to consolidate his relationship with Lucy Hollander, Stephen was, to his great annoyance, sent up to Yorkshire for a fortnight.

'Don't *scowl* like that, man,' Captain Grange had added, after he'd given Stephen the unwelcome news. 'Look, they've decided to make you up to first lieutenant. Orders came through today. So you can put another pip up.'

But Stephen, considering that his promotion was long overdue anyway, continued to frown. Captain Grange dismissed him. Ungrateful young hog, he thought. The barracks where Stephen was going had a reputation for looking after its officers, and fresh eggs, farmhouse cured bacon and well hung beef were rumoured to be regularly available in the mess. Captain Grange sighed. The food in Dorrington Camp was terrible . . .

Stephen took the train to Leeds and made his way to the barracks, a training camp in the middle of the Yorkshire Wolds. He was greeted by the commanding officer who asked him if he'd got his stuff ready.

'Stuff?' asked Stephen, mystified.

'Your lectures. Your talks.' The major frowned. 'You *are* the fellow who's going to give my rookies the lowdown on machine guns and weaponry in general? Bren, and that?'

'I wasn't told what I'd be doing here.'

'Oh. Well – ' The major riffled through some papers.

'S A Atherton – that's you, isn't it? Guards, temporarily attached to the Hampshires. Guff here says you're mad keen to be involved in training recruits. That not right?'

Stephen nodded, now vaguely remembering that he had mentioned something of the kind to the medical officer in Portsmouth. 'That's correct,' he said. 'Yes, I did ask if I'd be of any use in a training battalion. Only I was told – '

'Well, if this is what you wanted, don't look so bloody fed up about it! God, you youngsters – never satisfied!' The major went to the door and jerked it open. 'Halliday!' he bawled down the corridor. 'Halliday! At the double, you idle brute! Take this officer over to the mess and show him his quarters. Wake up, damn you, man!'

Stephen enjoyed his time in Yorkshire. When, at the end of the two weeks, the major asked if he'd like to stay on, he was very tempted. The work he was doing there was much more congenial to him than the wretched daily round of reports, documents and chits which bedevilled his life at Dorrington Camp.

Then he thought of Lucy. That day's letter from her was in his tunic pocket, warm against his heart. He was well aware that it was unusual to be given a choice. Routinely, at that stage of the war, one was obliged to go wherever one was sent. To Stephen, the fact that he could now decide for himself seemed like a portent. He turned down the major's offer.

In spite of the fact that Stephen was away from her, and in spite of missing him more than she'd have thought possible, Lucy was far happier now than she'd been a month ago. Two new recruits had recently joined her company, and these unfortunates were now the object of Agnes Lyall's baleful attentions and the butt of Rose Davies' witty asides.

In fact, since Lucy had become Lieutenant Atherton's

official fancy woman, she and Agnes had established a kind
of rapport which had gradually matured into an odd sort of
friendship. Each had developed a wary respect for the
other. 'Don't take any notice of Agnes,' Lucy told the
smaller of the recruits. 'She's just a bully, and a show-off.'
She giggled. 'Aren't you, Ag?'

'Says who, toffee nose?' retorted Agnes. Haughtily, she
stared at Lucy. 'Listen here, Lady Muck; I'll stick one on
you if you don't belt up.'

'You see?' Lucy smiled at the newcomer. 'But she
doesn't mean it. She's all talk.'

'Watch your step, Hollander. I'm warnin' you.' Agnes
grinned at the recruit. 'One of the snobs, Hollander is,' she
explained. 'Really thinks she's it. Only goes with officers,
see.'

'Jealous,' said Lucy. 'You're only jealous. No officer
would touch *you* with a disinfected bargepole. Cookhouse
orderlies – they're about your level.'

'Liar! Flamin' liar! Last week, I – '

And so it went on.

At the end of January, Stephen was transferred back to
Portsmouth. All the way south, standing in the crowded
corridor of a filthy, unheated train, he was singing to
himself.

Arriving back at the camp, he walked into the Nissen hut
where Lucy worked. She had not looked up as he entered;
so he stole up behind her and wrapped his arms around her
shoulders, causing her to mesh her typewriter keys and give
a little shriek of surprise. 'Hard at it, eh, Private Hollander?' he demanded softly.

'Stephen!' She turned round and looked up at him. 'Oh,
Stephen, I didn't know you'd be coming today!'

'Private Hollander!' Taking advantage of the fact that
Lucy's desk was shielded from public view by some filing
cabinets, Stephen leaned over and kissed her. 'Private
Hollander, you address an officer as *sir*!'

'Sorry, sir.' Lucy smiled at him, her delight at seeing

him only too obvious. 'Oh, sir, you can't imagine how I've missed you!'

'Lucy,' asked Stephen, later that evening, 'are you due for any leave?'

'I've seven days to come, but not until March.' Lucy sniffed. 'And I promised Daddy I'd spend that week with him and Mummy.'

'Oh.' Stephen grimaced. 'You could easily get a twenty-four-hour pass. Look, Lucy, we must have some time together. See what you can arrange, will you?'

'If I *can* get twenty-four hours, what shall we do at this time of year?'

Stephen considered. Walks in the countryside and rolls in the hay were out of the question at that chilly season. 'We'll go to a hotel,' he said. 'One of the other chaps knows a place; somewhere near the docks, I think.'

'We're not allowed to go near the docks.' Lucy frowned. 'Lois has put them out of bounds; I suppose she thinks we'll be enticed away by the Free Frogs. Stephen, if a redcap catches me – '

'Oh, for Christ's sake, stop making difficulties!' Stephen looked hard at her. 'You don't want to go on with this, do you?'

'I do! More than anything, Stephen!'

'Right, then. Apply for your leave, and I'll see what I can fix up.'

'I've booked us into an hotel in Lucan Street.' Stephen did not look at her as he told her this. 'Lucy, it was the best I could do.'

'Ah. Yes, I suppose it was.' Lucy, who these days felt that she was fast being sucked towards a whirlpool of debauchery and sin, sighed in resignation.

She could not imagine what had happened to her. Cool, calm Lucy Hollander, head girl at her school and top of the class at secretarial college, she could think of nothing but

251

Stephen, wanted nothing but his hands on her body, his mouth on her own. Day and night she saw his face in her mind's eye, day and night she imagined his arms around her. It was awful. She blushed. 'This place,' she murmured, in a small, embarrassed voice. 'It's not a brothel, is it?'

'Of course it's not!' Stephen's vehemence did its best to disguise a suspicion that a brothel was exactly what the Albany Hotel was. The receptionist had been so knowing, so arch. She had grinned at him cheekily and told him boldly that it would be cash in advance, my duck, no cheques accepted. He had seen at once that the place was no family boarding house or commercial travellers' home from home . . .

The room was at the top of the building. Its skirting boards were kicked and pitted, its sloping cream walls dirtied with the scuffed marks of innumerable grubby shoulders and its chairbacks shiny from the residues of countless greasy heads. Lucy looked around her appalled, taking in the awful chest of drawers which was cigarette-burned and battered beyond repair, the cracked and filthy wash-basin, and the horribly sagging bed. 'I'm sorry, Stephen, but I really don't think – '

'You want to leave?'

'No. But, Stephen, are the sheets clean?'

'Have a look.'

Lucy turned down the bedclothes and found a set of greyish, fraying linen. It didn't smell of washing soap and lavender – but at least it wasn't creased, or, worse than that, still warm. 'Perhaps,' she whispered, in a small voice. 'Well, perhaps – '

'Lucy, stop fretting about the bloody sheets.' Stephen smiled at her. 'Darling, come here.'

She did as he asked. He took her in his arms and stroked her neck. 'Look, my love,' he whispered. 'It's either here, in comparative comfort, or it's in the map cupboard, up against the wall of 47 block, or somewhere equally squalid

252

and public.' Stephen kissed Lucy's cheek. 'I wouldn't have chosen this place, but where else could we go?'

'I know. I'm being silly.' Lucy looked at him anxiously. 'Stephen, did you get some of those - er - things? I don't want to be made pregnant, and we were very foolish last time - '

'Yes, I've got some things. Don't worry.' Stephen opened the collar of Lucy's shirt and kissed her neck. 'Oh, God, you can't imagine how much I've missed you!'

'I can, as it happens, because I've missed you.' Lucy unfastened her lover's shirt and pulled it out of the waistband of his trousers. 'Where's your vest?' she scolded. 'Stephen, it's below freezing out there, and you - '

'Oh, shut up. You're as bad as my mother.'

'Sorry.' Lucy pushed his shirt open and now she ran her hands all over his chest, tracing the paths of scars which curved from his side round to his shoulder-blade, stopping where the metal had met bone. Seeing him in full daylight she could now appreciate the extent of the mutilation, and she grimaced at the sight. 'Does it still hurt?' she asked.

'No, not at all.'

'It's ruined your beauty.' Lucy frowned. 'I hate it!'

'I'm sorry.' Stephen looked past her, out of the window. 'If you find me repulsive,' he added coldly, 'we needn't take things any further - '

'I didn't mean that!' Lucy pulled off her shirt and threw it on to the floor. 'Oh, Stephen, let's go to bed!'

'These pillows smell of the dust and dirt of ages,' remarked Lucy, fastidiously wrinkling her neat little nose and raising her head from the offending stink. She laid her head on Stephen's chest. 'You *are* beautiful,' she added happily. 'Do you know what?'

'What?'

'You remind me of a toy panda. I had a lovely one once. He was just like you.'

'Did he growl?'

'Oh, yes! When I punched his tummy – '

'Don't try that with me.' Stephen grinned. 'And I'm not Chinese, you know. I'm descended from the dark, hairy Welsh.' He lifted Lucy's hand to his face, examined it closely. '*You're* as pale as pale,' he observed. 'I suppose you're a pure-blooded Anglo-Saxon?'

'Oh, yes. Well, as far as I know.' Lucy tickled his cheek. 'We're from quite different races, you and I.'

'It seems we're compatible, all the same.'

'Mm.' Lucy giggled. 'I think we are. Shall we make quite sure of it?' She gave an unequivocal wriggle, touching him where she knew it would excite him. 'Stephen, do you know what I mean?'

'*What*? Darling, really!' To Lucy's surprise, Stephen looked quite shocked. 'Ladies aren't supposed to make suggestions like that! Sweetheart, you shouldn't – '

'Women shouldn't be in the army, ladies aren't supposed to suggest making love.' Lucy kissed Stephen's nose. 'Don't you want to?' she asked.

'I – '

'Don't you fancy me any more?'

Stephen lifted her away from him and rolled her on to her back.

An hour or so later, both Lucy and Stephen realized that they were ravenously hungry. Reluctantly, they got dressed and went down the stairs and out into the grimy street. 'Next time,' said Stephen, 'we'll go to the Dorchester. We'll have the honeymoon suite, and I shall ring room service to order champagne and smoked salmon sandwiches.'

'Will you?' Lucy's eyes widened. 'How sinful!' she giggled. 'How divine!'

'Mm. But today, my poor darling, it'll be powdered egg omelette and greasy chips; and that's if we're lucky.' Stephen kissed his beloved. 'Shall we walk along by the docks? We can admire the seagulls and the barbed wire.'

'All right.' Lucy smiled at him, her fear of the military

police forgotten. 'Yes, we'll do that. Then we'll go and have some tea.'

'Right.' Stephen took her hand. 'What have you been doing with yourself these past couple of weeks?'

'This and that.' Lucy grinned. 'I've been out with three or four nice blokes, as it happens. One took me to the flicks and one gave me tea in town. I haven't been lonely!'

Stephen looked at her - then looked away. 'What have you been doing really?' he asked.

'I told you!' Lucy stared out to sea. 'I'm working my way up through the ranks,' she explained. 'I've been wined and dined by a lieutenant, a captain; and I intend to have hooked a field marshal by the time the war is over!'

Stephen let go of her hand. 'You started with a lieutenant,' he said stiffly. 'I'd prefer you to stay with that rank - until I'm promoted, of course.'

'I couldn't do that!' Lucy shook her head. 'Captains have more money than lieutenants. Oh, you needn't think I was pining for you,' she teased. 'All those chaps were going overseas, you see; so I let them spend their money on me, and in return I helped to make their last nights in Blighty memorable. It was my patriotic duty, wasn't it?'

'Was it?' A dark flush was, by degrees, spreading over Stephen's face. 'And did you enjoy yourself?' he asked, his voice so cold and dead that Lucy should have noticed he was angry . . .

But the wind was blowing against her ears and making conversation difficult, and she hardly heard what he said, let alone the tone in which he said it. More importantly, Lucy herself - though she hated to be teased - at least understood when someone *was* joking. It never occurred to her that, far from being able to take a joke, Stephen was habitually incapable of understanding that a joke was being made . . .

'Enjoy myself?' she asked flirtatiously. 'Oh, yes! I had a really good time!' She touched his cold hand. 'Now, don't be cross,' she went on, digging her grave even deeper. 'I only went out with old married men, chaps who love their wives. I held their hands and kissed them goodnight. It was all perfectly harmless, so you don't need to be jealous!'

255

'Well, I am jealous.' Stephen scowled at her. 'Very jealous!'

'Really?' Lucy laughed at him. 'I only hugged and kissed them, that's all. There's nothing for you to be jealous *about*!'

Stephen felt his throat tighten; a heart-wrenching spasm shook his whole frame. 'Nothing?' he demanded icily. 'You call hugging and kissing other women's husbands *nothing*?' He glared down at the pavement. 'God – what sort of a woman are you?' he muttered, almost to himself.

'What do you mean by that?' Lucy, herself rather put out now, folded her arms and stared at him. 'Come on – if you've anything to accuse me of, I'd like to hear it.'

'You know damned well what I mean.' His next words were unnecessarily harsh, forced out of him by the wash of misery which swept over and engulfed him. But such a betrayal! Such a deliberate, absolute betrayal! Made their last nights in Blighty memorable, indeed! Stephen felt tears behind his eyes. 'You're a tart,' he said curtly. 'A common little tart. That's all you are.'

'How dare you!' Lucy stopped walking. 'How *dare* you call me that! I suppose, out in the wilds of Yorkshire, you never so much as spoke to another woman?'

'I didn't! You're bloody well right, I didn't! I never even thought of anyone but you!'

'What a saint!' Lucy scowled at him. 'Listen to me, Lieutenant bloody Atherton,' she cried. 'You called me a tart. I'm not a tart – nothing of the kind! So, unless you apologize now, I shall go straight back to barracks and I'll never speak to you again for as long as I live!'

'Go then.' Stephen's head was aching. He wanted to take Lucy in his arms and cry on her shoulder, to be told he'd misunderstood, that she hadn't even looked at another man while he'd been away from her. But he couldn't climb down like that. 'Go away,' he muttered drearily. 'I don't want to see you; I don't want to listen to you any more.'

'Nor I to you! You pompous, stupid *oaf*! Here, you hysterical idiot!' Lucy took out the last letter he'd written

256

her, tore it across and threw it at his feet. 'Have your rubbish back!'

He watched her walk away. He wanted to run after her, but something held him back. He stood there, silent, the hammering of his heart loud in his ears, almost drowning out the screeching of the seagulls and the crashing of the grey waves on the sea wall.

Chapter Twenty One

THE LETTER FROM ALEC'S MOTHER arrived one cold morning in the middle of February 1941. Slitting the envelope, Helen wondered aloud what Mrs Townsend had to tell her. 'Perhaps Alec's got himself a medal,' she remarked, as she unfolded the paper inside.

The Allied victories of January and February had cheered the nation; the successes of their own troops against the Italian forces had provided the British with that best of tonics, the news of a series of military break-throughs.

But of course there had been casualties. And, as Helen read, she discovered that her fiancé had been one of them. During the battle for Tobruk that January, Alec's company had been decimated; and Alec himself had been injured.

Seeing Helen's face darken, Dora touched her daughter's arm. 'What's happened, dear?' she asked anxiously. 'Helen – '

'Just a moment.'

Helen read on. And now she learned that the wound made by an Italian bayonet had, though not initially serious, become infected – and that Alec had died of blood poisoning three days later.

'Oh, my poor darling!' Dora, her brown eyes welling with tears of sympathy, came round to her daughter's chair and embraced the girl. 'Helen, I'm so sorry! Look, have another cup of tea, let me fetch you a little brandy – '

'I don't want *brandy*!' Helen took her mother's arms from around her neck. 'I'll be late for work,' she said. 'I've already missed the bus – '

'You're not going to *work*?' Dora stared at her child. 'Darling, you don't need to go in today! I'll telephone, and explain what's happened. Tim,' she added, appealing to her husband for support, 'she doesn't need to go to work, does she?'

'It's up to you, Nell.' Tim looked at his daughter. 'If you feel up to it – '

'Oh, honestly, Tim!' Dora frowned at him. 'Have a bit of sympathy! You might at least tell your daughter you're sorry Alec's dead!'

'I'm sorry Alec's dead. Of course I am.' Tim drained his tea cup. 'Nell, shall I walk in with you?'

'Thanks, Dad. I'd appreciate that.'

Dora watched them walk down the path together. Obviously, Helen was in shock. Grief, tears and prostration would come later. But as for Tim! She was surprised at her husband. Habitually so kind, so thoughtful, so sensitive to other peoples' states of mind, he had practically pushed his daughter out of the house, and was now ambling along with her just as if they were setting off for a Sunday afternoon stroll.

A week or so went by and Dora, expecting Helen to give way to grief for her fiancé, was surprised to observe that her daughter showed no signs of distress. 'Good heavens, Mum,' she cried, when Dora asked how she was feeling, 'life must go on! He's *dead*; and there's no point in sitting around weeping and wailing for someone who's beyond help, is there?'

'I suppose not.' Dora shook her head, rather shocked by her daughter's apparent lack of feeling. 'Where did you get to last night?' she enquired. 'It was three o'clock before you came in. Darling, I know – '

'Actually, you don't. Mum?'

'What?'

'Might I bring a friend to dinner this evening?' Helen looked straight at her mother. 'You see, there's someone you ought to meet. So may I bring him here?'

'Of course you may.' Dora frowned. 'Who is he?'

'Just a friend.' Helen chewed her lower lip. 'Mum, you will make allowances, won't you?' she asked. 'And don't dress up, or anything.'

'I never *do* these days.' Seeing that her daughter was on edge, Dora wondered if the crisis was coming at last. 'Bring your friend by all means. I'd like to meet him.'

Helen had informed Tom that Alec had been killed. He had looked grave, said he was sorry to hear it; then changed the subject. And Helen had not mentioned Alec again.

Now that she had decided to take Tom home with her that evening, the prospect of introducing him to her parents was slowly reducing Helen to a nervous wreck. All that day she made mistakes; and her boss, seeing she was incapable of concentration, told her to go home early.

He patted her shoulder. 'Take it easy, Miss Atherton,' he said kindly. 'It's not something you get over just like that. I remember when my wife's nephew was killed at Dunkirk.' He sighed. 'Poor chap,' he murmured sadly. 'Only twenty-two. His whole life before him . . . '

Helen met Tom in Cornmarket. Telling him that they were in a hurry, she practically frogmarched him back to his digs and, taking out his best trousers and only jacket, she told him to go and wash all over. Since he was never anything but perfectly clean, this was particularly insulting – but Tom, seeing that Helen was in a state about something, did as he was bidden.

'What's all this about, then?' he asked as he came out of the bathroom, the hairs on his chest still wet and a towel around his waist. Seeing her grimace, he went up to her and took her in his arms, stroking her neck. 'What's the matter, love?'

'We haven't time for any of that.' Pulling the towel from around him she rubbed him dry, then handed him a clean

260

shirt. She looked about her for the box in which he kept his shoe polish, brushes and dusters. 'I want you to come to dinner – tea – at our house,' she said. 'Tonight.'

'Oh. All right.' Tom grinned. 'But I thought we were going to that new flick?'

'We'll go to that tomorrow.' Anxiously, Helen looked at him. 'You won't mind a change of plan?'

'No, why should I?' Now in his shirt and trousers, he began to towel his damp hair. 'It'll be a free meal, won't it?'

'If you want to look at it like that.'

Helen now fussed around him, knotting his tie with great precision and turning his collar down neatly. 'Here,' he said, kissing her forehead in an attempt to calm her down, 'stop fretting. I won't disgrace you. I won't eat peas with me knife, I won't be rude to your Mum and Dad – '

'It's not that.'

'Well, what is it, then?'

'I – well, you will be careful, won't you? You see, my Dad can be a bit sarcastic sometimes; he doesn't mean any harm, but if he says anything you don't particularly like – '

'He can say what he pleases.' Tom kissed Helen again. 'Oh, look, sweetheart. Your parents will see straight away that I'm an ordinary working man. You don't want me to pretend otherwise, do you?'

'No, of course I don't. Where's your comb?'

'On the washstand.'

'Keep still.' Helen made a parting and combed Tom's fair hair back from his face. She looked at him, and smiled. 'You'll do,' she said, using an expression of his.

'Jolly good show,' he replied.

Tim Atherton had been working hard all day. He had been commissioned to write a series of articles for a newspaper and this had proved more difficult than he'd expected it to be. Hearing the front door slam, he got up; and, still in his shirtsleeves, he walked out of his study and met Tom and Helen in the hall.

261

'Ah.' Tim held out his hand to the visitor. 'Mr Richardson, isn't it?'

'Good evening, sir.'

The two men shook hands. Tim kissed his daughter. 'Well, give Helen your coat,' he told the guest. 'And come through to the drawing room.'

Leaving Helen to hang up the coats, Tim led the visitor away. Rubbing his cold hands together, he held them out to the fire. 'Chilly night,' he observed. 'Will you have a drink, Mr Richardson? Gin? Or we've whisky. I don't know if you care for sherry. Can't stand it myself.'

Tom glanced at Helen, who had just come into the room and who now allowed herself a faint smile. 'I'd like some whisky, please,' he said.

'Soda in it?'

'No, as it is.'

'Good man.' Tim poured out the last of his pre-war Scotch. 'No sense in drowning it, eh?'

'I'll have a sherry, Dad,' said Helen. 'Dry.'

'Right.' Tim poured his daughter a drink. 'I don't know where Dora is,' he continued apologetically. He opened a box of cigarettes and offered it to the guest.

'No, thank you.' Tom shook his head. 'I've given up.'

'Have you?' Helen's father nodded ruefully. 'Very wise. I ought to, but I find I can't. How did you manage it?'

'It was difficult for the first few weeks.'

'I can imagine.' Tim lit up and inhaled a lungful of smoke. 'You've obviously got far more will power than I have.'

Helen became a little less tense, glad to see that her father was not going to savage the guest – or at any rate, not immediately. 'Really, Dad, you might go and put a jacket on,' she scolded. 'Er – look; I'll go and see if Mum wants any help.'

'Off you go, then.' Tim gulped down a mouthful of whisky. 'I'll look after Mr Richardson.'

Helen eventually relaxed, relieved that her father wasn't

disposed to embarrass her. And Dora, who was usually kind to her children's friends, put herself out to be especially pleasant to this one.

It was Sarah's day off; and since Dora had cooked the meal herself, she served it with some degree of diffidence. 'I hope you like meat pie, Mr Richardson?' she asked. 'I'm afraid it's nearly all vegetables,' she added, reddening slightly, feeling bound to explain that she wasn't trying to pretend the meal was something it wasn't.

They all began to eat. Tom was watched closely by Helen's mother. 'How do you find it?' asked Dora anxiously.

'It's very nice indeed.' Tom smiled at her. 'Excellent, in fact.'

'That's a relief!' Gratified, Dora smiled back; and she looked triumphantly at Helen, as if to say, 'there, you see? I can do as well as Sarah any day.'

For a few minutes there was only the most general kind of conversation. Then Helen's father decided that his visitor should entertain him.

'Well, Mr Richardson, Helen tells me you're a Royal Artillery man.' Tim poured his guest some white wine he'd been saving for no reason in particular and which he was now glad of an excuse to drink. 'At Dunkirk, were you?'

'Yes, I was.' Tom finished his meal and laid his knife and fork side by side on his plate, something Dora had been vainly trying to train Stephen to do for years. He swallowed a mouthful of wine. 'But I don't think Mrs Atherton would want to hear about that.'

'I would, though.' Helen's father topped up his guest's glass. 'Dora, don't listen. Now, Mr Richardson, were you anywhere near Fleurbaix?'

'I was, as it happens.' Tom nodded. 'We were told to pull out on the twenty-fourth. We left Lille – '

Soon, both men were deep in conversation. Helen and her mother, left out, talked about clothes, or rather the lack of them, for there was nothing new in the shops that spring.

*   *   *

Helen watched Tom walk down the path. Very reluctantly she closed the door on him; dragging her feet, she went back into the drawing room. 'Well?' she demanded.

'I'm tired. I'm going to bed.' Dora got up and looked meaningfully at Tim. 'Don't be too long,' she added, as she went through the doorway.

'Did you like him?' Helen sat down beside her father. 'Dad, *did* you?'

'He seems a pleasant enough sort of chap.' Tim lit a cigarette. 'Where d'you meet him?'

Helen looked at her hands. 'In a café in town.'

'Oh. I see.' Tim raised his eyebrows. 'How long does he expect to be out of service?' he enquired.

'He has a medical due in about three weeks' time. Dad – I – '

'What?'

'Thanks for being so nice to him.'

'Was I nice?' Tim smiled at his daughter. 'Am I ever otherwise?'

'Yes! You know you are!'

'All the same, I hope I'm not generally unpleasant, particularly towards people who are polite to me?'

'No, you're not usually. It's just that if you dislike someone it tends to show.' Helen chewed her lower lip for a moment. 'And Tom's – well, he's not – '

'The sort of man I have in mind for you?'

'Perhaps.'

'Mm.' Tom took his daughter's hand and chafed it between his own. 'What is he?' he asked. 'A sergeant? BSM?'

'A sergeant – I've no idea what kind. How did you know?'

'Oh, it was obvious. The way he talked; the way he looked; the way he behaved.' Tim grinned. 'Backbone of the British Army, that type.'

'Don't be sarcastic.'

'I'm not. Well, Helen – it's perfectly clear that this Richardson fellow likes you, and it's been plain for some time that you're not grieving for Alec Townsend.' Tim took another cigarette and lit it from the glowing butt of the previous one. 'So, what's going to happen now?'

'I suppose it depends on whether he goes back into the Army.' Helen looked anxiously at Tim. 'Dad, if he's discharged, could you help him find a decent job?'

'Oh, Nell, I doubt it! I haven't any contacts – I don't know what he's capable of. Anyway, he wouldn't want to be organized.' Tim shook his head at his daughter. 'He doesn't look that kind of man.'

'No, you're right, he isn't. He's very independent.' Helen smiled ruefully. 'Would you like to see him again?'

'Certainly. Bring him round in the evenings if you like. Then we can get to know each other.'

'Thanks. I shall.' Helen yawned. 'I think I'll go up now,' she said. And Tim heard her humming as she walked up the stairs.

The following morning Helen was up early. Her mother heard her singing as she walked along the landing, and at breakfast she looked happier than she had for weeks. She sat down at the table beaming. 'Dad liked my boyfriend,' she remarked, smiling at her mother.

'Your what?' asked Dora, who hadn't heard what Helen said.

'My boyfriend. Oh, Mum, it's an American expression in common usage here! Don't be stuffy! You can call him my fiancé, if you like.'

'That bad, is it?' asked Tim. 'I say, Nell; steady on – '

Dora silenced him with a look. 'Has he *asked* you to marry him?' she enquired.

'No, he hasn't. But he will; I'm sure of it!'

'I see. Well, in that case, I shan't say anything until he does.'

Helen left for work still ebullient, still too full of herself to allow her spirits to be dampened by her parents' apparent lack of enthusiasm for her schemes. 'You look much better today,' remarked her boss. 'It's amazing what a good

265

night's sleep will do,' he added, still somewhat mystified by the extraordinary change.

'He looks like you,' said Dora, pouring herself another cup of tea.

'What?' Tim opened the newspaper.

'Oh, for God's sake, Tim!' Dora banged her cup down on her saucer. 'That man! Helen's friend! Oh, I saw it as soon as I met him! He's *you*, thirty odd years ago. *That's* why she likes him!'

'D'you think so?' Tim frowned. 'Darling, aren't you getting a bit – well – Freudian?'

'I don't think I am. You've always been the light of her life. Oh, you said when she was born that she'd grow up to think you were the Lord God Almighty! You said *then* that you'd teach her to look up to you. And you've suc-ceeded – '

'Oh, really, Dora – '

'And now look what's happened. What's he called. Tom, isn't it? It's almost the same name, for heaven's sake!'

'Coincidence.' Tim laughed. 'Oh, darling, you're reading far too much into this!'

'*Oh* no I'm not. Helen loves you – more than that, she adores you, as you know very well. And you're *my* husband. So therefore – '

'Very interesting, Dr Atherton, very interesting. A fascinating theory.' Tim grinned. 'But you're wrong.'

'Am I?' Dora did not smile. 'Well, we'll see.'

'Did *you* like him?' asked Tim.

'Well, as it happens – '

'You did.'

'Mm.' Dora nodded. 'Yes, you're quite right, I did. There was something about him – '

'There you are then.' Tim folded his newspaper. 'He's just a nice bloke, who has a way with the ladies. Nothing more. Now – hadn't we better get moving if those kids are coming today?'

266

Chapter Twenty Two

THE SIRENS HAD GONE LONG ago, but Lucy Hollander was too miserable and too indifferent to her own well-being to go down to the dug-outs with the rest of her company. Alone in the little office which was situated on the ground floor of Dorrington Hall, she continued to fill in the forms which she'd volunteered to spend that evening completing.

No-one would miss her, she decided. And, if they did, they'd assume she'd finished her work and gone out for the evening, as she was entitled to do. Now, as she worked on, she found she was almost hoping that a particular German bomb had her name on it that night.

She'd tried and tried to speak to Stephen, but he wouldn't even acknowledge her presence. Without making a public scene, there was nothing she could do. It would not have done at all to have gone running across the parade ground to catch an officer by the sleeve and demand that he hold a conversation with her.

She knew he was on leave this weekend; he had a forty-eight hour pass. Then, from Monday, he would be at some barracks in London for a month. She suspected that he'd arranged that spell of duty quite deliberately and that he meant to get away from Portsmouth altogether if he could, Blitz or no Blitz. She wouldn't see him for – what was it – thirty-two days at least. Not seeing him at all was almost more distressing than being ignored. And what made everything particularly awful was that somehow Agnes Lyall appeared to have found out what had happened.

In fact, Agnes had merely put two and two together. 'They've fell out, I reckon,' she told Rose. Observing Lucy's red-rimmed eyes and miserable face, she'd drawn the obvious conclusion. 'They've 'ad a bust up.'

'So now's your chance, eh?' Rose Davies grinned. 'Well, kid – so what're you waiting for?'

'You 'ave to pick your time!' Agnes grinned back. 'He can take me to the flicks on Saturday.'

Agnes had sauntered over to Stephen's office that afternoon. She deposited a couple of files upon his desk and grinned at him. 'Have you anything else for me, sir?' she enquired, widening her eyes and positively leering at him.

She was back in her own office a bare two minutes later. 'Well?' demanded Rose, seeing that her friend was flushed. 'What happened?'

'Talk about curdle milk!' replied Agnes. 'God! I tell you, Rose, I thought 'e was going to 'it me!'

'Like that, was it?' Rose sniffed. 'Give up, then, do you?'

'For the time being, yes . . . '

Now Lucy realized that the planes were coming nearer. Let them come, she thought. These days, she wasn't afraid of bombs; for, along with most of the other people in the camp, she was a fatalist. If you were for it, you died, or you were injured, and that was that.

But, as she listened to the crashes and explosions which were now very close to the camp, she suddenly found that she *did* wish to live, after all. Although the idea of dying of a broken heart might be romantic, and although she suspected that if she were to perish in a raid Stephen would be sorry, it now seemed to be worth hanging on to life. She crawled under the desk and sat there. And, for the first time since she'd been a child, she began to pray.

A blast shook the old house. The windows of the room in which Lucy was sheltering blew in, and glass scattered all over the floor. Another bomb exploded, this time causing one of the wooden huts across the parade ground to burst into flames. Lucy heard excited voices shouting to each other and realized that now men were out in the darkness, meaning to tackle the blaze before it spread to the other buildings. Ten minutes, fifteen minutes, went by.

Then, like an angel's trumpet – or so it seemed to Lucy – the all-clear sounded. Relieved beyond measure, she crawled out from under her desk and stood up. She surveyed the damage in the room; told herself that in the dancing firelight it probably looked worse than it was. She decided to go and see what was happening.

In its heyday Dorrington Hall had been a very grand house. Its now shabby rooms were large, high ceilinged and graciously proportioned. When the army had taken it over, however, various jerry-built partitions had been put up, splitting the rooms up into smaller units.

As Lucy walked over towards the door, she did not notice the huge crack which had appeared over the lintel there. Nor did she realize that although the original fabric of the house was sound enough to have resisted the shock of the explosions, this partition wasn't anything like as solid.

As she opened the door, the partition gave way. A mass of wood, plaster and mortar rained down upon her. Half buried under the debris, a pile of masonry crushing her legs, Lucy tried to cry out; but already she was losing consciousness. When, half an hour later, they found her, her eyes were closed and she was cold.

'She was quite badly hurt, you know,' explained Dora, when Stephen telephoned that weekend. 'And it seems she has been asking to see you.'

'Oh?'

'Yes.' Dora frowned. 'Her parents have had her admitted to a nursing home near Dorchester. Steve, I know it's a long way for you to go, but Mrs Hollander did say – '

'I know what happened. She's broken her leg, that's all.' Stephen sighed crossly. 'I can't go all the way to Dorset,' he continued, the irritation in his voice apparent even over

269

a bad telephone line. 'One of her fancy men can visit her. She must be up to at least brigadier by now.'

'What *are* you talking about?' Dora wished she could see her son's face. 'Listen, darling,' she continued firmly. 'This poor girl's mother wrote to me; it's obvious that she's very worried about her daughter. So if Lucy's a friend of yours, I really do think it would be mean of you not to visit her. Steve, it's not like you to be so callous,' she concluded, appealing to his better nature. 'You're usually so considerate, after all.'

There was a kind of grunt from the other end of the line. 'Did Dad tell you I'd got another pip?' asked Stephen, changing the subject.

'Yes, he did; but I read your letters too, you know. Congratulations. What did you do to deserve it?'

'My spelling's improved,' replied Stephen sourly. 'How are your evacuees?' he added, determined to keep off the subject of Lucy Hollander. 'Have they settled in all right?'

'Yes, they're *fine*!' Dora laughed. 'Actually, darling, they're very nice little girls. Always demanding fish and chips, of course; always wanting bread and marge, refusing point blank to eat any fruit or vegetables, and their clothes were nothing but rags – well, I was expecting all that.' She drew breath. 'But, after some of the things I'd heard about East End children, I wasn't sure if these three would even be *human*; so on the whole I'm quite relieved that things have turned out so well.'

The three minute signal went. 'Look after yourself, Mum,' said Stephen, as he replaced the receiver.

'I shall. Goodbye, dear,' said Dora, to nobody.

Stephen folded his arms behind his head and considered what his mother had said. He wondered, sometimes, if he was being unreasonable. Cruel, even. In his more rational moments, he told himself that even if Lucy *hadn't* been a virgin when he'd first made love to her, it wasn't really any concern of his. But he also knew that if he admitted to

270

himself that he loved her – that he'd never stopped loving her – he'd be lost. He'd forgive her anything, even infidelity. Even though he was quite sure that infidelity to him would kill him . . .

He thought back over his month in London. His heart might have been bleeding for Lucy; but that hadn't stopped him from taking in the pleasures of the capital in a way he'd never had the nerve to do during peacetime. He now knew that he was not unattractive to women. Quite the reverse, in fact. And something he'd dreaded and anticipated with equal fear and longing had proved to be nothing very extra-ordinary after all.

He'd imagined that on the whole women disliked sexual congress. He couldn't have been more wrong. He had now discovered that girls enjoyed sex just as much as he did. They actually wanted him to screw them – he'd hardly had to ask, let alone persuade. In spite of the Blitz, he and a couple of other junior officers had had a splendid time in those clubs which were still open, and in the bars and cafés where young servicemen were welcomed with open arms and patriotic submission.

'If you could spare me just a moment, Stephen?' His immediate superior stood over him, looking quizzically at his junior. 'Come back to earth, there's a good fellow.'

'Sorry, sir.' Stephen reddened. 'I was thinking about something,' he explained.

'Evidently.' Leaving a pile of work behind him, Captain Roberts went over to the door. 'Buck up, now, Steve. I want that lot back by teatime.'

Stephen opened a folder and got on with some work. Brenda Gage, he thought, as he filled in a long report. Brenda Gage, that busty girl who worked for Captain Grange – she'd do. And there were another couple of girls he quite fancied – one blonde, one brunette, they both had that kind of look about them, they'd probably like to go to the pictures, or something . . .

Over the succeeding weeks, Stephen cut a determined swathe through the clerks, typists and secretaries of Dorrington Camp, spending more than he could afford and

271

earning himself something of a reputation. And, finally, it was Agnes Lyall's turn.

'You don't mean to say you've done it at last?' demanded Rose Davies sarcastically, as she watched Agnes painting her face and frowning at herself in the mirror. 'You don't mean to tell me you've actually got 'im cornered?'

'Shut up, you.' Agnes turned her skirt over at the waistband, revealing dimpled knees. 'Haven't got any decent lipstick, have you?' she demanded. 'This one cakes.'

'Here.' Rose passed hers over. 'So where you goin', then?'

'He said a pub. Then – I don't know.' Agnes applied lipstick, smudged it. 'Oh, *fucking* hell!' she cried, as she looked at the resultant mess. 'Where's me hanky?'

'I think you're scared.' Rose giggled. 'God, Ag, you've spent months and months working yourself up to this – an' now he's actually asked you out, you're scared!'

'No, I'm not.'

'Why you all shaky, then?'

'I – oh, shut up, Rose, will you?'

'Will you let him – you know?'

'Depends.' Agnes grimaced. 'He had Nora Wheeler, that's for certain. Don't know if I want her leavings . . . '

Stephen kissed Agnes with some fervour, patted her bosom experimentally; then got up and went over to the bar. He bought another couple of drinks, and, somewhat unsteadily, he made his way back to the table in the dark, nicely private corner where he'd left her. 'Here,' he said, offering her a gin and orange. 'Drink up.'

Agnes sipped the drink. Stephen sat down beside her, put his hand on her skirt and pinched her rather fat thigh. He had decided to get drunk, then to take Agnes back to the barracks and have her in the shrubbery behind the old house. From the way she was grinning and leering at him he didn't think she'd find the idea unattractive, and the nights *were* warmer now. Comforts for the troops, officers' groundsheets - he'd heard ATS girls so called, and thought it insulting to say the least. Now he knew the sobriquets were, in some cases anyway, well deserved.

Agnes watched Stephen tip back his fifth, or was it his sixth, whisky. She could see that her companion was now three quarters drunk, and soon she was taking liberties she'd never have dared to do if he had been sober. 'I remember when we first knew you,' she said, giggling into her glass. 'You wouldn't say boo! And now - well, you're the talk of the camp!'

'Am I?' Stephen grinned at her. 'I'm hoping to get a medal for it, you know,' he remarked. 'I'm hoping to be decorated one day - '

'Perhaps you will be.' Agnes sniggered. 'Ooh,' she squealed, as Stephen slid his hand under her skirt and then beneath her stocking top. 'Ooh, sir, careful now!'

'Don't you like it?'

'It's not that.' Agnes regarded him primly. 'But somebody might see!'

Too befuddled to care very much what anyone saw, Stephen shrugged. 'We could go somewhere more private,' he suggested. 'Then we could take things a little further, maybe.'

'You think I'm that sort of girl, do you?'

'Aren't you?'

Agnes looked at him. His narrow dark eyes were glittering, he was flushed, and she found him very attractive - in fact, almost irresistibly attractive. But he looked dangerous, as well. 'You wouldn't make a girl do something she didn't want to, would you?' she asked, in a small, almost frightened whisper. 'You wouldn't expect me to - '

Stephen leaned over and kissed her, opening her mouth with his. 'What don't you want to do?' he asked.

'I'm not a tart, you know.'

'I never said you were.' Stephen looked into her eyes. 'All the same, if two people like each other - '

'I expect a man to be careful.'

'I'm very careful.' Stephen kissed her again, licking off

273

the last of Rose's lipstick. 'There won't be any unpleasant consequences, I can promise you that. But, of course,' he added, tickling the inside of her thigh, 'if you don't want to – '

Agnes was tempted. Already she could feel perspiration trickling down the back of her shirt, already her stomach was fluttering expectantly. She looked at Stephen's sulky face and, more than anything, she wanted to see him smile at her again. 'All right,' she said, her voice slightly unsteady. 'Let me finish my drink, and we'll go.'

'Hurry up, then.' Stephen pushed his hands into his pockets and stared up at the smoky ceiling. 'Don't take all night.'

Agnes began to enjoy the sensation of keeping an officer waiting. She was determined not to let this bossy young man have it all his own way. Suddenly filled with an irresistible desire to tease him, she looked at him over the rim of her glass. 'Am I your third conquest this year?' she asked archly. 'Or your fourth?'

'How d'you mean?' asked Stephen.

'Well – first of all there was little Ellen Dyer; she was head over heels. And then there was Nora Wheeler, she's been telling everyone that you're her bloke now.' Agnes giggled. 'I had an idea you were sweet on little Lucy Hollander at one time.'

'Lucy?' Stephen grinned. 'Oh, nothing doing there. Miss Lucy Hollander only takes off her drawers for colonels and above.'

'What?' Surprised that Stephen could be so crude, Agnes choked on her gin. 'That's a good one,' she cackled, as she recovered. 'Colonels, indeed! Lucy's a professional virgin! Everybody in the camp knows that!'

'She's a tart, you mean.' Stephen spoke with a vehemence which made his companion stare. 'A common little tart, that's all *she* is.'

'She isn't!' Agnes shook her head. 'Oh, Christ Almighty, that girl's so bloody green she wouldn't know *how*!'

'She fucking well would!' Now Stephen banged his fist

274

down on the table, making the glasses upon it rattle. Other drinkers turned to stare; and he glared at them until they looked away again. But then, suddenly, he buried his face in his hands. 'She betrayed me, Agnes,' he moaned. 'Oh, Agnes, she betrayed me!'

'What the blazes are you talking about?' Agnes looked at Stephen, and saw that he was shaking violently, uncontrollably. His shoulders heaved, he might even have been sobbing, and he was obviously blind drunk. 'Look, sir,' she said gently, 'you're not well. Don't you think you'd better go home?'

'No, I don't.' Stephen knew he was maudlin; but now he wanted to talk, couldn't stop himself. 'I loved that girl,' he cried, gazing at Agnes piteously. 'I loved her! And she betrayed me!'

'Eh?' Agnes gaped at him. Absolutely astonished, she was momentarily dumbstruck. But she could see that he wasn't having her on; and in fact, she doubted now if he was as drunk as she'd thought. Plainly, the idiot believed what he'd just told her, sincerely believed that Lucy Hollander was a slut. 'You're talking rubbish,' she said at last.

'I'm not!'

'Stephen, you *are*!' Agnes shook his shoulder. 'Listen to me,' she rapped. 'Lucy Hollander, stuck up bitch though she is, isn't the sort to let a man do just as he likes with her. She's the kind of girl who's been brought up to believe that you *don't* mess about with men, that when you get married you must be *entitled* to wear white! Do you understand me? She'd never screw around, and you must be out of your mind if you think she does!'

'But Agnes, she goes out with men! She told me so! And she – '

'She goes to the pictures with boring old sergeants, she has tea with married corporals, she lets them hold her little hand while she looks at their photographs of their wives and kids! She kisses them goodbye, she tells them to go off and do their best for king and country; to be brave little soldiers! Chin up and not to cry! She *mothers* them, for

God's sake! That's all *she* ever does!'

'Is it?'

'Yes!' Agnes Lyall was suddenly stone cold sober. 'Lucy's not a whore, Stephen,' she said. 'I'll spell it out for you, shall I? She's not like me and all the rest of the women you've had up against the barrack wall on a Friday night!'

'Oh.'

'Is that all you can say?' Stephen's companion glowered at him. 'That explains everything,' she muttered. 'That explains why you've been working your way through the clerks like some overheated billy goat, why you've been screwing everything you can grab as it passes you by!' She looked at him with utter distaste. 'Oh, God! *Men!*'

Suddenly, Stephen retched. He managed, with difficulty, to swallow the vomit again; but he now felt absolutely sick with alcohol. And with guilt. With blinding clarity he realized that Agnes wasn't, couldn't be lying; that this wasn't a case of one woman covering up for another.

He looked at the girl beside him. 'I told her I didn't want to see her again,' he whispered. Passing his hand across his eyes, he blinked at Agnes quite pathetically. 'What shall I do?' he asked her. 'Oh, Agnes, what on earth shall I do?'

'Bloody obvious, isn't it?' Agnes scowled at him. 'On your next leave, you get over to that hospital and tell her you got it all wrong.'

'Right.' Stephen reached for his coat. 'Right. I shall.'

'Good.' Agnes swallowed the last of her drink. 'Here, where are you going?' she demanded, as Stephen fastened his buttons.

'To do what you said!' Standing unsteadily, balancing himself against the table, Stephen jammed his hat on his head. 'I'll go now. I can get a lift into town – I'll be there by morning!'

'The redcaps'll catch you!' Agnes grabbed his wrist. 'Stephen, you'll be in real trouble if you just clear off like this! Look, wait until you're sober, eh? At least wait until morning?'

'I'm going *now*,' he replied. Jerking away from Agnes, Stephen made his way out of the bar.

He travelled all night, hitching lifts, walking and finishing his journey on a goods train. He had a shave in a barber's shop in town, then took a taxi to the hospital, which was a mile outside Dorchester.

'It's not really visiting time, you know,' remarked the starched ward sister who looked Stephen up and down and obviously found him wanting. 'Couldn't you come back this afternoon?'

'I have to be back in barracks by six this evening,' he replied – which was true enough. 'Sister, please may I see Miss Hollander? Just for a minute or two?'

The sister pursed her lips and frowned; but then she relented. 'Very well,' she said. 'Wait here until someone comes for you.' And she disappeared into the depths of the building.

'Will you come this way, sir?' A ward orderly smiled at Stephen. 'You can't go into the wards at this time of day, you see,' she explained, as she led him down a long, twisting corridor. 'But you can talk to Miss Hollander in the day-room.'

She opened a door. 'Ten minutes,' she said. 'No more.'

Lucy was sitting in a wheelchair. Wrapped in a dressing gown and blankets, she was staring out of the window and did not greet her visitor. Stephen picked up a chair, placed it next to her and sat down. 'Lucy?' he asked softly. 'Lucy, won't you look at me?'

'Why should I?' she muttered. Folding her arms, she frowned down at her knees. 'Why are you here?' she asked.

'Your mother wrote to mine. She said that when you were feverish you asked for me. So I've come.'

'You took your time about it.' Still Lucy scowled. 'Well, I don't want to see you now, so you can just go away again.'

'No, I can't do that.' Tentatively, Stephen laid his hand on her arm. 'Lucy, don't get angry,' he pleaded. 'The nurse is outside. She'll send me away if you excite yourself.'

'Good.' Lucy looked at him now, her eyes bright. 'I'll scream, then, shall I? Throw a fit? Oh, for God's sake, go *away*!'

'Lucy, please – '

'Shut up!' She glared at him. 'I mean it! I'll raise the roof!' She opened her mouth wide . . .

Stephen got up. He walked out of the day-room into the corridor. Lucy heard his footsteps on the linoleum, and now she wished she hadn't been quite so harsh. She almost wanted to call him back . . .

Stephen went into the sister's office and smiled at her. 'It's a lovely morning,' he said. 'Do you think I might take Miss Hollander for a walk along the terrace?'

The sister considered. She glanced up at this nice-looking young officer; and, suddenly, she smiled. 'You wish to discuss something private, is that it?' she asked.

'That's right.'

'Oh, very well.' The sister nodded. 'Once along the terrace and back again. Five minutes only. Is that clear?'

'I thought you'd gone.' Lucy stared at him. 'In fact, I heard the door slam – '

'You were imagining things.' Stephen grinned at her. 'Come on, we're going for a walk.'

'Oh, don't be so stupid!' Lucy looked away. 'Sister Hobson – '

'I've spoken to Sister Hobson. She said I could take you along the terrace and back.' Stephen looked at Lucy, willing her to meet his eyes. 'Please, darling?' he asked humbly. 'Darling Lucy, please?'

'Oh, very well.' Lucy shrugged. 'If it's the only way to get rid of you.'

She couldn't imagine why he'd come or why he was so conciliatory. She was not going to forgive him, of that she was quite certain. He'd abused and insulted her. And over the past few weeks he'd shown that he was nothing but a philanderer after all. Agnes had written to cheer the invalid and had told Lucy all about Stephen's recent escapades . . .

Lucy had been shocked. Puritanical at heart, she had not found Agnes's revelations at all amusing. Having patched and bandaged her heart as well as she could, Lucy was now determined that she wasn't going to let any man, certainly not this one, break it again . . .

Stephen pushed the chair to the end of the terrace and sat down on the edge of a large stone urn. 'I'm sorry, Lucy,' he said. 'Very, very sorry.'

Lucy said nothing. She stared straight ahead of her; for, having by now successfully hardened her heart against him, she was wishing he'd go.

'It was a misunderstanding,' he added feebly.

'Misunderstanding!' This was too much. Lucy turned and glared at him. 'Is that what you call it?' she cried. Clenching her fists, she wanted to hit him. 'Have you forgotten what you called me?' she demanded.

'No. But Lucy – '

'*Have you?*'

'No.'

'Good. Well, it may interest you to know that Agnes has written to me. I know what you've been getting up to since I've been away. You're the talk of the camp! That's what you are!'

Stephen grimaced. 'Agnes does have a tendency to exaggerate,' he mumbled. 'Lucy, you know that.'

'So you deny that you've been having an affair with Nora Wheeler, you deny that you've taken God knows how many other girls out? It isn't true that you and Brenda Gage – '

'I – '

'I don't want to listen to excuses.' Lucy folded her arms. 'Go away,' she snapped. 'Just go away.'

Stephen wanted to cry. He was perfectly aware that he had no defence of any kind. After all, the plea that he had used other women merely to assuage his misery was hardly likely to endear him to another member of the female sex. 'You can't hate me more than I hate myself,' he began, trying again. 'Lucy, I know you can't forgive me yet, though if you – '

279

'Go *away*!'

'I shall, in a minute. But Lucy, before I do, you must understand something. I want you to know that in spite of everything I never stopped loving you. I love you still. And from now on I'll always be in torment, because of what I've done to you. Lucy, I – '

He found he couldn't say any more. He sat there in front of her, his face ashen, tears in his eyes. And, as Lucy watched, the tears spilled over. Running down his cheeks, they trickled past his chin and splashed on to his uniform jacket.

Lucy had never in her life seen a man cry. Now, the sight of it horrified her. She wished he'd make some effort to hide his emotion. For goodness' sake, it wasn't decent to be sitting there in broad daylight, weeping like a child. 'Haven't you got a handkerchief?' she asked, embarrassed for him.

He didn't answer. Instead he went on sobbing, his head bowed and his tears dyeing his tunic a deeper brown.

'Stephen, *stop* it!' Looking around her, terrified lest one of the nursing staff should come upon this ghastly scene, Lucy pulled out her own handkerchief and began to dab at his face. 'Stephen! For heaven's sake!'

He pushed her hand away. Leaning forwards, he buried his face in her lap. His shoulders still heaving with sobs, he wrapped his arms around her waist and held her.

The familiar feel of him softened her. Looking at the back of his neck she saw how the hair grew in a wavy pattern at the base of his skull, and she remembered that she'd kissed him there as he lay on his stomach in that awful bed in that equally awful so-called hotel. Unable to help herself, she leaned forward and kissed him there again. 'Don't cry, my love,' she said soothingly, stroking his dry black hair, hair which was more like an animal's fur than human tresses. 'Don't cry.'

He looked up at her. His face streaked and blotched, his eyes bloodshot, he was a truly horrible sight. 'You called me love,' he said. 'Oh, Lucy, could you love me again?'

'Love you?' Lucy shook her head. 'I didn't think so. But now I don't know. Honestly, I don't!'

'Because of what Agnes told you?'

'No – not because of that.'

'What, then?'

'Because you thought so badly of me, of course! How *could* you think I'd have behaved like that?'

'Well, you shouldn't have teased me.'

'So it's all my fault?'

'No, Lucy, it's not your fault. I lost my temper, I was very stupid.' Stephen raised himself and balanced one elbow on the armrest of Lucy's chair. 'Do you think that one day you might forgive me?'

'Don't be so silly. You know I've already done that.'

'What did you say?'

'You heard me.' Lucy shook her head at him. 'You know it's not possible for me to hate you!'

'Isn't it?' As if a tap had been turned off, Stephen's sobs abated. 'Then, Lucy, will you marry me?' he asked.

'What?' Lucy stared. 'Oh, don't be ridiculous.'

'I'm not being ridiculous! I mean it! Lucy, please? Will you be my wife?'

Lucy looked away and pursed her lips. 'I may do,' she said indifferently. Secretly delighted, she didn't smile. Surely he didn't expect her to be ready to accept him just like that, to agree just as if nothing unpleasant had happened? 'I'll think about it,' she told him. 'And let you know.'

'Lucy, don't tease! Yes, or no?'

'I'll tease you all I wish! I'm entitled to that, at least! Come and see me during your next leave, and I'll give you my answer. Come to think of it, Stephen, why are you here today?'

'I'm AWOL. I'll really be in the shit when I get back to barracks.' Weakly, Stephen grinned. 'I'll write to you every day,' he promised, rising to his feet. 'Oh, darling, I love you!'

The matron had come up behind them as they talked and now she was looking severely at Stephen. He hadn't upset her patient, but, goodness, he was in a state himself! 'I think, Lieutenant Atherton – ' she began.

'I'm on my way.' Leaning towards Lucy, Stephen kissed her. Then, standing up, he smiled at the matron. 'Goodbye, ladies,' he said.

And he marched off down the terrace, his easy stride, the slight but characteristic swagger which demonstrates that Guards officers think themselves only slightly lower than gods, making it plain that the young subaltern was feeling very much better than he had a few moments ago . . .

'Your friend seems a very emotional young gentleman,' observed the matron acidly. 'Miss Hollander, I hope he didn't upset you?'

'Not at all, Matron.' Lucy smiled; she liked the matron. 'In fact, he asked me to marry him.'

'Hm.' Ironically, the matron smiled back. 'Must I congratulate you?'

'No, not yet.' Lucy laughed. 'I said I'd think about it, you see.'

'Did you, indeed.' The matron began to push her patient back towards the day-room. 'Ah well, Miss Hollander, if I were you I'd take my time.'

'I shall.' Lucy leaned back and folded her arms. 'Yes, I shall take all the time I please.'

Chapter Twenty Three

IT WAS VERY ODD, BUT Tom's and Helen's affair now seemed to be going nowhere. True, she saw him as often as she ever had, she took him home for meals, she was in his company for whole days together at weekends. He came to know her parents well, and they appeared to like him. But his relationship with Helen was static.

In the end it was Helen herself who suggested marriage. 'Well, there's no reason why we shouldn't,' she told him, as she expounded the idea. 'Tom, wouldn't it be nice to be a properly married couple?' Bending down to pick a few spring flowers, she looked up and smiled at him.

To her surprise and chagrin, Tom thought she was joking. He laughed at the idea. Then, understanding that she was serious, he shook his head. 'You don't want to marry me, love,' he said, ruffling her hair. 'You don't want to tie yourself to *me*!'

He walked away across the lawn. Helen jumped up and followed him. 'Why not?' she demanded, tugging at his sleeve. 'Why on earth not?'

'I'm a lot older than you, and I've no money, no home. That's why not!' He detached Helen's hand from his sleeve. 'Oh, Christ, Helen – I'm not the sort of man your parents want for a son-in-law! And whatever would your uncle the professor say? Your uncle the baronet, or your brother the Guards officer?'

'They'd all be very happy for me, Tom. They'd be

pleased that I'd married the man I loved, whatever or whoever he was!'

'I doubt that! And anyway, I can't get married. I've
nothing to live on, I can't support a wife.'

'My father would help – '

'No, he wouldn't. I'd not take *his* money.' Suddenly, Tom
looked annoyed. 'So don't you think any more about it!'

'Hm.' Helen looked at him sideways. 'I'm good enough
to screw, but not good enough to marry.' She scowled at
him. 'Is that it?'

'*What* did you say?'

Helen scuffed the grass. 'You heard me.'

Tom glared at her. 'Don't you *dare* use language like that
to me!' he cried. For the first time since she'd known him,
he looked really angry. 'I can't stand women who talk like
that,' he muttered under his breath.

'Women who swear? Women who use slang?'

'Women who are foul-mouthed.' He narrowed his eyes
at her. 'I'll forget you said that.'

'Very generous of you.' Now Helen was angry too, had
almost forgotten that she'd been trying to interest him in
marriage. 'Mum was asking if you'd like to stay to dinner
this evening,' she added coldly. 'Though, in the circumstances – '

'That's kind of her. Yes, I would.'

'Really?'

'Yes!' Tom smiled now. 'Shall we take those kids to the
park for an hour?' he asked, proffering an olive branch.

'If you like.' Helen sniffed; then decided to accept it.
'Yes, that's a good idea. I'll fetch them, shall I?'

'Good girl.' Tom caught Helen's hand as she walked
past him. 'Sorry, love. Sorry I snapped at you.'

'That's all right.' Helen shrugged. 'Don't think anything of it.'

She went into the house and rounded up Dora's three
evacuees. Frannie, Dot and Peggy, learning that they were
going out with Tom, were glad to fall in with Helen's
plans.

Twins of eight and an elder sister of nine, these children

284

were self-opinionated little madams who had apparently decided that living in a big house in Oxford was a great lark. They had taken to Mrs Afferton, as they called Dora, straight away; and she was having none of the problems with them which some other Oxford women were experiencing with *their* not especially welcome guests.

'You're very good with them,' remarked Helen as she watched the children charging across the grass back towards Tom, who had outrun them. 'You ought to have children of your own.'

'Ah.' Tom looked at Helen. 'Now, don't start that again.'

Good with children or not, Tom had certainly found his way into the hearts of this particular trio, who treated him with an affectionate familiarity with which they did not favour the Athertons. 'Cheat!' Frannie, panting towards him, threw herself against his legs. 'Bloody cheat! You should've started last!'

'Language, miss!' Tom picked her up. 'Little lasses don't talk like that,' he told her, giving her a squeeze. 'Say you're sorry for cussing, an' I'll give you some sweets.'

'Bet you ain't got none!' Flirtatiously, Frannie grinned at him. 'Gimme the sweets first, an' then I'll say sorry.'

'Not likely. I know you!' Tom put her down and turned away from her. Seeing her sisters approaching, he crouched down and produced two sticks of liquorice from his jacket pocket. 'Here, one each. An' now I think it's time we were goin' home.'

While her sisters chewed, Frannie pretended to be unconcerned. She trailed after the rest of the group, regarding Tom from under her long eyelashes. Now and again she gave a loud, injured sniff.

'Ain't you got none, Fran?' Dot looked at her sister. 'Want a bite off the end of mine?'

Frannie tossed her head. 'Don't like that muck,' she replied haughtily.

'Don't you?' Peggy, the most tender hearted of the three, could hardly believe that. She twisted the end off the stick and offered it to her sister. 'S'nice. Try it.'

285

Shaking her head, Frannie pushed past Peggy and caught up with Helen and Tom. Grabbing at Tom's cuff, she looked up at him. 'Sorry I cussed,' she muttered, her little face scarlet. 'Sorry, Tom.'

'That's all right, sweetheart.' Tom took another piece of liquorice out of his pocket. 'There's yours.'

Frannie grabbed the sweet and ran back to her sisters. Delighted, she showed them what she'd got, loudly asserting that he'd given her the biggest bit.

'You have a way with women,' remarked Helen, as she watched the children running across the grass towards the park gate. 'Those three think you're the Lord God Almighty.'

'There's no need to be sarcastic, love.'

'I wasn't.' Helen regarded him coldly. 'It's the simple truth, isn't it?'

Helen was still annoyed with Tom when, later that evening, they sat in his room in East Oxford. Talking degenerated into arguing. Finally it all came to a head in one of those futile quarrels about nothing, and in the end neither of them knew what they were squabbling about. 'You're *always* criticizing,' cried Helen, lolling on the bed and punching the pillows. 'My clothes, my hair, my behaviour; nothing's ever right for you these days!'

'I only said that I preferred you in skirts instead of slacks. And that you look prettier with your hair loose.' Tom folded his arms and scowled at her. 'For God's sake, Helen, I'd have thought most women would be *pleased* to be told their legs were too nice to hide away!'

'And my hair? I ought to have that all hanging down my back, ought I? Like some bloody Rapunzel?'

'Stop swearing, you're only doing it to annoy me.'

'I'll swear if I please. What's it got to do with you?'

'Oh, Jesus, give it a rest!' Tom got up from his chair and walked over to the bed. He crouched down beside Helen and touched her face. 'What's the matter, love?' he asked kindly. 'You've been scratchy all day.'

286

'And you've been horrible all day.'

'I didn't mean to be.' Tom kissed her. 'Look, I'm sorry. Shall we go and have a drink, then I'll take you home?'

'I'd rather we stayed here. Tom, don't be mean to me!'

'I don't intend to be.'

'Shall we go to bed?' Helen loosened his tie and kissed his cheek.

Tom considered. 'All right,' he said, without any obvious enthusiasm. 'If you like.'

'Only if you want to. You don't have to, Tom. Not if you don't want to – '

'I said, all right! For God's sake, Helen, don't start all over again!'

'When's your medical?' asked Helen, half an hour later. 'When did the letter say?'

'Last week of April.'

'D'you think you'll be downgraded?'

'I reckon so. But I imagine I'll probably be kept on, all the same. They'll send me to a training battalion, I expect.' Tom grimaced. 'God, I hope they do,' he muttered. 'Can't stand much more of civvy street!'

After a couple of weeks in barracks a twenty-four hour pass seemed like a promise of unlimited freedom, and Stephen decided to go up to London for the day. He telephoned a friend stationed at Kensington Barracks and arranged to meet him for lunch. Jack Farley knew a place where they still used fresh eggs and where there was still a decent wine list. 'See you about twelve,' he said. 'I'll have to be back in barracks by three, but we can have a bit of a natter, eh?'

They had their natter, and, over a very good lunch, the two young officers finished a couple of bottles of what Jack said wasn't a bad Burgundy. They chased this down with coffee and then Jack produced another bottle to lace Stephen's second cup of rather bitter chicory extract. 'Drink up, old chap.' Jack grinned at his friend. 'Might as well finish it off.'

'Where d'you get that stuff?' Stephen looked at the label. 'My Dad wouldn't mind a bottle or two.'

'Fellow near Charing Cross can arrange a deal.' Jack tipped back a mouthful of almost neat spirit. 'I'll give you the address. It'll cost you though.'

'That's all right.' Stephen grinned. 'It's the old fellow's birthday next week.'

Stephen felt slightly unsteady as he walked out into the May sunshine. Since he still had a few hours to kill before catching the train back to Portsmouth, he decided to clear his head by going for a wander around the West End.

He was sure that it was Lucy. Even though, on one level, he knew it couldn't *possibly* have been, he was nevertheless certain it was her. An ATS private, a dark-haired girl swinging her gasmask on its strap, she was walking along Oxford Street towards Tottenham Court Road, twenty paces or so ahead of him.

The whisky Jack had given him at lunchtime had induced a slight headache, and Stephen was now feeling more than a little sleepy. He shook his head to try to clear it, and fixed his eyes on the girl ahead of him. He let his mind play on the pleasant fantasy that he'd catch her up in a minute or two, then he'd give her a kiss. Yes, it was rather nice to see a girl who resembled his beloved so closely, whom he could stare at as he daydreamed about Lucy herself . . .

He made his way along the busy street, intending to turn into the Charing Cross Road. He had a vague intention of ferreting out this fellow Jack had mentioned and seeing if he could get a bottle of malt for his father's birthday.

The sirens started to wail as he was almost at the station. Together with the rest of the people in the street Stephen automatically made for the Underground, and with hundreds of others he went down the steps into the warm, smelly mouth of the Tube. He saw Lucy's double several yards ahead of him, and felt relieved that she was safely inside.

The raid was a terrific one. The walls of the tunnel shook. Bits of masonry fell from the ceiling, children cried in terror, and even the most blasé of the adults were white-faced with fear.

Then it happened. A direct hit. Part of the wall at the eastern end of the platform seemed to explode outwards, hang suspended in the air for a moment and then crumble, collapsing with the most deafening of roars.

Thick smoke, together with blinding sheets of dust, contrived to add to the horror. Something hit Stephen on the side of the head, making him cry out in pain. And, by the time he opened his eyes again and could see properly, the sirens were sounding the all-clear.

He supposed he could only have lain unconscious for about five minutes or so, because the station was now chaotic. Looking around him, he saw bodies; and he realized that the damp patch on his sleeve must be someone's blood. Blearily, he gazed around him, still too dazed to think clearly. Unsteadily, he got to his feet.

And then he saw her. He could have picked her out of a million girls; her dark hair and pale face were quite distinctive. Half buried under some rubble, she was in that part of the station which was already cordoned off. He began to pick his way along the platform towards her.

'Come back, you!' An air raid warden grabbed at his arm. 'You can't go any further. Got to wait for the Heavy Rescue now!'

Stephen shook the man off, and went on.

'Somebody stop that stupid bugger!' The ARP man, trying to do twenty things at once, gesticulated towards Stephen. 'Come back here, sod you!' he shouted.

Stephen took no notice.

He clambered over the piles of bricks and rubble, carefully making his way towards the girl. His head was throbbing painfully and he felt sick and dizzy. As he moved he kept blinking. He couldn't focus properly, and he couldn't rid his mind of the idea that this was really some macabre dream. But, all the same, he kept going.

Inching his way, more gingerly now, he pushed aside

289

some lumps of brick. He stepped over a couple of concrete blocks and then skirted a pile of rubble perilously balanced on a framework of timber laths. He reached his objective.

He saw at once that she was very badly hurt. And, for a moment, he was surprised to find that she wasn't Lucy - she wasn't even in ATS uniform. She was simply a dark haired young woman - unconscious, her left arm a smashed and bloody mess, and her forehead bleeding profusely from a very deep gash. Lifting a beam which had fallen across her legs, he picked her up and stared at her face, unable to decide whether he knew her or not. Then, blinking, he realized that she was a total stranger. Her face was quite different from that of his beloved. Her body felt strange. Thin and very light, she lacked Lucy's solidity, this malnourished Cockney girl . . .

There was a rumbling just then, it was as if a train was coming into the station. 'GET OUT OF THE BLEED-ING WAY!' Even as the warning was shouted, Stephen scrambled clear. And, as he reached the platform, the rest of the wall collapsed. Another cloud of dust hid everything.

He laid the woman's body down and sat down himself. He couldn't stop shaking. Then he realized that someone was talking to him. Not swearing now, the ARP man was patting his shoulder. 'This young chap 'ere,' he was saying, 'he pulled her out. He should get a medal for that; proper 'ero he was. She your Missus, mate?'

The ashen-faced clerk at his side nodded. He bent down to look at his wife, adjusting the blankets which had been wrapped around her. Then he glanced at Stephen. 'You've cut your face bad,' he observed. 'S'bleedin' all down your jacket.'

'Is it?' Stephen wanted a drink, but he knew that if he tried to swallow anything he'd be sick. He dabbed at the blood on his sleeve.

'Thank you for fetching her out.' The clerk squatted beside the officer. 'D'you want a cup of tea?'

'No.' Although he was very thirsty, Stephen shook his head.

He was thinking of Lucy. If that woman, lying insensible

290

on the cold floor of the tube station, had been Lucy! Lucy had lain for half an hour in the rubble of Dorrington Hall and it had been by pure chance that she'd come out of it all with a mere broken leg and some bruises. Stephen leaned forwards and buried his face in his hands.

The ambulance men came; the clerk asked for Stephen's name and address; but Stephen pretended not to have heard him. And so, the clerk was obliged to go to the hospital ignorant of the identity of his wife's saviour . . .

Stephen hadn't thought of David for months. But now, as he sat in the train going back to Portsmouth, he could hear his cousin's voice. 'You'll get the opportunity to earn a bit of tin,' he'd said, that horrible sardonic smile playing across his face. 'You'll be a hero some day.'

The train picked up speed.

'Shut up, Dave!' Stephen ground his teeth and tried to blank out that mocking grin. 'Shut up, shut up, shut up!'

Chapter Twenty Four

STEPHEN RESIGNED HIMSELF TO PORTSMOUTH. He had by now decided that he would be stuck in the place for all eternity. He tried, very hard, to be content . . .

That September he arranged a week's leave, and he informed Lucy that he would take her to Scotland for a holiday. 'I'll borrow Dad's car,' he told her. 'We'll go to a hotel somewhere; we'll have a great time, you'll see.'

'Where will you get the petrol for this jaunt?' At first, Lucy thought the whole idea absurd. 'And we're not married, so won't the hotel – '

'I'll get the petrol somehow. And as for the hotel, that's simple, I shall book us in as Mr and Mrs Atherton. Lucy, don't make difficulties!'

Lucy shook her head. She was now able to walk again but still tired very easily. 'Mummy won't be at all keen. And – '

'I'll square Mummy.'

'She'll take one look at you and put her foot down straight away.' Lucy giggled. 'Oh, darling, the whole thing's ridiculous.'

'Won't you come?'

'It's not that. But Daddy did say he'd take us all to Aberystwyth – '

'He and Mummy can go together. You come with me.' Stephen stood up. 'Are they fetching you on Friday?'

'Yes.'

'Right. I'll come over on Sunday, and meet them.'

'You really think they'll let you whisk me away like that?'

'I shall charm Mummy. I shall dazzle Daddy. You'll see.'

And he had. Stephen's performance was so remarkable that Lucy herself was impressed. 'What a very nice young man,' said Mrs Hollander, after Stephen had departed with permission to carry off her daughter readily given. 'I'm sure you'll be in very good hands there. And his sister sounds a charming girl.'

Lucy nodded. Stephen had made much of the fact that Helen was to be of the party, and she wondered how he was going to explain her absence if Mr and Mrs Hollander should decide to meet up with them in Scotland . . .

A week later Lucy was delivered back to her home in Surrey suntanned and obviously in excellent spirits. Those few days spent in a hotel by the side of a loch, being fussed over by the proprietor who congratulated the newlyweds on bringing such splendid weather with them, had done more for Lucy than a whole summer in an expensive nursing home had.

'Your Mama thinks I'm wonderful,' said Stephen complacently, watching Mrs Hollander walk back into the house from the sunny garden.

'So do I.' Confident that neither of her parents were looking, Lucy kissed her lover on the lips. 'Stephen, thank you for a marvellous holiday.'

'My pleasure.'

'Will you come and see me again?'

'As often as I can.'

'I'm afraid Mummy's going to be all over you now.'

'I think I can cope.' Laughing, Stephen took Lucy in his arms. 'Do you think she knows about us?'

'No, of course not. She's decided that you're a perfect gentleman, so therefore – '

'Jesus. And I thought *my* mother was naive.'

293

'Mm. Poor souls, in their day things must have been so prim and proper. And dull!'

'Mm.' Stephen shook his head. 'Don't you believe it, Lucy. I'll tell you my family's history some day. It'll make you gasp and stretch your eyes!'

'Your family tree is a tangled mess of roots and shoots, is it? You come from a long line of adulterers, philanderers and kept women, I suppose?'

'As it happens, I do.' Stephen grinned at her. 'I'll tell you all about it after we're married.'

'I already know all about *it*.' Lucy grinned back. 'Stephen, I – '

'Don't be so vulgar, darling. Remember you're supposed to be a lady.'

'Oh, is *that* what you like about me? The fact that I'm so refined?'

'Refined? *You*?' Stephen thought back to the first night they'd spent together, their reunion after so many months' abstinence. 'My God, Lucy, you're the original Mata Hari! I bet Lola Montez had nothing on you!'

'Oh, thanks a lot.'

'That's okay.' Stephen slid his hands inside her blouse. 'Give me a kiss.'

'Why?'

'I want one, that's why.' His hands warm on her bare back, Stephen bit Lucy's ear. 'Come on, co-operate. Or I'll tear off all your clothes and ravish you, right here in your mother's shrubbery.'

'You're all talk.' Laughing at him, Lucy kissed him on the mouth. 'There. Satisfied?'

'Absolutely not.'

'Too bad.' Disengaging herself from Stephen's embrace, Lucy began to move towards the house. 'Come along, we'd better go in to tea.'

Lucy's injuries, which had included a complicated fracture of her shin and damage to her kneecap, took a long time to heal completely. It was the November of 1941 before she

294

was fit enough to return to Portsmouth. And in January 1942 she was told she would shortly be transferred to a training camp in the Midlands, to a place where raw recruits were turned into something resembling soldiers, and where she was to be a documentation clerk. A bare six weeks after she'd returned to Portsmouth, she was at the railway station, waiting for the train which would take her to Shrewsbury.

Stephen, recently promoted to captain and given Fred Andrews' job, assumed that *he* was as firmly entrenched in Portsmouth as ever. Gloomily he took Lucy to the station and saw her on to the train. 'You won't forget me, will you?' she asked, knowing the answer.

He looked at her and shook his head. 'There's no chance of that. Oh, Lucy, I was thinking that at last we'd have some time together! But I'll see less of you now than I did when you were convalescing!'

'I'll break the other leg, then, shall I?' Lucy kissed him. 'Stephen, do cheer up! I'll write every day! And,' she added, unable to resist teasing him, 'be careful! I'll be informed if you get up to any funny business – Agnes has promised to write.'

'Agnes!' Stephen winced. 'There's a rumour that she's going to be transferred. I hope it's true.'

'You can take a few girls out, you know.' Lucy grinned. 'As long as you're good, of course.'

'What about you?' He looked at her, his dark face sulky. 'How shall I know what you're doing?'

'Oh, *I'll* be good!' Lucy laughed at him. 'I shall stick to old married men who only want a bit of company in the pictures on a Saturday night.'

'Mm.'

'Stephen, you don't trust me, do you?' Lucy pinched his arm. 'You'd lock me up in a chastity belt if you could!'

'I trust you, Lucy. But I'll miss you so much!'

'Go on. You can always take a cold shower.'

He didn't smile. He took her face between his hands and studied her. 'Write to me,' he said. 'Every day.'

'I promise.'

The train pulled out. Melancholy civilians and military began to drift out of the concourse. Stephen sighed heavily and kicked an empty cigarette packet across the platform. The next few months were going to be impossible . . .

Another Army medical was scheduled, and Stephen went along to this quite indifferent to what the doctor might tell him. 'Well, sir?' he asked the major, as he dressed again. 'Am I better? Worse?'

'A bit better.' The doctor nodded. 'Yes, I'll be able to mark you up a point or two. You're not A1, of course, don't run away with that idea.'

Stephen now knew better than to ask to be transferred to a more active occupation. In fact, as he walked back to his office, he was wondering about trying to get himself discharged from the Army altogether. He had some fanciful idea of going to work on the land. His mother had relations who owned a farm in Herefordshire, which was very near Shrewsbury . . .

Could he become a farmer? His grandfathers had both been landowners. Presumably he must have farming in his blood? It was something to think about, anyway.

One March morning, his commanding officer sent for him. 'They want you back,' he announced, without preamble. 'Your regiment, that is.'

'What?' Stephen, unable to believe his ears, simply stared. 'Do they?' he managed to articulate at last, adding 'sir' as an afterthought. 'When?'

'Well, p.d.q. by the look of this.' The major waved a chit in front of Stephen's face. 'Training battalion. Some godforsaken place in Surrey.'

'Well – ' Stephen grinned. 'That's marvellous, sir!'

'Out in all weathers, getting a bunch of half-witted rookies through their basic training? Sliding on your belly through a bloody swamp, night exercises, all that skite?'

'Splendid, sir!' Stephen's dark eyes glittered.

'Hm.' The major sniffed. 'I'd have thought you had a cushy billet here?'

Stephen shook his head. 'When can I go, sir?'

'Soon as you like. We've got a new chap coming who can step into your shoes.'

Dismissed, Stephen almost danced across the parade ground. Elated, he wanted to throw his hat into the air and kick it along like a football. Now he'd be able to rip the beastly Hampshire hogs off his tunic. Now he'd be able to wear the eight pointed star again. At last, at last, he would be a Guards officer once more.

The rest of 1942 dragged on. Disaster after disaster made the newspapers gloomy reading. But in the autumn the breakthroughs in North Africa brought some light into the lives of those at home in England. After Alamein, it looked as if the Allies were at last going to break the stranglehold of the Axis powers, and talk of the invasion of Fortress Europe did not sound quite so fanciful as it had six months earlier.

'All the same,' said Stephen, 'I still can't see an end of it.' He and Lucy lay in bed together in a Midlands hotel. They were together for a couple of days, enjoying a break made possible only after extremely longwinded rearrangements of leave and duties. 'Look, why don't we get married?' he asked. 'Darling, we could get a nice house in the country somewhere, you could leave the service – '

'I'm not going to do that!' Lucy glared at him, mortally offended. 'I signed on for the duration. And although I may not be doing much towards winning this war, until it *is* won I shall continue to do what I can. So if you seriously think I'm going to chuck it all up, go and bury myself in the sticks and *knit socks*, you can jolly well think again!'

'Oh.' Stephen shrugged. 'It was just an idea.'

'A very silly one, too.' Lucy shook her head at him. 'Oh, darling, you don't really want a glorified housekeeper, do you? You're not one of those men who wants a bedwarmer, nanny and bottlewasher rolled into one, who thinks that a woman's place is in the home, for ever and ever and aye?'

'Well, I think a mother should always be with her

children, at least while they're small. A wife should look after her husband, she should – '

'Oh, God in heaven, *listen* to him!' Lucy pinched Stephen's shoulder. 'Listen to me, *sir*,' she cried. 'I'm not going to be your chattel! I'll never be a domestic slave! After all this is over, I'm going to have a job, make a career, *do* something with my life! If we win – when we win, I should say – I intend to have my share of the victory? Do you understand?'

Stephen looked at her. 'Well, I suppose so,' he said at last. 'Oh, yes, I know what you mean. You're right, of course.'

'You're just saying that.'

'No, you've convinced me.'

'I'm not just being selfish.' Lucy frowned at him. 'It's for England I want to do this. After the war is over, the country will need everyone to help to get it back on its feet – '

'Of course it will. And determined, modern women like you will be indispensible.' Stephen rolled on to his back and folded his arms across his breast, looking up to the ceiling. 'Could you do something else for England, d'you suppose?' he asked meekly. 'I'll just lie here and think of the place.'

'Don't be sarcastic.' Lucy folded her arms. 'You know you don't like it if I take the initiative in these things – '

'I've revised my opinions, repented of my heresies, let the light of revelation shine in upon my bigotry and ignorance.' Stephen continued to stare up at the ceiling. 'Shall I tell you what to do?'

'I know what to do!' With a growl, Lucy fell on him. 'Right,' she muttered, 'you've asked for it. You've really asked for it now!'

'What's happened to him? Why doesn't he *write*?' Miriam Lawrence, sifting through the morning's post, glanced up to see her daughter-in-law coming down the stairs. She laid the letters down on the hall table and followed Elizabeth into the drawing room.

298

'Elizabeth,' she began, 'I don't want to be intrusive, but I must know. The last time David was here, *did* you quarrel?'

'No.' Elizabeth picked Rebecca up, and shrugged. 'No, we didn't quarrel at all. In fact, as you can see from Becca here, we were pleased to see each other.'

'Then what's *happened*?' Miriam twisted her hands together and looked piteously at her grand-daughter. 'He doesn't even know about this little one! God in heaven, it's nearly two years now! And you don't seem bothered! Elizabeth, you don't seem to care!'

'I do care.' Elizabeth looked down at her daughter. 'Mum, I think about him day and night, I worry just as much as you do.'

'I wonder.'

'I do!' Elizabeth sighed. 'Look, I don't know how to say this. However I put it, it will sound as if I blame him, which I don't. The fact is, he doesn't write because he doesn't want to. I doubt if he ever thinks of me, or of – of anyone else here.'

'What ever do you mean?'

'I mean, he's not my husband any more; or at any rate not as far as he's concerned.' Elizabeth met Miriam's eyes. 'Oh, Mum, he should never have married anyone! He's selfish through and through! He doesn't *want* us – and that's all there is to it!'

'But I'm his mother!' Miriam shook her head, at a loss. 'He can't just pretend we don't exist!'

'Why not?'

'He can't, that's all!'

Elizabeth saw that she'd been too brutal. 'He could be – er – unable to write.' She looked away from Miriam. 'He could be – '

'Dead. A prisoner. Oh, we'd have heard.'

'We could ask Stephen to make some enquiries, perhaps?'

'Perhaps.' Miriam sighed. 'I don't blame you,' she said quietly. 'I know what he's like. But I never thought he'd cast us off completely. Elizabeth, he was my favourite child, my darling. My little one. I suppose I spoilt him. I suppose it's all my fault . . . '

David was crouched in a foxhole with half a dozen other men. He raised himself on one elbow and gave the signal to advance. Under covering fire from the artillery, Captain Lawrence's company of infantry moved forward, and passed a convoy of burnt out German tanks.

By now the enemy was on the run. Demoralized, the defenders of this particular little strip of desert had retreated even as the British advanced, and the new position was established without any casualties at all.

That evening, David and his men were in possession of a German trench. Eating their usual sandy supper, swatting away the habitual flies and waiting for the African night to drop, like a pall, upon them, they chatted to each other and agreed that the Hun had had it . . .

A stack of mail was delivered the following morning. 'Here's yours, sir,' said a private, giving David a dozen envelopes, all addressed in different handwriting.

For half an hour there was virtual silence. Men read, sighing, swearing or laughing depending on what they learnt. The company sergeant major, sitting on an ammunition box a couple of feet away from David, watched as his officer skimmed through his correspondence. 'You're not a married man, are you, sir?' he enquired, as he refolded a particularly affectionate letter from his wife, and thanked heaven for her and the kids.

'Me?' David shook his head. 'I was once,' he said. 'But my wife and I – well, it was a mistake. We haven't actually divorced, but I daresay that one day she'll tell me she wants to marry someone else.'

'Sorry to hear that, sir.' The sergeant major coughed. 'Didn't mean to be nosy,' he muttered. 'No offence meant.'

'None taken.' David opened his fourth letter. 'None taken.'

Chapter Twenty Five

MEDICALLY DOWNGRADED SEVERAL POINTS BUT kept in the Army, Tom Richardson was eventually pronounced fit for service. Posted, by chance, to a training battalion near Abingdon, he had almost as much opportunity to see Helen Atherton as ever he had before. And to improve his acquaintance with her parents . . .

Dora and Tom had taken to each other right from the beginning; but nowadays, as Helen sourly observed, they seemed to be living in one anothers' pockets. Helen found that Tom would turn up at her home when she wasn't even there. In due course she grew accustomed to returning home from work to find Tom and Dora seated in the drawing room, drinking tea and gossiping together.

Not that Tom was practising the role of ideal son-in-law. Indeed, the possibility of marrying him appeared to grow more and more remote. He never mentioned marriage; on the contrary, he went out of his way to avoid the subject. 'Have you thought any more about what I asked you?' enquired Helen, a couple of months after she'd first mentioned the idea.

'No,' he replied shortly. 'No, I haven't.'

'Do you intend to?'

'Perhaps.' He sighed. 'I'll let you know.'

And with that, Helen was obliged to be content.

It would have puzzled a stranger to decide upon the relationship between the four of them; Tim, Dora, Helen and Tom. Towards Dora, Tom behaved like a sort of esquire; a John Brown to Dora's Queen Victoria. He held her garden trug while she cut flowers; he walked with her when she went shopping; he carried her laden baskets home for her.

Watching Tom and Dora coming up the path one Saturday afternoon, Tom holding two overflowing shopping baskets and trailing Dot and Peggy in his wake, Helen suddenly felt very, very jealous. She went into the kitchen, ostensibly to help her mother unpack but really to complain. 'I was supposed to be at the convent this afternoon, you know,' she said, as she unwrapped the cheese.

'Were you, dear?' Dora filled the kettle. 'Then why didn't you go?'

'Because I thought I'd be spending it with Tom, of course!' Helen fetched cups and saucers and banged them down on to a tray. 'He told me he'd be over - so naturally I assumed he'd want to see me! But instead, *you* lugged him off to town!'

'Darling, he offered to come! I didn't know you had other plans!'

Helen muttered something her mother didn't catch. 'Did you manage to get Peggy some shoes?' she asked.

'Oh, yes, we did - in the end! We walked the town, you know; Elliston's had nothing and the other shoeshops were empty, but then Tom suggested a shop just over the other side of Magdalen Bridge and do you know, they had just what we wanted! I'd never have thought of those little shops down there, but Tom said - '

'Did he?' Helen grimaced. 'So I suppose Dot had to have some too?'

'Well, Tom said that since it's so difficult to get things nowadays, it might be as well - '

'What about Frannie?'

'I asked the man if he had any size twelves, and he said not in stock but he'd see what he could do. So Tom said he'd take her over there next weekend, and see if anything had come in. Those girls have such little narrow feet, I'm sure you were in ones or twos at their age!' Dora drew

302

breath. 'Kettle's boiling, dear,' she went on. 'Could you bring everything into the drawing room? Milk for the children, they do so need building up! Now, I just wanted to ask Tom – '

Dora disappeared through the kitchen doorway, and a minute later Helen heard her mother's giggle followed by Tom's deeper laugh.

'You seem to prefer my mother's company to mine these days,' remarked Helen, when Dora had gone to see about the evening meal.

'I like your mother.' Tom pushed Peggy off his lap and told her to run away and play. 'She's a lady,' he added inconsequentially. 'A real lady.'

'And I'm not, I suppose. What do you talk about? You're always nattering together! What do you say to her?'

'Oh, nothing in particular. We just chat.'

'About what?'

'Just things!' Tom sighed. 'Oh, for God's sake, Helen, we don't discuss you, if that's what you're getting at!'

'I should hope you don't.' Suddenly, Helen wanted to upset him. 'My mother's parents weren't married, you know,' she said. 'And so, whatever you may think, she's not a lady. Her mother was a servant, some peasant girl from my grandfather's estate whom he seduced when she was sixteen.'

Tom stared at her. 'Why did you tell me that?' he demanded.

'I don't know.' Helen shrugged. 'But perhaps it explains why you and she and those noisy little brats all get on so well together.'

'You mean that we're all as common as muck, is that it?' Tom leaned over and took Helen by the shoulders. 'Well?' he demanded. 'Is that what you mean?'

'No.' Helen looked at him, unshed tears making her eyes very bright. 'I didn't mean that at all. Oh, Tom, why are you so cruel to me?'

'I'm not, love, I'm not!' Tom got up and crouched down

303

beside her, taking her hands in his. 'Helen, what's the matter?'

'Why won't you marry me?'

'I – oh, sweetheart, I can't explain.'

'You're married already. That's it, isn't it?' Helen began to sob. 'That's why you're so careful; that's why you don't want me to get pregnant! You think that if I were to start a baby, I'd be able to blackmail you! Tom, for God's sake tell me the truth! I won't grumble or shout at you – '

'I'm not married.'

'Then why won't you marry me? *Why*?'

'I'm too old for you.'

'You're not! Tom, you're not!'

'Your father wouldn't want you to marry an NCO.'

'Nonsense!'

'It's not nonsense. Good God – if you seriously think that your father would welcome me into the family with open arms, you must be off your head!'

'He likes you! Honestly, Tom, he does!'

'He still wouldn't want me as a son-in-law. For Christ's sake, Helen, just think of it! Imagine a christening, a wedding or something – there'd be all the professors, the officers, the landed gentry there; and then there'd be me! "Oh, yes," they'd say, "Helen's husband, he's rather a rough character. We did warn her, but she took no notice; of course, we keep him in his place – " '

'Our family isn't like that! Tom, it isn't – '

'Come on, you two. I called you five minutes ago!' Dora came towards them. 'What are you arguing about?' she asked innocently.

Tom and Helen walked down the High Street and crossed Magdalen Bridge. Having nowhere else to stow his belongings, Tom had kept the room in East Oxford, and now he and Helen climbed the grimy stairs to the little eyrie in the roof.

Helen lit the gas fire and put the kettle to boil on the

ring. 'Make yourself at home, won't you?' remarked Tom, watching her.

'I shall.' Kicking off her shoes, Helen unbuttoned her cardigan; she took it off and then lay down on Tom's bed. 'Come over here,' she said. 'Come on, love; give me a kiss.'

Tom had been looking out of the window, over the roofs towards the fields, but now he knelt down beside her and kissed her. 'Those women who sit on rocks in the river,' he murmured. 'Those girls who lure sailors to their deaths. What are they called?'

Helen smiled at him. 'Sirens?' she asked.

'Probably.' Tom rubbed his eyes. 'That's what you are.'

'Rubbish.' Helen began to unfasten his shirt. 'I'm not trying to destroy you,' she said. 'All I want to do is marry you, make you a home, have some children, perhaps. I just want to be your wife, and belong to you.'

'That's another way of saying exactly the same thing.' Tom pulled his shirt out of his waistband, unfastened the rest of the buttons and took it off. Taking Helen's face between his hands he looked at her. 'Why d'you torment me like this?' he asked miserably.

'I don't torment you!' Helen kissed his face and ran her hands over his chest. 'Darling, I don't!'

'You do.' He laid his face on her shoulder. 'Sweetheart, you'll be the death of me,' he added, almost in despair.

Later, Helen made some coffee and took Tom a cup. Sitting on the edge of the bed, she pushed his hair out of his eyes. 'I love you,' she said.

'Mm.' He caught her hand, and held it. 'D'you know what?'

'No.' She shook her head. 'What?'

'When we were in bed together just now, you called me something. Something you've never called me before.'

'Did I? What?' Helen smiled at him. 'What was it then? Love? Sweetheart? Darling? I must have called you all those things before?'

305

'You called me Dad.' Tom looked at her. 'Oh, Dad, I do love you.'' That's what you said.'

'You're a father figure, that's why.' Helen laughed at him now. 'You're always telling me how much older and wiser you are. I'm beginning to believe you!'

'Is that all it is?'

'Yes!' Helen giggled. 'Look, I don't want another father, not when I have a perfectly splendid one already! I want a *husband*!' She put her cup down and stroked his face. 'Tom, *will* you marry me?'

'I don't know.'

'Yes or no! You must say! Darling, it's mean to keep me in suspense like this!'

'Look, love, think about it. Is it what you really want?'

'Yes! Yes, yes, yes!'

'Sure?'

'Certain!'

'Mm. Oh, all right. Yes.' He shrugged helplessly, a victim. 'But God knows what we'll live on.'

'We'll be fine!' Helen beamed at him. 'I'll carry on working; but when the children come, my parents will help us out – '

Tom pushed her hand away. 'Time you went home,' he said.

'I'm not going home tonight.' Helen snuggled against him. 'I'm not leaving until tomorrow morning.'

'You're going *now*. Your mother will be frantic if you don't go home! Come on, Helen, get dressed.'

She saw that he meant to be obeyed. And, for once, she did as she was told.

Chapter Twenty Six

LUCY HAD FORMALLY AGREED TO marry him, and had been introduced to his parents as a prospective daughter-in-law. She had accepted an engagement ring and now wore this symbol of ownership upon her finger, signifying that she was more or less his property. At last Stephen was more at peace within himself.

He no longer clung to his forlorn hope to distinguish himself in action. And although he had spent most of his war service either working in an office or training recruits on the firing ranges of Surrey, he no longer felt that he was a failure as a man.

The successful conclusion of the campaign in Africa in May 1943 did, however, provoke the odd twinge of envy. But for a malicious providence, he might have been there; he could have been with the Eighth Army as it smashed the German battalions into the desert sands. A recent letter from David, who was now living it up in Alexandria, had described the past few months in graphic detail. And Stephen had been filled with regret for what *he* might have done . . .

'You might have been a conquering hero,' agreed Lucy, as she lay next to her fiancé in the bedroom of a country hotel. 'But on the other hand you might have been a blackened corpse, you might have been a decaying body with the flies slowly eating you up.' She shuddered. 'Think of the PBI going forward in the face of the enemy, being

shot down like animals. Dying like insects. Surely you
don't think that's an enviable fate?'

'You don't understand.' Moodily, Stephen picked at the
corner of the sheet. 'If I *had* been killed, I'd have died an honourable death. I'd have died serving my country, and – '

'And now, the choir will sing Land of Hope and Glory.'
Lucy kissed his shoulder. 'You're silly.'

'I'm not.'

'You are.' Lucy grinned. 'I've got my first stripe,' she
added. 'You didn't even notice.'

'I did! I was about to say – '

'Fibber.'

'No, it's true. But Lucy, I was so delighted to see you
that it went right out of my mind.' He pushed the bedclothes back from her shoulders. 'Sit up,' he ordered. 'Let
me look at you.'

'Why?'

'I forget what you're really like. I find I can't remember
all the details. But if I study you now, I can commit every
bit of you to memory, then think about you when I'm
alone.'

'You mean, you'll meditate on my left ankle or my right
shoulder blade?'

'That sort of thing, yes.'

'How very odd.' Lucy giggled. 'I think about all of you.'

'That's greedy. Oh, I find it too disturbing to think
about all of you, I have to ration myself.'

'I see. Well, Stephen, all of me is here now. So why
don't you indulge yourself for once?' Sitting up cross-
legged, Lucy put her hands on her head. 'There,' she said,
turning this way and that. 'One head, two arms, two
shoulders. Moving downwards, various other parts which I
have been far too well brought up to mention by name, but
which you may now examine at your leisure. Starting from
the other end, two feet, two ankles, two knees – '

She got no further. Her lover grabbed her round the
waist and pushed her on to her back, then continued to
catalogue her various components for himself.

When Stephen had finished his inventory, he sat up

beside her. 'You shouldn't be so wicked, Lucy,' he said severely. 'Tonight, when I'm back in barracks, I shan't be able to resist thinking of you sitting up in bed and flaunting yourself like that, and I'm very much afraid I'll set my blankets on fire.'

'You poor thing. Where's your self control?'

'It doesn't exist where you're concerned.' Stephen stroked Lucy's shoulder, allowed his hand to trace the outline of one breast. 'You're very wanton,' he said. 'Is your mother like you?'

'How on earth should I know? It's not the sort of thing we discuss.' Lucy laughed. 'I don't think she can be. She wears terrible flannelette nightdresses in bed, awful linty things which I imagine would destroy the most intemperate lust! And in winter she wears pink bedsocks, too.'

'When we're married, there'll be no flannelette nightdresses. No curlers, no cold cream, no hairnets either. And certainly no bedsocks.'

'Really.' Lucy scowled at him. 'Well, Captain Atherton, you can just stop laying down the law. If there are going to be lists of conditions, I shan't marry you at all!'

'Oh, but you can make conditions, too. This will be an equal partnership; that's what you wanted, wasn't it?' Stephen kissed her. 'What about a walk before lunch? A bit of exercise would do you good - it might help to firm up your thighs.'

'There's nothing wrong with them!' Lucy narrowed her eyes. 'Is there?'

'You're just a little bit chubby in that area. Don't worry, most English women are.'

'How do you know?'

'Mass observation.'

'What? Stephen, you rat - '

'Well, you said I could take girls out - '

'I never said you could examine their - oh, how *could* you?'

'My darling, I didn't. But I'm not blind, you know, and I do have a very good memory. I can recall summers before the war, when the beaches were full of women in bathing

309

costumes which displayed their legs to advantage - or not, in some cases.'

'And in all your enormous experience, you've never seen a fatter, more hideous pair of legs than mine, is that it?'

'Well, as I said, they're just a bit chubby - '

'Pig.' Lucy folded her arms and glowered at him. 'I release you from the engagement,' she snapped. 'I shan't marry a man who says I have fat legs.'

'You have marvellous legs.' Stephen grinned at her. 'Oh, I didn't mean it,' he added. 'You have lovely legs, the most beautiful legs in the whole wide world! Ouch, that hurts! Lucy, don't hit me, I was only teasing - '

But Lucy continued to hit him until he caught both her wrists, turned her on to her back and pinned her underneath him. Breathing heavily, she glared at him. 'You're a rat,' she said, when she could speak. 'A horrible, ugly, hairy rat, and I *hate* you.'

'You're beautiful.'

'Get off me! D'you hear?' Lucy bared her teeth. 'Stephen, if you don't let me go, I'll kick you where it'll hurt; they taught us how, you know! And Sergeant Dawes said I was a natural!'

'I could thrash Sergeant Dawes any day of the week. And as for a little thing like you - '

'Bighead.' In spite of herself, Lucy giggled. 'Oh, you stupid, ugly brute, get up! Do you hear me?'

Stephen kissed her. 'I love you,' he replied.

From Surrey it was easy enough to get to Oxford and Stephen often managed an evening or a weekend at home. One Saturday he strolled down the Banbury Road and called on his aunt. He found Miriam and Elizabeth in the kitchen, giving Rebecca her tea.

'You've heard from him?' As Stephen mentioned her husband, Elizabeth started. 'Steve, he wrote to you?'

'Well - yes.' Puzzled, Stephen looked at his cousin. 'Why shouldn't he? This is the first letter I've had this year, though,' he added.

310

'He hasn't written to me at all.' Elizabeth offered Rebecca a piece of bread and butter. 'Is there – I mean, could you tell us anything about him? How he is?'

'You can read the letter, if you like.' Horribly embarrassed, Stephen fished in his pocket and touched the envelope – but then he remembered that David had described his time in Alexandria in rather lurid detail, and he took his hand out again. 'I must have left the thing at home,' he said lamely. 'Well, he's in excellent health. He seems to have had a decent time in the desert. Look, Elizabeth, you *must* have heard from him! When Rebecca was born – '

'I sent a letter – in fact, I sent two or three – to his regiment, asking if they could be forwarded. He didn't reply.'

'Oh.' Stephen looked at his hands. 'I'm sorry,' he said. 'I've really put both my big feet in it, haven't I?'

'No.' Elizabeth tried to smile. 'I'm glad to hear that he's safe.' She got up and, leaving Stephen with his aunt, she went out of the room just as Rachel came into it.

'Stephen's heard from David,' said Miriam.

'Oh?' Rachel took off her coat. 'Any tea in the pot?'

'I said, Stephen's had a letter from your brother!'

'So, you expect I should dance the polka?' Rachel shrugged her shoulders. She looked enquiringly at her cousin. 'Well, Steve – where is the schnook?'

Stephen grimaced. 'In Egypt,' he replied.

'Nice for him.'

'He's well,' put in Miriam. 'Well, and happy.'

'There's no justice.' Rachel sniffed. 'Any of that chocolate cake left? Some of my sugar ration went into it, so I hope you saved me a piece?'

'Oh, get it yourself!' Angry now, Miriam pushed her chair back and went out of the kitchen.

'Temper.' Rachel sat down. 'And how's my little darling, how's my naughty little brother's lovely little girl?' she asked, smiling at her niece. 'Well, Steve, tell all.'

'I wish I hadn't told anything.' Stephen poured Rachel some tea.

'I suppose he's having a fine old time.' Rachel bit into a piece of bread and butter. 'Oh, yes, I can just imagine what

311

he'll be up to. Wine, women and song. Have you told Liz?'

'Yes. Well, I told her that he's in good health. She's a bit upset, I think.' Stephen chewed his lower lip. 'Oh, God, I wish I'd never mentioned that damned letter!'

'Not your fault, Stevie, not your fault. Give.' Rachel held out her hand.

She read the letter through, shook her head, and returned it. 'Haven't shown this to Liz, have you?' she enquired.

'Good heavens, no!'

'I hope he picks up some nasty, disfiguring disease; it would serve him right.' Rachel leaned back in her chair. 'I always did have a sneaking admiration for patient Griselda,' she observed reflectively. 'The Clerk's Tale, you remember? All about the sweet, obedient wife who takes whatever her husband dishes out, and loves him in spite of everything.'

'I do remember. Vaguely.' Stephen shrugged. 'I don't understand women. I mean, she has every reason to hate him. But she obviously doesn't.'

'*I* hate him.' Rachel scowled. 'If I had him here, I'd murder him; God forgive me, I'd strangle him with his own tie!'

Rachel stroked her niece's fine, black hair. 'Don't grow up to be like your Daddy,' she told the baby. She replaced her teacup. 'Steve, is there any more tea?'

'I'll make you some.'

'Thanks.' Rachel sighed. '*Men*!' she added crossly. 'Not you, Steve - God knows that ATS girl's lucky to have a chap like you. But honestly, isn't he disgusting? Elizabeth's his wife - she's had his children, she loves him - and he repays her like this!'

'We don't know all the circumstances, Rachel. Perhaps we shouldn't judge - '

'That's right, stick up for him - you always did think he was Rob Roy, Clark Gable and Hercules rolled into one!' Rachel gave her niece a piece of chocolate cake. 'Well,' she went on, 'we won't fall out over my horrid little brother.

312

Tell me, how's Helen these days? Haven't set eyes on her for weeks.'

'She's okay, I think.'

'Still in love with the dashing white sergeant?'

'Who? Oh, Tom Richardson. Yes, I believe so.'

'What d'you think of him?'

Stephen considered. 'He's a bit wary of me. Doesn't say much when I'm there. He and Mum are as thick as anything, though.'

'That's what we heard.'

'Do you like him?'

'Me?' Rachel laughed. 'Oh, Steve, she hasn't brought him round to meet the Jews! She's not that stupid!'

'Rachel! Why do you say that?'

'Oh, I don't know.' Rachel shrugged. 'Though I did wonder if she was deliberately keeping him away from us. Her tall, blond, handsome Aryan, that is.'

'Oh, honestly, Rachel!' Stephen poured water into the teapot. 'I don't know why she hasn't brought him to meet you,' he said. 'But I'm sure it's not because of that.'

'You are, are you?' Rachel paddled her teaspoon in the dregs of her cup. 'Well, I can't think of any other reason for keeping him away.'

Stephen shrugged. 'He's a nice bloke,' he said, sitting down again. 'Quiet, sensible, decent; the sort I'd be glad to have with me in a sticky situation. He certainly hasn't any fascist sympathies – the few remarks he's made about the Germans show how much he despises everything the Nazis represent.'

'I shall go and look him over.' Rachel poured herself another cup of tea. 'Now, I wonder if we Yids will get invited to the wedding?'

Chapter Twenty Seven

HELEN HAD NOT EVEN THOUGHT of introducing Tom to her relations in the Banbury Road. She was far too busy thinking of herself to consider that Rachel might be hurt by her young cousin's neglect . . .

The feeling of euphoria which had followed Tom's agreeing to marry her was quickly dispelled by his now habitual sullenness and his almost constant criticism of her. Helen could not help noticing how he avoided being alone with her, engaging her mother in conversation and excluding Helen herself, or jabbering to her father about military matters of which Helen knew nothing. She could not help understanding that he felt he'd been forced into an agreement which he'd never intended to make.

There was to be no more lovemaking, it seemed. Although he still paid rent on his room in East Oxford, the narrow little attic wasn't often used as a trysting place these days. For Tom obviously had other things on his mind. Now he was back in the Army, he was making his contribution towards winning the war.

'There's a lot to be done,' he said stubbornly, when Helen remarked that he always looked exhausted nowadays, and asked why he needed to volunteer for all that extra duty. 'Don't you understand? We've all got to pull our weight! God, Helen, this rotten little country has its faults sure enough, but it's still the nearest thing to heaven on earth! It's worth fighting for!'

'Rule Britannia.' Helen scowled at him. 'I suppose you mean that I shan't see you next weekend, or the one after?'

'I'd have thought you had enough to keep you busy.' Tom scowled back. 'If you've time on your hands, I expect those nuns could find you something to do.'

'Don't be so patronizing! I hoed over the whole potato patch last Saturday. My hands are raw!'

'They look all right to me. You can't pretend that *you're* going all out to help the war effort, can you, love? You do what suits you, no more.'

'That's not fair! And anyway, what else could I do?'

'You should be in the Forces. A young, healthy woman like you ought to be in the ATS or the WAAFs, not sitting on her backside in an office all day and pottering about in a garden at weekends.'

'Sometimes, you are hateful.'

'I say what I think, that's all.'

'Exactly.'

She knew he didn't want her, and the knowledge of it left a permanent sour taste in her mouth. For a week or so after that conversation Helen thought constantly about Tom, about herself, about what their future together might be like. And she realized that she couldn't hold him to the bargain.

On the following Monday morning she did something she'd thought she'd never do. She took an early lunch break and walked into town. The May sunshine was streaming through the trees, the gracious buildings looked as beautiful as Helen had ever seen them; the idea of leaving Oxford appalled her. But, all the same, she went into the Army recruiting office. 'I want to join the ATS,' she told the officer there.

Tom had arranged a twenty-four-hour pass, and that Sunday he took Helen for a walk along the river, then back to his room. He was in an unusually good temper that day;

Helen supposed the sunshine and the splendid news from Africa had cheered him up.

'You're nice when you're happy,' she told him, as she made some tea. She sat down beside him on the bed. 'And I've something to tell you which will make you happier still.'

'Oh, God, you're not pregnant?' He took his cup and looked at her. 'Well, if you are, we can't get married straight away. And – '

'I'm joining the ATS.'

'What?'

'You heard me.' Helen stirred her tea. 'I went to the office last week. I've a medical tomorrow morning.'

'Honestly?' His relief was plain, his enthusiasm for the idea almost insulting. Obviously, he couldn't wait for her to be posted and out of the way. 'That's marvellous!' He beamed at her. 'Oh, love, that's splendid news! Well! My little Helen in the Army! Who'd have thought she would – '

'There's no need to have a fit.' Helen scowled at him. 'I thought you'd be pleased,' she added bitterly.

'I am! Well, what brought this on, eh? And why the ATS? I'd have thought the WAAFs had a bit more class. Nicer uniforms for a start – '

'Oh, shut up!' Helen felt tears come into her eyes. 'As if I care what the uniform's like!' She grabbed his arms and shook him. 'That's all you think I care about, isn't it? That's what you think of me; that I'm a frivolous middle class tart, who's amused herself by pretending to be in love with an ignorant proletarian lout! And now that she's tired of that game, she's going to play at being a soldier, instead!'

'What?'

'Oh, God!' Helen pinched him, hard. 'You don't know what you've done to me!' she cried. 'You're too stupid to understand!' Her eyes very bright, she was determined not to cry – or at any rate, not in front of him. 'I loved you,' she said. 'I loved you with all my heart. And you've destroyed everything, thrown it all back in my face. Well, I release you from our engagement. You don't have to

316

marry me, after all. Look, I'll give you that in writing. Have you got a pencil?'

'No.' Tom sighed. 'I'll miss you,' he said evenly.

'I bet! Just now, when I told you I was going to join up, you could hardly contain your delight!' And now, unable to control herself any longer, Helen began to sob.

'Don't cry, love.' Still somewhat bemused by her outburst, Tom took her in his arms. 'Oh, sweetheart, you're getting all worked up about nothing! Look, you mustn't cry!'

'I'm not crying!' Angrily, she pushed him away. 'You don't think I'd cry for you, do you?' she demanded. 'Why should I cry for a man who's used me, who's turned me into a whore? Oh, God, how could I have been so stupid? You wanted a woman - and I let you have me!'

'As I saw it, we wanted each other - '

'You were wrong.' Helen turned away. 'You're rubbish, you are,' she muttered, now really determined to hurt. 'You're nothing but a guttersnipe, you're worse than dirt. Born and bred in the slums - probably somebody's by-blow - '

'Helen, stop it!'

'Somebody's by-blow, that's all you are, somebody's bastard! All that stuff about your father dying and your mother abandoning you, that's just some story you've dreamed up - '

'Helen!'

'Somebody's little mistake, that's you, a misbegotten thing conceived by some ignorant slut on her Saturday night out - '

She'd gone too far. Pulling her round to face him, Tom slapped her, raising red weals across her cheeks. 'Don't you speak to me like that,' he murmured softly, threateningly. 'I'd *cripple* any man who said such things to me!'

'Oh?' Too angry to feel fear, Helen stared back at him. 'Well, I suppose that's the way with your sort! Violence is the answer to everything, isn't it? You hit your women; and if a *man* offended you, you'd try to kill him. Bloody stupid, that's what you are.'

317

'Don't swear at me. Helen, I warn you – '

'Damn you!' Helen wrenched herself free. 'Damn you, sod you, bugger you; I hope you burn in Hell! There! Bad language! You don't like it, do you? You like women to have their legs open and their mouths shut! You like – '

'Helen!' Tom caught her wrists, made her meet his eyes. 'Helen,' he said gently, 'I know I've upset you, and I'm sorry. I shouldn't have hit you. Sweetheart, don't speak to me like this!'

'I'll speak to you how I please! God, I don't have to do as *you* say, I'm not some mill-girl with her hair done up in a scarf, some street tart grateful for a quick screw up against a factory wall! A dirty little Liverpool whore – '

'Stop it!' Now Tom was shaking her. 'Helen, I shan't tell you again – '

'Let me *go*!' Squirming out of his grasp, Helen picked up her coat. 'I don't want to see you again,' she said. 'I never want to hear from you, I'm going to forget you exist. And another thing. While I'm away, don't you dare go near my parents! If you do, I swear I'll kill you.'

She let herself out of the house and walked back into the city, staying in the shadow, afraid of the bright sunshine, feeling sickened by what she'd just done. A voice inside her was insisting that it was still possible to go back, to apologize – to make everything all right again . . .

Helen kept walking.

'You heard what I said, Mum. I'm not going to say it again.' Helen lay back on the sofa and closed her eyes. 'I don't want to discuss it any more.'

'Why don't you go up to bed?' Dora reached across and touched her daughter's hand, still hardly able to take in what Helen had said. 'A good night's rest – '

'Will make everything better again.' Helen opened her eyes. 'I'm going to have a bath.' Getting to her feet, she walked out of the room.

'She's very upset, poor thing.' Dora looked at Tim. 'I wonder what they quarrelled about?'

'I suppose matters came to a head. I *had* wondered if something like this was about to happen.'

'Oh.' Dora went to sit beside her husband. '*I'd* assumed that they'd get married,' she said. 'Tim, it's not anything we've done, is it?'

'I suppose we haven't helped.'

'Whatever do you mean? Oh, for goodness' sake, Tim, we've bent over backwards – '

'That's just it. And a touchy chap like that must have noticed.' Tim sighed. 'I think I was so determined not to let his background, or lack of it, count against him that I was a bit too friendly. Patronizing, perhaps.'

'Rubbish.' Dora sniffed. 'You spoke to him just as you speak to everyone else. I liked him,' she added wistfully. 'I really liked him. I understood why Helen wanted him.'

'They might make it up.'

'It's possible, I suppose. Well, there's no reason, is there, why he shouldn't come to see us? I'd miss him, you know. And so would the girls.'

'All the same, I doubt if he'll come.' Tim looked gloomily into the twilight. 'This ATS business,' he said. 'This going for a soldier; will she cope?'

'I think so.' Dora stood up. 'And she'll meet other men now, which might be all to the good.'

'Maybe.' Tim shrugged. 'If she gets herself involved with someone from her own sort of background – '

'I don't think that's important.' Dora frowned. 'After all, the baronet's son married a peasant's bastard.'

'Don't call yourself that.'

'And if you'd been killed at Passchendaele, Helen would have been a bastard herself.'

'Don't, Dora.'

'You don't like to look at it like that, do you?'

'It's irrelevant, darling. It doesn't matter.' Tim got up. 'Come on, Dora – time for bed.'

Chapter Twenty Eight

THE HOT, ARID CONDITIONS OF the North African desert had been the worst possible preparation for an autumn campaign in the mountains of southern Italy. Arriving on the mainland in September 1943, the men of the battalion in which David Lawrence was a company commander realized almost at once that they were in for a bad time.

Even before the Italian Armistice, several German divisions had been moved into the country with the express intention of stopping the Allied advance. Given the task of pushing the Germans northwards – and eventually out of Italy altogether – the rain, the mud, the biting, numbing cold and the impossible terrain all combined with the enemy to make the autumn of 1943 the most dreadful any Allied soldier could remember. And the knowledge that the winter would be many degrees worse did nothing at all for the Eighth Army's already low morale. Sunny Italy. That was a joke . . .

The mountains, which spread in a series of ribs from the central spine of Italy down to the coastal plains, offered the German defenders superb attacking positions. In fact, the whole geography of the country was on their side. The rivers ran fast and treacherously from the summits to the sea and were deep and difficult for the Allies to ford; the roads, with their hairpin bends and terrifying gradients, were perilously narrow for most wheeled vehicles, and easy to destroy.

Hitler had ordered his troops to prevent the Allies from

advancing more than half way up the peninsula. To this end, long lines of defensive positions had been established, which straddled the country from east to west. The Winter Line, a mass of wire, bunkers and machine gun positions south of Rome, was backed by the formidably engineered Gustav Line; towards which the Germans were retreating, as slowly as possible. Destroying bridges, bombing towns and villages, laying waste everything as they went, they left behind them a wilderness of ruined homesteads and barren land.

There seemed no reason why the Germans should give an inch more than they chose. The Allies' task looked hopeless.

For David Lawrence and his fellow captain Keith Mulholland the pleasures of a summer in Alexandria were soon to become nothing but a distant memory, a fading dream. By the middle of November they, and all their men, had been in the mountains for five awful weeks; and they had completely forgotten what it was like to be warm, dry and well fed.

'Bugger all this!' Captain Mulholland, peeling off his saturated battledress jacket and hanging it over an arrangement of sticks to dry, stared gloomily into the smoky little fire. 'Sod this for a lark,' he muttered, opening a packet of damp cigarettes. 'Sergeant Aylesford, come and have a fag.'

'Thank you, sir.' After much inhaling, the sergeant managed to get the cigarette to draw. 'Mr Lawrence all right?' he enquired.

'He's okay. Just gone down to see that the men are nice and cosy.'

'Hm.' The sergeant grimaced. 'They'll think they're in the bleedin' Savoy 'otel tonight. I mean, cowsheds – that's flamin' luxury compared with what they've 'ad to put up with this week.'

Two companies of infantry commanded by David Lawrence and Keith Mulholland were spending the night in a derelict farmhouse, which was perched on the side of a barren mountain a mile or so from what was now the German front line. As was their habit, the Germans had, before retreating, blown the place up, but enough remained of the building for it to provide rudimentary shelter for the British troops.

All that week the men had been engaged in an offensive against a couple of hundred Wehrmacht infantrymen, crack troops left south of a line of German bunkers, whose task it had been to delay the Allied advance up one particular valley. This they had done. The fighting had been fierce, and the courage of the Germans had impressed their enemies.

For both sides, conditions had been terrible. Wading through freezing rivers, driving or footslogging up barren hillsides, sheltering at night in ruined houses or, more often, lying down to sleep wrapped in their anti-gas capes with nothing but these waterproofs between them and an inclement climate, the British soldiers were now close to exhaustion.

Inadequately clad, without blankets or dry clothes, the men were also permanently hungry, for rations had been slow in coming. They had, in effect, lived off the land, scrounging where they could, bargaining for food with Italian peasants who were in any case too frightened to deny the soldiers anything. For days now their diet had consisted of assorted vegetables, coarse bread, and acorn coffee.

Then, one morning, the Germans had suddenly made a bolt for the safety of their lines, leaving the British in possession of a little wasteland, a desolation of ruined villages and lethal minefields.

David pushed what remained of the door open and came into the kitchen where the officers and senior NCOs were conferring. 'Bloody awful night,' he observed, accepting a cup of coffee and drinking it down. 'Any of that stew left?'

'Yes, sir.' Sergeant Aylesford handed his officer a dixie full of a disgusting grey concoction, together with a hunk of equally unappetizing dry bread. 'Men okay?' he asked.

'Fine.' David grinned. 'They've put together a meal of sorts. And Corporal Wayland has a couple of chickens; he's making a kind of curry by the smell of it, though I can't think where he got the ingredients.'

'He 'ad some German beer last week. Was hawkin' it round the platoon.' Sergeant Aylesford inhaled a mouthful of smoke and coughed. 'Oh, Wayland's the sort who'd find peaches an' oranges at the bloody North Pole. That bloke'd come up with sardines in the middle of the Sahara Desert; so of course he could get a tin of curry powder from some Wop! He's probably had it in his kit since we were in Taranto.'

The sergeant shifted closer to David and squatted down beside him. 'Look, sir,' he continued urgently, 'the transport's in a bad way. One truck's got a broken gearbox, one's got no brakes, all their tyres are in shreds. An' then there's the lorry that stupid bugger Charlton drove over the edge of the road; that's bust its axle. Sir, when are we goin' to meet up with the rest of the brigade?'

'On Tuesday, according to Mr Mulholland. Eh, Keith?'

'What?'

'Sergeant Aylesford is concerned about the deplorable condition of our transport. And he's missing his friends in the Worcestershires.'

'They'll be here by Monday night.' Captain Mulholland yawned. 'We've just got a bit ahead of ourselves, that's all. As for the trucks, we'll be getting new ones, had a message from GHQ.' He lay back and closed his eyes. 'And now, I'm going to have a bit of kip. I don't wish to be disturbed. So, even if the entire German Army comes thundering over the ridge, I am to be left to die in my sleep, okay?'

David nodded. 'I'll leave a note pinned to your sleeve. "No flowers by request. Donations may be sent to a charity of your choice." How's that?'

'Donations to the Jewish Widows' and Orphans'

Holiday Fund.' Keith Mulholland folded his arms across his chest. 'Right, Dave?'

'Right.'

Sergeant Aylesford glanced from one young officer to the other, and shrugged. 'It's all very well for you and Mr Mulholland to joke, sir,' he told David sourly. 'You're too young to remember the first war. But my brother, he was at Passchendaele. An' I'll tell you this for nothin' - *that* was a Girl Guides' picnic compared to what we're goin' to get this winter.'

And with this comforting assurance he got up and went out of the kitchen, intending to post sentries and then get his own head down in the luxury of an Italian farmer's byre.

Sergeant Aylesford's gloomy prognostications were fulfilled. Battering its way up the Adriatic coast of Italy, the Eighth Army was up against an enemy which was better provisioned and often better equipped than the Allied soldiers were. Barbed wire, minefields, mud; fortified pill-boxes and lines of defences too strong to be broken by mere infantry attacks, all combined to make the campaign as bloody and almost as costly as any action in the Great War; and comparisons with the slaughter at Passchendaele were routinely made by men whose friends and relations had told them about it.

In the grey dawn of an early December day David's battalion stormed a village on the southern slopes of a barren mountain and entered the main street literally seconds after the retreating Germans had fled. The Italians themselves had run away, or been killed. Most of the houses had been set on fire, and now their wooden rafters blazed merrily in the gloomy chill of the winter morning. Apart from the crackling of these bonfires, there was no sound at all.

This particular village was, in appearance at any rate, no different from a thousand others which clung to the mountainsides, whose inhabitants had for centuries tried to

324

win a precarious living from their small fields. The houses looked Neanderthal; built of great blocks of undressed stone, they seemed to grow out of the rock on which they stood. And others *were* in fact caves, excavated from the sides of the mountain itself.

Before the Italian Armistice, however, this particular place had been a Fascist stronghold. After the Italian army had surrendered, *this* village had actually welcomed German soldiers. Its people had willingly co-operated with their new masters in exchange for certain privileges, or so the peasants from further down the valley maintained . . .

'Collaborators,' the patriarch of their nearest neighbours had told David. 'They were Fascists; and they're Fascists still, most of them. They're all one family, you see; they've intermarried, they've always kept themselves to themselves, and they've always done as their Fascist masters told them. Sir, they're not to be trusted. Be careful.'

Looking at the silent desolation all around him, David was inclined to believe what his informant had said. If the villagers had collaborated with the Germans, they had probably run away into the high mountains; abandoned by their Nazi friends, they would now be afraid of reprisals from their own people. And if this was the case, it might explain the total absence of life.

For, almost immediately after entering all the other villages they had captured from the Germans, the British troops had been welcomed by bands of peasants coming out of their hiding places in the hills, out of caves near at hand, even out of ditches. All smiling and shouting with delight, they had been thrilled to see the British soldiers. 'The English, the English!' they had cried, overjoyed that the Germans, who had lorded it over them, eaten their food and made free with their possessions, had been routed. And out had come the hidden casks of wine, out had come bags of flour, the people had fed and fêted their liberators. But here, there was still silence.

'I don't like this, Dave.' Keith Mulholland followed David up the village street under cover of an overhanging wall and wiped his face on his sleeve. 'I reckon it's a trap.'

Suddenly, he started. 'Oh, God,' he cried, 'what's that?'

'What?' David stared at him.

'Listen!'

It was a squeaking, chittering sound – and it appeared to be coming from behind the door of the ruined house close to which the two officers were standing. Now, David heard it too. 'Rats?' he hazarded.

'Rats!' Captain Mulholland sniffed in derision. 'Look out.' Pushing David aside he kicked the door open. 'Mani in alto!' he shouted. 'Hands up. Now!'

Nothing happened. But the chittering was now louder, and added to this there was a sort of strangled moaning, as if of a creature in dreadful pain. David peered into the darkness; saw what was making the noise, and walked into the room.

Two women, one quite young, one middle-aged – perhaps mother and daughter – crouched in a corner of the kitchen, huddled together for warmth and mutual comfort. The chittering noise appeared to be coming from the older of the pair. 'Ah.' Captain Mulholland rubbed his eyes, smearing more dirt across his grimy face. 'Vermin. Dave, there're your rats!'

Obviously terrified, the women stared.

'Stand up!' Keith Mulholland glared at them. 'Up! Capisce? Stand *up*! Aufstehen! Presto!' Like many Englishmen, he imagined that if he yelled at foreigners in a loud and threatening manner, they'd understand and obey. It appeared, in fact, that these two women *did* understand, for, as the captain continued to bawl at them, they struggled to their feet and stood against the wall.

'Aus!' Captain Mulholland looked towards the entrance to the kitchen. 'Outside, damn you!' And, with more than necessary violence, he pushed the women towards what had once been a door.

In the daylight, the women blinked and the older one hid her face in her shawl. David looked at them. Both dressed in black; they were very shabby. On their feet they wore coarse boots which looked as if they'd been made out of cardboard, and under these they had thick, cream-coloured socks. In such outlandish garb they hardly looked like German officers' molls. 'What shall we do with them?' he asked.

'Dunno.' Keith Mulholland looked from one woman to the other. 'If we send them down the valley, I suppose the partisans there'll finish them off?'

'If they're Fascists, yes. I wonder why they didn't go with the others?'

'Ask them.' Keith Mulholland shrugged. 'You're the scholar, Dave – ask them.'

The older woman had now stopped whimpering, but she was evidently still terrified. She muttered something to her daughter, whose eyes widened in alarm.

David caught what she said. He wished he could speak Italian well enough to reassure them that there was no danger of violation. He managed a kind of smile; and then, speaking very slowly and clearly, he attempted to explain that he – and the rest of his men – were too tired and too hungry to hurt women in that way.

'I understand.' The girl, speaking in a sing-song accent, now surprised him by answering him in English. 'My mother is very ill,' she went on. 'She needs a doctor.'

'Ah.' David nodded. 'Where did you learn to speak English?' he asked.

The girl pushed her hair out of her eyes. 'I was in London before the war,' she explained. 'My uncle's family has a restaurant there, you see, and I was a waitress.' She paused for breath. 'When the war began, I was arrested. My relations were interned. But I – '

'Yes? You what?'

'I – ' The girl was almost gasping for air now, white with the effort of talking. 'But I was told that I could – '

'All right.' David saw a platoon of soldiers coming up the street. 'Well?' he asked the lieutenant in charge.

'Nobody around, sir.' Lieutenant Harper shook his head. 'They've all scarpered. There's a nice little cache of rifles and ammo in one of the cellars, though – it might come in useful.' He looked curiously at the two women.

'Who're your lady friends, sir?' he enquired, grinning. 'Didn't you keep one for me?'

'Watch it, Mr Harper, just watch it.' Captain Mulholland scowled at the girl. 'Where are the others?' he demanded.

'Ah.' The girl narrowed her eyes. 'They - er - '

'See, Dave?' Keith Mulholland grimaced. 'Bleeding Wops. I tell you, Dave, these two are definitely collaborators. And any minute now, their mates'll be back, we'll be caught - '

'The others have gone.' The girl hung her head. 'When the Germans pulled out, they left us.'

'She was ill, Keith. She had a fever of some kind, she needed medical treatment.'

'So, Sir Galahad, you decided to waste our supplies on a pair of Fascist tarts.' Keith Mulholland crouched over the fire and shivered. 'Dunno what's the matter with you these days,' he grumbled. 'I know you like women - I remember when we were in Alexandria - but all the same!'

'The fact that they were women had nothing at all to do with it.' David scowled at his friend. 'Nothing, d'you hear?'

But Keith Mulholland wasn't listening. He had let his mind wander back to happier times. 'Those were the days,' he murmured dreamily. 'That month in Alex. Paradise. And do you remember that leave we had in Beirut? You had that black-haired girl - Lisa, wasn't it?'

'As it happens, I don't remember her name.'

'Well, you wouldn't. She'd have been one of dozens, wouldn't she? But, for all that,' he added, coming back to the present, 'I honestly don't see why you have to stick up for the enemy's trollops!'

'Oh, shut up, Keith.' David poked the fire with a stick. 'Just give it a rest, eh?'

'You're not ill, are you?' Keith Mulholland looked closely at David. 'You're not sickening for something?'

'I'm just cold, that's all. Cold, fed up and tired - like

328

you.' David pulled his gas cape closer around him and went out of the kitchen where he and Keith had been eating their supper. He walked over to the men's quarters and looked in. 'Corporal Daly here?' he asked, squinting into the gloom of a cellar.

'Sir?' The NCO, who had been peacefully chewing his way through a plateful of some kind of stew, looked round and got to his feet. 'What is it, sir?' he enquired.

'Is Sergeant Aylesford back yet?'

'Dunno, sir.' The corporal picked up his jacket. 'I'll go and see.'

A few minutes later Sergeant Aylesford came stumping into the officers' quarters. 'Well, sir,' he said drearily, 'they'll be all right now. Mind you, the girl's in a bad way.'

'The girl?' David frowned. 'I thought it was the mother – '

'Yeah, well, the old bag had a bit of a temperature. They give her an aspirin or two.' The sergeant accepted a cigarette. 'But the daughter was really sick – had a knife wound in the side, a nasty thing it was, septic. Just missed her heart, the MO said.'

'But how – '

Sergeant Aylesford coughed. 'Some Jerry done it,' he replied. 'Vicious bastard.'

'Why did they hurt her?'

'Dunno, sir.' Sergeant Aylesford shrugged, as if to convey that he didn't care either. 'Perhaps she'd been a naughty girl. Perhaps she wasn't naughty enough. Perhaps she wouldn't do as she was told. Sir, how the hell should I know?'

In the kitchen of the house where he and Keith Mulholland had found the women, and which was now Battalion HQ, David and his fellow officers sipped their acorn coffee and made themselves as comfortable as they could, intending to take a few hours' rest. It was pleasant not to be shivering in slit trenches; it was nice to have a decent fire for once.

Accustomed, by now, to huddling together for warmth, the officers clustered together in groups, and David lay

329

down beside Keith Mulholland. He propped himself up on one elbow. 'I wonder how they are?' he asked.

'They'll be okay.' Keith Mulholland grinned, then yawned. 'I expect the pretty little Signorina will end up a general's doxy. Her Mum can keep house for them all.'

'She *was* a pretty girl, wasn't she?'

'Trust you to notice.' Keith snickered. 'Yes, she was. Fancy her, did you?'

'God, no.' David laughed too. 'And if I had, I wouldn't have had the energy to do anything about it.'

'Me neither.' Keith reached for his kit, pulled out a packet of cigarettes and lit one. 'Do you know, Dave – if Betty Grable herself walked in here, stark naked and begging for it, I doubt if I could get excited – '

Long after Keith Mulholland had gone to sleep, David lay awake. Something about that girl's face had disturbed him. Eventually, he realized what it was. That look of patient suffering; he'd seen it before, on another equally pretty face.

But there was more to it than that. The girl had had blue eyes. Her hair, dirty and matted though it was, had been fair. Blonde – almost flaxen. And, as she'd looked at him and Keith Mulholland, it was as if it had been Elizabeth standing there.

Elizabeth. David realized now that he hadn't thought of her for months. For years, even.

He closed his eyes and tried to sleep. At dawn, he was still only half dozing. He got up and walked out into the chilly morning.

He let his mind play on an image of Elizabeth. Her hair had always smelled of flowers; for some reason, he remembered that. Her eyes were blue, clear and beautiful, the contrast between the blue and the white as sharp as upon willow pattern china. And now, inexplicably, tears came into his eyes.

He lit a cigarette. Calling to one of his lieutenants, he walked quickly over to the men's quarters, and was unusually curt with Lieutenant Harper as he went.

*   *   *

330

'You're daydreaming again.' Keith Mulholland shook David's arm. 'Come on, now, Dave - get on with it!'

David yawned. Lathering his face as best he could, he began shaving. He wondered if that village had really been a Fascist stronghold. Or if, perhaps, the villagers had been terrified into collaboration - had been threatened with the rape of their women and the burning of their homes? Well, they'd lost their homes now . . .

In the raw cold of the winter morning, David watched the company coming to life. But, as he gave orders, as he observed men going to and fro, as he planned the day, he found he was still thinking of his wife.

'Come on, Ben. You're going to be late for school!'

'Can't find my pencil case.' Benjamin Lawrence rummaged in his school bag and frowned at his mother. 'Have you seen it, Mum?'

'I expect it's on your table upstairs. You were colouring those pictures of planes last night, remember?'

'Yes!' Ben's dark eyes lit up. He raced upstairs, two at a time, and came back holding the missing case. 'Thanks, Mum!'

'My pleasure.' Elizabeth looked affectionately at her son. 'Darling, you must GO!'

'Will you come and meet me?'

'Yes. I'll take Becca to the clinic and call for you on the way back.' Elizabeth wrapped her son's scarf around his neck and kissed him. Opening the front door, she shooed him off down the drive.

She was lucky in her son, she knew that. Whereas most boys of his age hated to be seen out in public with their mothers, Ben liked to be in the company of his. He talked to her, he asked her advice, he loved her; he almost made up for his father's cruelty . . .

The house in the Banbury Road was full to bursting. Presiding over a menage of women and children, Anthony was the patriarch of a veritable tribe. His grandchildren - Katherine's twins, Eleanor's two sons, Elizabeth's son

331

and daughter – ran riot in both house and garden, and would look back on the war years as the happiest of their childhoods. And Anthony and Miriam, while concerned for their sons, who were both overseas, found that their children's offspring gave them plenty to occupy their minds.

Rachel, still unmarried and evidently happy to remain a spinster, now mystified her parents by volunteering for munitions work. All able-bodied childless women were now expected to undertake some kind of war work, and Rachel had opted for what appeared to be the most disagreeable kind . . .

'I don't mind making bombs,' she'd said blandly, when her father had told her of a job going in one of the Ministries, a job for which Rachel was well qualified.

'Why won't you consider the Forces?' Miriam looked enquiringly at her daughter. 'Dora tells me that Helen likes the ATS. And *she's* even less of a jolly hockey sticks type than you are!'

'I'd *hate* the ATS!' Rachel grinned at her mother. 'Oh, Mum, imagine it! Regulation bloomers, itchy stockings, cross country runs in the cold light of dawn! Enough drill to make you seize up, followed by PT to finish you off altogether! Ragging in the dorm, initiation ceremonies! That's all right for youngsters, but I'm nearly forty!'

'I suppose you are. You don't look it, though.' Miriam shook her head. 'I worry about an explosion, you know,' she said. 'All that gunpowder – '

Elizabeth gradually became the centre of the children's world. Rachel, watching her sister-in-law coming in from the garden, followed by a horde of rosy children, thought she resembled some kind of female Pied Piper. And she also looked happy – which was pleasing.

'I think you ought to divorce him,' Rachel told Elizabeth, as she and her cousin sat together in the kitchen one evening, drinking watery cocoa. 'I really do. And Mum and Dad would agree with me.' Rachel offered Elizabeth a biscuit. 'Eleanor and Jon think he's disgusting. And so does Katherine. We're all on your side, you know.'

'I can't divorce him.' Elizabeth dipped her biscuit in her drink. 'He may be a prisoner,' she said. 'He may be lying in some hospital, wounded. He might even be dead.'

'We'd have heard.' Rachel sniffed. 'Liz, loyalty's all very well, but don't you think – '

'No, I don't.' Elizabeth finished her drink and got up. 'I've had his children,' she said calmly. 'And, whatever he might have done to me, I love him.'

'Still?'

'Still.' Elizabeth collected the cups. 'Rachel, I do see your point, I understand what you say. But, all the same, I'll always be David's wife. Or, at any rate, I'll never be anyone else's.'

Rachel shrugged. There was nothing of the martyr about Elizabeth. The days when she had gone sobbing about the house, hurt and puzzled by David's appalling behaviour, had long since passed. She had now, it appeared, accepted her husband for what he was. And she still loved him – that fact was as unalterable as the certainty that the sun would always be in the sky.

Chapter Twenty Nine

THE NORMANDY LANDINGS IN THE summer of 1944 provided the turning point. While the Eighth Army continued to slog its weary way up the Italian peninsula, the troops under the command of General Eisenhower had much more dramatic successes.

A little over four years had passed since Stephen had been brought back rather more dead than alive from the debacle at Dunkirk. And now he was back in France once again, on the staff of one of the generals.

He was glad to be there. Even in the capacity of a glorified clerk, it was better by far to be directly involved, to hear the sounds of battle and to know the Allies were winning through, than to be left in England wondering what exactly was going on.

By the time Stephen had arrived in Normandy, the fine summer weather was over and there was now a sharp bite of autumn in the smoky air. 'Chilly today, Steve,' remarked a fellow officer, as he made his way across a cobbled yard towards the requisitioned manor house which was now Divisional HQ. 'Seen the old man this morning?'

'Actually, no.' Stephen grinned. 'I heard a rumour that he's gone for a little ride in his motor car. He's not expected back until this evening.'

'I suppose he's gone to a high level conference?'

'Of course.'

'And maybe he'll stop off and visit his lady friend?'

Stephen laughed. 'Major Freeling was wondering about

that. He thought it likely. Madame Desmoulins apparently keeps a good table.'

'She must have been a collaborator, then.'

'I dare say she was.'

'Tut tut. *What* an example to impressionable young chaps like us!'

'Just what I was thinking.'

Madame Desmoulins might have been prepared to make welcome a high-ranking Allied commander, but it was plain that on the whole the French civilians were not disposed to shower their liberators with flowers and champagne.

The general attitude appeared to be that the British and Americans had taken their time in coming; and that the invading armies needn't think the French were going to kiss the feet of a mob of soldiers who were now making a horrendous mess of the countryside and causing more damage than the Germans had ever done.

It was with some pleasure therefore that Stephen's immediate superior received an invitation to send a couple of his junior officers to dinner at a farm some three miles away from the town where they were stationed.

'You'd like a decent meal, wouldn't you, Steve?' he asked. 'You wouldn't mind spending an evening chatting to a mob of Frogs, showing them what decent chaps we British are?'

'That doesn't sound too arduous, sir.'

'No. And you speak the lingo, don't you?'

'I did an intensive course in it a couple of years ago.'

'Yes, it's on your record.' The major unscrewed his fountain pen. 'Who'd you like to take with you?'

'Mike Davies speaks fairly fluent French, sir.'

'Right. He'll do.' The Major scribbled down an address. 'Friday night, then. Wear your best clothes, eh? Do things in style.'

That Friday evening Stephen and Mike Davies set off

together in a jeep. They had run the gauntlet of comments from their friends and colleagues who assured them that they looked perfectly beautiful but that a bit of lipstick would improve things still further. If they couldn't be good they should be careful and they must be sure not to speak to strangers.

'I'll *castrate* Robertson one of these days,' muttered Lieutenant Davies, as he reversed out of the courtyard and drove off down the road. 'He's too sodding cheeky by half.'

'He's only jealous of your beauty.' Stephen glanced at his companion and grinned. 'You *are* looking fetching tonight, Mike,' he added, smoothing the creases in his own tight trousers. 'With your figure – '

'And you can shut up, too.' Mike Davies scowled. 'Sir,' he added, as an afterthought.

Mike's striking looks were a burden to him. He was a pretty, blond boy whose tendency to chest infections and bronchitis had prevented him from going on active service. His huge but short-sighted blue eyes looked at the world from behind a fringe of tawny lashes; and his heart-shaped face with its finely modelled, almost girlish features, had sent a shiver of delight down many a soldier's spine. In camp, he was called Daisy. He let it be known that he hated this. He was consequently ragged almost to the point of violence . . .

Oudenay-sur-Charette turned out to be a small village set in a pleasant valley, in an area of great natural beauty which had not, apparently, suffered too much from the fighting of recent months. The two officers drove through the village and – having overtaken a wrecked glider and, later, a very dead horse which was putrefying by the side of the road – they eventually came to a large farmhouse which appeared to be their destination.

'Was it you who suggested I came on this stunt?' asked Mike, as he parked the jeep.

'Yes.' Stephen looked at him candidly. 'I knew you spoke the language; so I didn't think you'd mind – '

'But my French isn't anything near as good as yours. Did you take a degree in it?'

'I did a course in oral French a year or two back.' Stephen got out of the vehicle and scuffed the gravel with his foot. 'I had a vague idea of volunteering to be dropped into France, you see. To do undercover work, or something.'

'Fancied yourself as a leader of the Maquis, did you?'

'I suppose I did.' Stephen grimaced. 'Stupid, really. I knew I'd never be anything like fit enough.'

'Never mind, sir.' Mike Davies jumped out of the jeep. 'They also serve, and all that.'

'I suppose so. Look here, Daisy, you can dispense with the formalities this evening. Christian names, okay?'

'Good evening, gentlemen. And welcome.' Alain and Jean-Louis Gaultier stood on the steps of their home, beaming at their guests. As the two British officers were ushered inside, smiling wives and a dozen or more children appeared, and the welcome became a noisy one.

'Come in – come in.' Jean-Louis led his visitors into a warm, whitewashed kitchen, in which the smells of cooking made the Englishmen's mouths water. 'Now. Captain Atherton, isn't it? I'm sorry, that's a difficult name for a Frenchman, you must excuse me if I pronounce it badly. And Lieutenant Davies? That's much easier! Gentlemen, make yourselves at home!'

The meal, which was delicious, took hours to consume. Course followed course, and each dish was accompanied by some kind of alcohol. Finally, over glasses of brandy from a huge, blackened bottle which Stephen assumed must have been buried in the ground during the Occupation, Jean-Louis leaned close to his guests and asked if they had enjoyed their dinner.

'Monsieur Gaultier, it was excellent.' Stephen smiled tipsily at the two wives hovering in the background. 'Madame Gaultier and Madame Gaultier, I congratulate you!'

'I second that.' Mike Davies grinned. 'A splendid effort!'

Gratified, murmuring something to the effect that they'd

never *seen* a soldier as altogether pretty and charming as Lieutenant Davies, the two women smiled back. And then, at a signal from one of their husbands, they left the kitchen.

For half an hour more the four men sat drinking together. And then, as Stephen was beginning to wonder if he'd be able to drive himself back to headquarters - obviously, Mike Davies wouldn't be able to do so - Jean-Louis rose to his feet. 'And now, gentlemen,' he intoned, swaying above his guests, 'you British are well known to be fond of animals. So would you like to see our pets?'

'Pets, Jean-Louis?' asked Mike - for they were all on Christian name terms by now, a happy band of drunken brothers - 'what pets are these?'

'Some we've had for a few weeks now. We keep them in the cellar.' Jean-Louis winked at his brother. 'Do come and have a look.'

'Oh, very well.' Stephen got up from the table, wondering what on earth the Frenchman was keeping mewed up in darkness. 'Lead on, Jean-Louis. Lead on.'

The two British officers followed their hosts from the kitchen, then went with them down a rickety flight of steps towards a heavily padlocked door. 'What's he on about, *pets*?' muttered Mike Davies, who rather fancied another shot of brandy.

'Dunno.' Stephen shrugged. 'Humour the fellow, eh? These pets, Jean-Louis?' he demanded loudly. 'Are they rabbits?'

'Rabbits?' Jean-Louis turned round, and, taking a key from his trouser pocket, he inserted it into the padlock. 'No, Stephen, they're not rabbits.'

He pushed open the door of the cellar and held up a lamp. 'Look,' he invited genially. 'Pigs. Prime pigs.'

The smell made Stephen retch. Unable to see into the gloom, he screwed up his face in disgust. 'What the hell - '

'Christ!' Mike Davies, peering into the murk, pushed past the Frenchmen and walked into the cellar. 'Stephen - look!'

Blinking, his eyes adjusting now, Stephen did. And what

he saw made him retch again. Clamping his jaws together, it was as much as he could do not to throw up . . .

Jean-Louis and his brother, however, were not so squeamish. While Jean-Louis kept guard, Alain strode briskly across the slippery floor of the cellar. He stood in front of his pets. 'Stand to attention!' he ordered. He flicked at them with a stick. 'Out!' he barked. 'Up the steps! Now!'

Encouraged by threats and kicks, the three young German soldiers hobbled out of the cellar. Unsteadily, they walked past the British officers who stood gaping at them, and made their way up the wooden steps. When at last they were in the kitchen, they stood in the centre of the room, leaning against each other. Their faces ashen, they glanced nervously at Jean-Louis. And when Alain picked up a poker and rammed it into the heart of the kitchen fire, the smallest soldier began to cry.

'Shut up!' Jean-Louis regarded him with a baleful stare of absolute hatred. 'Shut up! Do you hear?'

With evident difficulty, the boy – for he could not have been more than seventeen or eighteen, and he was small even for that – stifled his sobs. He fixed his eyes on Alain, and waited.

'We found them in one of the barns,' explained Jean-Louis. 'Deserters, I imagine. We've had them about a month now; so I think they'd welcome a change of scene. And I'd like to get my cellar straight again.' He sauntered over towards his captives and grinned at them. 'You're going with these gentlemen,' he told them. 'Well, aren't you pleased?'

Stephen now looked more closely at the soldiers. He saw that, apart from having been starved and kept locked up in the most squalid of conditions, they'd been ill-treated. The ears of one had been raggedly cropped. Another's hands were blackened with dried blood; obviously some of his fingernails had been pulled out. The third, who was staring fixedly at the poker with terror, had rows of festering burns across his forehead and down his cheeks.

'Barbarian.' As good as sober now, Stephen glared at

Jean-Louis Gaultier. 'You're a monster,' he cried. 'A butcher! Don't think you'll get away with this! I shall report you to the authorities, and I shall see that you and your brother are punished! I shall have you – '

'Yes, Captain Atherton?' Jean-Louis, unmoved, shrugged his shoulders. 'Sit down, pigs,' he barked at his prisoners, who obeyed him without demur. 'And you sit down, Captain,' he added, rather more politely. 'You too, Lieutenant. Make yourselves comfortable. Have another drink, perhaps, while I tell you a little story.'

Stephen was about to protest more vigorously, and demand that the Germans be handed over into his custody without further delay. But then he glanced at Mike Davies; and, looking at Jean-Louis, at the cold-blooded torturer who stood so relaxed and languid before him, he changed his mind. As obedient as the Germans, he and Mike did as they were told.

The Frenchman walked across the room, turned and walked back. 'Now, you British officers,' he began, 'you splendid English soldiers with your regimental traditions and your sense of fair play, listen to me!

'I don't doubt that nowadays the English are congratulating themselves and planning celebrations, for they have won this war. They have beaten the Germans – no-one doubts that. They have liberated France – for which, gentlemen, we cowardly Frenchmen are most humbly grateful – and shortly they will have Adolf Hitler on his knees begging for mercy.

'I do not question the fact that, for the past five years, the English have been suffering. Or think they have. I can assure you, gentlemen, that compared with what the French have endured, the English have not even begun to feel pain! But let that pass.

'Captain Atherton, you look bored already. "Why is that idiot ranting and raving like this?" you ask yourself. Well, I shall come to the point.

'In 1942, there was a Gestapo headquarters not far from here. In a pleasant, pretty house a few miles away, the local branch of the SS set up home. And to this place many men and women were taken; some of whom, I can assure you, would sooner have foregone the excursion.

'As for the Gaultiers, we knew who our masters were. We tried to keep out of trouble. But then, one day, a high-ranking German officer was killed. Shot. As he walked from his staff car into the pretty house, about to begin his day's business, he was murdered in cold blood.

'A terrible thing, you may say. What barbarian could have done this? And the Germans thought it was terrible, too.

'They decided that someone should be punished for this monstrous act. Then, one of them had a better idea. Why not make one particular village an example? Why waste time interrogating and torturing individuals when a whole community could be made to pay? No sooner thought of than done. One day, a squad of SS drove into a little hamlet a mile or two away and rounded up all its inhabitants. They took them to a meadow not far from here. In fact, the meadow was on my land.

'So, there they were. A community of seventy or eighty souls, from the old too decrepit to walk to the babies at their mothers' breasts, the boys and girls, the wives and working men.

'Captain Atherton, these people were farmers. They were not in the Maquis. They had committed no crime. But, all the same, they died. Before they died, the men were made to dig a grave. And then all the people were shot.'

Jean-Louis looked at Stephen. 'You may say,' he went on remorselessly, 'that to be shot is to die a clean death. But, let me tell you, it is not always so. Those butchers did not make it easy. This was no military firing squad, there were no neat white crosses pinned to these peoples' hearts.

'My brother Alain and I, we were picked up that evening. We knew what had happened, and we thought we were to be murdered too. But they only wanted us to fill in the grave.

'We buried them. We buried little children, a boy of six or seven who had been shot through the stomach and who must have taken hours to die; a baby whose brains were splashed across its mother's chest. We buried young virgins ready for marriage who had been shot in the face at close range, their beauty deliberately destroyed?' Jean-Louis stared hard at Stephen. 'Captain Atherton, you called me a barbarian. What do you call people who can do *that*?'

Stephen shook his head. 'I don't know,' he conceded. 'I don't think there *is* a word to describe such - such animals.' He rose to his feet and, as tall as the Frenchman, he stared straight into the torturer's eyes. 'But all the same, Jean-Louis, you ought to have handed these men over to the authorities; you shouldn't have taken justice into your own hands!'

'Justice?' Now Alain Gaultier fondled the handle of his poker, and grinned. 'Oh, Captain Atherton, this isn't justice! This is revenge! Something quite different!'

'You still had no right to torment these men. You had no quarrel with *them*!' Stephen scowled at Alain Gaultier; and, reaching past him, he took the poker out of the fire and plunged it into a bucket of water, making it sizzle. 'Look at your victims,' he snapped. 'They're little more than children; drafted a matter of months ago, I shouldn't wonder. Half-trained conscripts - '

'Steve, watch it.' Mike Davies, looking from one farmer to the other, understood that it would be unwise to irritate their hosts further. 'They've had some provocation,' he added. 'Steve, in their place, I daresay that you - '

Not understanding English, Alain Gaultier nevertheless caught Mike's meaning. 'Ah, no,' he sneered, grinning. 'Captain Atherton is an officer and a gentleman, he would never have stooped to such base behaviour! Well, I assume not. Of course, he has not seen his neighbours butchered, his friends' children murdered. And I hope he never will.'

The Frenchman picked a shred of meat from between his teeth. 'We were going to shoot them,' he said pleasantly. 'Then we wondered about handing them over to the local gendarmerie - *they* would have had a little fun with them, there's no doubt about that! But then we thought no, we will give them to our liberators, who will deal with them

342

fairly, according to the provisions of the Geneva Convention.' He laughed. 'Well, gentlemen? Do you like your present?'

The soldiers, crammed unceremoniously into the back of the jeep, sat mute and uncomplaining as Stephen drove away. Concentrating on the potholed road ahead, Stephen did not want to think about anything else. And the men in the tattered Wehrmacht uniforms had more sense than to draw attention to themselves.

Mike Davies hadn't even noticed that his revolver was lying on the seat. But someone else had. As the vehicle slowed down at a crossroads, one of the Germans lunged forward. Grabbing the weapon, he leapt out of the jeep and ran into the gloom of a wood.

Stephen stopped the jeep. Then, to his companion's surprise, he too jumped out. Mike Davies made a grab at his cuff, but missed. 'Come back!' he shouted into the night. 'Steve! He's armed!' Mike covered the other Germans with Stephen's own revolver and bawled another warning.

But Stephen ignored him and ran on, through the murk, determined to catch the runaway.

Chapter Thirty

STEPHEN COULD HEAR THE MAN crashing through the wood. Breaking branches, leaving a clear path of trodden undergrowth, he was easy to follow. Confident that the prisoner would be retaken without difficulty, Stephen ran after him. But by now, he'd completely forgotten that the German soldier had a gun . . .

He saw the flash of metal in the moonlight. As Stephen came up to him, the soldier levelled the revolver at the Englishman's chest. 'Halt!' he shouted. 'Halt, or I fire!'

It was only afterwards that Stephen realized just how stupid he'd been. But, having drunk a great deal of Jean-Louis' excellent red wine, having been upset and disgusted by his host's revelations, he had only one idea in his head, and that was to catch the prisoner. Disdaining to take orders from a Hun, he ran on, straight at the German and with a flying tackle remembered from his basic training, he brought the man down. The gun flew out of his hand and disappeared into the thick undergrowth of the wood.

The two men were hardly well matched. Small, thin, weak from lack of food and debilitated by the rigours of confinement, the German was easily overpowered. And now, to Stephen's surprise, he made no further attempt to escape. He glanced up at his captor; and then, with a hopeless sigh, he shut his eyes, as if resigned to death. Looking at the man's closed eyes, Stephen saw tears sliding from under the lids.

He released his hold on the German and rolled away

from him. He found a handkerchief and handed it to the boy, who was now sobbing bitterly. 'There's nothing to cry about,' he said lamely, well aware that as far as the German was concerned there most definitely was.

The boy muttered something in German. Stephen, who had learned the language at school, racked his brains for something to say in reply. 'Don't cry, you mustn't cry,' he repeated eventually, using the familiar *du* instead of the formal *Sie*. 'Oh, come on; get up.'

The boy sniffed. 'I'll be a prisoner?' he asked, as he struggled to his feet.

'A what? Oh, a prisoner. Yes, you will.'

'Then, I wish to die now.' The soldier covered his face with his hands. 'Will you kill me now?' he pleaded pathetically. 'Please – will you kill me now?'

'No!' Stephen scowled at him. 'No, of course I shan't kill you! You can go to the cages, with your friends. And then, when the war's over, you'll be free again.'

But the German wasn't comforted. 'The British torture prisoners,' he sobbed. 'British soldiers cut out tongues, they burn out eyes. Our colonel said so.'

'He's a liar.' Losing patience, Stephen grabbed the boy's arm and began to haul him back through the wood. 'We treat our enemies well,' he muttered. 'We don't go in for torture. Unlike you lot.'

They made their way to the edge of the wood. Stephen gave the soldier's arm a vicious jerk. 'Come on,' he said roughly, angry now. 'You can go faster than this.'

'You can go faster than this!' Tom Richardson, losing patience, swept Dot into his arms and began to run, making the little girl giggle with delight. He caught up with her sisters and deposited Dot on the grass beside them. 'Peggy won, Frannie was second, Dot didn't finish the course. Now, who wants a piece of chocolate?'

'You got chocolate?' Frannie looked incredulously at him. 'Bet you ain't!'

'How much?' Tom pushed his hand into his pocket.

'Here,' he said. 'It's American.' And he gave the girls a whole bar each.

They were soon too busy eating to say anything else. Like three obedient puppies they trailed out of the park after him, following him up the Banbury Road and eventually turning into the avenue where the Athertons lived. 'Seen your Mum recently?' Tom asked Frannie, who had slipped her hand into his.

'She come up last week.' Frannie grinned. 'Mrs Afferton asked 'er if she wanted to stop the night, but she said she 'ad to get back. I reckon she's 'avin' it off wiv a Yank.'

'And what does a young lady like you know about things like that?'

'I 'ears people talking.' Frannie winked. 'An' she 'ad silk stockin's on, so I reckon – '

'I see.' Tom shook his head. 'You know, Fran, you don't want to believe all you hear.'

'Had a nice time?' Dora met Tom and the children at the front door and stood aside for them to enter. 'Go and wash your hands,' she told the girls. 'Tom, could I have a word with you?'

'What is it?'

'Helen's here.' Dora twisted her hands together. 'I didn't know she was coming today. When I told her you were out with the girls, she – well, I don't know how to describe it really. I thought she was going to faint – '

'I'd better go.' Tom took his coat from the peg. 'Look, Dora – Helen did say she wasn't very keen for me to go on seeing you, I expect that's why she's annoyed.'

'If *I* invite you over, I really don't understand why Helen – '

'I'll see you.' Tom leaned over and kissed Dora on the cheek. 'Tell Frannie I'd like her to go on writing to me. An' if the others want to do some more drawings for me, I'll stick them up on my locker with the rest.'

'Tom, you *could* come in! Honestly, I don't see why Helen should – '

'It'd be better if I go. Don't forget – tell the girls.'

346

He opened the door and walked off down the path. As he turned into the Banbury Road, Helen caught up with him.

'Going into town?' she asked coolly.

'What?' He looked down at her; and realized, with a sudden jolt of tenderness, that he'd forgotten just how pretty she was. 'Yes,' he replied. 'Yes, I am.'

'So am I. We could walk together.' Cheekily, Helen grinned at him. 'That is, unless you have any objection?'

'I - no, I've no objection.' Tom pushed his hands deep into his coat pockets and stared straight ahead. 'So, Helen, how am I going to die?'

'What?'

'You said, if I ever went near your parents again, you'd kill me.'

'Did I?' Helen shrugged. 'I don't remember saying that! Tom, how are you?'

'Fine.'

'You look awful.'

'Thanks.' Tom glanced at her. 'You look very nice in uniform,' he said. 'Not many girls do.'

'I look like a sack of potatoes, and I know it.' Helen grimaced. '*You've* been overdoing things,' she said. 'And you're much too thin. Why don't you eat more?'

'Why don't you mind your own business?' Irritated now, Tom stopped outside a newsagent's shop. 'Did you have anything to say to me?' he demanded.

Helen looked at the touching attempt at a window display. 'I wondered why you hadn't written,' she replied.

'You thought I would?' Tom stared at her. ' "I never want to see or hear from you again." That's what you told me! And you seriously expected - '

'I was angry.' Helen scuffed the pavement with her shoe. 'And you'd just hit me.'

'I was provoked. And I apologized.'

'So that makes it okay?'

'No. I wish I hadn't done it.'

'Mm.' Helen looked at him. 'I quite like the ATS,' she said. 'Did Mum tell you where I was stationed?'

'Yes, she did.' Tom met her eyes. 'I expect the social

347

life's quite hectic? What with the Army camp down the road and the RAF place almost next door, I daresay you don't get lonely?'

'No.' Helen grinned. 'And we've the Yanks as well, don't forget the Americans! *They're* always hanging around offering us stockings and chewing gum. God, they're pathetic!'

'Mm.' Tom shrugged. 'Well, I wanted to get a paper. If you're in a hurry, don't let me keep you.'

'Get your paper in town.' Helen pushed her hand through the crook of his arm. 'Tom, don't be so stuffy. I want to talk to you.'

'I'm not sure we have anything to say to each other.'

'I think we have.' Helen smiled at him. 'Oh, don't worry; I'm not going to nag or start droning on about the past. I just want to chat, that's all. Do you mind?'

Tom merely shrugged in reply.

They walked on. 'Do you still have your room in Iffley Road?' asked Helen, as they came to St Giles.

'Yes.' Tom looked straight ahead. 'I need somewhere to keep my things.'

'When you're there, d'you think about me at all? Do you remember when we were together?'

'Sometimes.'

'I often think about you.' Helen pushed her hand into his pocket and plaited her fingers around his. 'I'm going out with a captain in the Pay Corps,' she went on. 'Well, he wasn't always in the Pay Corps. He was badly wounded in the course of a raid on some island or other, so now he's unfit for service overseas. He's tall and fair-haired, a very nice, gentle man. He reminds me of you, in a way. And he – '

'I don't want to know about your boyfriends.' Tom took Helen's hand out of his pocket and folded his arms.

'Tell me about your girlfriends, then.'

'There aren't any.' Tom grimaced. 'I'm not bothered about women these days.'

'Oh.' Helen shrugged. 'Don't get the wrong idea about me,' she said. 'I don't sleep with Michael, you know.'

348

'I don't care what you do with Michael, or what you don't do. I told you, I'm not interested in your men. Or in you, come to that.'

'Ah.' Such bitterness made her wince and brought tears to her eyes, so she took out her handkerchief and dabbed at her face. 'I've a bit of a cold,' she said. 'One of those you can't seem to shake off, d'you know what I mean? My eyes keep watering, and some mornings I'm quite hoarse.'

'I have caught an everlasting cold. I have lost my voice most irrecoverably.'

'I've heard that before. Where's it from?'

'I've no idea.' Tom sniffed. 'As a guttersnipe, as an ignorant, stupid product of the slums, I can't be expected to know things like that.'

Chastened, Helen walked along in silence for some minutes. Then she tried again. 'Can I come and have a cup of tea or something?' she asked humbly. 'Tom, could I come home with you?'

He glanced at her. 'Why d'you want to do that?'

'I think it would be nice. I like your room, you know – I made it quite comfortable, didn't I? With all the cushions and things.'

'Did you want all that stuff back?'

'No! Oh, Tom, look – I only want to talk to you!' Helen's voice was now unsteady, not under her control at all. 'I only want to – to chat, for heaven's sake! And surely the best place to do that would be your room?'

'Maybe.' He sighed heavily. 'I don't want to go to bed with you, you know.'

'I didn't assume that you *did*!' Helen managed to force a faint smile. 'Honestly,' she added, in a firmer voice, 'why do men think of nothing but bed?'

'Oh, shut up.' Tom stopped walking. 'Look, Helen,' he said, 'you've had a little bit of fun. You've informed me that you've got yourself a new boyfriend, you've as good as told me that you don't miss me. You've seen that I'm as miserable as sin, and that must please you no end. I think we ought to part company, don't you?'

'I think we ought to go to your room.'

'I have some things to do in town.'

'Will you be long?'

'Don't know.' Tom shrugged. 'Helen, I don't want you tagging along behind me, if that's what you were thinking of doing.'

'I'll go on, then, and make some tea.' Helen smiled at him, forcing a gaiety she did not feel. 'I'll get a few things to eat, some milk - I'll have it all ready by the time you get back.' She held out her hand. 'Key?'

He put his hand in his pocket and looked searchingly at her. 'Helen,' he began, 'you mustn't think - '

'Come on, hand it over.'

He looked down at the pavement. 'You're sure?' he asked, finding the key on the ring. 'Helen, do you realize what you're doing?'

'I'm only going to make you some tea, for heaven's sake! What's the harm in that?'

'None, I suppose.' Tom held the key in his hand. 'Well, then - '

'Don't be long.' Helen took the key and walked off down Cornmarket, leaving Tom staring morosely after her.

'I enjoyed that.' Pleasantly full of tea and some rather ersatz sponge cake which had nevertheless contained - she could have sworn it - real raspberry jam, Helen smiled at Tom. 'Well, I have to be back in camp by nine o'clock tonight, so I'd better - '

'Get moving.' Tom rose to his feet. In spite of Helen's having made room for him on the bed beside her, he'd insisted on sitting opposite her in the single arm chair. 'Right, then. I'll come with you.'

'There's no need.'

'I *said* I'll come!' Tom scowled at her. 'Unless you'd rather I didn't?'

'I'd like you to come.' Helen pushed her feet into her shoes and fastened her jacket. 'Don't glare at me, Tom; I'd *like* you to come!'

Conversation during tea had been very heavy going; and

350

now that they were walking along the river bank, Tom seemed just as ill at ease. Helen glanced sideways at him and wondered if she should say anything. She decided against it, but then she shook her head. 'Oh, damn it!' she thought, 'if I have to tie his hands together and *drag* him to the altar, I'll get him there!' She looked up at him. 'So?' she asked mildly, 'have you reconsidered at all?'

'Reconsidered what?' The river, grey in the fading light, mirrored the branches of the willows which grew along its banks and seemed to cast an eerie light on the faces of those walking beside it. Shivering slightly, Helen moved a little closer to Tom. And now he could smell scent, a sweet, flowery perfume, and he wondered sourly which of her many boyfriends had given it to her. 'Reconsidered what?' he asked again.

'Getting married, of course!' Taking Tom's hand in hers, Helen pinched his fingers. 'Tom, we could still get married! We could! We – '

'It wouldn't be a good idea.' Tom sighed. 'Look, sweetheart, I don't want to argue! But, oh God, Helen, just accept it, can't you? It wouldn't flipping *work*!'

'*Why*?' Helen shook his arm. 'Why wouldn't it?'

'Because – because of your relations, for one thing. I tell you, Helen, I *won't* marry into a family in which I'd be looked down on, belittled, snubbed; at best patronized, tolerated – '

'They don't look down on you! They *don't*! Tom, my mother thinks you're wonderful; it's Tom thinks this and Tom said that – '

'Your mother's okay. But the rest of them! God! Your brother looks at me as if I'm less than dirt and as for your father – well, talk about the decent officer always willing to hear the NCO's side of things, talk about the fair-minded commander always ready to humour the other ranks! Christ, Helen, your father's so sodding *pukka*, I feel – '

'So your feelings are more important to you than I am?' Helen looked down at the ground, keeping her temper with some difficulty. 'Tom,' she added carefully, 'you know that if anyone insulted you, I'd – '

351

'I can fight my own battles, thank you.'

'Exactly!' Now Helen was really angry. Meeting Tom's eyes, she glared at him. 'Exactly! And if no-one *wants* to fight you, you go looking for trouble! Don't you?'

'Rubbish. Helen, that's tripe.'

'It isn't. It jolly well *isn't*! It's *so*! Tom, you *want* people to annoy you, to upset you, you *want* – '

'Oh, you don't understand!' Tom pulled his fingers away and thrust both hands deep inside his pockets. '*You* come from a decent, middle class family. *You've* been loved and cossetted from the moment you were born. *You've* never been hungry – for food, for affection, for anything! So don't damned well tell me what I want or don't want! *I* know what I want, and I *don't* need – '

'You don't need me.' Helen stamped her foot. 'You're determined that you won't need me! You're *scared* of needing me!'

'What?'

'You heard!' By this time Helen was beside herself. 'You're scared,' she cried. 'Scared, scared, scared! You're scared to commit yourself! All that stuff about being patronized by my family, all that rubbish about being too old for me, beneath me, not good enough for me; that's so much eyewash! You're scared of me! That's all it is!'

Drawing breath, she glared at him. 'Admit it, why can't you?' she demanded. Grabbing his lapels, she shook him. 'Tom, listen to me! You say I've never been hungry for affection! Well, I've never been afraid to give it, either! But you – *you're* afraid! Any love given to you, you take it and *hoard* it! It never so much as occurs to you that love is something to be shared!'

'Oh, shut up!' Trying to squirm free, Tom would not meet Helen's eyes. 'You read too many books,' he muttered. 'Helen, you're not a psychiatrist, you don't know – '

'I do!' Now Helen shook him even more violently. 'Look, I know your early life must have been hard! That as a child you must have been sad, lonely, afraid! Your experiences have made you scared to trust *anyone* – '

'Oh? And how do you know all this?'

'That girlfriend you had once. Annie.' Now Helen looked into Tom's eyes. 'It *was* Annie, wasn't it? *Did* she jilt you? Or did you leave her?'

'I don't want to talk about Annie.'

'You left her.' Helen, calmer now, let Tom go. 'You left her, didn't you? She fell in love with you; she wanted you to marry her, she wanted your children, so you left her. I'm right, aren't I?'

'Sort of.' Tom scuffed the path with his shoe. 'Well, sort of.'

'Sort of, my foot! I'm *exactly* right! Annie wanted more than you were prepared to give. And *so do I!*' Now Helen knew precisely what to say next. 'Tom,' she murmured, just loudly enough for him to hear, but still so quietly that he had to lean towards her to catch what she was saying, 'Tom, I love you. There's no limit to the love I can give you. It's not metered, it's not rationed; it's a commodity which is in inexhaustible supply! So won't you take it? And give me just a little from *your* precious hoard, in return?'

'I – '

'Tom? Answer me!'

'Well . . . ' Blinking rapidly, Tom looked down at her. Beginning, at long last, to accept the truth of what she was saying, he swallowed hard. 'I suppose I could,' he replied slowly. 'I suppose – '

'What did you say?'

'I said, I suppose I could.'

'You could love me?'

'I could – I could love you.'

The admission, forced out of him against his will, left him white and shaking. To steady himself, he laid his hands upon Helen's shoulders. And then, the desire to confess, to admit everything, made him begin to talk. 'I did love you, in a way,' he said wretchedly. 'But when I first knew you, you told me that you had a regular boyfriend, so – '

'You felt safe. And when Alec was killed, you panicked.'

'No!'

'You did!'

'Mm.' Tom shrugged. 'Yes, I suppose I did.'

'I love you.' Helen looked up at him with tears in her eyes. 'I love you more than life itself. Tom, dear Tom; can't you just accept that? And admit to yourself that one day you might be able to love me as much? All right, don't marry me. We'll live in sin, I don't care. But we can't do without each other. Can we?'

'No.' Drawing Helen into his embrace, Tom kissed her on her forehead. 'No, love, we can't.'

The Italian winter of 1943-44 had been every bit as terrible as Sergeant Aylesford had predicted. In an abortive attack on a German stronghold, the original company had been decimated; and now most of the men under David's command were new faces, replacements sent up the line from the base, not particularly eager to do their duty under such appalling circumstances.

Now it was spring and all the rivers were in flood. The snows had melted, the ground had thawed and there was mud everywhere. Waist deep and sticky, it made movement of men and transport almost impossible. But, true to the best regimental traditions, and in spite of renewed enemy action of previously undreamed of ferocity, the advance somehow continued. In the face of shellfire which never stopped and which made the mountains ring, the Allies pressed on.

David had managed to put up with the unceasing racket of explosions and had found he could just about endure the terrible hardships of crossing increasingly inhospitable terrain. More than that, he had remained in good spirits when all the time other men were being sent down the line shell-shocked, rendered useless by nervous exhaustion; or, simply, raving mad. But losing Keith Mulholland was a devastating blow . . .

*   *   *

Detailed to attack a hilltop fortress, the companies had to cross an area which was heavily mined. The men followed the trail laid by the advance party, but inevitably there were casualties. Captain Mulholland stepped on a mine, detonated it and, as it was designed to do, the thing exploded at waist height. It ripped a hole in the officer's stomach and, as Keith mumbled just before he died, destroyed his chances of ever being a father. 'Let go, you stupid bugger,' the injured man muttered as David dragged him on through the minefield. 'Let go – I'm not going to survive this!'

David half dragged and half carried his friend to the comparative safety of a rocky overhang. 'I'll send someone back for a stretcher party,' he said, as he applied field dressings to the injured man's horrible wounds. 'I'll stay with you until they come.'

'Don't be daft.' His eyes closing in pain, Keith Mulholland grabbed at David's hand. 'You get on and take that bloody bunker,' he whispered. 'Go on! Do it for me! And Dave – '

'Yes?'

'For God's sake don't let any of the bastards get away! If you leave enough of them alive to mount a counter attack, they'll reoccupy the place – and you'll have to take it all over again.' He tried to grin. 'Think what a bloody bore *that'll* be!'

David led a successful attack. Anger and sorrow making him reckless, he reorganized his and Keith Mulholland's companies into one fighting unit; and, infected by their leader's determination, the men followed him up the hillside. Supported by the artillery, the infantry stormed the stronghold and, taking no prisoners, killed every German in sight, even those who surrendered.

By evening, the British were in possession of another line of German defences. David and another captain made a tour of their new position, congratulating each other on their achievement as they went.

Then, rounding a corner, they came across a corporal being sick. Crouched between a couple of other men who, rather green in the face, were squatting down next to him, he was vomiting his heart up, and crying as he did so. As the officers approached, his companions jumped shakily to attention – but the corporal didn't move.

'At ease.' The captain with David nodded towards the corporal. 'What's up with him?'

'In there, sir.' One of the men jerked his thumb towards a bunker. 'Direct 'it, sir.'

David and the captain looked into the bunker.

It was burnt out. Corpses of men had melted, stuck to the floor and were melded to the walls. Now and again a blackened, grinning skeleton, stirred by the wind which was blowing hard against the mountainside, shifted in a kind of grisly dance. The stench was overpowering.

'Get two men from C Company up here, with shovels.' The smell of burnt flesh, although distressingly familiar by now, always made David retch. Turning away from the bunker, he gulped in a mouthful of comparatively fresh air. He glared at the private whom he'd addressed. 'At the double, man!'

'Sir.' The soldier stumbled off.

David and his fellow officer stood over the corporal. The man was no longer vomiting, but he was shaking uncontrollably and still he wept. 'You'd better get him to the MO,' said the captain, to the corporal's companion. 'Come on, let's have him on his feet.

'I've never seen a man break down at the sight of dead Jerries,' remarked the captain, as he and David continued their walk. 'At the sight of dead mates, yes. But Jerries, no.'

'They're *all* men.' David was shocked. 'No-one ought to die like that. Surely such a reaction is normal, human pity?'

'Eh?' The captain shrugged. 'Didn't notice *you* showing much normal, human pity this afternoon,' he observed. 'That Jerry on the ridge had his hands up, no mistake about it. And you just cut him down.'

356

'Mm.' David nodded. 'That was in the heat of battle, though.'

'That makes it all right, of course.' The captain looked sideways at David. 'I heard the CO say they'd be recommending you and Mick Astley for the DSO.'

By May, David knew he was near breaking point. His sleep – when he slept – was full of nightmares. If he closed his eyes for a moment he saw blood and corpses; and all the time he could smell the sweet stench of putrefaction and decay. Sleep, once as desired as the most delightful of mistresses, became as dreaded as death.

The campaign ground on remorselessly. One morning, as he crouched with a couple of his men in a recently captured pillbox, waiting for reinforcements to arrive, David watched a rat sitting close to the door. The animal was nibbling something, a bluish lump. The rodent was tearing at it with his teeth, and David realized that it must be a bit of lung. There was a decaying corpse in the corner of the pillbox, and David understood now that this body was the animal's personal larder. He gazed at the creature, mesmerized.

The body of the German soldier was very high, and the men had already been complaining about it. It would, however, have been foolish to try to get it outside, for the pillbox was under enemy fire; and in any case, the body smelled so revolting that it would have been almost as noisome outside as it was within. David noticed that the man had had fair hair. Blond, it had been. Flaxen . . .

He wondered if that woman who had reminded him of Elizabeth was dead. Now, thinking about her, he decided that *she* must have been the child of some other German soldier, of an Austro-Hungarian adventurer who had strayed into Southern Italy in the course of the previous war and left his mark in that mountain village.

David now knew that he wanted Elizabeth. He wanted to see her, to touch her, to lay his head on her shoulder and shut his eyes against the world. As he sat there in the

357

pillbox, hearing the gunfire, he let the idea of her fill his mind. And, somehow, he was comforted.

The battle for Rome that June went down in the history of the war as an Allied victory. Yet the city was taken at such a tremendous cost that it was difficult, at the time, to see it as such. By the autumn the Germans were still in control of much of Italy. And, as October came on and the Allied advance ground to an exhausted halt, as the troops braced themselves for another foul winter, David thought increasingly of his wife. He clung to the image in his mind; now, when he closed his eyes, he could make himself think of Elizabeth. This, he was sure, was what now kept him sane.

Eventually, he decided to write to her. Sitting in a bombed out farmhouse, he drafted and redrafted the lines, composing the most difficult letter he'd ever had to write. A simple thing for most men, it was hard for this husband to tell his wife he loved her.

As he wrote, he decided that Elizabeth must be his own lucky charm. Many of the men had lucky charms: amulets, love tokens, or other bits of rubbish it would have broken their hearts to lose. While the Catholics had their holy medals, the Jews had their phylacteries, little boxes containing passages from the Torah. To ward off madness, men carried about with them photographs of wives, children, sweethearts; and after an action, exhausted soldiers would sit in their trenches or bivouacs, simply looking at these images, comforted by them. Now David, too, had a talisman; he had the image of Elizabeth in his heart.

For a while, he carried the letter about with him. But then, when the better weather came and he was ordered up the line again, when the letter was crumpled and becoming tattered at the edges, he finally posted it.

358

Chapter Thirty One

Elizabeth took one look at the handwriting on the Forces lettercard and tore the paper open. She scanned the contents; racing on towards the end, she hardly took in what David had written. Half fearful, half hopeful, she did not give herself time to digest what he told her . . .

She reached the last paragraph. He'd said nothing about being wounded, or ill; and for that she was grateful. But now, these last few sentences made her frown in disbelief.

'I think about you all the time,' he had written. 'Day and night, you're with me. Believe me, my darling, I did love you. I *do* love you. I know I've behaved very badly – I do not make excuses for myself – but you must know that if I ever see you again, I shall try to make amends. God bless you, Elizabeth. If you pray at all, then pray for me.'

He signed it, simply, 'David'. There were no kisses, no empty-sounding protestations of undying affection. Just his name.

As Elizabeth read and re-read, her sister-in-law came into the hallway. 'What've you got there?' demanded Rachel, as she tied up her hair in a scarf.

'A letter from David.'

'No!' Rachel stared. 'Well, what does *he* have to say for himself?'

'You can read it, if you like. Here.'

Rachel read. Now and again, she grimaced. 'Well,' she murmured, as she handed it back. 'Well, what a turn up!'

'Rachel!'

'Well, honestly!' Rachel snorted. 'What do *you* make of it?' she asked. 'All that stuff about God bless you and pray for me – talk about maudlin! It doesn't sound at all like our Davy, you must admit!'

'There's no need to mock.'

'I wasn't mocking. But I do wonder if the army chaplain's been giving my little brother the third degree!'

'Aren't you late for work?' Annoyed with her sister-in-law, Elizabeth stuffed the letter into her pocket. 'You'll miss the bus if you don't hurry.'

'I shall indeed.' Rachel wound a scarf around her neck and buttoned her coat. 'See you, cousin. By the way, Steve's in town; he said he'd look in today.'

Elizabeth found Stephen a far more responsive source of sympathy than Rachel had been. Turning her letter over in her hands, she looked at the Forces' Postal Address which David had given her. 'So, where do you think he can be?' she asked. 'Steve, what's going on in Italy?'

'It's stalemate, as far as I can gather.' Stephen shrugged. 'The Germans are beaten, that's for sure; but up in the North they're still holding on like grim death. It must be awful out there.'

'Thanks, Steve, you do cheer me up.'

'Sorry.' Stephen looked at his cousin. 'Will you write to him?'

'I expect so. Though I don't really know what I'll say.'

'No.' Stephen sighed. 'I can see it might be difficult. Liz, do you want him back?'

Elizabeth shrugged. 'I'm not sure,' she replied. 'It's just that – well, I'd got used to the idea of not seeing him again. Of knowing that if he wasn't actually dead, he was dead to *me*.'

She got up and walked about the kitchen. 'I'd put all the bad things out of my mind,' she continued. 'I'd decided that I'd remember only the good. Steve, I was determined that having been married to David was not going to ruin *my* life, as well.'

'How do you mean, as well?'

'As our grandfather's cruelty ruined my grandmother's, of course.'

'Oh, I see.' Stephen frowned. 'Liz, none of us knows exactly what happened there.'

'No. But it's odd, isn't it, how my own life has followed the course of hers? I look like her, you know – my mother was always remarking on it. Perhaps I'm like her in other ways, too. Perhaps, in my marriage, I made all her mistakes.'

'So, you want to put it all behind you, to concentrate on the children, that sort of thing?'

'I think so. Yes, Stephen, I think that's what I want.'

'So if he comes back, you'll divorce him?'

'Perhaps. I used to think I'd never do that. But – oh, Steve, I don't know! I don't know, I don't *know!*'

'Mm.' Stephen shook his head. 'Look, I do know a chap in Intelligence, who owes me a favour or two. I could try to get some information for you. How's that?'

'I'd be grateful if you could.'

'See what I can manage.' Stephen stood up. 'Shall we take Rebecca for a walk? I've nothing else to do.'

'You're at such a loose end that you'd even prefer your boring old cousin's company to no company at all?'

'Elizabeth, you're looking almost happy today.' Stephen grinned at her. 'I do believe you could smile – if you really put your mind to it!'

Walking through the Parks with Elizabeth, clowning about to entertain Rebecca, Stephen felt pleased with life; so much so that when Rebecca burbled a silly little song which she'd learned at kindergarten, he found himself joining in.

'You really ought to get married, Steve,' remarked Elizabeth, looking at him with affection. 'You and Lucy, you ought to settle down, have children . . . '

'Marriage is a state you recommend, eh?' Stephen caught Rebecca in his arms and swung her up into the air. 'Speaking from personal experience, you – '

'Steve, that's not fair!' Elizabeth frowned at him. 'And I'm sure you know what I mean.'

361

'Yes, I suppose I do. Sorry.'

'That's all right.' Elizabeth took her daughter into her embrace. 'After the war is over,' she continued, 'will you stay in the Army?'

'I imagine so.' Stephen kicked a pebble across the path. 'If, of course, they'll have me.'

'You sound as if you don't much care one way or the other.'

'Funnily enough, I don't.' Stephen pushed his hands into his pockets and stared into the distance. 'Do you know, Liz, when I got my commission in the Guards, I felt as if I'd really achieved something? That the worst thing which could possibly happen to me would be to be kicked out of the regiment? When I got back from Dunkirk and they sent me to that bloody awful barracks in Portsmouth, I felt it was the end of the world. Do you know what I mean?'

'Steve, to me one Army camp looks very much like any other.'

'Well, they're not.'

'I'll take your word for it. So, you were in the depths of despair. Booted out of Paradise, consigned to outer darkness, all that. What happened next?'

'I found, in the end, that it didn't matter to me any more. Well – not so much, anyway.'

'Why?'

'I met Lucy, I suppose. Oh, I don't mean that having her made up for *everything* – '

'Oh, of course not!'

'Liz, I'm trying to explain!'

'Sorry. Go on.'

'I don't know – I mean, it doesn't seem so important now. It's not that I don't want to stay in the Guards; I do. But if I had to leave, it wouldn't break my heart. I suppose, well, it's like falling out of love. One still likes the person one adored, but it's not the same as it once was. When I was in France last year; well, I think that was when everything came to a head – '

'If they *do* invalid you out, what will you do then?'

'Try farming, perhaps. My mother's family – well,

they're your family, too - they were all farmers. Mum's cousin still manages an estate in Herefordshire. In fact, I wrote to him a week or two ago, and he told me I could visit if I liked.'

'It's serious, then?'

'It's something I'd like to consider. The more I think about it, the more I like the idea. So I shall go over to Ashton Cross next month, and see what I can make of it all.'

'Mm. Farming. Do you know, I can see you with mud on your wellies and straw in your hair.'

'So can I, actually.' Stephen grinned. 'Come on, Liz! Race you to the pavement!'

'*I* can't run!'

'You can! You've got two good lungs, which is more than I have; it'll be a doddle!'

Elizabeth reached the park gate first. Holding her side, she turned to look at Stephen.

'There you are,' he said. 'An easy winner.'

'You were carrying Rebecca.'

'Mm.' Stephen tickled the little girl. 'Come on, Becca, giggle! Make Mummy smile!'

The results of Stephen's enquiries were not calculated to make anyone smile. He had eventually discovered where David's battalion was probably deployed. And, a few days later, he found out that it had been involved in an action which had resulted in the virtual annihilation of a couple of companies. Of those few who had not been killed, the rest were either taken prisoner or unaccounted for.

And, a fortnight later, the telegram arrived. David was missing. Missing. Miriam crumpled the paper and pushed it into her pocket. She wiped her eyes with the back of her hand, trying to comfort herself with the idea that at least it wasn't the worst of news, that at least he might still be alive . . .

* * *

By May, the war in Europe was over. Stephen, home for a weekend's leave, helped Ben to make a bonfire in a spare piece of the large vegetable patch which had once been the elegant garden of the Banbury Road house. 'What d'you think's happened to my Dad?' asked the boy, piling rotten, unusable wood on to the flames.

'I don't know.' Stephen shrugged. 'That's the worst of it, I just don't know. Ben, do you remember your father?'

'Not really.' Ben looked at Stephen. 'I try, but all I can see is a tall man in uniform, and I wonder if I'm imagining *that*.' The boy raked a stray piece of wood towards him and cast it into the heart of the blaze. In common with many of his schoolfriends, he was hardly missing a father he'd scarcely known anyway. 'Mum says you and he were very good friends.'

'We were.' Stephen kicked a burning branch, making sparks fly. 'You ask Rachel. She'll tell you how I used to follow him about. I must have got on his nerves no end; but he was always patient with me.'

'He liked you, that's why. He wrote to you, didn't he? He never wrote to Mum, but he wrote to you.'

'Ben, that's not true. She had a letter from him a couple of months ago.'

'Before that, he hadn't written at all.' Ben frowned. 'And he didn't write to me. Some of the boys at school have fathers in the Forces, or who are prisoners. *Their* fathers have written home. Why has my Dad never written to *me*?'

'Oh, Ben, I couldn't tell you!' Stephen shrugged. 'I honestly don't know!'

'But *I* do. I hear what Rachel says, you see.' Ben threw a pile of rubbish on to the fire. 'They think I'm too young to understand what they're saying, but I listen all the same. And I *know*!'

'Don't judge your father.' Stephen touched Ben's shoulder. 'He was worth loving. Whatever Rachel says about him, however much she goes on about his faults, the fact remains that he was basically a decent man.'

'Was he really?' Ben met Stephen's eyes, gazing

candidly into his cousin's face. 'You talk about him as if you're sure he's dead.'

'I think he must be.' Stephen looked at the grey wood-smoke drifting across the garden, and sighed. 'Come on, this'll burn itself out. Let's go and see if there's any tea.'

Miriam was adamant that David could not be dead. 'He must have been taken prisoner,' she said, over and over again. Pacing about the twilit drawing room one evening, she eventually went to sit with her husband on the sofa. 'If he was dead,' she insisted, 'I'd know!'

'Would you?' Anthony was aware that his wife was a little unhinged these days. He laid his book aside and took her hand. 'Darling, it's months now, we must begin to accept – '

'He *can't* be dead.' Her brown eyes bright, Miriam pinched her husband's fingers. 'You see, Anthony, he's not among the ghosts . . . '

'Ghosts, darling?' Anthony took his wife in his arms and stroked her hair. 'Don't talk nonsense, love.'

'It's not nonsense! I see them, Anthony, I see them all the time!' Miriam let the tears which had filled her eyes trickle unhindered down her cheeks. 'The babies, Anthony! The toddlers, the mothers with infants at the breast, the little children too small to walk! So many of them!'

'I know.' Anthony hugged his wife and tried to soothe her. 'But, darling, it's all over now – '

'I used to think I hated them.' Miriam laid her head on his shoulder, and sobbed. 'I used to think hatred was enough. But it isn't. What they've *done* – '

'Don't cry so, Miriam. Darling, you mustn't cry like this. Please!'

Miriam made an effort to control her tears. 'If they'd come in 1940,' she murmured, 'would you have let them take me?'

'No, I wouldn't. They'd have had to kill me before they harmed you. You know that.'

'Mm.' Miriam shrugged. 'It's a nightmare I've had all my life,' she said. 'Anthony, I was born afraid. Such a childhood I had; full of fear, for myself, for my parents, for my relations . . . '

She closed her eyes. 'I think I want to die,' she whispered. 'I don't think I want to live any more, not in a world where I'm hated for being something I can't help!'

Anthony could think of nothing to say to that – nothing, that was, which was neither trite nor patronizing. He rocked his wife in his arms, hoping she might fall asleep. 'Why is it, I wonder?' asked Miriam dreamily. 'Anthony, *why* is it unforgiveable to be a Jew?'

'It isn't, darling! It isn't unforgiveable!' Anthony, willing her to doze, continued to rock, continued to stroke his wife's soft, dark hair. He thought she was falling asleep at last, but then she began to talk again. 'I remember,' she began, whispering, 'Anthony, I remember – '

'Remember what, love?'

'When I was eight or nine, it must have been.' Her voice expressionless, Miriam seemed to be murmuring to herself. 'In a village near our town, in – where was it – Mitorovsk? Yes, that was the name. Anthony, in Mitorovsk one day, a Gentile child went missing. Oh, he turned up again, of course. He'd wandered off along the river bank, a farmer had found him; but since he was busy with the harvest the man hadn't been able to spare the time to take him home straight away. He kept him for a few days, then he brought him back.

'But, meanwhile, the people in the village didn't think of any of that. *They* were sure the Jews had taken him. You see, there was a part of the village where some Jews lived. They kept themselves to themselves. They caused no trouble. They were mild, peaceable people; shopkeepers mostly. Well, the villagers told the authorities that they suspected the Jews. A band of Cossacks came. They rounded up all the Jews, took them to the village square, and waited for the magistrate to arrive.

'The magistrate was old and deaf. The villagers tried his patience, I think. They insisted that the Jews had stolen the child. They talked about ritual slaughter, they said that the Jews had used the child's blood in some gruesome rite – all that horrible nonsense.

'The magistrate shook his head over the whole business. He told the villagers that they had no evidence to support their accusations, and suggested that they try to find some. He said he would reopen the case in a few days' time, and that in the meanwhile, a search for the child should be got under way.'

Miriam sighed. 'But no search was organized. Instead, the Gentiles said they would teach the Jews a lesson. They went into the Jews' houses, pulled out all the furniture, piled it up in the village square and set fire to it.

'The Cossacks had been in the village tavern all day, and now they were drunk. But they were still thirsty for blood. When they heard about the bonfire, they came out to watch. They laughed. Then one of them picked up a Jewish child, cut his throat, then tossed him into the flames. And the others followed suit.'

Anthony did not wish to listen to the rest. But still Miriam's voice murmured inexorably on; and, fearful of upsetting her even more, he had no choice but to hear. 'They killed all the children then,' she said. 'They stabbed them, hacked them to pieces, and threw their bodies on to the fire. As for the babies, they just flung them into the blaze. They shot the women. The men were killed too.

'I heard the grown-ups talking about it.' Now Miriam twisted round and looked up at her husband. 'I heard them, whispering and muttering; I knew what they were discussing. I listened at keyholes, I sat outside my parents' bedroom door and heard them speak of it. And I thought that Satan had come to Russia and had made his home in Mitorovsk.

'But, later, do you know, I was comforted. As I grew up I thought, what happened in Mitorovsk was the worst thing; that was the ultimate horror, the most terrible cruelty. And it had *happened*. It was past, and God would never let such a thing take place again.

'But now I see that what happened in Mitorovsk was

367

nothing.' Miriam was weeping helplessly now. 'Nothing, Anthony! Two hundred Jews murdered! Why, that was nothing! Nothing at all!' And she rocked herself backwards and forwards in an agony of grief and despair.

'She's not at all well. I think Anthony ought to take her away, for a holiday.' Dora poured tea for her husband and son. 'She looks just like she did when David and Elizabeth were first married, when she was so worried about the Leitners and all her other friends.'

'I don't think a holiday's the answer.' Tim shook his head. 'She'll be more contented at home. Then, if David does come back, at least she'll be there to greet him.'

'Anthony wrote to the War Office. They've no information about him. I really think we must accept that he's – well, that he's not coming back.'

'All the same, Miriam ought to stay at home. It's where she's happiest, after all.'

'She'll never be happy again!' Dora frowned at her husband. 'Tim, she went to see those ghastly newsreels again last week. Why does she keep torturing herself?'

'I think I understand why; but I can't very easily explain. Dora, I know it's a cliché, but time *will* heal, if only a little. You and I are well aware of that.'

Stephen coughed, to remind his parents of his presence. 'Oh, darling, I'm neglecting you!' Dora smiled at her son and helped him to sandwiches. 'Now, Steve, I'll put Lucy in Helen's room; it's bigger and there's more space for her clothes. What time do you think she'll get here?'

Chapter Thirty Two

THAT FINE SUNDAY AFTERNOON, STEPHEN and Lucy borrowed some bicycles and rode out into the countryside for a picnic. After they had eaten, Lucy lay back on the rabbit-bitten turf with her head pillowed in Stephen's lap. 'I'm tired,' she murmured sleepily. 'After all, we must have cycled at least a hundred miles.'

'We didn't.' Stephen shook his head. 'It just seemed that way.'

'Mm.' Lucy closed her eyes. 'How far *did* we come?' she demanded, yawning.

'Don't really know.' Tickling her face with a strand of her hair, Stephen laughed at her. 'Poor old thing, you're not fit, are you?'

'Mm.' Lucy wriggled her shoulders; then, turning towards him, she rubbed her face against the rough serge of his trousers. 'Is that nice?' she asked wickedly.

'It's very disturbing. Can't you tell?'

'Actually, I can.' Lucy giggled. 'Aren't I terrible?'

'Yes. Lucy, stop it.'

'Why?'

'Because I say so.'

'Because I say so!' Lucy mimicked him. 'Oh, Stephen, do all Guards officers think they're God?'

'Probably.' Stephen looked up into the sky. 'Lucy, I don't think I'll *be* a Guards officer for much longer.'

'You'll be invalided out, you mean?'

'Possibly. And if I'm not - well, I may try to get out anyway.'

'Really? Goodness. What will you do then?'

'I wondered about farming. In Herefordshire.' Stephen looked down at his fiancée. 'Do you fancy being a farmer's wife?'

'Don't mind.' Lucy pulled at a blade of grass and stuck it into her mouth. 'Oi reckon Oi could learn to shear sheep, milk cows, all that koind o' thing - '

'Lucy, be serious!'

'Stephen, I wouldn't mind being a farmer's wife. A soldier's wife, a farmer's wife, as long as I'm *your* wife it doesn't matter to me.'

'When I suggested buying a house in the country, you thought it was a dreadful idea.'

'But the war's over now. Or as good as.' She smiled at him. 'We'll buy a little cottage in - where was it you said - Herefordshire. Where on *earth*'s Herefordshire? I'll keep chickens and breed ducks, you can grow oats and wheat and barley and ride to hounds at weekends.'

'Hops, it'll be.' Stephen twisted a piece of grass around his fingers. 'They grow hops in Herefordshire. And they breed cattle.'

'All right, you grow hops. And sugar cane!' Lucy giggled. 'Now, give me a kiss.'

'No more kisses.'

'Why?'

'Too disturbing.'

'Rubbish.' Lucy slid her hand inside Stephen's shirt. 'Are you ticklish?' she asked.

'Lucy, *stop* it! Oh, for God's sake, do as you're told!'

'Just listen to him! And what if I *don't* do as I'm told?'

'I'll rape you. I'll rip off all your clothes and I'll - what's that expression the Sunday papers use - I'll *interfere* with you!'

'Oh, bliss!' Lucy licked her lips. 'Go on, then.'

In reply, Stephen leaned over, kissed her; and pushed her aside. 'How's your mother these days?' he asked.

They talked about mutual acquaintances and discussed

old friends. 'Agnes is off to Berlin next week,' said Lucy. 'She's looking forward to that.'

'I'm sure.' Stephen laughed. 'She'll find herself a rich Yank or three, and she'll have a high old time out there.' He turned to Lucy. 'Do *you* fancy a trip to Germany?'

'No, not at all.' Lucy folded her legs underneath her. 'In fact,' she added, 'I shall be demobbed soon. I think I'll be able to get out with the next batch.'

'I doubt that.' Stephen tossed a pebble into a rabbit hole. 'You'll have to wait your turn.'

'I don't think so.' Lucy took Stephen's hand and laid it upon her stomach. 'There,' she said. 'What d'you think of that?'

'Don't know.' Stephen shrugged. 'You're rumbling a bit – are you still hungry?'

'Oh, you *are* dense!' Lucy giggled. 'Listen, I'll give you a clue. D'you remember my birthday? You got a thirty-six-hour pass, you came up to see me and we, well, we went back to your hotel and you'd left your bag at the station, so you hadn't any, um, things. And I said, oh let's anyway, it won't hurt for once?'

'Oh, Jesus!' Stephen stared at her. 'Lucy! You're not!'

'I am!' Lucy beamed at him. 'Yes, yes, I am! There's a little black-haired Welshman cluttering up my nice neat Anglo-Saxon womb, and aren't you thrilled? Say you are, please say you are, because *I* am!'

Stephen continued to gape at her. 'Your mother will have forty fits,' he said at last. 'Oh, God, Lucy, she'll have hysterics!'

'I know, I know!' Lucy was still grinning. 'You look as if you will, too!'

'Do I?'

'Yes.' Lucy frowned at him. 'Stephen, you *are* pleased, aren't you?'

'I – well, I suppose so.' Still Stephen looked more surprised than anything. 'But what about your career?' he demanded. 'What about sharing in the rewards of victory, and all that stuff?'

'Oh, I shall have that, too.' Airily, Lucy waved her

371

hands in the air. 'I shall be a teacher. Or a writer. Yes, a writer, like your father; I can sit at home and write books. Or I'll be a lecturer – I shall go back to college, I shall take a degree, and – '

Stephen stopped her mouth with a kiss. 'And, apart from all that,' he said, 'you're going to be my wife. We'll have a special licence, shall we? We'll find a house we like, we'll – '

'We will, will we? And with what will you buy this house?'

'If I become a farmer, we'll get a tied cottage or something. Oh, my cousin Elizabeth is rich, she'll lend me some money.' Suddenly, everything seemed delightfully simple, and Stephen grinned. He lay back on the grass, his arms behind his head. 'Come here, woman,' he added. 'Come and lie on me.'

'There you go again, ordering me about. Why should I lie on you?'

'Why do you think? Come and disturb me again.'

Stephen kissed Lucy's face. He unfastened the collar of her shirt and kissed her neck. Then, opening his eyes, he looked up at her. 'Tell me when to stop,' he said. 'I mean, this is a public place; we don't want to get too carried away.'

'Hardly matters if we do, now!'

When Dora was informed by her son that he was getting married by special licence, she looked at Stephen and guessed. 'Well,' she said calmly, 'she's a very nice girl. And, do you know, I rather fancy being a granny.'

'Really, Mum!' Stephen blushed. 'I don't know why you should think – '

'Think what, dear?' Dora smiled at him. 'You young people,' she said, 'you assume your parents are stupid. Don't you?'

'No. But all the same – '

'You'll have to write to Helen. You will invite her, won't you?'

'Yes, of course. Look, Mum, if Lucy and I make out a

guest list, perhaps you could telephone Lucy's mother – '

'Perhaps Mrs Hollander wishes to arrange all this herself?'

'I don't think so.' Ruefully, Stephen chewed his lower lip. 'I have seriously blotted my copybook there. In fact, I am definitely persona non grata at the Hollanders' just now.'

'Are you?'

'Mm.' Stephen grimaced. 'Lucy and I went over to see them, to confess all. There were ructions. They had thought better of me; that, at any rate, is what Mr Hollander said. His wife was lying on the sofa with the vapours, you see, unable to speak.'

'Oh, dear.' Dora shook her head. 'Poor Lucy! Well, I expect they'll come round in the end.'

'I hope so.'

'I'm sure they will.' Dora smiled encouragingly. 'We'll have everyone back here then, shall we?' she asked. 'That might be best – '

The train to Oxford was crowded and dirty. Lugging a kitbag so full and unwieldy that he was seriously considering jettisoning the whole thing, David finally found himself a seat. The train pulled out of the station and, leaving the suburbs of London behind, it was soon puffing through green, unspoilt countryside. David was surprised to see how perfect England was, how undamaged, how unchanged . . .

'Gasper?' The elderly man opposite him offered a packet.

'Thank you.' David took the cigarette and accepted a light.

'Going far?' asked the man.

'Only to Oxford.' David inhaled. 'Look, I don't want to seem unfriendly, but I'm a bit tired. Do you mind if I don't talk? I know it's rude of me – '

'That's all right.' The man shook his head. 'You relax. You look dead beat.'

373

'You have a little sleep.' The man's wife smiled at David. 'We'll wake you when we get to Oxford.'

'Poor chap.' The man looked at David, at his less than immaculate uniform and the black circles under his now closed eyes. 'Reckon he's had a time of it,' he whispered. 'Look at his hands – all cut and bruised, and the nails are black and blue.'

'Nice looking boy.' The woman nodded approvingly at the sleeping soldier. 'I 'spect there'll be flags out for *him*, eh?'

Oxford hadn't altered, either. As he walked up the Banbury Road, David wondered how this could be so; how, with Europe in ruins, England could be so relatively unharmed. He turned into the drive.

The front door was open, as it always had been. The hallway was cool and silent as always. He dropped his kitbag on to the floor; and, momentarily, the desire to run away again, to take off for somewhere else, to be anywhere but here, came into his mind.

'Elizabeth?' His own voice sounded strange in his ears. He called again. 'Elizabeth!'

The door of Anthony's study opened, and a boy came out. 'Who are you?' he demanded. Curiously, he stared up at David. 'Did you want to see my mother?' he asked.

'Is she at home?'

'She's in the garden.' Now, the child was coldly polite. 'Come through, if you like. I'll show you the way.'

'It's all right, Ben. I already know it.' Hesitantly, David touched the boy's arm and turned him round to face his father. 'It *is* Ben, isn't it?' he asked.

There were footsteps just then; someone had walked in through the french windows. 'Come along, darling, tea's ready. Whatever are you doing indoors?' Elizabeth's voice carried across the drawing room and into the hallway beyond. 'Ben?' she called.

David and Ben looked at each other; and, all at once, the

374

child's face became hostile. 'In the hall, Mum!' he replied stonily. 'You have a visitor.'

'A visitor, dear?' Elizabeth, holding Rebecca in her arms, stood in the doorway of the drawing room. 'Oh, my God!' she whispered, as she saw who was standing next to her son. 'Oh, God in heaven . . . '

'Why did you come back, David?' asked Elizabeth, later that evening. She stood with her husband at the bottom of the garden, leaning against the trunk of an ancient pear tree.

'You'd rather I hadn't?'

'I honestly don't know what I'd rather.' Wanly, Elizabeth smiled. 'But your mother was pleased to see you,' she added. 'No doubt about your welcome there.'

'Poor Mum.' Recalling Miriam's tears, remembering her obvious, unalloyed delight when she'd realized who he was and had satisfied herself that he wasn't a ghost, David shrugged. 'Did she worry a lot?' he asked.

'Of course she worried!' Elizabeth glared at him. 'Did you think she'd write you off? Did you think she'd say, ''oh, he's gone, he's missing – that's the end of him, so now let's get on with the baking''. Well? *Did* you?'

'No. I suppose not.' David took a step towards his wife. 'What about you, did you write me off?'

'Don't touch me!' Shivering, Elizabeth drew her cardigan tightly around her shoulders and hugged herself. 'David, if you think you can carry on just where you left off, that I'll forgive you everything and welcome you with open arms – '

'You want explanations and apologies, do you? You want me on my knees, grovelling; you want the sinner begging to be forgiven?'

'No.' Steadily, Elizabeth looked at him. 'I doubt if you *could* explain, even if you wanted to. And as for apologies; well, they're not what I want from you.'

'Aren't they? Well, then, what do you want?'

'That's just it, I don't know.' Elizabeth sighed. She

walked away from him, across the straggling patch of un-tended grass amid which the fruit trees grew. 'I just don't know . . .'

David followed her. 'You're angry,' he said, at last. 'Is anger all you feel for me?'

'I don't really know what I feel. David, do you think you'll *ever* change?'

'I think I have altered. A little.'

'Oh. In what way?' Severely, she looked at him. 'Are you any less selfish? Less greedy?'

'I was never greedy.'

'You were! Oh, you *were*!' Elizabeth nodded violently. 'Anything you saw; if you wanted it, you took it!'

'Including you?'

'Including me.' Elizabeth glanced up at him. 'I suppose you've suffered,' she said. 'No, I don't just suppose, I can see that you have. And I imagine that a *dutiful* wife would have made you welcome by now, would have given you a hero's reception and not kept you out here in the cold, cross-examining you, lecturing you – '

'Don't be bitter, Liz. That's not like you. Not like my wife.'

'I have a right to be bitter!'

'Mm. Perhaps.' David shrugged. 'Shall I go, then?'

'Back indoors?'

'Out of the house altogether, if you like. Out of Oxford, out of England – '

'Don't be silly.' Elizabeth sniffed. '*Do* we have any chance of happiness together?' she asked. 'Is there any point in staying married? David, since you went away, how many other women – '

'A few.' David had the grace to look abashed. 'But, since I was sent to Italy, none. Elizabeth, for the last couple of years, I've thought of no-one but you.'

'Liar!' Angrily, Elizabeth rounded on him. 'Liar! David, I know you, and I'm perfectly well aware – '

'That I've never lied to you.' David looked at her. 'Liz, whatever else I may be, I'm not a liar, am I?'

'Well – ' Elizabeth thought about it. 'Perhaps not.' She

studied him. 'You're dirty,' she observed. 'You're absolutely filthy in fact; your face is grimed and your hands are like a navvy's. What have you been doing?'

'I'll tell you sometime.'

'Not now?'

'Not now.'

'Later, then.' Elizabeth held out her hand. 'Come into the house,' she said, as if talking to a child. 'You need a wash – no, I'll run you a bath.'

'*Will* you?' Taking her hand, David actually laughed. 'And you'll scrub me clean?' he demanded, squeezing her fingers. 'You'll soap me all over, wash away my sins? And then towel me dry?'

'What?' Elizabeth looked at him. His laugh, remembered from the days when she'd first known him, warmed her. 'Would you like that?'

'Yes. Yes, I would. Better than anything!'

They made their way towards the house. 'I don't know how you mean to behave now,' said Elizabeth evenly. 'But you must realize that you've lost your power over me. You can't make me miserable any more. If you sleep with other women, if you humiliate me, if you neglect your children – '

'I shan't – '

'If you do, though, it won't touch me. I'm beyond being hurt in those sorts of ways. I'm innoculated against you.'

'You're proof against my wickedness?'

'Indeed I am.' Elizabeth glanced at him. 'So, do you want to be my husband still?'

'Yes.'

'I'd be hard on you, you know. And you'd have your work cut out with Ben. You realize that, don't you?'

'He'll come round.'

'You're sure?'

'He'll understand that you've forgiven me, and he'll do likewise. I'll be a reformed character, Liz, I'll astonish you. I'll make you love me again.'

'We'll see.' Elizabeth began to walk up the garden path. 'I've promised you nothing, you know; I've not even said I'll stay married to you – '

377

'Elizabeth, I can't argue with you, not tonight. I'm too tired. All I want is that bath, then to go to bed.'

They entered the house and walked up the stairs. Sending David to run his bath, Elizabeth fetched two large bath-towels from the airing cupboard on the landing. She went into the bathroom. Seeing that the bath was half full she turned off the taps. Then, glancing at her husband, she observed that he was still only half undressed. 'Come along,' she said sharply. 'Hurry up and get in. I'll wash your hair for you.'

'In a moment.' And now David embraced her. His arms tight about her waist, he kissed his wife's neck. 'Come on, Lizzy,' he cajoled. 'How about a little kiss, a bit of a cuddle? To celebrate the warrior's return?'

'Don't!' Elizabeth squirmed. 'David, *don't*! I don't *want* you! Or at least, not in that way!'

'Yes, you do.' Releasing her, David took her face between his hands and studied her. 'Your eyes are huge,' he murmured. 'You're sweating – '

'It's *hot* in here!' Angrily, Elizabeth pulled away. 'David, stop all this fooling about. For God's sake get your clothes off, have your bath and come to bed!'

'In a *moment*, I said! There's no hurry.' Now, David yawned. Letting himself more or less collapse, he slid down against the bath and sat upon the floor. He patted the space beside him; and so, resignedly, Elizabeth sat down too. 'You look pretty when you're angry,' he remarked.

'Do I?' Very much aware of his bare shoulder close to her own, Elizabeth frowned. 'Do I really?'

'Yes.' David rubbed his eyes. 'Anger suits you. I've never seen you angry before. Liz – '

'What?'

'Will you kiss me?'

'No, I won't!' Elizabeth glared at him.

'You don't fancy me any more, is that it?' David sighed. 'I know I've changed,' he said. 'I know my hair's going grey and that I've lines on my face now. But I didn't think I'd become repulsive.'

'You're not repulsive; you'll never be that! But you're

378

too thin.' Elizabeth eyed him critically. 'Much too thin!'

'Yes, I know.' Pushing a folded towel behind his head, David looked back at his wife. 'Don't worry,' he said, yawning again. 'I'm not going to force myself upon you, to demand my - ah - rights. But, oh, for God's sake, Liz! Just lean against me, can't you? Put your arms around me?' His eyes bright, David was now blinking hard. 'Please?'

'Mm.' Elizabeth did nothing. She folded her hands in her lap and continued to stare at him.

He was older now, much older than his years. Haggard. Not handsome any more. For David was the kind of man whose beauty had, essentially, been that of youth. Once slim, he was now gaunt. Once finely chiselled, his features were now too sharply cut. His hair had streaks of grey in it. He would not age well.

She sighed. Perhaps one little embrace wouldn't matter? Perhaps, poor man, he deserved some comfort, some affection? She reached across and took his hand. 'Why, David?' she asked. '*Why* didn't you write?'

'I don't know!' Drawing his wife into his embrace, David laid his head on her shoulder. 'I thought - I suppose I decided - that we weren't right for each other. Oh, Liz,' he cried, his voice rising to a wail of anguish, 'you were so good! So uncomplaining! So bloody saintly! You *suffocated* me!'

'I never meant to!'

'No. I understand that now. I'm to blame; I admit it. I'm entirely to blame.'

'What made you come home?' Elizabeth could feel him shaking now, and she realized that he was trying not to cry.

'I wanted you.' David hugged his wife more tightly. 'When I was in Italy, I thought of you; I thought of you all the time. The idea of you kept me sane.'

'I see.'

'You don't.' Now David looked up at her. 'When I was in Italy, I fell in love again.'

'Did you?' Elizabeth stiffened slightly. 'Who with?'

'An idea. With the idea of you.' Rubbing his face, he

swallowed hard. 'When we were together before the war, you see, I thought I loved you. I *did* love you. But – oh, it's so difficult to explain! I suppose what I mean is, away from you I had the chance to think everything through. And I know now that you're part of me. You belong with me; without you beside me, I hardly exist.'

His eyes wide with anxiety, David looked at his wife. 'Liz, there's so much you'd have to forgive, but if you could come round to feeling the same way about me . . . '

'Mm. Perhaps we'll try again, then, shall we?' Stroking his hair, Elizabeth felt – not love, and certainly not desire, but pity. And an overwhelming tenderness for him. 'Come on now,' she murmured gently. 'Let's get on. Or the water will be stone cold!'

Although he was quiet and moody, although he would not speak of his experiences – would hardly speak at all, except to his wife – David's return lifted everyone's spirits. The fact that he was alive was, at present, enough for his family. He had come back; and the rejoicing over this lost sheep returned to the fold was, although mostly silent, all pervasive. Miriam went about with a permanent smile twitching the corners of her mouth, and Elizabeth's face had taken on the radiance of an angel's.

Somehow, Miriam persuaded her butcher to find her a chicken. 'We'll give him chicken soup today,' she said, displaying her somewhat elderly prize and positively beaming at her daughter-in-law. 'He needs building up. Elizabeth, did he have a good night's rest?'

'He fidgeted a lot, but I think he *did* sleep.' Elizabeth smiled back. 'I told him to stop in bed this morning; I think he's so exhausted he needs to take all the rest he can.'

'Yes.' Miriam nodded in agreement. 'Yes, he does. Poor boy,' she added, 'he's skin and bone, no flesh on him at all.'

'We'll soon alter that.'

'Yes, we will.'

And, like conspirators, the two women smiled at each

other. Coming into the kitchen, Rachel grinned at them. 'Killing the fatted calf?' she enquired genially.

'Rachel, don't be so sarcastic.' Miriam, busily dismembering her precious chicken, frowned at her daughter. 'He needs – '

'Building up. Oh, yes, I quite agree.' Rachel giggled. 'Look,' she added, 'there's a woman at work who can get some fresh eggs, at a price. I've asked her to keep me a dozen. You can make him – oh, I don't know. Something nourishing!'

'Oh, you're a *good* girl!' Miriam hugged her daughter. 'A good girl, a very good girl!' She dabbed her eyes with a corner of her apron. 'You hide your feelings, I know,' she went on. 'But you've a good heart!'

Lucy married Stephen just before, as Lucy herself put it, it began to show. A fine, sunny autumn afternoon saw the Lawrences and Athertons, together with a few embarrassed Hollanders, assembled at a small Oxford church.

Glancing round to see if everyone had arrived, Stephen looked enquiringly at David and was given an encouraging wink in reply. 'She'll come,' whispered David, looking at Stephen's anxious face. 'Don't worry, Stevie, she'll turn up!'

'Have you got the ring?'

'Somewhere.'

'*Have you?*'

'Yes! Now look, calm down!'

A sudden rustle at the back of the church made most of the guests turn to see – not Lucy, but Helen, in uniform and breathing as heavily as if she'd been running. Anthony glanced round and, squinting hard – for he'd forgotten his spectacles – he recognized his niece. 'It's Nell,' he said. 'And she's got some fellow with her.'

Miriam was too well bred to gawp. 'Who is he?' she whispered.

'I don't know. He's tall, fair; in uniform. An Army sergeant.'

'A sergeant?' Curiosity got the better of good manners and Miriam glanced round. 'They look as if they're good friends,' she murmured. 'Hand in hand, they are.'

'Mm.' Anthony shrugged. 'I suppose she'll introduce him to us later.' He turned round again. 'And here's Lucy,' he added.

'About time, too.' Miriam sniffed, and began to rummage in her handbag. 'Where is it?' she muttered.

'What's the matter, darling?' asked Anthony, concerned.

'Nothing.' Miriam dabbed at her eyes with her handkerchief. 'Oh, dear,' she said, 'it's this silly music. It always makes me cry!'